The unforgettable *Star Wars* saga continues with The New Jedi Order adventures . . .

They had been living on the very edge of disaster for so very long, fighting battles, literally, for decades, running from bounty hunters and assassins. Even the first time Han and Leia had met, on the Death Star, of all places, and in the gallows of the place, to boot! So many times, it seemed, one or more of them should have died.

And yet, in a strange way, that close flirting with death had only made Han think them all the more invulnerable. They could dodge any blaster, or piggy-back on the side of an asteroid, or climb out a garbage chute, or . . .

But not anymore. Not now. The bubble of security was gone.

To Han Solo, the galaxy suddenly seemed a more dangerous place by far . . .

—from *Vector Prime*

Also in The New Jedi Order series

VECTOR PRIME
by R. A. Salvatore

Dark Tide I
ONSLAUGHT
by Michael Stackpole

Agents of Chaos I
HERO'S TRIAL
by James Luceno
. . . coming in August 2000!

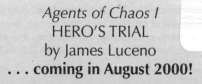

THE NEW JEDI ORDER

DARK TIDE
RUIN

MICHAEL A. STACKPOLE

A Del Rey® Book
THE BALLANTINE PUBLISHING GROUP • NEW YORK

A Del Rey® Book
Published by The Ballantine Publishing Group

www.starwars.com
www.randomhouse.com/delrey/

Library of Congress Catalogue Card Number: 00-190326

ISBN 0-345-42856-0

Manufactured in the United States of America

First Edition: June 2000

10 9 8 7 6 5 4 3 2 1

To *Star Wars* Fans

Your knowledge and dedication makes
writing these books a challenge.
Your passion for the universe makes
writing them indescribably rewarding.
Until we meet again . . .

TINGEL ARM

EMPIRE
BELKADAN
(HELSKA)
BASTION
DUBRILLION (SERNPIDAL)
MUUNILIST
YAGA MINOR
DANTOOINE
GARQI
AGAMAR
DATHOMIR
HYDIAN WAY
ALMANIA
CORPORATE SECTOR
ITHOR
YAVIN
MERIDIAN SECTOR
WAYLAND
MYRKR
PERLEMIAN TRADE ROUTE
ORROA-SKAI
TION CLUSTER
HAPES CLUSTER
CRON DRIFT
MON CALAMARI
KASHYYYK
THOLATIN
BIMMISAARI
HUTT SPACE
KESSEL
NAL HUTTA
HONOGHR
YLESIA
RIM
BARAB I
GAMORR
PZOB

HYDIAN WAY
PERLEMIAN TRADE ROUTE
RALLTIIR
RHINNAL
ESSELES
BRENTAAL
CHANDRILA
CORULAG

STAR WARS: THE NOVELS

44 YEARS BEFORE *STAR WARS: A New Hope*	32 YEARS BEFORE *STAR WARS: A New Hope*	22 YEARS BEFORE *STAR WARS: A New Hope*	20 YEARS BEFORE *STAR WARS: A New Hope*
Jedi Apprentice #1–2	*Star Wars:* Episode I The Phantom Menace	*Star Wars:* Episode II	*Star Wars:* Episode III

3 YEARS AFTER *STAR WARS: A New Hope*	3.5 YEARS AFTER *STAR WARS: A New Hope*	4 YEARS AFTER *STAR WARS: A New Hope*	6.5–7.5 YEARS AFTER *STAR WARS: A New Hope*
Star Wars: Episode V The Empire Strikes Back Tales of the Bounty Hunters	Shadows of the Empire	*Star Wars:* Episode VI Return of the Jedi Tales from Jabba's Palace THE BOUNTY HUNTER WARS: The Mandalorian Armor Slave Ship Hard Merchandise The Truce at Bakura	X-Wing: Rogue Squadron X-Wing: Wedge's Gamble X-Wing: The Krytos Trap X-Wing: The Bacta War X-Wing: Wraith Squadron X-Wing: Iron Fist X-Wing: Solo Command

14 YEARS AFTER *STAR WARS: A New Hope*	16–17 YEARS AFTER *STAR WARS: A New Hope*	17 YEARS AFTER *STAR WARS: A New Hope*	18 YEARS AFTER *STAR WARS: A New Hope*
The Crystal Star	THE BLACK FLEET CRISIS TRILOGY: Before the Storm Shield of Lies Tyrant's Test	The New Rebellion	THE CORELLIAN TRILOGY: Ambush at Corellia Assault at Selonia Showdown at Centerpoint

— What Happened When?

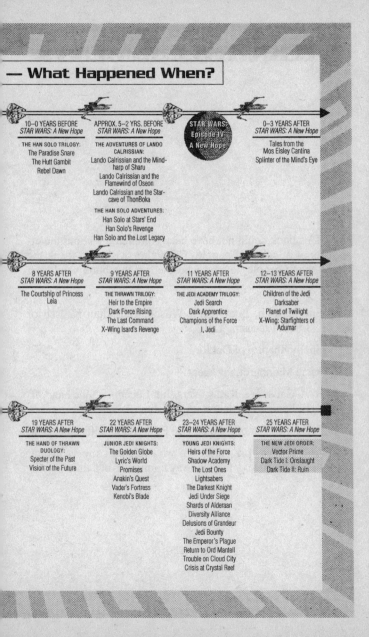

10–0 YEARS BEFORE
STAR WARS: A New Hope

THE HAN SOLO TRILOGY:
The Paradise Snare
The Hutt Gambit
Rebel Dawn

APPROX. 5–2 YRS. BEFORE
STAR WARS: A New Hope

THE ADVENTURES OF LANDO
CALRISSIAN:
Lando Calrissian and the Mind-
harp of Sharu
Lando Calrissian and the
Flamewind of Oseon
Lando Calrissian and the Star-
cave of ThonBoka

THE HAN SOLO ADVENTURES:
Han Solo at Stars' End
Han Solo's Revenge
Han Solo and the Lost Legacy

STAR WARS:
Episode IV
A New Hope

0–3 YEARS AFTER
STAR WARS: A New Hope

Tales from the
Mos Eisley Cantina
Splinter of the Mind's Eye

8 YEARS AFTER
STAR WARS: A New Hope

The Courtship of Princess
Leia

9 YEARS AFTER
STAR WARS: A New Hope

THE THRAWN TRILOGY:
Heir to the Empire
Dark Force Rising
The Last Command
X-Wing Isard's Revenge

11 YEARS AFTER
STAR WARS: A New Hope

THE JEDI ACADEMY TRILOGY:
Jedi Search
Dark Apprentice
Champions of the Force
I, Jedi

12–13 YEARS AFTER
STAR WARS: A New Hope

Children of the Jedi
Darksaber
Planet of Twilight
X-Wing: Starfighters of
Adumar

19 YEARS AFTER
STAR WARS: A New Hope

THE HAND OF THRAWN
DUOLOGY:
Specter of the Past
Vision of the Future

22 YEARS AFTER
STAR WARS: A New Hope

JUNIOR JEDI KNIGHTS:
The Golden Globe
Lyric's World
Promises
Anakin's Quest
Vader's Fortress
Kenobi's Blade

23–24 YEARS AFTER
STAR WARS: A New Hope

YOUNG JEDI KNIGHTS:
Heirs of the Force
Shadow Academy
The Lost Ones
Lightsabers
The Darkest Knight
Jedi Under Siege
Shards of Alderaan
Diversity Alliance
Delusions of Grandeur
Jedi Bounty
The Emperor's Plague
Return to Ord Mantell
Trouble on Cloud City
Crisis at Crystal Reef

25 YEARS AFTER
STAR WARS: A New Hope

THE NEW JEDI ORDER:
Vector Prime
Dark Tide I: Onslaught
Dark Tide II: Ruin

ACKNOWLEDGMENTS

This book could not have been completed without the efforts of a legion of people. The author wishes to thank the following people without whose effort this book would not exist:

Sue Rostoni, Lucy Autry Wilson, and Allan Kausch of Lucas Licensing Ltd.

Shelly Shapiro of Del Rey.

Ricia Mainhardt, my agent.

R. A. Salvatore, Kathy Tyers, Jim Luceno—Nice handoff, Bob; here's the baton for you, Jim.

Peet Janes, Timothy Zahn, Tish Pahl, and Jennifer Roberson.

And always, Liz Danforth, who tolerates my vanishing into the galaxy far, far away for months at a time.

DRAMATIS PERSONAE

Gavin Darklighter: Rogue Squadron colonel; human male
Corran Horn: Jedi Knight; Rogue Squadron; human male
Traest Kre'fey: New Republic admiral; Bothan male
Deign Lian: Yuuzhan Vong warrior; male
Gilad Pellaeon: Imperial Remnant admiral; human male
Shedao Shai: Yuuzhan Vong commander; male
Luke Skywalker: Jedi Master; human male
Anakin Solo: Jedi Knight; human male
Jacen Solo: Jedi Knight; human male
Jaina Solo: Jedi Knight; Rogue Squadron lieutenant; human
    female
Leia Organa Solo: New Republic ambassador; human
    female
Wedge Antilles: Rogue Squadron general; human male
Mara Jade Skywalker: Jedi Master; human female

CHAPTER ONE

Shedao Shai stood in his chamber, deep within the living ship *Legacy of Torment*. Tall and lean, long-limbed with hooks and barbs at wrist, elbow, knee, and heel, the Yuuzhan Vong warrior had pulled himself up to his full height and held his open hands out away from his sides. A slender, fleshy umbilical connected his ship to the cognition hood he wore. The tiny cable snaked up and out through the cabin's yorick coral wall where it was grafted into the ship's neural tissue.

Shedao Shai saw what the ship saw and knew what it knew, there, orbiting Dubrillion. Only the void of space surrounded him, with Dubrillion being a blue and green ball slowly spinning beneath his feet. The system's asteroid belt stretched over him in a mobile arch, and the distant brown world Destrillion hovered away in the near-empty darkness like a cowardly suitor.

This is what it feels like to be a god. Shedao Shai hesitated for a second, barely a heartbeat, letting fear of having blasphemed run through him. He smothered the fear, knowing that Yun-Yammka, the god known as the Slayer, would allow him his conceit as a reward for having successfully taken so many worlds from the infidels. The priests had told the Yuuzhan Vong that their new home was here, in what the infidels called the New Republic; and to Shedao Shai fell the hideous responsibility of leading the attack that would make the priests' prophecy a reality.

1

Using the ship's senses as his own, Shedao allowed himself to slip the bonds and concerns of his body and spread his intellect over all he saw. The Yuuzhan Vong had traveled far, in great worldships, seeking this new home. Scouts had located this galaxy over fifty years before, and the report of the survivors had brought reality to the Supreme Overlord's prophecy: a new home was at hand at last. Later, agents had been infiltrated into it. Intelligence had flowed back to the worldships, and a whole generation had been trained to cleanse the galaxy of the infidels.

Shedao Shai smiled as he gazed down at Dubrillion. One truism of war was that even the most careful plan could shatter against the opposition; and so it had here. Nom Anor, a Yuuzhan Vong agent provocateur, had conspired with his brethren in the intendant caste to usurp the role of the warriors. A premature attack had been launched and repulsed by the New Republic, though not without losses to the infidels. Shedao Shai's initial assaults had to be shifted to the worlds where the Yuuzhan Vong had been driven off, so their conquest could be completed and the shame of defeat effaced from Yuuzhan Vong honor.

The Yuuzhan Vong commander closed his right hand, his smile broadening. *Were your throat in my grasp, Nom Anor, my pleasure would be boundless.* Though the warrior did not deign to imagine how the priests or other intendants would explain away Nom Anor's action, Shedao felt certain the gods would punish him. *When next you come to Changing, Nom Anor, you will find your perfidy rewarded.*

Shedao Shai reached his mind into the memories stored within *Legacy of Torment*. He plucked one from a slave that had been employed as a soldier in the ongoing pacification of Dubrillion. The short, stocky, reptilian humanoid Chazrach had served the Yuuzhan Vong well in their wars, with some of them being celebrated enough to be allowed into the warrior caste at its most basic levels. As Shedao Shai pulled the memory to himself and donned it like an ooglith masquer, it felt odd, since the creature was much smaller than he was. It took him a moment to accept the discomfort of wearing the creature's flesh, then he pushed through and began to live the Chazrach's mission on the planet below.

As missions went, it was not very challenging. This Chazrach and his squad had been assigned to clean out one of the warrens the infidels had created amid the rubble of Dubrillion's main city. The Chazrach each carried a coufee—a large, double-edged knife—and a breed of amphistaff that was shorter than that employed by Yuuzhan Vong warriors. Not only was it more suited to the Chazrach's shorter stature, but it remained largely inflexible, since the slaves seemed genetically incapable of mastering the whip skills needed to use an amphistaff to its full capabilities.

Shedao Shai shifted his shoulders, still poorly suited to the alien flesh he wore, but allowed his mind to plunge into the memory. Through Chazrach eyes he saw the soldiers move into narrow, dark recesses. A sour scent assaulted his nostrils and the Chazrach's heart quickened. Two of his compatriots jostled and moved forward as their passage broadened. The Chazrach fingered his amphistaff and raised it out of the way as another slave slipped past him.

A red energy bolt exploded from the darkness, momentarily dispelling shadows, then burned into the Chazrach formation. Clutching hands to its blistered and smoking face, a screaming slave spun away. With his amphistaff still raised, the Chazrach Shedao wore sidestepped his wounded companion, then looked up as the scrape of metal against stone and a spark alerted him to new danger.

On a ledge above the passage's mouth an infidel had hidden himself. He swung a heavy metal bar, which sparked against the chamber's ceiling. The bar whistled down toward the Chazrach's head, but the slave parried it with the amphistaff, then lunged up with the amphistaff's sharpened tail. The staff punctured the meaty part of the man's leg, allowing salty blood to spurt out when the slave yanked the amphistaff free.

The man came with it, spinning through the air and landing hard on his back. Bones cracked and the lower half of the infidel's body went limp. Blood still pulsed from the hole in his leg, and his hands grabbed for it. The infidel looked up into the slave's eyes, fear widening his own orbs until the white balls looked as if they would rattle around in the skull. The mouth formed words that came with piteous tones, but a quick whirl of the amphistaff brought the flattened tip down to slash through the man's neck, silencing his voice and ending his life in one stroke.

All around Shedao's Chazrach other soldier-slaves attacked and fought. More energy bolts lit the further recesses of the warren. Slaves went down, writhing, hands clawing at leaking wounds. Infidels, shrieking out their last moments, collapsed in bloody heaps. Slaves stepped over bodies—both those of other Chazrach and of infidels—pushing themselves to get at more of the enemy. The ambush had become a rout, with the infidels seeking escape, but the flood of Chazrach made that impossible.

Then Shedao Shai felt the soothing sting of pain. It entered his back just above his right hip and cut toward his belly. He felt the Chazrach try to suppress the pain as he spun away from it, to the left. This allowed the weapon that had stabbed him to slip free of the wound, minimizing the pain a bit, but doing nothing to stem the panic rising as the Chazrach realized he'd been seriously wounded.

Coming around, the Chazrach brought his amphistaff up and almost missed killing his foe. The infidel that had stabbed him was female and certainly juvenile. The stroke that would have taken an adult across the throat slashed her face at eye height. The weapon crushed bone and ripped through the braincase. The infidel jerked as the weapon came free, spraying blood against the broken ferrocrete of the warren's walls. She fell to the ground like a discarded wet cloak, yet the vibroblade she'd used to open the slave's side remained clutched in her hand, buzzing in an abominable imitation of life.

Shedao Shai arched his back and tore the cognition hood from his head. He did not fear the Chazrach's reaction to the wound, his going into shock and collapsing. Shedao Shai had lived through that sort of thing many times before. This time, though, he would not have himself sullied by the impressions of a coward. *I will not be tainted.*

The Yuuzhan Vong commander opened his arms and breathed deeply there in the cavity at the heart of *Legacy of Torment*. He knew others would find his fastidious rejection of the Chazrach's final impressions to be an affectation. Deign Lian, his immediate subordinate, certainly would, but then Domain Lian had a more glorious history than Domain Shai, at least until recently. *A history of successes allowed them to become sloppy and weak. Lian has been given over to me so I may instill in him the proper passions of a warrior.*

Shedao Shai knew that what he had sensed in the Chazrach would be seen as a minor thing by many, but it was not the Shai way to allow himself to be tainted. The pain the slave had felt when the vibroblade—a blasphemous weapon that corrupted an innocent and injected her into the war—had been met with rejection. The Chazrach had been given a clear path to salvation, yet had turned from it.

Pain was not to be rejected, but embraced. As Shedao Shai saw it, the only true constant in reality was pain. Birth was pain, death was pain, all change required pain. To reject pain was to deny the very nature of the universe. Personal weakness distanced people from pain, which was not to be worked past, but woven through one so a being could become transcendent and be transfigured into the very likeness of the gods themselves.

Shedao Shai walked to one of the pitted chamber walls and caressed a pearlescent orb embedded in it. As if it were black beach sand being washed away, color drained from the wall, rendering it transparent. Behind it, arranged in a pyramidal hierarchy, lay relics of Domain Shai. Only a fraction of them had been stored here. By no means would so valuable a collection be entrusted to one person, and certainly not placed on a vessel like *Legacy of Torment*. The relics had been chosen by the domain's elders specifically to inspire this one of their scions.

Shedao Shai played a hand over the barrier between him and the bones therein encased, pausing only at the open spot in the lower left corner. He intended to enshrine there the relics of Mongei Shai, his grandfather, a valiant warrior who had perished on a scouting mission to a world known to the infidels as Bimmiel. Mongei had arrived there as part of a scouting mission preparatory to the invasion. He had courageously remained behind to send information to those of his party who were flying back to the waiting fleet. His sacrificial death resulting from his attention to his duty had brought great honor to Domain Shai and had, in very large part, made it possible—no, *vital*—that Shedao be chosen to lead the invasion.

Shedao had dispatched two of his kin to recover the relics, but they failed in their mission. Neira and Dranae Shai had been slain by *jeedai*—the most perplexing of the infidels that Nom Anor had sent information back about. *These* jeedai, *they claim kinship with and mastery over life, yet their emblem is a lightsaber—a weapon that can destroy both life and abominable mechanicals with ease. They set themselves as above and outside life, using this mythical Force to hide their wallowing in mechanistic blasphemy.*

The Yuuzhan Vong commander shook off a shiver, then turned away from the relic wall and crossed the chamber. There he stroked a red bar on a wall. That end of the chamber began to transform itself, with the yorik coral wall flowing down into a platform. Triple-jointed appendages, six of them, unfolded from the wall. Turning again to face the relics, he held his arms up and out.

The upper two appendages each exuded a leathery tentacle that encircled his wrists and snugged tight. The lower four similarly produced straps that trapped his ankles and thighs. He felt himself lifted by his wrists, with the lower arms resisting. Joints popped and little explosions of pain shot down his arms, making his fingers tingle. His feet then left the floor. They came up above the height of his head, forcing him to crane his neck back so he could study the relics in the golden glow from above.

The light rendered the uppermost skull's eye sockets into black pits. Shedao Shai stared at the left one, the more irregular one, his gaze tracing the concave edge of the orbit. Though he had never seen this female alive, and could barely keep straight the number of generations back she had lived, he could imagine her cold gaze being as merciless in life as her shadowed stare was now.

Firmly settled in the Embrace of Pain, Shedao Shai began to struggle against his restraints. The creature's limbs contracted, twisting Shedao's arms and arching his spine. The pain slowly began to build, so Shedao Shai fought harder, pulling and pushing, trying to tug his arms free. The creature that was the Embrace of Pain wrenched his limbs and shifted so his shoulders turned one way and his pelvis another. Glancing back over his left shoulder, he could see his right heel. *But I cannot see enough of it.*

He wrestled with the Embrace more and harder, letting silver agonies replace the red traces of pain working up and down his body. He sought the pain, tasting it, savoring it, trying to quantify it and describe it, yet secretly luxuriating in the fact that it was too much, too great for him to possibly ever do. Even knowing that this task was beyond him, he forced himself to push against the Embrace, mustering himself for one more explosive act of resistance.

The Embrace shifted again, cranking his wrists up to where they all but rested on the back of his neck. Stretching his fingers out, he caught at the fringes of his hair and tugged his head back so he could stare at the relics. Sheer torment raced through him, igniting every nerve fiber in his body. He could not begin to catalog everything he felt. It came too much, too quickly, overwhelming him with pain until . . .

. . . until all I am is pain.

His true goal achieved, he let his lips peel back from jagged teeth. The infidels did everything they could to save themselves from this sort of pain. *They divorce themselves from all reality. This is why they are an abomination that must be cleansed from this galaxy.* It did not matter to him that the infidels had been here first; it mattered only that the gods had given the Yuuzhan Vong the galaxy and the mission of ridding it of these unbelievers.

Wrapped in agonies all but unimaginable, Shedao Shai again dedicated himself to the sacred mission given the Yuuzhan Vong. *We have come to give them the Truth. Shriven in the*

*crucible of pain, the fortunate will know salvation before they
die. The others*—He paused as a hot jolt curved up his spine to
burst in his skull. —*The others will become as lifeless as the
machines they embrace, and the gods will rejoice at the ful-
fillment of our destiny.*

CHAPTER TWO

The hiss-crack of lightsaber smashing against lightsaber drowned out the sharp intake of Luke Skywalker's breath. He watched as the blow that had been struck drove Mara Jade Skywalker back and had her stumbling. Luke could feel the way the Force flowed around her and through her. Jagged, precipitous lines seemed to attack her, to trip her up. He reached out with a hand, ready to smooth sharp lines into gentle curves.

Yet even before he could do that, Mara used the physical momentum of her retreat. She rolled down onto her right hip, then came around, slashing wide and level with her blue lightsaber. Her red hair shone with reflected highlights as it lashed from one shoulder to another. Her green eyes blazed with another sort of light, one that matched the feral snarl on her face, betraying no sense of weakness from her debilitating illness.

The foe leapt above the slash, though not as high or as gracefully as other Jedi might have. Corran Horn landed and shifted his silver lightsaber to his left hand and stabbed it toward the ground. It sparked as it caught Mara's return cut. Corran then pivoted on the ball of his left foot and snapped a side kick at Mara's head. She ducked back, rolling through a somersault, then came up on her feet.

Her blade came up in a guard high by her right ear. Corran faced her, his blade held in two hands and running from his

9

belly toward a point beside his right instep. The light from their blades turned their sweat into an iridescent sheen visible on Mará's face and bare arms and on Corran's dripping torso.

Mara attacked and Corran parried. They exchanged blows, each retreating and attacking in turn. Luke marveled at the complexity of the Force flows around them. He had seen greater displays of the Force—*years ago before I understood the Force's subtleties*—and more fluid displays of swordsmanship, but the fight he witnessed here was altogether different. Mara and Corran, longtime friends, each sought to push the other to the limit, and relied on guile and skill and strength to do it. They shifted from defense to attack, and through a myriad modes of each. The object was not to do damage, but to force the other person to prevent damage.

What made it even more remarkable was that neither of them was in full, good health. Mara had been battling a disease that sapped her strength and defied Luke's best efforts to help her. He knew things could have been worse: of a hundred people diagnosed with the ailment, only she had survived. *Her strength in the Force has sustained her, and in combat she lets the Force race through her.*

Corran had only recently completed bacta therapy for life-threatening wounds he'd earned in a fight with the Yuuzhan Vong on Bimmiel. While the injuries had healed, including the long-term effects of a biotoxin, getting his conditioning back and regaining his combat edge was not easy. Luke could see Corran's chest heaving with the exercise and smiled. *Neither of us is as young as we once were.*

Mara crashed her blade against Corran's, driving him back. Corran's right ankle twisted, dumping him to the workout room floor. He rolled back through a somersault and came up on his right knee, with his left flank closer to Mara than his right. He held his lightsaber in toward his belly, then rotated his right hand. The weapon's internal assembly shifted, more than doubling the length of the lightsaber's blade and infusing it with a deep amethyst hue.

Mara laughed sharply and swung her blade at the slender purple energy rod opposing her. While Corran's weapon did give him reach on her, a simple beat attack would swing the blade wide, then she could dart forward and spit Corran with a lunge. The surprise of Corran's blade-lengthening tactic had worked on enemies before, but Luke knew Mara must have been expecting it and had long since worked out a strategy to deal with it.

She swung her blue blade to batter Corran's blade aside, but got no spark and no hiss from a collision of the blades. Her mighty swing spun her around, and as she completed the circle, the blue blade carved an infinity symbol in the air before her. She dropped back two steps, then thumbed her blade off and bowed in Corran's direction, before slumping to her knees with sweat pasting locks of hair to her cheeks.

Luke arched an eyebrow at Corran. "How long have you been waiting to use that tactic?"

Corran shut his blade off, then rotated the assembly back into its original position. He slid off his right ankle and onto his butt, then sat cross-legged on the floor. "The Vong got me thinking about it. We can't feel them through the Force, so we can't *feel* where they are. That makes them difficult to defend against."

Mara snorted. "Turning your blade off in the middle of a fight like that is a foolish thing to do."

"I know, but I could have just as easily switched blade lengths as you went to beat my blade aside. A stop thrust is very effective against an incoming enemy, if you know the enemy is incoming. I figured you'd have to press your attack. I doubled the blade, giving you a way to take my weapon out of play, then killed the blade as you went to knock it aside. Another touch of the thumb and you get spitted."

Luke felt a chill run down his spine. He recalled his teacher, Obi-Wan Kenobi, raising his lightsaber in a salute, then killing the blade even as Darth Vader killed him. *It worked that time as a tactic, too. The ultimate in self-sacrifice for the ultimate in victories.*

The Jedi Master smiled and opened his hands as he walked to the center of the training floor. Above and around him, through a great transparisteel dome, he could see the orderly flow of airspeeders and hovertrucks moving through Coruscant's sky. Everything seemed so natural and normal when he looked at the outside world, yet beneath the dome, in the Jedi headquarters on Coruscant, things boiled like storm clouds on the horizon.

"Both of you did very well, all things considered."

Mara forced herself to her feet. "We can do better. We have to do better. C'mon."

Corran shook his head, spraying sweat from his brown hair and beard. "I've got at least one more go-around in me, I think."

Luke frowned. "No, right now, this was enough for you both."

Beyond the two of them, striding boldly through an archway, came a Jedi with a black cloak billowing behind him. Slender and sharp featured, the Jedi had an incendiary gaze. His upper lip curled with a hint of contempt, then he smiled carefully. *And coldly.* "Good afternoon, Master Skywalker." The way he spoke the word *Master* made it a simple title, draining it of any sense of respect.

"Good afternoon to you, Kyp Durron." Luke kept his voice even, despite his dislike of Kyp's tone. "I thought you'd be here later."

Kyp stopped on the other side of the sweating combatants. "I convinced the others to speed their arrangements." He waved a gloved hand back toward the archway. "We're ready to convene the council of war right now."

Luke raised his chin slowly. "This is not a council of war. The Jedi do not go to war. We are protectors and defenders, not aggressors."

"With all due respect, Master Skywalker, the difference is a mere semantic one." Kyp clasped his hands together at the small of his back. "The Yuuzhan Vong are here and are intent on conquering at least some, if not all, of our galaxy. As defenders we have already failed, and yet, as aggressors we knew success. Ganner Rhysode and Corran attacked on Bimmiel and came away with their prize. We defended at Dantooine and were driven away."

Corran sighed. "Bimmiel belongs to the Vong now, too, Kyp, in case you hadn't noticed. And Ganner and I did what we did to protect some people taken prisoner. It was that simple."

Kyp frowned at Corran, allowing annoyance to ripple off him. "Semantics again. You attacked the Yuuzhan Vong and slew them, which is the only way you succeeded in getting your charges freed. Regardless, I have the others here with me. They are waiting below in the auditorium. What shall I tell them, Master?"

Luke closed his eyes for a moment, then nodded once, wearily. "Tell them I appreciate their coming here so quickly. I wish them to relax. They should spend this evening in contemplation of the Force. Their input will be treated with respect and considered fully. We will meet with them tomorrow."

"Tomorrow? I understand and obey, Master." Kyp bowed once, quickly and shallow, then spun on his heel and marched out very precisely. Luke noticed Corran watching the other man's departure, his thumb caressing the black ignition button on the lightsaber's grip. Mara spared no glance for Kyp, but flashes of fury came off her like bursts of radiation from a pulsar.

"I know you find him annoying . . ." Luke said.

Corran turned at the sound of Luke's voice. "Annoying? Either I'm covering my feelings, or you're being kind. If I had any talent for telekinesis at all, I'd have strangled him with his own cloak."

"Corran!" Mara frowned as she looked at him.

"Sorry, I suppose that would have been out of character for me—"

"Out of character to be so obvious." Mara's green eyes narrowed. "You need to be more subtle. Locate a partially blocked artery in his brain, then just pinch it off. Bang, he's down and it's over."

Corran smiled. "Now I'm *really* sorry I don't have TK."

"Stop it, both of you." Luke shook his head. "Even joking that way compounds the problem we have with Kyp and his faction. They've all grown up in the post-Empire era. They've always had dreams of being Jedi that could destroy the greatest evil we've ever known. What I did fighting the Empire, what I had to do fighting the Empire—that's how they think we should handle *all* evil. The slash of a lightsaber is the last word in justice. They know better than that, but the Yuuzhan Vong, because they are outside the Force, seem to leave us with only the lightsaber to deal with them."

The Corellian Jedi flicked sweat out of his beard. "I suppose that killing two Vong at Bimmiel didn't help dispel that impression, did it?"

"You had no choice, Corran, and you came very close to dying on Bimmiel." Luke sighed heavily. "That lesson was lost on Kyp's faction, too. You got hurt; they see you as weak. They're missing how good the Yuuzhan Vong are. Since Kyp's followers see themselves as better than you, your ability to defeat the Yuuzhan Vong means they, too, can defeat them, and easily."

Mara nodded. "And Anakin killing even more of them on Dantooine likely has encouraged some to severely underestimate the Yuuzhan Vong. The lesson of Dantooine is a terrifying one. The Yuuzhan Vong care more about doing their duty than worrying about death. Those Jedi who use fear or intimidation to keep enemies in check should be terrified of an enemy that isn't afraid to die."

Luke pressed fingertips to his temples. "That's what has me worried the most: fear and terror, pain, envy, and contempt. They're all of the dark side."

"Yes, but, Master, we have to be realistic." Corran clipped his lightsaber to his belt. "The Vong are formidable and merciless. We can't sense them with the Force. This takes away a lot of the abilities most Jedi have come to rely on. The loss of our edge has got to bring fear."

"No, Corran, you're wrong." Luke made his right hand into a fist and thumped it against his heart. "Being Jedi is what we are. It's not the power we wield and the weapons we carry. I don't stop being a Jedi when stripped of the Force by an ysalamiri. The others are letting fear distance themselves from this basic truth. We serve the Force, whether our enemies are part of it or not."

Corran frowned as he thought for a moment, then nodded. "I see your point, but I'm not sure they will. Face it, a normal reaction to fear is to strike out at that which frightens us."

"Or," Mara added in ominous tones, "to curry favor with it in the hopes of being spared."

Luke hissed. "I don't like the sound of that, Mara." On Belkadan he had seen beings that had been enslaved by the Yuuzhan Vong, but he had wondered if some of them had accepted their role or welcomed it. *Fear can motivate people to do all manner of irrational things.* Having to fight people of the New Republic to fend off the Yuuzhan Vong was something Luke didn't want to consider.

"Still, Corran's point is good. Kyp's calling this gathering a council of war is a clear sign that some want to strike hard at the Yuuzhan Vong." Luke rubbed a hand over his forehead. "The missions for us, as Jedi, are simple. We go to the frontier worlds and help evacuate the helpless. We go and coordinate defensive postures. Dantooine seems like a poor example of how that sort of thing can turn out, but we did allow some people to escape who would not otherwise have made it."

Mara looked up sharply. "What about scouting missions? That's what you did on Belkadan and it was useful. We learned a lot from your being there. Corran and Ganner brought back useful information from Bimmiel, too, including those samples of biotech the Yuuzhan Vong use and that mummified Yuuzhan Vong body. The more intelligence we can gather on the Yuuzhan Vong, the better off we'll be in dealing with them."

"I agree, but with fewer than a hundred Jedi, and with hundreds of worlds as potential targets, how do we allocate our people?"

Corran nodded. "Well, there is no winning the political battle here, I think we all know that. If no Jedi is on a world the Vong hit, we'll be blamed. If too few Jedi are there to stop them—and we know that's a given—we lose again. I'm not suggesting that we do nothing, but we have to know that we're never going to satisfy those that we can't help.

"On the other hand, Mara's point also carries with it a truism: the only place we know for certain that we can find the Vong is on worlds they've taken. I can review data on the conquered worlds and see if there is any way we could get a mission in. It won't be easy."

"None of this will be easy, Corran." The Jedi Master reached out and took Mara's left hand in his right. "We'll just have to make sure that the Jedi do everything we can to fulfill our mission. I'm less afraid of criticism from outside than I am that failure on our part may shatter the Jedi from within. If that happens, the Yuuzhan Vong will face no opposition at all."

CHAPTER THREE

Something about returning to the suite of rooms where he'd spent much of his time on Coruscant felt very odd to Jacen Solo. He would have said he'd grown up there, but he knew that wasn't close to the truth. He'd traveled all over the New Republic with his parents, then spent a lot of time at the Jedi academy.

The place didn't look that much different than he remembered it. His room was down the hallway; his parents' suite was upstairs. C-3PO still puttered about, dashing from one seeming crisis to another, stopping only to say how good it was to see Jacen again. The golden protocol droid's antics, while annoying, made up one of the elements Jacen still found familiar about the place, and for some reason even that made him uneasy.

The unsettling nature of the suite bothered him. Anakin, his younger brother, stood over by the transparisteel viewport, studying the lines of speeders tracing their paths through the sky. Jacen got almost no sense of Anakin through the Force, as if his brother were a continent away. What little he did get was somber and tinged a bit with apprehension.

Jaina, his twin, on the other hand, brimmed over with bright emotion. Seeing her, dark hair gathered into a thick braid, dark eyes bright, brought a smile to his own face. Her joy at having joined Rogue Squadron infected him, broadening that smile. As twins, they had always been close and shared much; still, the way Jaina had blossomed in this new role had taken him by surprise.

But a pleasant surprise.

Jacen enfolded her in a hug after he stepped down into the large living room area. "I've missed you. The squadron has been keeping you busy, has it?"

Jaina returned the hug fiercely, then gave her brother a kiss on the cheek. "Yes. We're recruiting new pilots and I'm helping to screen them. I monitor their reactions when we show them what the Yuuzhan Vong do in combat. We work on weeding them out based on performance and such things."

Jacen smiled. "Jedi senses are good for that sort of thing."

"I know, but what's amazing is this: We compile our reports after simulations and interviews, and everyone on the board does it independently. Wedge Antilles and Tycho Celchu are helping, and it's weird, but without using the Force, they seem to flag the same people I do as being unsuitable. Years of experience is serving them the way the Force does me."

Anakin laughed lightly. "I don't think years of experience will lift big rocks."

Jaina gave him a big-sister frown. "You know what I mean."

Jacen moved past his sister and seated himself on the tan couch. "Experience is one thing that can help anyone, including Jedi. Learn from things, don't repeat mistakes."

Anakin nodded, then resumed staring out the viewport. "Good thing some mistakes can't be repeated."

His sister sighed and started toward him. "Anakin, it wasn't your fault—"

Anakin held up a hand, stopping her. He didn't resort to the Force to do it, but Jacen sensed he would have, had Jaina not stopped and lowered her arms. "Everyone keeps telling me that, and I know it, deep down in my heart. Being cleared of blame, though, doesn't mean I don't still feel some responsibility. Maybe I didn't kill him, but was there something I could have done that would have saved him?"

Jaina shook her head. "There is no way of knowing that."

Anakin turned, and somehow banished a haunted expression. "If you are right, Jaina, then I'm doomed. I have to believe there is, so when there's a next time—"

Jacen sat forward. "You've been through your 'next time,' Anakin. You saved Mara."

"Sure, right up to the point where you and Luke saved me and her. Don't think I'm not grateful, I am." One corner of Anakin's mouth cocked itself into a grin. "You got me halfway to an answer. I just have to get myself the rest of the way."

Jacen nodded. It had not escaped him that Anakin had not actually spoken the name "Chewbacca." The Wookiee's death had hurt them all, terribly and deeply. He had always been a part of their lives, and when he was taken away, they saw how vastly and to what depth he had been involved with them. His death opened up a gaping wound that, for Jacen, had not yet begun to heal.

All three of them fell silent, turning inward. Anakin looked out the viewport again, but his eyes were focused too distantly to be watching any one thing. Jaina folded her arms across her chest and flounced down on the couch next to Jacen. Her brows furrowed, and Jacen could almost read the memories of Chewbacca radiating off her. For himself, he remembered the softness of the Wookiee's fur and the gentle strength in his arms, his sense of humor and his infinite patience with human children possessed of Force powers.

"Hey, it's so quiet down there . . ."

Jacen looked up at the stairs and saw a man standing there, but it took him a heartbeat to realize it was his father. The voice had helped, but the hitch at the end, and the raw nature of it, surprised him. His father's clothes hung looser, and his flesh was tinged with a gray pallor instead of the rich bronze from being kissed by so many suns. Han Solo had swept his hair back out of his eyes, but wore it longer than Jacen could ever remember. The length hid some of the gray, but not all of it, especially at the temples.

The greatest discontinuity with his father, though, was the way his initial comment tailed off. Jacen had to have heard him utter the same line a hundred times, usually when things were grim, when the family needed tension broken. His father would smile, open his arms, and say, "It's so quiet, did somebody die?" *That you can't say that, Father, tells me just how bad it really is.*

Jacen heaved himself up from the couch. "Good to see you, Dad. I came as quickly as I could after I got Threepio's message."

"I know you did." Han gave him a confident nod, then started down the stairs. "Goldenrod, you haven't gotten them anything to drink."

"Well, Master Solo, the usual custom is—"

"Usual custom? These are my children." Han smiled. "What will you have?"

Jaina shook her head. "Nothing, I'm good to go."

"Jacen, you must want something." Han turned to the protocol droid. "I think I'll have—"

"It's okay, Dad, I don't want anything."

Han frowned. "Well, I don't want to be the only one drinking."

Anakin raised his left hand, waving away any drink request, without turning from the viewport.

The elder Solo shrugged, uneasily, awkwardly, as if his joints needed lubrication. "Well, I guess I can wait until later."

Jaina looked up at her father. "The message sounded pretty urgent. What's going on?"

Han took a deep breath, then let it out in a long sigh. He seated himself in a chair, then motioned to Jacen that he should be seated, too. Han then glanced at Anakin and made to wave him over to the couch, but Anakin couldn't see the gesture.

Han waited a moment for Anakin to move, then, when he did not, just sat forward and rested his elbows on his knees. "Look, I don't know how to tell you this. It's not easy . . ." He stared down at his clasped hands, rubbing one over the other. "Losing Chewie . . ." His voice failed for a moment, then he swallowed hard.

"It's okay, Dad, we know." Jaina gave her father a brave smile. "We all loved Chewie, too."

Han ran his hand down his face. "Losing him, you know, made me think what else I had that I could lose. That scared me the way I've never been scared before. I mean, me, Han Solo, scared."

Anakin's chin rose. "Not an easy thing to admit for anyone."

Their father nodded once, curtly. The gesture was accompanied by a flash of anger and grief that drilled into Jacen.

Jacen moved to stand at his father's right hand, awkwardly patting him on the shoulder. "We understand, Dad, we really do."

But his father had already shut him out. "Yeah, well, there's nothing to understand."

Jacen sighed. *We may beat the Yuuzhan Vong, but will my family survive the battle?*

CHAPTER FOUR

Leia Organa Solo slowly rose from her chair in the tiny briefing room. Leaning forward on the edge of the table, she posted her body up on her arms. Her head dipped for a moment, surrendering to the ache in her shoulders, but she looked up quickly enough. She knew the others in the room had to be just as tired as she was, but given the events unfolding, none of them could afford to rest.

Above a holoprojector plate built into the heart of the black table hung a representation of a rimward portion of the New Republic. New Republic worlds and the space between them glowed a soft gold. Up on her left, the Imperial Remnant had been shaded in gray, with the worlds little black pearls. Stabbing into the New Republic like a vibroblade were brown worlds and space. A string of them carved a wedge in the New Republic, just skirting the Remnant border.

"Data just keeps flowing in. The silence from Belkadan, Bimmiel, Dantooine, and Sernpidal should come as a surprise to no one since the Yuuzhan Vong have taken those worlds and they didn't have much population on them to start. From Dubrillion we still get some reports, but those are becoming fewer and farther between. It does look as if Dubrillion is going to serve as the Yuuzhan Vong headquarters, at least in the short term. From Garqi we're not getting much, but all indications are that the Yuuzhan Vong have landed, assumed control, and are putting programs into effect for whatever their ends are."

Admiral Traest Kre'fey, a young Bothan whose violet eyes were flecked with gold, smoothed his snowy white mane. "Refugees are moving through Agamar fairly quickly. We are debriefing qualified witnesses, but your own story of what happened on Dantooine is typical of the sorts of reports we're getting. The Yuuzhan Vong seem to be using proxy troops for most of the cleanup or hard assault operations. We have reports of slaves being turned out and some rumors about collaborators, but the latter are little more than gossip at this point."

Borsk Fey'lya, leader of the New Republic, screwed his face up into a snarl. "It is to be expected that some people cower and cling to the strongest force around. We saw plenty of that under the Empire."

Leia shook her head. "The Yuuzhan Vong are much worse than the Empire ever was."

"From your perspective, Leia. The Empire dealt with non-humans as dispassionately as you describe these Yuuzhan Vong doing with humans. Now you know what we faced."

She let one quick guffaw contract her belly, then gave the Bothan a smile full of teeth. "They destroyed my homeworld, Borsk."

"Ah, yes, we are yet again reminded . . ."

Borsk Fey'lya's remark died as Elegos A'Kla, a Caamasi, reached out with a hand and settled it over the Bothan leader's forearm. Leia saw muscles bunch in Elegos's arm, and the resulting start from Fey'lya.

The Caamasi's voice remained even. "While our fatigue may shorten our tempers, we must be mindful of our duty here." He inclined his head toward the other human in the room. "I notice that General Antilles seems to have a datapad full of notes."

Wedge Antilles looked up and blinked his brown eyes, then smiled. "I've been looking at things the same way I used to look at Imperial installations and moves, and I've got some basic questions that need answering."

Borsk Fey'lya rubbed at his freed forearm. "Such as?"

"Well, first, Sernpidal. They drew a moon down into the planet, setting off a hideous cataclysm. We know we didn't get all the people off the world. If you check with planetary physicists, civilization would be completely disrupted, and if all living creatures haven't been killed off completely, they'd be reduced to scavenging for whatever they could find."

Fey'lya sniffed. "The Empire destroyed Alderaan, as Leia has pointed out a time or two. Sernpidal was meant to be a message to us."

Wedge shook his head. "Doesn't make any sense that way. Remember, they used some sort of creature to pull the moon from orbit. The resources that must have gone into growing a beast of that size and power have to be incredible."

Elegos raised a gold-furred finger. "How can you be certain of that, General?"

"We've had reports of the sort of ships and weapons they use. While their propulsion and defenses rely on creatures that can manipulate gravity in some form or another, none of them have but a fraction of the power that it would have taken to pull a moon from orbit. If creating that sort of creature was easy, the ships and defenses we've seen would have been vastly more powerful than they have been."

Elbows on the table, Wedge pressed his hands together, fingertip to fingertip. "We know the creature on Sernpidal was killed before the moon crashed down. It did not escape before the moon hit; and since disrupting the orbit made the crash inevitable, it's safe to suggest the Yuuzhan Vong never intended to recover the thing. They considered the result worth the cost of the means necessary to create it. This tells me that they have something else going on at Sernpidal."

Traest frowned. "I understand your reasoning, Wedge, but your model is based on a profitable return on an investment. What if they don't think that way? What if such a creature was considered, um, unclean because of what it did? Perhaps they didn't recover it because they would have been tainted by it."

"That's possible." Wedge shrugged. "If it is, if their thought patterns are so alien to what we know, then anticipating them and countering their movements is going to be impossible."

Leia scratched at the back of her neck. "While I think the point about expanding our view of the Yuuzhan Vong is important, the sort of facilities my brother found on Belkadan suggests that they actually do need to use the resources of the worlds they've taken to replenish or reinforce the things we've destroyed. Toward that end I do wonder what they're doing with Sernpidal's remains. I've read some of the same reports Wedge has, and most folks, save for the Givin, would find the resulting world uninhabitable. Discovering that the Yuuzhan Vong could survive there would expand what we know about them."

Borsk Fey'lya sat back in his chair, letting the lights from the map dapple his fur with golden highlights. "I understand well the value of learning as much as we can about our foe, but my concern, as leader of the New Republic, is containment of this scourge. I assume, Admiral, that you have redeployed forces to adequately contain these Yuuzhan Vong?"

Traest and Wedge exchanged bemused glances, then the younger Bothan nodded. "As far as it is possible, I have done that, yes. We are staging from Agamar and sending patrols out along known transit routes to gather in any refugees. We organize them into convoys, which we bring to Agamar, load to capacity, and send to the Core. So far we're not seeing any more Yuuzhan Vong aggression, but our patrols are heavily armed and should acquit themselves well. And we vary the nature of the patrols—their timing, composition, and the like—so planning an ambush would be difficult and very costly for the Yuuzhan Vong."

Borsk's violet eyes half lidded. " 'As far as it is possible,' you said."

"I did. We're talking here about a vast amount of space. While a computer can draw a very comforting and pleasing map for us to study, this graphic representation really has nothing to do with the reality of space." Traest punched a few buttons on his own datapad, and the map shifted radically.

The worlds remained in place and retained their color, but

instead of the shading around them, each world sprouted tendrils that linked it to the other worlds. Some were long and looping, others short and direct. As Leia watched, some blinked out of existence, while others stretched and new ones were born. What amazed her the most is how interconnected the worlds were, and how the borders on the previous map stood for nothing.

Traest pointed to the new map. "These are the routes that link these worlds together. It's shifting because as planetary bodies orbit, the transit times between worlds alter. Routes develop breaks that have to be worked around in realspace; *and* these are just the routes that lead from star to star. If someone wanted to jump into deep space and jump back out, they could hit almost any world from any other world—it would just take a *long* time, which is militarily impractical. So, setting our military to be able to intercept Yuuzhan Vong forces and drive them back is impossible."

Borsk frowned darkly. "Then you are suggesting there is nothing we can do to stop them?"

Wedge shook his head vehemently. "No, Chief Fey'lya, not at all. What we are doing is organizing system defenses on the worlds we think they will hit. Our goal is to slow their attacks long enough that we can bring overwhelming forces to bear to drive them back. We all know that forces bent on taking a planet are most vulnerable as they transit from space to surface. If we can hold them up and slow this transition, we have far longer to bring firepower to bear on them. That's how we'll stop them."

"You're baiting traps for them."

"Setting traps, yes, but not baiting. We don't know what they want, so bait is not something we can offer." Wedge sighed. "This brings us back to the earlier point about not knowing enough about them. I mean, we know they use slaves, we know they hate machines, we know their weapons are all organics, and we know they have a thing about pain; but the significance of any of this has not been assessed."

"Easy, Wedge." Leia patted his hand with hers. "I know your frustration. We can detail operations to go out and learn as much as we can. I'm sure Luke will lend us some Jedi for covert runs at worlds, just as they did on Belkadan and Bimmiel."

"No, no Jedi." Borsk Fey'lya shook his head. "I won't have them involved in this."

Leia looked at him. "What?"

Fey'lya's face became an impassive mask. "Do not think I do not know the value of the Jedi, Leia. I do remember how your brother and you headed off the crisis that would have consumed Bothawui, but the people don't respect them anymore. While my read of the reports about the battle for Dantooine tells me that were it not for the Jedi, the entire contingent of refugees would have been slain, that is not the only reading of the reports. Read most uncharitably, it indicates that the Jedi were powerless to prevent the slaughter of hundreds.

"Moreover, the Yuuzhan Vong have slain Jedi. The most powerful of the Jedi—your brother—was induced to leave Belkadan, abandoning an unknown number of slaves. According to one of the students rescued from Bimmiel, the Jedi there introduced genetically altered creatures that could forever disrupt the cycle of life on that world, sterilizing it. Add to that the rumors that Jedi Force skills are less than adequate against the Yuuzhan Vong, and you can see why there is no confidence in the Jedi. If we use them to spearhead operations, we will look foolish and confidence in us will waver. We will cause a panic."

Pain arced temple to temple in Leia's head. She'd heard the various reports coming from students and from Dantooine survivors and even the interviews with a few Jedi concerning their dealings with the Yuuzhan Vong. While she would have preferred a complete news blackout concerning things until they had a better understanding of what was going on, to keep the people ignorant presented a much more difficult problem. Since leaks could not be stopped, official denials of the leaks would erode confidence in the government and start a panic. But having an informed public meant they could express opinions on matters like the Jedi. Politicians like Fey'lya tried their best to work within the guidelines set by the will of the people.

She sat back down and cradled her head in her hands. "By refusing to use the Jedi, we're cutting off a resource that is invaluable. The Jedi we have out there are folks who have traveled widely, have dealt with crises in discrete and flexible ways. They are the perfect agents for missions to places like Garqi or Dubrillion. More importantly, I don't think we can stop Luke from sending his Jedi out to help people. You do realize that."

"Oh, I do, Leia, I certainly do." Fey'lya's lips peeled back in a feral grin. "My only concern is that we cannot be seen to sanction them. They will have to operate without our support."

Wedge arched an eyebrow. "If we got a distress call from a Jedi behind Yuuzhan Vong lines, you're telling me we can't do anything?"

"Unless there was a vital strategic or operational goal involved, no, I don't see how you could, General."

Traest looked at Wedge. "I guess that means we'll just have to set up our own operations and use our own personnel."

"We have no choice."

Leia closed her eyes for a moment, then sighed. "If we are unable to use the Jedi, then I suppose my mission to Bastion will be out, as well?"

Fey'lya's smile broadened. "Oh, no, not at all. If you want to go and talk Pellaeon into using as much of his firepower and personnel as possible to defeat the Yuuzhan Vong, I would applaud it. I wish you all speed and good fortune on that mission, Leia, I really do."

Leia glanced at Elegos, and they nodded to each other. In discussing her idea to ask the Imperial Remnant for help, the two of them had run through various scenarios, and no matter which one they reviewed, it always turned to a political advantage for Borsk Fey'lya. If Leia succeeded in getting the Remnant to come to the aid of the New Republic, she could easily be painted as a collaborator with a reactionary element, while Borsk could position himself as the heir to the traditions of the Rebellion. If the Remnant refused, they would be vilified, and Leia along with them, for having such poor judgment to try to deal with them. Everything else in between resulted in the same impression: she would be collaborating with an enemy.

"I am so glad you approve, Borsk. Senator A'Kla and I will be leaving in two days for Bastion."

"Senator A'Kla?" Fey'lya shook his head. "I'm afraid the senator will have pressing business here, on Coruscant, Leia. He won't be going with you."

"If you think—"

Elegos held a three-fingered hand up to forestall Leia's reply. "He's right, Leia, I won't be going with you. Even so, Borsk, I will not be here, either."

Leia blinked. "What? Where will you be?"

The Caamasi sighed and sat back, staring up at the dark ceiling. "I've listened to all of you, your discussions, your arguments. I think you are all on the right course for dealing with this problem. You have covered all aspects of it save one: what the Yuuzhan Vong want. I intend to go to Dubrillion to ask."

"No, impossible." Leia shook her head adamantly. "We were at Dubrillion before and tried to communicate with the Yuuzhan Vong. They didn't want to communicate with us."

Traest nodded in agreement. "We've no evidence they understand the concept of truces. They certainly don't treat captives well—we have ample evidence of that. You'll be putting yourself in mortal danger."

"And you and your soldiers will not?"

"That's our job, Senator."

"In reality, is it not my job, as well?" The Caamasi leaned forward, his long-limbed body moving with a serene fluidity. "As a senator, I bear responsibility for millions of people. I do not want to see them dead or dying. It is my responsibility to do what I can to avert this war. You know my people are pacifistic, yet you know I fought with you at Dantooine, and I have fought before. I do not wish to fight again, so to Dubrillion I must go."

Leia stared at him, a lump rising in her throat. A chill

shook her, a chill she wanted to put down to exhaustion, but one she could not. She knew the Force could provide a flash of insight concerning the future. The dread she felt welling up inside her seemed so strong that she hoped it did not mean that Elegos' mission was doomed.

"Elegos, at least take some Noghri with you, someone to protect you."

"That is a kind suggestion, friend Leia, but the Noghri will best serve elsewhere." Elegos canted his head to the right a bit and smiled at her. "This mission must be undertaken. If I am successful, we will all be saved."

Borsk snorted. "Are you really so naive as to think your mission can succeed?"

The Caamasi stared at the Bothan for a moment, then half-closed his eyes. "The chances are slender, perhaps nonexistent, but can anyone here tell me the risks are not worth it if this war can be stopped?"

Leia shivered. "And if you are not successful?"

"Then, my dear, my fate will matter little, given the gravity of what will come."

CHAPTER FIVE

Luke entered the auditorium and saw he'd made a tactical error in leaving the arrangements to Kyp. Tables and chairs had been set up on the stage, facing out toward the amphitheater where Jedi sat. The two tables on the stage were at right angles to each other, forming a wedge centered on a podium. To the left were Kyp Durron, Ganner Rhysode, Wurth Skidder, and the Twi'lek, Daeshara'cor. Her presence on that side surprised Luke because she'd always seemed to view Kyp's rhetoric as being extreme.

At the other table there were only three chairs. Corran Horn and Kam Solusar stood by two of them, conversing. Luke expected Mara to take the third, then sensed she was not behind him. He glanced back at the top of the stairs and saw her taking up a position in the auditorium's shadows.

Luke smiled. *How like her to watch, assessing who is with me and who is not.*

The Jedi Master mounted the steps to the stage with no ceremony. At the top of them he paused and nodded to Kyp. The younger Jedi Master waved a right hand to indicate that Luke should move to the podium, but instead Luke spun and bowed to the sixty Jedi occupying the seats. "I welcome you. Not so long ago we had a meeting, and now events have drawn us together again."

Kyp moved behind the podium and adjusted the microphone, sending an audible squeak through the room's sound system. "Master, the lighting and sound are better from back here."

Luke let himself chuckle once, then nodded and sat on the stage, letting his feet rest on the steps. "That may be true, Kyp, but those who know the Force will be better served trusting in their impressions that come through it, rather than their eyes or ears."

A wave of surprise pulsed off Kyp, then was cut off immediately. From the back of the room Mara gave Luke a nod. To his right, Kam and Corran came to the edge of the stage, then jumped down to the floor to keep themselves lower than he was. This pressured Kyp and his confederates to do the same thing, though Daeshara'cor seated herself on the edge of the stage and gathered her lekku around her like a shawl.

"Thanks for joining me. You worked hard setting this up, but I didn't really want it to be too formal. It made this too much of a council of war. What we need is a meeting of sapient beings who will decide the course of our future."

"Master, you are first among equals." Kyp bowed his head to Luke. "Your wisdom will guide us."

Oh, Kyp, how surprised you would be if I used that opening to dictate what we will do. Luke could feel a sense of quick victory boiling off Corran, urging him to snare Kyp in his own web, but he shook his head. "Insight granted by the Force is not mine alone."

Wurth Skidder smiled carefully. "You suggested, Master, that this is not a council of war, yet we find ourselves at war with an enemy that is merciless and invading the New Republic. Is it not to counter threats like this that the Jedi were created?"

"That *is* our goal, yes. How we get there is what we need to discuss." Luke pressed his hands together and fell silent for a moment. "The Jedi are meant to protect and defend the people of the galaxy. The distinction between protectors and warriors is critical to avoid the seduction of the dark side."

Ganner Rhysode, tall and dark, with a hard, blue-eyed gaze, eclipsed Skidder. "Perhaps, Master, the confusion we suffer comes from the point where an offensive action can be defensive. A preemptive strike at a target, for example, is merely proactive defense."

Corran ran a hand over his mouth before speaking. "It's semantic games you're using there, Ganner. The way you frame that statement doesn't take into account the scope of the operations you're talking about. In a tactical situation where disabling an enemy's ability to respond would guarantee the safety of others, you're right, the strike is defensive. Staging a planetary assault to root out the Vong before they can spread and hit other worlds, on the other hand, is distinctly offensive in nature."

"Corran, your argument plays exactly to my point: what are the guidelines that determine where offense and defense switch one to another? I look for intent, you look at size. All of these variables must be balanced, clearly, and I think we all seek wisdom in marking the difference."

"A very good point, Ganner." Luke smiled at him, then looked out at the Jedi gathered there. Humans and aliens of all genders, they projected keen interest, with concern tainting the edges. The Jedi Master nodded thoughtfully, felt the concern begin to drain away, then looked up.

"The point of balance comes with the focus of the danger. The Yuuzhan Vong have taken a number of worlds. Now many beings are in jeopardy, but that jeopardy is unfocused. Until the threat goes from general to specific, we can't use proactively defensive tactics against it. Corran's example points out that on a tactical level, finding the danger's focus is much easier than on some grander scale."

The green-fleshed Twi'lek's head-tails twitched. "Then you are saying that until we detect this focus, we can do nothing?"

Luke held his hands up. "Not what I'm saying at all. We do have things to do. We need to be out there, on the front, so we can be ready to react when a focus is detected. We have to be out there helping calm the refugees, inspiring them to take heart."

Kyp frowned. "But, Master, if we are not out there fighting the Yuuzhan Vong directly, how can we inspire? Will we not

be seen as weaklings who are just as afraid of the enemy as
the refugees are?"

"Those very questions, Kyp, go back to a wrong way of
looking at the Jedi." Luke sighed. "It is my fault, because I
emerged from the Rebellion cast as a warrior who had destroyed Death Stars, Darth Vader, and the Emperor himself.
Later missions kept that myth alive. Given a choice between
calling upon a bounty hunter or a Jedi, folks turned to the Jedi
because we worked for free and *are* concerned about collateral damage."

"Master, you have not been alone in creating that impression."

"No, Kyp, but it was up to me to see the error of it and take
steps to counter it. Again, the failure to do that has been mine.
Now, better than any other time, we must project the correct
image of the Jedi. We have to inspire hope for the people."

Daeshara'cor launched herself from the stage and landed
in an agile crouch. She straightened up slowly, then bowed
her head to Luke. "With all due respect, Master, I think you
are wrong."

The Jedi Master kept his voice even. "Please, Daeshara'cor,
explain."

The black-eyed female began slowly, her voice low enough
to demand the attention of everyone in the room. "So much
was lost during the dark time of the Empire, Master, that we
do not know a lot about the Jedi; yet what we do know flies in
the face of what you are saying. You were trained by Obi-Wan
Kenobi and Master Yoda to be a warrior. Three times you engaged Darth Vader, and you survived or defeated him. For
you to say now that Jedi are not warriors is to deny your success and the freedom of billions that your efforts won."

She glanced at the white-haired woman seated in the third
row. "Tionne has been tireless in collecting all the Jedi history she can, and what do we find: ballads and tales that cele-
brate great victories by Jedi. The martial aspect of our
tradition can't be denied, Master, and I think it is to this tradition we need to look again to defeat the Yuuzhan Vong."

Kam Solusar, his white hair cut short, folded his arms

across his chest. "You've got a huge flaw in your logic there, Daeshara'cor. You say we've lost so much, then you build a whole based on the parts we *do* have. Fact is that for every grand battle a Jedi might have had, there could have been thousands of little victories. Victories just like the ones the Master is saying we'll need to deal with the Yuuzhan Vong.

"More importantly, his point about focus is critical. It's obvious to everyone here. Kyp almost died fighting the Yuuzhan Vong. Miko Reglia did die fighting them. Why? Because they engaged the Yuuzhan Vong when they didn't know who or what they were."

Kyp snarled. "But Corran had the benefit of my knowledge and his own scouting of the Yuuzhan Vong, and he came far closer to death than I did."

Corran nodded. "Yes. On Bimmiel the danger was very focused, and still I almost ended up dead. When we know enough to launch good missions, we'll have a much better chance of success. Much better than with a series of amorphous efforts to attack and defeat the Vong."

Luke held a hand out. "We need to cool down here for a bit. We don't want emotions flaring and things getting out of control. Regardless of beliefs in offensive or defensive postures, we all can see the wisdom of dealing with the Yuuzhan Vong when danger focuses itself, right? As Corran said, once we have a focus, we can plan and use our abilities to the best in dealing with the danger. Agreed?"

Most of the Jedi nodded their heads, Kyp included—which made Luke feel a bit better. *He may not agree with the course of action we will take, but he has agreed that his course requires limits, and that is a victory I'll gladly take.* Daeshara'cor was the only notable holdout, but she'd always been reasonable in the past.

The Jedi Master smiled slowly. "I do have some bad news. We're going to have some limits placed on our efforts. I learned from my sister yesterday that the New Republic will not sanction or support any Jedi operations in the invasion corridor."

"What?" Kyp's surprise exploded out like a supernova.

"That's pure madness. We're their best hope, and they won't have us working with them?"

Octa Ramis, a strongly built young woman from a high-gravity planet, shook her head. "It makes zero sense for them to do that. Then again, if that's how the government's thinking, being free of them might not be a bad thing."

Ganner scowled. "We have to make them change their minds. They have to see reason."

Luke waved away the comment. "Actually, I'm somewhat pleased with this decision."

"How, Master?"

Luke sighed. "Octa was close to the mark. No sanction, no support, no answering to politicians. We'll be free to use our own best judgment in handling problems."

Ganner ran a hand over his goatee. "But it strips us of resources we could use to handle problems."

"Then you'll just have to be creative, won't you?"

Daeshara'cor shook her head. "How could they abandon us like this? After all we have done?"

"It's better they have." Luke held his arms out. "We are perhaps a hundred in number. A hundred Jedi. If the New Republic was relying on us, they'd pitch us into the battle and expect us to take care of things. They did it before, more times than I care to remember."

He lowered his hands to the stage. "Face it, of late, our exploits have been less than awe inspiring. The problem at Rhommamool, for example, and even the loss of Dantooine. As Leia noted, the politicians can't support the Jedi. This does not mean, however, that we will be totally alone out there. The military will be unable to help us overtly, but they are very sympathetic to us."

Kyp snorted. "What a surprise, warriors liking warriors."

Luke shook his head. "The leadership knows what is truly going on. Having us out there to deal with civilian difficulties will free up their people to do what they do best."

Skidder groaned. "So we baby-sit refugees while others do the fighting?"

"We will protect them and guide them. If danger presents itself, then we take steps."

Kyp Durron raked fingers back through his dark hair. "And we do nothing more? We get no more active missions? Nothing going into Yuuzhan Vong territory?"

Luke shifted his shoulders uneasily. "One mission. Corran is being sent to Garqi."

"Figures he'd be your choice."

"He wasn't, actually, Kyp." Luke smiled carefully. "That choice was taken away from me."

"What?"

Corran's mirth at Kyp's surprise leaked out through the Force. "I used to fly with Rogue Squadron and resigned my commission there five years ago. That left me in the military reserve, and they just reactivated me."

Luke nodded. "Colonel Horn will lead a team of six commandos and two civilian observers into Garqi to study the Yuuzhan Vong, coordinate with any resistance movement, and set up operations to try to get people off the world."

Ganner rested his fists on his hips. "A half-dozen commandos against a planet full of Yuuzhan Vong?"

"They're Noghri, Ganner." Corran shrugged. "Besides, I figured to tap you as one of my civilian observers. Figured you had to be the equal of another dozen Noghri, right?"

Ganner's harsh expression lightened. "Noghri. The mission has merit."

Corran looked out into the audience. "Jacen, I've talked with Master Skywalker, and he's consented to having you be the other observer. Want the slot?"

Luke could feel the different emotions warring inside Jacen, but grudging adherence to duty won out.

The youth stood. "I'm, ah, honored to be asked. If you think I should go, Master, I'll go."

"Good, Jacen, I knew I could count on you." Luke clapped his hands once. "I'm in the process of preparing assignments for the rest of you. They should be ready by the end of the week. We're only waiting on transport scheduling. I know that what you're being asked to do may not be what you think needs to be done. You may think your skills are being wasted. I appreciate that, but these are the tasks that need doing."

Fury arced from Daeshara'cor. "Then this meeting was all a sham?"

Luke frowned. "Not at all."

"But if you were preparing assignments, you had already made your mind up. You knew what you were going to tell us to do. You weren't willing to think about being wrong."

"That's not it at all. The orders could be changed easily. Had there been a convincing argument to show this course of action was wrong, I'd have changed them." Luke held a hand out toward her. "Your effort was excellent, but lacked enough support to be convincing."

"And yet Kam's counterargument lacked any evidentiary support at all. He argued that a complete lack of evidence to the contrary of my evidence was somehow evidence that my point was invalid." She balled her hands into fists. "That is wrong and you are wrong. If we persist in this course, we will find the Yuuzhan Vong right here, on Coruscant. I know it. I can feel it."

"You may be right, Daeshara'cor. I hope you are not." Luke's expression hardened. "But if we follow your course, if we become warriors and go totally on the offensive, the Yuuzhan Vong being here would be the least of our worries."

Her eyes narrowed. "They would never make it."

"No, but in their place would be something worse." Luke's voice sank into a harsh whisper. "In their place we would have a hundred Darth Vaders, and that should fill all of you with more fear than anything we face now."

CHAPTER SIX

Jacen Solo sat alone in the *Ralroost*'s meditation cabin. Located in the aft of the Bothan Attack Cruiser, the room featured a transparisteel arch that provided a clear view of the light tunnel of hyperspace. Jacen had seen such lights all his life, so they were no longer remarkable to him; yet, even so, he found it hard to concentrate and focus his thoughts.

The week just past had been a very full one, but it was not the packing and farewells, the briefing and training that weighed on him. All of those things he had done long before—though he did admit to himself that to be heading off into such grave danger made a big difference in what he said to his mother and father and even his little brother.

"Thought I'd find you here."

Jacen turned and gave Jaina a smile. "Join me?"

"Sure." She appeared only as a silhouette in the cabin doorway. When it closed, returning the room to contemplative darkness, she floated forward like a ghost and seated herself next to him. "Emperor's black bones, Jacen, you really *can* use some time meditating, can't you? I don't think I've ever felt you this agitated."

"Nor, apparently, ever found me this much out of control of my emotional broadcasting."

Jaina laughed, and Jacen luxuriated in the familiar sound. "We're twins, Jacen. We had a head start on reading each other before we got to know anyone else. Still, you do seem to be leaking here a bit. What's wrong?"

"I'm not sure. I mean, I guess the enormity of what we're doing has finally hit me." He looked at his sister. "Mom and Dad had the Empire to fight, and that was very big and powerful. Well, the Yuuzhan Vong are our Empire, and at first scan, they're more powerful than what Mom and Dad faced."

Jaina nodded. "Before, the Force has always tipped the scales in our favor. Here, we just have to be ourselves and do the best we can. Of course, I've got great examples to follow in doing that."

"Colonel Darklighter?"

"Yes, him, the rest of the Rogues, General Antilles, Colonel Celchu. None of them have the Force, but they're ace pilots. I mean, I have a hard time imagining life without the Force, and these guys are doing great things without relying on it."

Jacen laughed lightly. "Not having the Force has to be like being color-blind, but it doesn't affect them." He held his hands out and curled them down into fists. "And that's what's getting to me, Jaina. We have all these people here willing to put their lives on the line, trusting in their leaders, the traditions that govern them, their own sense of right and wrong, their guts. It's a whole army doing that, going off to defend people on worlds that orbit stars that they can't see from their own homeworlds. As Jedi, that's what we do, but . . ."

His sister glanced down and picked at her fingernails. "It can be overwhelming if you look at it on that grand a scale, I guess."

"How can you not?"

She glanced over at him. "You look at the situation, you take responsibility for the things you can handle, and you trust others to shoulder their burden. I'm just one pilot in the squadron. I'm responsible for my wingmate. I'm responsible to Colonel Darklighter. I carry out my orders as best I can. If I try to think beyond that, I'll be distracted and then I won't be of use to anyone."

"But, Jaina, you're a member of Rogue Squadron. All the tradition—how can you not carry that with you?"

"I don't have time for it, Jacen. I concentrate on what I

have to do now, not worrying about the past or what might happen in the future." She turned to face him, allowing the light from the viewport to scroll in warped stripes over her right profile. "I'm kind of surprised that all this has hit you so suddenly. Or, rather, that it hasn't hit you before."

He frowned. "What do you mean?"

"You've always been looking beyond things, Jacen. You always wonder if whatever you have is it, if it's all it could be. It's not a question of whether or not a mug is half full or empty, but whether or not it's the right mug, and the stuff in it is the appropriate stuff." She shrugged. "Because you're smart and talented, you've been able to blow past most problems and still function being concerned with these grander things. In fact, you roll over most problems without even thinking about them."

"That's not true."

"Sure it is. On Belkadan, you went out to free slaves without giving any real thought to your own safety. Why? Because there was a bigger issue there, whether or not the Force had granted you a glimpse of the future. And even after things went badly, you're concern wasn't about your injuries, but about *why* the vision failed you."

He shook his head. "You have that all wrong."

"Jacen, this is your sister. I know you." She sat back, holding herself up with her arms. "Even being a Jedi is something where you look for more. At first you acted as if *Jedi* was synonymous with *hero*. It isn't. Being a hero isn't what all these folks are here to do. They're here to do their jobs."

Jacen stood and paced over to the viewport. "I know that and I respect it."

"But you're still looking for more. You aren't sure if what you've learned about being a Jedi is what you were supposed to have learned about being a Jedi. You want to find a way to become the ultimate Jedi."

"Oh, and you don't question what we've been taught? You don't want to push yourself beyond?"

"Beyond what, Jacen?"

Her question startled him. "Um, ah, I guess I don't know."

"So you're searching for something that may not exist." Jaina gathered her legs beneath her and stood. "Look, I take each job as it comes along. Now I'm a pilot with Jedi skills. I want to be the best pilot I can be. Once I'm there—*if* I get there—then I can look for the next thing."

"There's the problem, Jaina. I have no current job, which is why I'm looking beyond."

"No, Jacen." She reached out and playfully cuffed him on the back of the head. "You have a job. You're a Jedi and you have a mission coming up."

"I know. I'm all ready for that. I did the training. I've studied all about Garqi. I'm set there."

"It's just like when you were younger, Jacen. You're prepared for the job, but you've not done it yet. You're off thinking about the next big thing, and the little thing in front of you might eat you up. The Yuuzhan Vong aren't one of the little adventures we've had in our lives. They are totally serious, and if you look past them, you won't *get* past them."

Jacen turned and looked at her for a moment. The determination on her face and in her voice convinced him that her read was dead-on. *Which means I've got a whole lot more thinking to do.* "And you believe that my experience on Garqi is going to help me perfect being a Jedi?"

"It can help you perfect being yourself. You've got two very different Jedi on the mission with you: Corran and Ganner. You can learn a lot from them—both what to do and what not to do. Slow down a step. Learn. Give yourself a chance to learn."

"It certainly gives me a place to focus." He sighed. "Now you're going to tell me that you knew all this stuff because girls mature faster than boys."

"*Women,* Jacen, women mature faster than boys." She tried to maintain a stern expression on her face, but it cracked quickly. She drew her brother into a hug. "Look, neither of us is playing kids' games anymore. We either have to be as sharp as we can, or we end up being very dead. And a lot of other people with us."

"I know. You're right." He clung to her as if it would be the last time they would see each other. "You'd better fly fast and shoot straight, Jaina. Don't let them get you."

"And you'd better remember that there are nasty creatures lurking in the purple botanical paradise that's supposed to be Garqi." She pulled back, smiling. "Take care of yourself, Jacen. May the Force be with you."

"Thanks, Jaina. It will." He looped an arm over her shoulder. "C'mon, we've got time for a cup of caf before our missions run. I'm going to have to be a great Jedi, and you a great pilot, but, for now, maybe we can just be brother and sister for a little bit longer."

Seated in the ship's galley, Jaina stiffened as she looked past Jacen. He turned to follow her gaze, and what he saw killed his smile. "Did you need me? I think my comlink is on, isn't it?"

Corran Horn smiled easily. "Not a problem, Jacen. Good to see you, Lieutenant Solo."

"Thank you, Colonel." Jaina reached over and pulled a chair away from the small table where she and her brother were seated. "If you want to join us . . ."

Corran ran a hand over his newly shaved jaw. "No, I was just coming down here to get some caf. Chances are, it's the last we'll have once we set down on Garqi. They grow plenty of the beans there, but never mastered the art of brewing it. At least, that was true two decades ago."

Jacen glanced in his own half-empty mug. "If this caf is considered good by Garqi standards . . ."

"Too late, Jacen, no backing out of the mission now." Corran patted him on the shoulder, then looked over at Jaina. "I understand you've taken well to being a Rogue."

"Yes, sir, I like it a lot."

"Different sort of responsibility than being a Jedi, but just as important a one. Colonel Darklighter suggested that when we get back from Garqi, I should run a sim against you and see how good you are."

Jaina blushed. "I'll disappoint you, Colonel. General Antilles and Colonel Celchu regularly vape me in exercises."

Corran shrugged. "Well, they still vape me. Perhaps *we* should sim against them, teach them old guys a lesson or two."

"I'll look forward to that, sir."

Jacen glanced up at Corran. "Do you prefer being back in the military to being a Jedi?"

"It was nice to see the uniform still fit, and I like the extra pip. Even got rid of my beard." Corran grinned. "But I'm no less a Jedi in this uniform than you are or Jaina is. It's a convenient fiction to get done what needs to be done. I'd prefer it were otherwise, but if we have to play games to save some lives, I'll play."

Corran set his empty mug on the table. "That being said, the mission on Garqi will be anything but a game."

"I know. I've studied up on the terrain and surroundings, the natural resources, the communications network, transit links and routes, energy generators and distribution patterns." Jacen frowned as he ticked things off on his fingers. "I've also worked on sims of all of our basic equipment and know the workings of my sample scanner backwards and forwards."

"Good. I expected no less from you. One thing that is going to be very important—something I know your sister is learning with Rogue Squadron—you're going to have to follow orders. I know that independent action the two of you took at Helska 4 saved Danni Quee. I also know your running off to free slaves on Belkadan didn't end so well. Right now you're going to be part of a team. We all depend upon each other, so no running off on some wild tear just because you think you know what has to happen. I'm never going to say no to something just to say no. If it makes sense, I'll consider it. Understand?"

Jacen nodded. He appreciated what Corran was telling him, and didn't miss the very fatherly tone the older man was taking with him. "Yes, sir, I understand."

"Good. One other thing I think you should know: I chose you for this mission because of your experience with the Vong and because of the heart you've shown dealing with them. My own experience with them has not been pleasant, and given an option, I'd not be here. Your willingness to come back again is admirable."

Jacen glanced down again at his mug. "Thank you."

"If we do this mission right, we'll be in and out and the Vong will have scant evidence we were ever there. I'm not expecting anything to require the sort of reckless heroics your family is famous for." Corran smiled warmly. "On the other hand, knowing we've got a good dose of Corellian disdain for the odds, backed by Noghri combat skills, is enough to keep me confident about our chances for survival."

Jaina lifted an eyebrow. "What about Ganner?"

"He's from Teyr—he wouldn't know odds from groats." Corran retrieved his mug from the table. "He's good in a fight, though, and smart when he thinks before acting. And handsome, too, as you've probably noticed."

Jaina blushed again. "Well, it's hard not to."

"His preening all the time kind of makes it obvious." Corran winked at Jacen. "We probably can keep that between us, though. Kind of outside mission parameters."

"Understood."

"Well, I'm off. Take some time with your sister, then double-check your gear. We have a day or two until we deploy, but being ready early is never a vice."

"Will do, Corran."

Jaina nodded. "Good to see you, Colonel."

"And you, Lieutenant. Keep improving that Rogue Squadron reputation, will you?"

"Yes, sir."

Jacen waited until Corran had passed on before arching an eyebrow in his sister's direction. "You were being awful formal there."

"In the military, Jacen, familiarity flows downhill, not up." She smiled. "We're playing by different rules now, I guess."

"Same goal, different paths." Jacen sighed. "Which *could* get me thinking beyond the mission at hand, but I won't. First things first. Get through them, and then worry about the future."

"That, my brother," she allowed as she clicked her mug against his, "is a winning strategy."

CHAPTER SEVEN

Leia Organa Solo sat silently in the passenger compartment of the *Marketta*-class shuttle *Chandrila Moon*. Her two Noghri bodyguards, Olmahk and Basbakhan, sat behind her in the craft's narrow cabin. In contrast to the woman seated in the row in front of her, Leia sensed only calm from the two Noghri. Danni Quee, on the other hand, threw off fear the way a fire gives off heat.

Leia forced herself to breathe in deeply, then slowly exhale, letting her tension slowly bleed away. *Some of it, anyway.* The journey from Coruscant to Bastion had been undertaken under the tightest security possible. The ship kept away from heavily traveled routes, plotted a convoluted course to its destination, and then, when the *Victory*-class Star Destroyer *Protector* arrived at the Bastion system, it waited at the edge, its shields down, weapons unpowered.

Bastion's reaction was swift, sending out an *Imperial*-class Star Destroyer—the *Relentless*—to query the *Protector* concerning the intentions of the New Republic. Leia had indicated she had information she needed to communicate to Admiral Gilad Pellaeon. The Remnant ship had broken off communications for two hours, then instructed Leia that she, her personal staff, and two pilots could bring a single shuttle into the system.

Admiral Aril Nunb of the *Protector* had insisted that for Leia to comply would be to put herself in the hands of the enemy. Leia acknowledged this was true. Many of the Remnant's people still clung to the former glory they had known in the Empire. A whole new generation had grown up since the Emperor's death, and all the wants they felt were blamed on the Rebellion. Leia, as a leader of same, and the chief of state for the New Republic during all but the final battles with the Remnant, became the focus for much bitterness. *People from the Remnant tried to disrupt Luke and Mara's wedding, and it would be foolish to assume I'm safe here.*

Still, if the greater threat of the Yuuzhan Vong was to be dealt with, the Remnant would have to be informed of what was going on and convinced their fate and that of the New Republic were intertwined. She once again pressed Danni into service as a witness to the depredations of the Yuuzhan Vong. She assumed the Imperials would find Danni as convincing as the people of Agamar had.

Leia reached forward between the seats and patted Danni on the shoulder. "It's not going to be a disaster, Danni."

"Thank you." The younger woman covered Leia's hand with her own. "Every time I start feeling sorry for myself, I just remember where Senator A'Kla is going, and I know I have the easy course."

"I'm afraid you're right." Leia sat back in her seat. She remembered back to seeing Elegos off on his solo mission to Dubrillion. She'd been surprised that she caught no fear from him despite the risks he would be taking. She commented on that fact, eliciting a smile from the gold-furred alien.

"The truth is that I feel no fear." He blinked his big eyes. "I know this mission could end in death for me, but that seems a small concern weighed against a war that will kill many. And, I must confess, I have an immense curiosity concerning the Yuuzhan Vong. I would assume they have a similar curiosity about us, which means we have a currency of exchange between us. This will make negotiation possible and, I hope, fruitful."

Leia had hugged him and relished feeling his strong arms around her. "You don't have to go, Elegos. There are other ways."

He'd held her out at arm's length. "Are there, Leia? The Yuuzhan Vong hate machines, so sending any sort of droid or mechanical device to convey our best wishes to them would be an insult. Based on Anakin's experience on Dantooine, we know they respect boldness, hence this mission. If I return, perhaps more bloodshed can be forestalled."

"And if you do not?"

"Then your knowledge of the Yuuzhan Vong will be that much greater." He gave her a simple smile. "I know the danger I am in, but for me to live in peace without taking this chance is impossible. You could no more abandon your acceptance of responsibility than I can. You just make wiser choices in exercising it than I do."

Leia had agreed then, but as the screen in the front of the cabin showed the *Chimaera* looming larger, and Bastion's customs station yet larger, she had second thoughts. She'd last seen the ship when the peace between the Remnant and New Republic had been signed. Her focus on New Republic internal affairs and her subsequent retirement from government had insulated her from contacts between the Remnant and the New Republic. She found herself lacking a sense of the Remnant, which meant she didn't know how difficult it would be for Admiral Pellaeon to offer help.

Even the briefing documents she'd studied on the way out had not given her as complete a feel for the politics of the region as she might have liked. While a number of unreconstructed Imperials had fled to the Remnant, taking a vast amount of wealth with them, economic development of the region had gone slowly. Only a few pockets had the amenities of Coruscant available, and there were portions of worlds where people lived in grinding poverty. The availability of cheaper goods from the New Republic had crippled several industries, and outbreaks of rioting connected with imports had been reported.

On the diplomatic front, things had remained cordial between the two nations. Leia put a lot of that down to the efforts of Talon Karrde. At the time of the peace he had proposed and created an agency that facilitated the exchange of intelligence data between the two realms. This bled off much of the paranoia by hard-liners in each nation, though limited suspicions did remain. According to the files Leia had been given, little or none of the data about the Yuuzhan Vong had been released to Karrde and the Remnant, so while they might know something was going on, they wouldn't have details.

If that has spiked their paranoia, this mission might be doomed before it starts.

The pilot's voice echoed through the cabin. "We have permission to set down in the primary docking bay at the customs station. Estimated time of arrival is three minutes."

Danni turned around in her seat, came up on her knees, and peered down at Leia. "We'll actually be meeting *the* Admiral Pellaeon?"

"It's possible, and if true, a very good sign." Leia sighed. "Diplomacy can be a game, Danni. When we went to Agamar and asked to speak to the Agamarian Council, the fact that I had been chief of state of the New Republic pretty much guaranteed I would be granted access and allowed to speak. My addressing the council was seen as an honor for them."

Her eyes narrowed. "Pellaeon may have factions within the Remnant that oppose the New Republic, and if they are strong enough, it might be political suicide for him to meet with me. In that case a functionary will conduct the preliminary negotiations. If it's a lowly staffer, our mission is doomed. If it is someone higher up—a deputy minister of state, which is roughly my equal as protocol is concerned—we have a chance of pushing our case and getting favorable results."

Danni smiled. "I think astrophysics is easier than diplomacy or politics."

"Oh, I don't know. In politics we have black holes, pulsars, things that give off more heat than light." Leia smiled up at Danni. "I can't remember a time when politics was not part of my life. I'm fortunate that I took to it well. I will admit, though, retirement was fun, and I look forward to it again."

The gentle hum of the shuttle's wings retracting was followed by a bump as the shuttle settled to the customs station's deck. The egress hatch hissed open—the hiss being more than enough to mask the sound of Basbakhan crossing to the landing ramp to forestall any assault. Olmahk stood between the gantry and Leia, then nodded at her to come forward when his partner indicated all was clear.

Leia moved past the gray-skinned aliens. The Noghri, with their small stature, appeared almost childlike, save for their fierce features. She knew from experience just how powerful and deadly they could be, either bare-handed, or wielding the lethal knives they wore. The Noghri were quick and dedicated to her safety.

The Yuuzhan Vong killed Bolphur on Dantooine, which is why I now have two *Noghri to accompany me.* A shiver ran down her spine. Twenty years earlier she couldn't have imagined any creatures more deadly than the Noghri, but a Yuuzhan Vong warrior had killed Bolphur with his bare hands.

Leia descended the landing ramp and was pleased to see two squads of stormtroopers lined up beside a white walkway painted on the deck. The formality and ceremony of the welcome boded well for the mission. Beyond them were three officials in Imperial uniforms, though one of them bore no rank insignia. She let Basbakhan precede her through the gauntlet of stormtroopers, then she paused and waited for the envoys to come forward.

The civilian, a woman only slightly taller than Leia, did so. "Welcome, Consul. I am Miat Temm. This is Colonel Harrak and Major Pressin."

Leia shook hands with each in turn, then waved Danni forward. "This is Danni Quee, my aide."

The Imperials acknowledged Danni with a nod, then Miat pointed toward a turbolift. "If you would come this way, the admiral is waiting."

As they rode up in the lift in silence, Leia gently used the Force to get a sense of the Imperials. From the two military men she caught insecurity masked by arrogance, and a fair amount of confusion about her and their being asked to attend her. From Miat she got almost nothing. *She's blocking me!* Leia suppressed a smile and wondered if any of Pellaeon's enemies knew Temm had Force abilities.

The lift opened, and Miat led them into a large reception room that had a wall of transparisteel that allowed them to look out at the *Chimaera*. Leia took this as a very good sign. Beyond it sat her ship and, below, the world of Bastion, all looking very peaceful.

Admiral Pellaeon, clad in the white uniform of a grand admiral, stood at the far end of a white table. He had no guards with him and wore no weapons. He smiled as they entered, and waved Leia toward the seat at his right hand.

"It is good to see you again, Consul Organa Solo. Please, come, be seated, and tell me what has prompted your visit." He nodded to his own people, indicating their place was along the other side of the table. "If you need any refreshment, this can be arranged. You have a comlink, yes, Major Pressin?"

"Yes, Admiral."

Leia smiled. "Nothing right now, thank you." She shook Pellaeon's hand and returned his smile, then introduced Danni as her aide.

Pellaeon greeted her with a nod of his white-maned head. "Please, be seated."

Leia sat and noted how Pellaeon turned his chair to face her, leaving his back to his aides. Miat did not seem to mind, but the two officers were clearly put out. *Pellaeon wants them off guard and unsettled for some reason, but why?*

Leia leaned in toward Pellaeon, capitalizing on his openness. "I have come to correct a problem we've had sharing information with you. Something very important has happened, something that could determine the future of both the New Republic and the Remnant."

Pellaeon nodded slowly. "You're referring to the fall of Dubrillion."

Leia managed to cover her surprise, but Danni could not. "How did you know?"

The flesh around the admiral's dark eyes tightened. "Dubrillion and other New Republic worlds that border our space are of interest to us. I'm certain, Consul, it will come as no surprise that we had agents on Dubrillion. While the messages they got out did not contain a lot of information, we knew something was amiss. The cessation of their communications confirmed it was a serious problem."

He lifted his chin. "I will also tell you that I know of Danni Quee. We had an agent on Belkadan, at the ExGal project. Any site designed for the gathering of intelligence has an interest for us. We've not heard from our agent since what we presume to have been the facility's destruction."

Danni blinked. "Who?"

Pellaeon shook his head. "Let's leave the dead, dead, shall we?"

Leia nodded. "You know some of what has gone on, then. I have a data card that will fill in the technical details, but the brief is this: Humanoid aliens from outside the galaxy have attacked or destroyed half a dozen worlds on the Rim. They exhibit an extreme technophobia, are merciless in combat, take slaves, and are ruthless in dealing with them. They are called the Yuuzhan Vong, and we, as yet, have established no direct diplomatic connection with them. Danni was one of their captives for a while and has had the most direct contact with them among our people."

The admiral sat back, lacing his fingers together and letting them rest against his chin. "You have come to us to ask for aid in dealing with the Yuuzhan Vong?"

Leia nodded. "You, perhaps better than anyone, know the difficulty of dealing with an enemy who can strike anywhere. And let me speak frankly, internal dissent within the New Republic is not at the boiling point, but New Republic military forces are needed to police disputes. At the same time there are vocal segments of the population who, because of the peace accords, think the military should stand down, demobilize, and that no more money should be budgeted to defense. While the Yuuzhan Vong invasion, if it goes unchecked, could bring everyone together, the unity would come too late. We need to stop them now. We have a force that will function very well as an anvil, but we need a hammer."

A grim grin tugged at the corners of Pellaeon's mouth. "I would have thought the Jedi would act as your hammer."

"As the data files will point out, the Yuuzhan Vong are resistant to Force powers. The Jedi are doing all they can to help in this situation, but there aren't enough of them to be able to handle a problem of this magnitude."

Pellaeon glanced back at the two military men. "Your request has not gone unanticipated, Consul. These men have told me, at various times, that any military cooperation with the New Republic would be a trap. You would lure our ships away from our home and destroy them, then finish your conquest of Imperial space. They had not anticipated this very scenario, but their cautions are not easily dismissed. To them, this threat is a sham."

Leia smiled coldly at the two men. "Your intelligence forces must already know that my daughter, my sixteen-year-old daughter, has joined Rogue Squadron. She did so at Dubrillion, and your sources would have told you that the squadron has just replaced over half its personnel. If I did not think the Yuuzhan Vong were a grave threat, do you think I would allow my child to have joined the military?"

Colonel Harrak ran a finger around between his neck and the uniform's collar. "Your children are Jedi."

"And as I said, the Jedi have little edge against the Yuuzhan Vong."

Pellaeon raised a finger, cutting off Harrak's reply. "All right, Consul. I will review the material you have brought. I am not unsympathetic to your plight, and I, as well as many others in the Empire, do feel a responsibility for the people of the New Republic. They may have rejected us, but we have not rejected them. If we are able, we will help."

Leia nodded. "I can't ask for more than that."

"You could, Consul, you could." Pellaeon returned her nod. "Let's hope this will be enough."

CHAPTER EIGHT

Luke Skywalker reached out and tapped the Force to re-
fresh himself. Energy pulsed into him, sending a tingle over
his flesh. He smiled, luxuriating in the warmth flooding him.
He did not often use the Force in this manner these days, pre-
ferring passive acceptance of its gifts, but exhaustion had
seized him. With no time to sleep, he needed the boost.

He glanced down at the datapad on his desk. Compiling
the assignments for all the Jedi had not been as simple a task
as he had hoped it would be. It seemed those Jedi given solo
missions wondered why they were being sent out alone.
Those who were traveling in pairs or larger groups wondered
if Luke doubted their abilities, or they resented the extra
burden of nursemaiding another Jedi. Protests arose over the
nature of the missions themselves, or the nature of the solutions to be used on them—the philosophical split among the
Jedi raising the smallest of conflicts to a whole new level.

He massaged the back of his neck with his mechanical
hand. "Well, Artoo, I thought saving the galaxy was hard work.
Being a bureaucrat is even worse."

The little droid's head swiveled around, and R2-D2 tootled
at him. The droid had plugged its interface into a computer
connection and had been helping Luke track the Jedi as they
headed out on their transports. As news of their making their
connections came in, R2-D2 updated their files, letting Luke
know if his people were getting where they needed to be.

Mara appeared in the office doorway. "Luke, we may have a problem."

"What?"

She entered the office and waved Anakin in after her. "Anakin found the initial stuff. I'll let him explain."

The brown-haired youth smiled. "To help plan missions in the future, I created a computer program to analyze the usage of our data library. By tracking the files accessed after assignments were made, we'd learn what kind of information the Jedi needed to complete their missions. In the future we could add those files to the mission assignments, saving some time. It would be on the data cards, and their only need from that point on would be for updates."

The Jedi Master smiled broadly. "That's very good thinking."

"Thank you." Anakin beamed. "The program just peeled off requests for data. No one knew it was running. When I did a breakdown of the requests for information and cross-checked my data against the computer system's control log, I found a problem."

Luke arched an eyebrow. "And the problem is?"

"My program caught fifteen more requests than the official control file had listed in it." The youth shrugged. "The fifteen that aren't recorded could be trouble. Artoo, if you can, pull up the anomaly file and send it to Uncle Luke's datapad."

The droid whistled a low tone. Luke glanced down at the screen and saw a list of fifteen files scroll past, with descriptions for each appended. "Maw Installation, Death Star, Sun Crusher, Darksaber, *Eye of Palpatine* . . . These are all about superweapons and the places they were built."

Mara nodded. "The files contained the complete technical specifications for those things. There's a ton of data there, and we have no idea what they were looking for in pulling them up. The implication, though, is not good."

Luke sat down at his desk and stared at the list of files. "The reason the control file didn't list these fifteen requests is because whoever asked for the files went in and deleted the requests, right? Covered her tracks?"

"Or his, yes." Anakin shook his head. "I tried to go through and see if I could pull the data from memory, but the appropriate memory sectors had been overwritten twice. Whoever did it is very good."

Luke sighed, then looked up at his wife. "You have suspects?"

She nodded slowly. "I checked our files. There are a handful of Jedi who have the necessary computer skills. I ruled Anakin out immediately, ditto Tionne. Most of the others I'm not concerned about, but Octa Ramis could be a problem."

Luke called to mind the dark-haired woman. "She was close with Miko Reglia, wasn't she?"

"Tionne said they had a romance at the academy. She thought they'd drifted apart after graduating and going their separate ways, but the logs of their travels suggest they were able to meet several times." Mara shrugged. "I don't recall her being particularly distraught at his memorial service on Yavin 4, but I was not in the best of shape then."

"I was preoccupied. You notice anything, Anakin?"

"She wasn't weepy or anything that I saw, but then I didn't pay that much attention to her. I'm sorry."

"That's okay. It's not your responsibility." Luke nodded. "Do you think she pulled these files down to try to build a weapon to use against the Yuuzhan Vong? I can't see the sense in that."

Mara shook her head. "It would take years to build another Death Star. The fastest to build would be a Sun Crusher, but the facility for doing that is gone. I can't imagine anyone, no matter how much in grief, would look at building one and causing stars to go nova just to get rid of the Yuuzhan Vong."

"That would be extreme, yes."

"But isn't that what Kyp did?" Anakin frowned. "To avenge his brother's death by the Imperials, he destroyed Carida."

"And found out his brother wasn't dead after all, but died when the planet did, yes." Luke sighed heavily. "The ends never justify the means. You've checked on Octa?"

"She has boarded her ship and is on her way."

Luke sat back and ran a hand over his jaw. "Interesting. Her associates?"

Mara smiled. "She's been on a number of missions with Daeshara'cor."

"But Daeshara'cor is on the *Durastar*, going off to Bimmisaari. I mean, Artoo reported to me that the *Durastar* suffered a drive failure so came out of hyperspace early, but Corellia is supposed to be sending ships out to ferry the passengers on to their destination."

The droid shrilled confirmation of Luke's comment.

Luke's wife nodded. "If you look at the standard emergency rescue report appended to the request for aid, you'll see one rather significant item. There are zero Twi'lek females listed on the passenger manifest."

"What?"

Anakin smiled. "I figure she boarded, planted some memories on the staff, then left the ship before it departed. The list of passengers was made up based on the folks who reported to evacuation stations."

"And you'd have to think, Luke, that a Jedi would be very hard to miss in that sort of emergency situation."

The Jedi Master closed his eyes. "Something here doesn't make sense. Octa looking for superweapons does make sense. The Yuuzhan Vong killed Miko. I can see her wanting to seek revenge, even if it's of the dark side. But what is Daeshara'cor's motive? Were she and Miko ever close?"

Mara shrugged. "I don't know, but I think motive is secondary right now. We need to find out where she went."

Anakin laughed. "That should be easy. There are only so many places where a superweapon could be built, right? The shipyards at Kuat . . ."

The Jedi Master stood. "Building a superweapon isn't something that can be done in secret anymore, and the resources to do that just aren't available. She's after something else."

He glanced at the droid. "Artoo, pull up the docking bay data

on the *Durastar*. I want a list of ships—and their destinations—
that took off from that docking bay within four hours either
way of the *Durastar*'s departure."

"That could be dozens of ships, Luke."

"I know, Mara, but we have to start somewhere." Luke
took his lightsaber from his desk and clipped it to his belt.
"We don't need a rogue Jedi running around, and especially
not one looking for a planet killer."

An airspeeder got them to Docking Bay 9372 quickly
enough. The cavernous enclosure bustled with activity. Load-
lifters shifted cargo; passengers snaked through the chaos in
long lines; idle workers clustered together drinking, laugh-
ing, gambling. Mara and Anakin split up to hit the ticketing
offices for the commercial shuttles that would transport people
from the surface to ships waiting in orbit. R2-D2 accessed a
local terminal node to get the data Luke had requested.

Luke opened himself to the Force and wandered through
the docking bay. A torrent of emotions poured into him. He
smiled at the petty anger arcing between a couple whose
sense of *on time* differed radically. He passed by people anx-
iously trying to remember if they had packed this or that. He
nodded at ships' captains calculating profit with each crate
loaded or unloaded from their freighters' holds. The excite-
ment from folks heading into space for the first time broadened his smile, and the passion of a couple heading off on a
honeymoon prompted him to blush.

As he strolled along he did his best to immerse himself
in Daeshara'cor's mind-set. She had an interest in superweapons and had access to fairly confidential files concerning them. She knew she was expected to be in Bimmisaari in
five days, so she had that much time in which to operate before any alarm could be sounded. That narrowed down her
choice of destinations.

Luke immediately rejected her having traveled to the Maw
Installation near Kessel. The *Durastar* would have taken her
to Bimmisaari, from which Kessel was a short hop. More importantly, the files she'd accessed would have left no doubt

that Admiral Daala had destroyed the lab complex. While it was possible some portions of it still floated in space, the chances that anything useful still remained were minimal.

Before Luke could figure out what Daeshara'cor had been looking for, he felt something through the Force that seemed out of place. It began as curiosity, but spiked immediately into fear. Discipline immediately masked the fear, but did a fairly poor job of it. Luke looked to his right and saw a man hastily pulling up the hood on his cloak and turning away.

The Jedi Master gestured easily. "Wait, don't go."

The cloaked man halted in midstride as if he'd frozen solid. Though he fought against Luke's suggestion, his torso turned and his head came up, letting the cloak slip back. "M-me?" the man stammered.

Luke nodded slowly and smiled as he crossed to where the man stood. "I think you can help me."

"I don't know anything."

"Perhaps." Luke shrugged easily. "The fact is that you are here often, and you make a living by spotting needs and fulfilling them, isn't that true?"

"I, ah, I . . . I've done nothing."

A security officer came walking over. "Is Chalco here giving you trouble, Master Skywalker? I will deal with him, write up a report."

Luke casually waved a hand. "Thank you, not necessary. Nothing here to report."

The security officer blinked once, then continued on his way, passing between Luke and the surprised docking bay denizen.

"What you do here, Chalco, is of no concern to me right now. I think you may be able to help me, though."

The heavyset man ran a hand over his bald head. "How so?"

"You observe things. Two days ago a Twi'lek, a Jedi, was here. She was supposed to leave on the *Durastar*, but she did not embark on the ship. You saw her, yes?"

The man slowly nodded. "I find it convenient to keep an eye out for Jedi, you know, ah, in case I can help them."

"That's very nice of you."

"Yeah, well, she came through and I noticed her. She boarded the ship, but I never seen her come off." He scratched at his unshaven throat. "Then, later, I saw her talking to a mate on a freighter. She did that thing with her hand that you did there, and the mate, he just turned away from her like she wasn't even there. I looked away at that point, figuring I didn't want her to see me and do me like she did him, you know. I heard those stories about losing your mind and everything."

Luke's eyes narrowed. "What was the name of the freighter?"

"*Lucky Star II.* Tramp freighter, makes stops all over the place. Half of them aren't on the flight plan. I think they were making for Ord Mantell, but I don't know."

"Good, thank you."

The man opened his hands. "Hey, I helped you. You gonna do something for me?"

Luke crossed his arms over his chest. "What would you have me do, Chalco?"

The man shrugged. "I dunno, maybe make all the security guys here forget what I do. You know, make them forget me?"

"If I did that, there would still be the surveillance holo-cams." Luke openly appraised the man, noting that despite having thickened around the middle and being somewhat short, he was still a powerfully built man. "Let's try this. I think I'm going to need someone to help me locate the Jedi. If you come with me and we succeed, I'll speak to the authorities on your behalf."

Chalco hesitated. "You'd do that?"

"Speak to them, yes."

"No, trust me to come with you?" The man's brown eyes narrowed. "You know what I am, that I make my living as I can, doing whatever."

"And here's a chance for you to make it doing something beneficial." Luke nodded once. "So, yes, I'll trust you. Meet me back here in an hour all packed and ready to go."

Chalco thought for a second, then nodded. "I'll be here."

Mara came walking over as Chalco departed. She glanced at her husband. "Picking up strays?"

The Jedi Master gave her a sidelong glance. "Daeshara'cor's

mother was a dancer who traveled very extensively. As a youngster Daeshara'cor spent a lot of time in docking bays in spaceports. She knows her way around, and we're going to need help catching her. If Han were himself, I'd ask him to help. As it is, we'll have to trust this one."

Mara nodded. "Daeshara'cor will be worrying about *us* tracking her and likely won't see *him* coming. I understand. The office I checked with didn't have anyone heading out that answered to her description."

"They wouldn't. Chalco noticed her hanging about. Chances are, she took a freighter that was destined for Ord Mantell, but might have made some stops along the way."

"Then she could be anywhere."

"I doubt it. My recollection of star charts isn't flawless, but there's one world out in that direction that will help Daeshara'cor." Luke gave his wife a smile. "We've got to get a ship. We're bound for Vortex."

"Vortex?" Mara took Luke's hand in her own. "There's nothing there but the Cathedral of Winds. Daeshara'cor is going there to listen to music?"

"Nope." Luke smiled and gave his wife a kiss on the cheek. "She's going there to talk to someone who helps make the music."

CHAPTER NINE

Shedao Shai spun on his heel before the harsh, hoarse scream had a chance to echo down the street. A ragged human slave, flesh coated with dust, beard patchy and unkempt, broke from the work detail and rushed at him. The slave's eyes blazed past the nubbins of the coral growths on his cheeks, and he raised a piece of duracrete debris to smash the Yuuzhan Vong leader down.

Two younger warriors belatedly moved to intercept the assassin, but Shedao's sharply barked warning held them back. Clad in vonduun crab armor, with his rank baton, the tsaisi, coiled about his right forearm, the Yuuzhan Vong leader had little fear of injury. He flowed forward, keeping his center of gravity low, then came up, catching the slave's throat in his right hand. He lifted the man effortlessly, then battered the debris aside with his left hand.

The slave grabbed Shedao's right wrist. His eyes widened as the tsaisi hissed and rose up, ready to strike. The human's lips peeled back in a feral snarl, then he looked into Shedao's eyes defiantly. Unable to speak because of the hand crushing his throat, the man nodded, once, sharply, as if to demand death from the Yuuzhan Vong leader.

Shedao's thumb pressed up along the man's jaw, slipping past the curve of the bone, touching the skull right behind his ear. The two combatants watched each other, both knowing that with a simple increase of pressure Shedao Shai would pop the man's skull free of his spine, killing him. The man, with spittle flecking his lips and beginning to ooze down into the Yuuzhan Vong's gauntlet, nodded again, daring Shedao to kill him.

The Yuuzhan Vong commander shook his head once, then cast the man toward the two warriors who were overseeing the work group. "Take this one to the priests. Have them prepare him. If he survives, he will be of use."

The two warriors each grabbed an arm and bowed respectfully, tugging the man back down the street.

Shedao Shai allowed them to get ten paces away, then added, "And while there, ask the priests for a regimen of contemplation for warriors who are slothful."

The warriors bowed again and set off, but at a pace noticeably quicker than before.

Deign Lian, his direct subordinate, resumed his place a half pace behind Shedao, at his left hand. "Was that wise, my leader?"

"Easily as wise as your questioning my judgment, here, in the streets." Shedao Shai was pleased that his face mask hid the crooked smile born of Deign's flinching at that remark. "The warriors will return chastened, enlightened, and more dedicated to their duty."

"It was not that, Commander, but sending the man off with them. He attempted to murder you. The other slaves will see his survival and exaltation as a license to try to kill you again."

Shedao Shai continued his tour down the broad Dubrillion street in silence, knowing his lack of an answer would weigh more heavily on his aide than any rebuke. The destruction caused by the conquest of Dubrillion had not been overwhelming. Much of the cityscape was recognizable, and the work details were making much headway in clearing debris. Soon the slaves would be trained in how to use gricha to repair minor damage, and gragricha would be brought in to produce proper Yuuzhan Vong buildings.

"I believe, Deign Domain Lian, you are looking past the obvious to explore a realm we may never approach. Your question presumes the slave will survive inculcation. We do not know this. Yes, I chose him because he had spirit. He didn't shy from pain. More importantly, he wanted me to kill him. He had embraced his insignificance, which means our inculcation can give him new significance. He is a vessel ready to be filled with the truth of the universe. If he can contain what he learns, he will be of great use to us."

"This I understand, Commander Shedao Domain Shai." Deign bowed his head as he spoke.

His using Shedao's full, formal title—aping Shedao's formality—acknowledged his subordinate status. Shedao knew this acknowledgment was halfhearted at best. Domain Lian wished for a return to its former days of glory, and Deign was its best chance for such a return. In his aide Shedao had a feral amphistaff clutched to his breast, and he knew he would feel the sting of its bite when he could least afford it.

"Perhaps then what you do not understand is that despite the work of our agents like Nom Anor, we do not know our foe well at all. This New Republic is curious in how it approaches warfare."

"They are cowards at heart, my leader."

"To make that judgment so coldly, Deign Lian, is to deny that we have much to learn." Shedao glanced left, catching a spark of hatred in his aide's eyes. "Enlightenment is always useful, and we need more, much more, concerning these people."

Shedao Shai ignored Deign's fatuous mouthings about his wisdom. The New Republic and its response to the Yuuzhan Vong invasion had him puzzled. Nom Anor had provided a succinct political analysis of the situation within the New Republic, which is why they had chosen the invasion corridor they did. They hit the New Republic at a point where it was weakest, along a line joining it to the Imperial Remnant. That was pure military strategy: any force is weakest where two commands meet. The Remnant had not reacted and attacked the flank, which freed up units Shedao had held against that possibility.

The New Republic still had not struck back, and this puzzled

Shedao Shai. He did know of the galactic civil war, and it did strike him as possible that some peoples would not want to see a return to a conflict. Still, the actions of the slave showed that these people were capable of martial conduct. A total acquiescence to the invasion did not seem to be a rational response, which led him to suspect deception.

He was willing to admit, as well, that of the worlds taken, only Dubrillion had true significance. The others had been sparsely populated and largely undeveloped, so their losses would be insignificant to the galaxy. Garqi, to which he had sent Krag Val to oversee occupation and transformation, did produce a lot of foodstuffs, but its loss could easily be compensated for since many of its products were geared for consumption by the elite, not the masses.

In their military engagements, the New Republic forces had fought a series of rearguard actions. Shedao Shai refused to acknowledge their destruction of the Yuuzhan Vong base at Helska 4, because that had been a Praetorite Vong operation. *When politicians seek to play at being warriors, one must anticipate disaster.* He glanced again at Deign. *The reverse can also be very bad.*

Shedao Shai found his foes admirable, after a fashion. That they were corrupt and weak was not in doubt. Their reliance on abominable mechanicals pointed out their moral decay, but the facility with which they employed their tools did impress him. The military response to initial encounters with Yuuzhan Vong biotechnology had neutralized the invaders' advantages, leaving their starfighters on even terms.

The land battle on Dantooine had likewise shown how formidable the New Republic's personnel could be. When Shedao Shai reviewed a report listing the casualties among two training cadres of warriors in pursuit of a pair of refugees, he felt his belly begin to tighten. Given that the two being chased were *jeedai*, some casualties were to be expected, but the escape of the quarry was not. Domain Lian lost four warriors in that escapade, which only partially dulled the sting of Domain Shai's losing two warriors to a *jeedai* on Bimmiel.

In his grudging admiration for the enemy, Shedao Shai

wondered if their reluctance to attack centered around the same problem he was having: that the New Republic did not know enough about the Yuuzhan Vong to be able to formulate a solid strategy. *If they need more intelligence, we will have insertions of forces on conquered worlds. They investigated Belkadan and likely know we have been producing coralskippers there. What else they gleaned from there I cannot imagine, but I shall have to assume they know all.*

Shedao Shai mounted the steps to the building in which he had situated his office. The building both irritated and soothed him. The irritation came from the predominance of straight lines, hard edges, and exposed piping, all of which had been described to him with the vulgarity *industrial*. The building was no more elegant than a big stone box, and the uniform shade of gray it had been painted did little to enhance it.

The reason he chose it as his headquarters, however, was because of the purpose to which it had been put. The building had been the Dubrillion Aquarium and was filled with scores of transparisteel tanks teeming with sea life from Dubrillion and other worlds. A central column filled with water dominated the building's heart, and through it swam a rainbow riot of fish, including huge emerald sharks.

Shedao Shai did not acknowledge the guards at the doors as he swept into the building. He mounted the stairs to the right, then cut back to the left, to the central chamber. Fish swirled in a lazy cyclone through the column and eclipsed three figures whose outlines were distorted by the water. The two taller figures were his own people, but the golden pyramid between them intrigued him.

He circled through the chamber to the right and saw seated on the floor a long-limbed creature covered in golden down. The creature's long legs were crossed, his hands folded into his lap and his spine straight along the duracrete wall at his back. Purple striping flowed back from the corners of his eyes and over his shoulders. He wore a simple purple loincloth, gathered with a gold cord.

When Shedao Shai moved into view, the individual rose to

his feet without touching his hands to the ground. The guards were a heartbeat late in restraining him, clearly not having anticipated his action. *He has lulled them into carelessness, which marks the placidity with which he allowed himself to be borne here.* By the same token, the supple strength in his body and the ease with which he slipped his shoulders from beneath the guards' hands marked him as a potentially dangerous enemy.

The Yuuzhan Vong commander halved the distance between them with two long strides. "I am Commander Shedao Domain Shai." He spoke first in his own tongue, then repeated his introduction in the halting, clicky tongue native to the galaxy.

The creature blinked his big violet eyes. He spoke slowly but strongly, allowing Shedao to capture his words easily. "I am Senator Elegos A'Kla of the New Republic." He bowed his head for a moment. "I apologize for not having mastered your tongue."

Shedao looked at the two guards flanking Elegos. "You are dismissed."

Deign looked at him. "Commander?"

Shedao spoke in the New Republic's tongue. "I have nothing to fear from you, Elegos?"

The Caamasi opened his three-fingered hands and displayed them as empty. "My mission here is not one of violence."

The Yuuzhan Vong leader nodded slowly. *He does not say that I should not fear him, but just should not fear violence at his hands. It is a difference that Deign has missed entirely.* "You see, Deign?"

"Yes, my leader." The subordinate bowed. "I shall leave you."

"Wait." Shedao reached up and stroked the vonduun crab making up his helmet and face mask. The creature relaxed, allowing him to slip the helmet off, baring his head and face. Shedao shook his head, freeing his black mane and spraying sweat onto Deign's armor.

He handed his aide his helmet. Even though Deign's face lay hiding behind a mask, there was no disguising his shock at seeing his leader show his naked face to the enemy. "You will take this to my contemplation chamber, then return with refreshments. You will hurry."

"Yes, Commander." Disbelief and disgust threaded through his words. Deign bowed deeply, then backed away until the fish-filled cylinder shielded him from Shedao's gaze.

The Yuuzhan Vong leader returned his attention to Elegos. He watched him for a moment, slowly organizing the words of his enemy's tongue. "I was told you appeared in a small ship at the edge of this system. You used a villip to request transport here on one of our ships. Why?"

Elegos blinked once. "It is believed you see machines as abominations. I wished to offer no offense."

"Your respect of our sensibilities is appreciated." Shedao Shai stepped toward the cylinder. He stripped off his left gauntlet and pressed his hand to the transparisteel. The warmth of the water slowly filtered into his flesh. "Your mission here is?"

"One to promote understanding. One to see if the course our peoples are on now is the only course possible, or if we might plot another one, together." The Caamasi pressed his hands together. "I was at Dantooine. I would not see that happen again."

"And I reviewed the aftermath of Dantooine. I was also at the place known to you as Bimmiel." Shedao's dark eyes hardened. "There is much that separates our people. Much that would speak against any peace between us."

"Perhaps our ignorance of each other's nature and ways is what makes it appear that we are falling into a black hole of conflict." Elegos lifted his chin, exposing his slender throat. "I would enlighten you and learn from you."

Shedao smiled and caught the reflection of his twisted visage in the transparisteel. "Do you know what you ask, what you suggest?"

"In your mind, apparently not."

The Yuuzhan Vong gestured toward Elegos with his right hand. The tsaisi slithered down into his grasp, then stiffened into a blade the length of Shedao's forearm. "You know that I could kill you at my whim. Praise would be heaped upon me for slaying you, for you traffic in abominations. To some of us, there is no redemption for your kind."

Elegos bowed his head. "Already I learn. And, yes, I knew my life could be forfeit in coming here. This did not deter me."

"A commitment to mission above the preservation of self—this I understand. This I respect." Shedao spun the baton in his hand, then flicked it back so it slapped against his forearm. The tsaisi flexed, then coiled around his vonduun bracer. "What you are willing to teach me will contain no tactical information that would be of use."

"I am not a tactician, nor am I privy to their counsels." Elegos regarded him closely. "What I would learn from you would likewise be useless."

"Is knowledge ever useless?"

"No, and this is another place we agree."

Shedao Shai nodded slowly. "I will place you under my protection. I will teach you. I will learn from you. We will understand each other."

"And find a new path to bring our people together?"

"Perhaps. You will know if this is possible when you know us better."

Elegos clasped his hands together at the small of his back. "I am prepared to learn."

"Good." Shedao Shai nodded once. "Your lessons will begin now. Follow me. To understand us, there is but one place to start. I will introduce you to the Embrace of Pain."

CHAPTER TEN

Corran Horn glanced up from his datapad. "Everything on the checklist is covered. I think we are ready to go."

Admiral Kre'fey nodded slowly and escorted Corran across the *Ralroost*'s deck. The proximal docking bay had been cleared of starfighters, leaving a decrepit freighter as the sole occupant. "My engineers have assured me that the *Lost Hope* will be able to make it off the ship. How much longer it will hold together after that they will not say."

"I understand, Admiral. We've all known this was a gamble from the start." Corran sighed and slipped the datapad into a thigh pocket on his flight suit. "If it works, great. If it doesn't, well, make sure others learn from our mistake."

"Certainly."

The problem of inserting a scouting team onto an enemy planet was one that had perplexed military strategists for ages. Ships often tried to slip in disguised as space debris, streaking toward a planet like a meteorite, then veering off under power once they were too low to the ground to be tracked. While the lack of an impact would tip the enemy to the fact that something was odd, the scout team could be well away from the area and safely gone to ground by the time investigators tried to puzzle out where they had gone.

With the Yuuzhan Vong, things got a bit more complicated because the New Republic wasn't certain about the technical capabilities of their scanners. The fact that the Yuuzhan Vong used biologically based tools suggested severe limitations, but without actually knowing, there was no way to put together a sure plan to slip in unnoticed. Absent the ability to go in unseen, the New Republic decided to go for the other extreme and make sure the Yuuzhan Vong knew, beyond a shadow of a doubt, that their security had been penetrated.

Corran boarded the *Lost Hope* and retracted the gantry. He went up front to the bridge and waved at the admiral. He refrained from touching anything in there. Since the Yuuzhan Vong would undoubtedly investigate the crash, the New Republic knew they'd need trace biological matter in the ship to make the enemy believe the crew had not survived insertion into Garqi. Biomatter had been synthesized and sprayed around in all the logical locations, so any inquiry would have plenty of data to sort out in reconstructing the deceased crew of the *Lost Hope*.

He worked his way back to the main cargo hold and climbed into a much smaller ship, one of the tiny shuttle craft found on luxury liners. All six of the Noghri were jammed in the back and strapped in place. Ganner sat back with them, looking very large and uncomfortable since his feet rested on equipment and his knees were tucked under his chin. Corran slipped past Jacen and took his place in the forward of the two seats in the cockpit. He buckled on his restraining belts, then pulled on a helmet and opened a comm channel to the *Ralroost*.

"*Lost Hope* reporting in. Ready to go."

"Copy, *Hope*. Two minutes to reversion."

Corran initiated the start-up sequence. Both sublight engines came on-line, but the starboard one was producing only 75 percent of its usual power. "Jacen, can you see about bringing *Hope*'s starboard up at least another 10 percent?"

"As ordered."

The older Jedi hit a button on his console and reports concerning the *Lost Hope* vanished, to be replaced by the monitors for *Best Chance*, the smaller shuttle craft contained within the freighter's hold. Corran brought its engines on-line, and each reported 100 percent output. Repulsorlift coils reported operational. He hit a button that sealed *Chance* and made it spaceworthy.

"I've got *Hope*'s engines balanced."

"Thanks, Jacen. The charges are set and functional?"

"Yes, ready to go on your command."

"Good, we're perfect." Corran forced himself to smile. The plan was simple enough. The *Lost Hope* would leave the *Ralroost* and head down, then suffer a catastrophic engine failure. As it plunged into Garqi's atmosphere, the ship would break apart. Debris would be strewn everywhere, and *Best Chance* would be able to fly away free. By the time the Yuuzhan Vong collected all of the *Hope*'s parts and figured out something was going on, the survey team would have returned to the New Republic.

The only Hutt spoiling the party was the lack of a hyperdrive on *Best Chance*. Without it, the only way the party could leave the system would be by rendezvousing with a larger ship, like the *Ralroost*. The lack of a hyperdrive made emergency extraction very tricky, but Corran knew that if they needed to get off Garqi in a hurry, they'd already be in enough trouble that there was no guarantee they'd ever get a chance to escape into hyperspace.

Corran flicked his comm unit over to address Ganner and the Noghri. "Get set for a wild ride. No guarantees on this one, but with any luck, we'll all get out of it alive."

Jaina's X-wing shot free of the magnetic containment bubble over the *Ralroost*'s belly launch bay. She brought the fighter around on a heading that tucked it into the Rogue Squadron formation above Garqi. Anni Capstan, Jaina's wingmate, designated Rogue Twelve, came up behind her, then Rogue Alpha, a recon X-wing piloted by General Antilles, completed the formation.

Colonel Gavin Darklighter's voice came strong and steady through the comm channel. "Two flight, you're on the snoop; One on my polar, Three below. Lock S-foils in attack position."

Major Alinn Varth followed Gavin's orders with a quick comment. "On me, Three. Tighten it up, Sticks."

Jaina suppressed a smile. Because she was a Jedi and carried a lightsaber, and because she used a flight stick to control the X-wing, her compatriots had given her the call sign Sticks. She took it as a sign of acceptance, which was good, since she was a lot younger than the others in the squadron and didn't have a fraction of their experience. They didn't look down on her for those lacks, however, and had even bragged about her to some of the new recruits.

"As ordered, Nine." She nudged the stick to port, bringing her into proper position in the formation. Jaina glanced back at the R2 unit riding behind her. "Sparky, pipe up if I slip out of formation again."

The droid beeped an acknowledgment.

Colonel Celchu's voice came through the comm channel. "Rogues, Flight Control here. We have ten skips coming up from Garqi. Intercept is plotted, being sent now."

Data scrolled up on Jaina's primary monitor, and Sparky tootled as he assimilated it. The skips—more properly, coral-skippers—were single-pilot fighter craft, similar in purpose to X-wings. *But utterly dissimilar in design.* Unlike X-wings, which were manufactured, skips were grown, forming a symbiotic union of various creatures that provided a hull, propulsion, navigation, and weapons for the stony ships. The pilot interfaced with the fighter through a hooded device that fed impressions to him and received his orders by reading his brain waves.

Jaina shivered. Her uncle had tried on one of the cognition hoods and experienced the contact with the alien fighter. She'd not been offered the opportunity to do the same, nor would she have taken it. Her experience as a Jedi built in her a dislike for anything trying to pick up stray thoughts, and having her head enclosed in a gelatinous membrane while that was going on was just not something she wanted to think about.

She looked at her monitors as the *Lost Hope* deployed from the Bothan Assault Cruiser's belly bay. "Nine, I have two skips breaking off to go after *Hope*."

"I copy, Sticks. You and Twelve are on them."

Anni hit her comm unit's talk switch twice, sending a double click through the channel in acknowledgment of the order. Jaina broke to port and pulled back on her stick, coming around in a tight turn. She inverted, then dived and cut to starboard to make her first run at the skips.

"I have lead, Twelve." Jaina flicked a thumb over her weapon-selection switch and linked her lasers for quad fire. She nudged the stick around and dropped the aiming reticle over the lead skip's ovoid outline. She hit the fire-control button beneath her middle finger, starting the lasers through a fast cycle that spat out dozens of little red energy darts.

The scarlet bolts flew on target until ten meters from the skip, then they bent inward. The dovin basals that manipulated gravity fields to provide the skip with propulsion likewise shielded it by creating gravitic anomalies. These little voids sucked the light in like a black hole.

Jaina kept her fire steady, but let the targeting point shift up and back. To properly shield the skip, the dovin basil had to move the void, taxing its energy much as absorbing the bolts did. Finally a few stray bolts got past, scoring the black rock hull. Jaina then hit the primary trigger and sent a quartet of full-powered laser bolts into the skip.

A void picked one off, but the other three hit the skip's aft hard. Yorik coral bubbled and evaporated in some spots, became fluidly molten in others. In the frigid vacuum of space, the mineral shell hardened almost immediately into an icicle trailing behind the Yuuzhan Vong fighter. The hot stone burned dovin basals and scorched neural tissue that allowed for control of the ship, sending the lead skip into a tight spiral that curled it back down toward Garqi.

The second skip proved to be more evasive. It juked and dove, cutting to port and starboard at random. Shots missed entirely instead of being absorbed by a dovin basal. The pilot had clearly learned that agility in space combat was worth as much or more than shielding. He used his skills as a pilot to avoid the X-wings and to draw ever closer to his target.

"Cover me, Sticks."

"Got it, Twelve."

Anni Capstan's X-wing cruised forward and broke hard to port, bringing it in on a slashing attack at the skip's starboard aft quarter. She sprayed laser darts all over the ship, using her etheric rudder to keep the fire on target, and the Yuuzhan Vong pilot finally had to deploy a void to keep her shots off him. She cut loose with a full quad shot, but the void sucked all four of those bolts in, then the skip bounced up above Anni's line of flight.

Jaina saw the nose of Anni's fighter come up and wondered for a second why she hadn't fired another burst. It occurred to her that Anni's lasers might be recharging, since she had sprayed a lot of energy around to little effect. The skip boosted forward, pulling away from the X-wing, and Jaina thought Anni would lose him since he could now use the dovin basal that had been shielding him to provide more propulsion.

Then fire blossomed on either side of the X-wing's slender nose.

Throughout the time snubfighters had engaged in combat, a debate had raged over the efficacy of employing proton torpedoes against other starfighters. There was no doubting that the missiles would obliterate a starfighter. The weapons were designed for damaging much larger ships. To use them against a snubfighter was the equivalent of using a vibro-ax to kill an insect—gross overkill.

Then again, in combat, can overkill ever be gross?

Jaina couldn't be sure if the Yuuzhan Vong pilot realized that Anni had waited for him to pick up speed before she fired, or if he died assuming she had just gotten lucky. He did try to deploy another void, but it was late in materializing and only slightly altered the course of the second torpedo. The first one flew straight and true, slamming into the skip's belly. It detonated in a burst of argent fire that fed up through the fighter like lightning. The fragmenting coralskipper disintegrated before her eyes, with the second torpedo flying through the heart of the blast and detonating a hundred meters beyond it.

"Great shot, Twelve." Jaina smiled as she looked up at the

Lost Hope. She could feel her brother on board. *You're safe now, Jacen.*

Then a terrible explosion ripped apart the freighter's port side, and the stricken ship started falling toward Garqi.

Hitting Jacen harder than the jolt from the explosion was Jaina's shocked anguish. He'd tried to steel himself for it, having anticipated it, but the grief and sense of loss rolled through the Force all raw and jagged. He wanted to reach out to her, through the Force, and tell her all was well, but he could not.

Instead he pulled himself in, shutting down his presence in the Force. He'd not liked having to deceive his sister about how the *Lost Hope* would be used to get them onto Garqi, but fooling her had been necessary. No one knew how much the Yuuzhan Vong could read in terms of communications or emotions. *Just because we are blind to them through the Force, we've no call to assume they are blind to us, too.* Only by having the people on the ship and in the fighters think their freighter was going down could they be sure the emotions and communications would be genuine.

"Jacen, my screen is showing a faulty linkage at J-14. Bad switch or—"

"Just a second, Corran." Jacen's fingers flew over his console. "Looks like the explosion kicked metal back. J-14 is broken and has released prematurely. J-13 and J-15 are still holding, but pressure is beyond spec already."

"Sith spit." Corran turned in his chair enough to glance back at Jacen. "Get the secondary charges ready to go. Blow them in sequence two on my mark. Be sharp. Can't be worrying about your sister right now."

"Yes, sir." Jacen brought up the pattern diagram of the sequence two explosions. Six of the eight charges glowed green, but two others showed red. *The two nearest J-14.* "We have a problem, Corran. The charges near J-14 are bad."

"Got it."

Jacen looked past the pilot's head and at the holographic feed occupying the area of *Best Chance*'s forward viewport.

The feed came from holocams mounted on the *Hope*'s hull, allowing the pilot to see what things looked like as the doomed freighter hurtled at the planet. The freighter was just beginning to hit the edge of the planet's atmosphere. Little pieces of the hull began to glow from the friction, with scraps of paint ablating off as sparks.

Corran keyed a comlink. "Ganner, look out the starboard viewport. Can you see the two charges there on the stanchion? They're blinking red."

"I see them."

"Can you use the Force to compress the det-chargers to the point of exploding?"

"Never done it before."

"Well, we have to do it now. If you can't get both, just focus on the upper one. On my signal."

"I copy."

"Jacen, get ready. Once his goes, you blow yours."

"As ordered."

The freighter bucked as the atmosphere became denser. Corran's hand danced over the command console. He fed power into the repulsorlift coils, which slightly insulated the ship from the tremors wracking the *Hope*. The *Chance* shimmied a bit, and stresses mounted on some of the other connectors holding the two ships together, but nothing else released.

The freighter started to turn to port as the jagged hull there began to drag in the atmosphere. Corran fought it and tried to get the ship oriented on a simple flight path, then hit a switch that cut the power on the *Hope*'s engines. The whole craft lurched, then twisted as the atmosphere battered it.

"Everyone stand by. This won't be fun or pretty." Corran hit some switches on his console. "Ganner, blow the charges, now!"

The Force gathered behind Jacen and focused itself on the explosives. The first one blew easily and vanished from Jacen's screen. Without waiting for the second, the young Jedi hit a button on his console, lighting off the other explosives in a rippling sequence that shattered the aft hull.

Corran hit a switch, and the connectors holding *Best Chance* inside *Lost Hope* all released. The smaller ship tumbled free of the shell that had brought it into the atmosphere. Corran made no attempt to direct its flight or stabilize it, he just let it twist like any other piece of debris. As the ship came around, Jacen managed to look through the viewports and catch a glimpse of the *Hope*'s fiery descent to Garqi.

The altimeter built into Jacen's console scrolled off the meters to the planet's surface dizzyingly fast. Six kilometers shrank swiftly to four, then three and two. Jacen recalled a single klick being their margin of safety and sought any sense of anxiety from Corran as the small ship plunged past that barrier.

He got none, which brought a smile to his face. He could easily imagine his father sitting in the pilot's chair, waiting and waiting to bring the ship to full power, pushing safety margins that he considered overly generous. Jacen didn't necessarily think this willingness to undertake risks was part and parcel of being a Corellian as much as it was an artifact of the Rebellion. Pilots then had had to do outrageous things to win the freedom of everyone in the galaxy. For them, prudence gave way to efficacy.

Five hundred and seven meters above Garqi's rain forest–covered surface, Corran boosted full power to the repulsorlift coils. This marginally slowed their descent but didn't prevent the ship from plunging into the trees, shearing off limbs, splintering wood, and scattering a colorful cloud of birds. The *Best Chance* crashed down through the upper canopy and through the midlevel before the repulsorlift coils met enough resistance in the planet's mass to bounce the *Chance* back up.

Corran let the small ship hang there in the air as the purple leaves and gnarled branches strewn over the forward viewport began to shrivel and smolder against the hot hull. "Everyone okay?"

"I'm good." Jacen glanced back at the others as they all reported in unharmed.

The small ship's comm speakers crackled. "This is Flight

Command *Ralroost* recalling all fighters. Evac countdown has commenced."

"Rogue Eleven here. We have a freighter down."

"We're aware of that, Eleven. The ship broke up. No life signs."

Jacen felt a shiver run down his spine. Jaina's X-wing's sensors would be too weak to pick up life signs at this great a range, so she had to believe he was dead. Just for a heartbeat he wanted to open himself up in the Force so she'd know he lived, but he stopped himself.

Corran turned and nodded to him. "I know it's tough, Jacen, but she'll be told the truth once the *'Roost* pulls out."

Jacen shook his head. "I don't think I've ever done anything like that to her before—to anyone before."

"It would be great if you never had to do it again, either, but there are times when a little cruelty now saves more a lot later. It's an unfortunate part of growing up." Corran gave him a smile.

"I copy." Jacen hit a button on his console and punched up a specific frequency. "I have a locator beacon on our contact frequency. Heading two-one-nine."

Corran ruddered the ship around on that heading and fed power to the engines. The small ship began to move forward sliding through the forest. The branches scraped along the hull, and furry anthropoids scurried away in terror. The ship moved on, letting the purple world of Garqi swallow it and, hopefully, hide them and their mission from the Yuuzhan Vong.

CHAPTER ELEVEN

Once the *Pulsar Skate* came out of hyperspace and began its descent toward Vortex, Luke Skywalker could feel the peace of the Vors lapping against him like waves on a shore. He traveled from the lounge amidship in the long, slender freighter to the cockpit and smiled. Mara sat in the copilot chair, and R2-D2 had plugged himself into a restraining socket build behind her chair. Opposite him a green and white R2 droid had taken a similar position behind the pilot.

Mirax Terrik Horn, her long black hair gathered into a braid, turned and regarded Luke with a steady, brown-eyed gaze. "We made it. With Whistler and Artoo both doing nav plots, we shaved a good distance off that run."

The droids tootled happily in unison.

The Jedi Master smiled. "Once again, I am happy you were willing to make this run for us."

Mirax shrugged. "I regularly have Whistler monitor request traffic for courier runs. Anything with Jedi appended to it gets a high priority from me. Besides, with Corran off out there somewhere, my children at the academy, and my father doing whatever he's doing, I'd just be sitting at home."

Mara smiled. "Better doing something than just waiting."

"Waiting is so boring."

Luke raised an eyebrow. "I don't seem to recall the word *boring* ever being applied to times when the two of you are running around together. In fact, I recall—"

Mara held a hand up. "We were exonerated."

"And we *could* have been at your academy during those years instead of off on our adventures. Your students would have loved *that* distraction." Mirax nodded. "Besides, the collateral damage was never really that bad."

The Jedi Master smiled. "I think the Vors are rather particular when it comes to the issue of collateral damage."

"Agreed. We've got a landing clearance at their primary Cathedral docking bay. After Admiral Ackbar and Leia's unfortunate accident, the Vors established a two-kilometer no-fly zone around the Cathedral so no one else will plow a fighter into it." Mirax turned back around to look out the viewport. "Atmosphere in fifteen seconds. Buckle in if you don't want to get bounced around."

"I'll let the others know." Luke turned and walked back up the corridor to the lounge, where Anakin and Chalco both sat. The two of them had played a game on the holotable, but ended up squabbling about the other cheating. This offended Anakin, who only partially accepted the explanation that the tables Chalco normally played on had had their code sliced so often that the only way to win was by cheating the other guy better.

"Since you were winning and I couldn't cheat, I figured you had to be cheating," he'd offered.

Luke smiled. "Strap in. We're hitting atmosphere."

Anakin complied with the order, but Chalco just gripped the arms of his chair with white-knuckled hands. Luke shook his head as he walked over to a bench seat and fastened restraining straps about himself. "Chalco, you don't have to do everything the tough way."

The heavyset man shrugged and almost bounced out of the seat as the *Skate* bucked. "I know you Jedi have power, but that's not everything, you know. Us normal folks are capable, too." As he spoke he jabbed a thumb in the center of his chest.

Another jolt shook the ship, and Chalco came half up out of the chair. Luke gathered the Force to settle him back down, but discovered Anakin had already managed it. *And he did it so gently that I doubt Chalco knows he's been helped.* "Please, Chalco, just strap in."

The man grumbled a little, but reached for the restraining straps. "Well, the ride is a bit bumpy. I mean, if you Jedi are going to strap in, can't hurt, can it?"

Luke and Anakin shared a smile, then the Jedi Master shook his head. "Can't hurt at all. When we get down, Mara and I will go see the person we need to speak with. The spaceport here is not much, so I'd like you two to stay with the *Skate*."

Anakin's expression immediately soured. "But I was hoping—"

Luke held a hand up. "Stretch out with your feelings, Anakin. Can you feel Daeshara'cor here?"

The youth hesitated for a moment, then shook his head. "No."

"No, indeed."

Chalco frowned. "You didn't expect to find her here?"

"Not unless something highly unusual is going on. I think she came here for information." The Jedi Master sat as far forward as the restraining straps would allow. "We will learn what she learned, then move on. That's when we'll need you, Chalco."

"What about me?" Anakin asked.

"You're vital to all this, too, Anakin, that much I know."

His nephew's expression brightened. "What am I going to be doing?"

"I'm not certain. The Force hints at times, and hints are all I have. And the hint for right now is that you'll be staying with the *Skate*."

"You wouldn't be saying that because it's easier than telling me to stay because you're my uncle, right?"

Luke arched an eyebrow at him. "Anakin!"

The comm speakers in the lounge crackled for a second, then Mirax's voice poured from them. "We are on final approach. A landspeeder is waiting for us. We'll be on the ground in a minute."

Luke smiled. "And if all goes well, we'll be off again inside an hour."

A temperate world with almost an equal mix of land mass and ocean, Vortex consisted primarily of vast grassy plains of blue-green grasses that whipped this way and that by the gusts of wind. The Vors themselves were a humanoid species of mammalian stock. Hollow-boned, with leathery wings that let them glide on the thermals rising from the plains, the Vors had an incredible sense of harmony within their species and with their world. This harmonic nature had inspired them to create the Cathedral of Winds.

As the landspeeder approached it, threading between two large colonies of thatched dwellings, Luke found the Cathedral to be something at once tied to the world, yet something completely alien to it. While the Vors were clearly capable of advanced materials manipulation—since without these skills the tall crystalline spires could never have been raised—they reserved such construction for special projects. Their homes were of the world and would nourish the world, whereas the glassy towers were made to be more permanent and impressive.

The winds fed into the Cathedral, rushing through hollows, twisting through clear tubes. Thin walls vibrated, filling the air with a ringing peal that undulated in tone. Transparent louvers connected to gears that, in turn, were connected to propellers, making the louvers rise and fall, sharpening and softening sounds. The very building seemed almost a thing alive, giving voice to thousands. And during the Concert of Winds, the Jedi Master knew, the Vors would use their bodies to shift the sounds, truly making that performance into a living symphony.

Mirax slowed the landspeeder, then brought it to a stop, allowing Mara and Luke to disembark five hundred meters from the towering cathedral. Standing there between the two Jedi and the crystal structure was a tall, blue-skinned female. She wore a gown of midnight blue that set off her flesh color and pearlescent feathery hair. Luke had once heard the term *ethereal* used to describe her, and here, at the Cathedral of Winds, it seemed so appropriate. Willowy and even fragile, she seemed a phantom composed of the melody washing over him.

As he approached, he smiled at her and was a bit dismayed to see that she did not return his smile. "Greetings, Qwi Xux."

She nodded. "Greetings, Master Skywalker. It has been a long time. I am sorry you came all this way. I cannot help you."

Mara frowned. "How can you say that?"

The frail Omwati smiled knowingly. "I know many things, Mara Jade. I know that when, with Wedge, I helped repair the damage here I did something that was good. After leaving him, I realized that this was the only place where I found peace. I returned and begged the Vors to let me continue my work here. It is my hope that through the songs of the winds, the laments of my many victims will be given voices. Once that happens perhaps I will finally know complete peace."

Luke nodded solemnly. "I can understand the desire for peace."

Qwi sighed. "Very few do. Here I have a chance to create something of beauty which might counteract the horrors I created."

Luke and Mara exchanged a grim glance before Luke spoke. "I'm sorry if my appearance here reminds you of past pains. I wish you all the best in seeking this peace. If there is anything I can do to help . . ."

A quick smile contorted her face for a heartbeat. "I had hoped, perhaps, that Kyp Durron might come here. I don't know if he is haunted as I am, but I would hope he would hear the people of Carida singing here."

"That is a request I will relay to him." Luke glanced down at the ground for a moment. "Kyp could use some peace."

Mara brushed her red-gold hair back over her shoulders. "Why is it you think we're here?"

"You are after the Twi'lek Jedi. She was here." Qwi's voice tightened. "She came to me to ask after superweapons. She knew of the third partial Death Star at the Maw. She wanted to know if there was yet one more, or another Sun Crusher, or perhaps other abominations that no one knew of save me. She noted the Emperor seldom had only one of anything produced."

Luke nodded. Even the first Super Star Destroyer, the *Executor*, had had a twin being produced at the same time. It had become the *Lusankya* and was given over to Ysanne Isard as her personal playground while the first one was presented to Darth Vader. *I've always assumed there are more of his vicious little toys waiting to be discovered out there.*

Mara frowned. "So, was there a second Sun Crusher?"

Qwi shook her head. "Not to my knowledge. The armor was a breakthrough. Some of the quantum crystalline technology was used here, to rebuild the Cathedral. Unless the Emperor had a parallel facility matching the Maw's work, he could not have produced another. Had such a facility existed, its lethal harvest would have already been seen. As it was, the Maw produced enough terror weapons that he must not have felt a need for another facility."

Luke's head came up. "There was nothing else?"

Qwi thought for a moment. "Well, there *was* the *Eye of Palpatine*. Its mission failure caused the Emperor to support the Maw. Perhaps the Eye has a twin. Daeshara'cor seemed to think it might have."

"Did she ask you if you knew of plans for other things that had not yet been produced?" Luke asked.

"Or for knowledge of scaled-down prototypes or anything else that could be used as a weapon?" Mara added.

"She asked and I told her that all the memories from that time were gone, destroyed by Kyp Durron."

The Jedi Master's eyes narrowed. "But you just said you used the Sun Crusher's armor technology in the Cathedral. She would have picked up on a lie."

The woman laughed lightly, but the sound came mirthlessly. "Kyp stole the memories, but I still possess the foundation upon which all that work was built. Reviewing files, experimenting, I now know what I once knew then. I can see how I did what I did. I did not lie, so no lie was detected. Regardless, never again will I create things that maim and kill. Never."

Mara snorted. "Never say never, Qwi. There's a threat out there that might require a Sun Crusher or Death Star to deal with it."

The blue-skinned woman shook her head. "It does not matter. I stand by what I said, no matter the price."

Mara's hands curled into fists. "How can you say that? Your work could save billions."

"How, by killing billions?" Qwi pressed a hand to her breastbone. "You are heroes. You may have killed, but it was in battle, defending yourselves. I created weapons that shattered worlds and murdered billions in an eye blink. Innocents were vaporized. You may have felt that through the Force, but I have felt it by studying about the worlds I destroyed. I know the names, know the images, and with them I work to give those extinguished lives a voice. I strive to let those people contribute to the beauty here."

She sharpened her gaze. "I know it can sound insane, dwelling on such things, but someone has to. Without accepting responsibility and resolving to atone for what I did, I would leave myself open to believe that things weren't really so bad. I would do what you suggest, I would create only silence. Death would be preferable to that."

Mara blinked hard. "Philosophically I understand pacifism, but to adopt that as a stance in the face of an overwhelming evil, I just . . ." Her fists opened and closed slowly.

Luke rested a hand on his wife's shoulder. "It is better she has made a principled stand and would defend it with her life, than it is for her to become the tool of those who would use her work for ill."

"But, Luke, what if there is no other way to stop the Yuuzhan Vong?"

"Then, my dear, we must question whether they are meant to be stopped, or if we have missed the other solution." Luke gave his wife a confident smile. "I don't like having options eliminated, but neither do I like having weapons that can destroy planets and stars being made available. I have a question for you, since you knew the Emperor. Would he have had only one ship named *Eye of Palpatine*, or would the Emperor have had two eyes?"

As Mara thought, a stiff wind coaxed a high keening from the Cathedral. "If he had a second and it was employed at the same time, perhaps the same problem would have resulted in its loss."

Luke smiled. "That problem was a pair of Jedi."

"And there were plenty of pairs of Jedi to go around back then." Mara shrugged. "It's possible there's another *Eye* out there."

Qwi brought her slender-fingered hands together. "It's my hope that if there is another *Eye* out there, you find it before it is employed. Giving a voice to the dead is a noble pursuit, but it is one that I hope, someday, will no longer be necessary."

"That's my wish, too, Qwi." Luke sighed and set his shoulders. "I have a feeling, though, that particular day is a long way off."

CHAPTER TWELVE

Anakin watched his uncle, Mara, and Mirax race off in the landspeeder. He didn't like being left behind, but he fought against his discomfort. *Being angry is childish, and I don't need to be childish.* He was about to drop into the copilot seat and look over the *Skate*'s controls when the scuff of a boot on the floor turned him around.

Just for a moment, Chalco froze like an animal trapped in a spotlight. Then he grinned and straightened up, projecting an air of confidence that almost completely masked his shock at being discovered. "I was just going out. To look around."

"Master Luke told us to stay here."

"He's your master, kid, not mine." Chalco rested his thick-fingered hand on the landing ramp control switch. "You stay here, like he told you to."

Anakin folded his arms across his chest. "You aren't supposed to go out there."

"You think you can stop me?"

"You think I can't?"

Chalco's dark eyes narrowed, thick flesh bunching up around them. "You sure you want to try?"

"Master Yoda told my Master that there was no try, 'only do or do not.' " Anakin suppressed the immediate desire to use the Force to pin the man against a bulkhead. Mara had gotten after him about using the Force for tasks that didn't require it. Since he'd been able to keep Chalco in his seat during the atmospheric entry, Anakin knew he could easily stop the man from moving.

And because I know I can do that, I don't need to do it. There has to be another solution. Anakin shrugged easily and let his hands hang loose at his sides. "You know, if you're not on the ship when we go to leave, you'll be stuck here. This isn't exactly Coruscant when it comes to ships and traveling and making a living. The Vors are a bit uneasy about foreigners, so you'll be put on a manual labor detail. But you can do what you want to do."

Chalco's expression eased into a mask of puzzlement. "You really think you could stop me?"

"Does it matter? If you want to go out there and spend your time pulping grasses, pulling fibers, weaving them into cloth, why would I want to stop you?" He recalled a conversation he'd had with Mara on Dantooine. "Lots of folks think of the Jedi as people who will come in and save them from their own stupidity. If we were, we'd never have a free moment."

"You think I'm stupid?"

Anakin ignored the twin piping from the two droids. "If you were stupid, Master Luke wouldn't have you along with us. I guess I think you just are like a lot of folks. You live for today and don't think about tomorrow. That doesn't let you get ahead."

"Think that's so, kid?" The question came loaded with pique, but Chalco relaxed and leaned against the bulkhead, so Anakin assumed the tone was more for show than reflective of any true upset.

The young Jedi shrugged. "I haven't known you for very long, but I think you have the same problem as some of the Jedi. You are concerned with image and what others think of you. You trade a lot on your reputation. Does it wear on you the way it can on Jedi?"

The stocky man ran a hand over his unshaven jaw. "Maybe there are times, you know. Sure, it gets tiring. People always pushing, testing. You get a reputation and people want a piece of it."

"Yeah, I know." Anakin spun the copilot chair around and

sat on the edge. "My father's had to put up with that forever, and the Jedi, well, everyone pushes us to see what we have. Some folks are just afraid and stay away. Others are afraid and push just to prove they aren't afraid. Lots of wasted effort there."

Chalco nodded. "Your father's Han Solo, right?"

"Yes."

"I saw him a couple of times recently. Kinda torn up about his partner's death."

Anakin nodded slowly, fighting against the automatic—and now familiar—pangs of guilt over Chewbacca's death. "It hit him very hard."

"They must have been good friends." Chalco let a half laugh shake him. "Never had much truck with Wookiees myself. Don't know that I've ever been that close to anyone."

"They'd been through a lot together. Chewie was a constant in my dad's life, and in mine. He was always there and, now he's not." A jolt of pain ripped through Anakin, choking him. The vast gulf Chewie's death had left in his life opened up before him.

He tried to speak, but couldn't. He held a hand up for a second, then swiped at a tear. "Sorry," he croaked.

Chalco shifted his shoulders stiffly. "Look, kid, I, ah, may not have had a close friend like that, you know, but I can understand the hurting. You get used to people being around. Seeing them at a spaceport, having them in the next cell, that kind of thing. And, you know, one day you wake up and they've been paroled or something. You never know if you're going to see them or the credits they lost to you playing sabacc. I mean, look, I'm not good expressing myself here, but . . ."

Anakin nodded and felt relief roll off the man. "Thanks, I understand. When you get to know someone, you can be hurt if they go away suddenly. The hurt is really big and really strong. Chewie, well, he was always there, smiling, joking, never complaining when I climbed all over him or messed up something he was doing. He was just a rock, and when that goes away . . ."

"But he wasn't the only rock in your life, kid." Chalco nodded off toward the Cathedral of Winds. "You have your uncle and your mother and your father."

"Well, you saw my father. He's been, um, distant." Anakin sighed. "My mom has had things to do. She's been supportive, but we've been apart. Uncle Luke, he's been great, but he has a lot to do. It's okay, though, because this is an adult thing and that's what I need to be learning to handle."

"Don't grow up too fast, kid." The short man shrugged ruefully. "But you gotta grow up. You don't, you become like me. Maybe growing up fast isn't all that bad."

"Well, the key is just growing up, I guess, fast or slow, no difference." Anakin glanced at the landing ramp's controls. "You still want to head out there?"

Chalco thought for a moment, then shook his head. "Not that I'm afraid of a little hard work."

"Never thought that."

"Didn't figure you did." The man smiled slowly. "Then again, helping Jedi track a Jedi, that's plenty hard work, I'm figuring. Harder than anything I've ever had to do before, and it's about time I start pushing myself. After all, it's the grown-up thing to do."

Admiral Gilad Pellaeon hated being seated in a big chair on a dais at the Moff Council. Only four of the moffs had attended in person; the rest were present in holo only, with their appearances costing more than the admiral thought their input was worth. Everything he had to tell them he could have sent out in a communiqué, but the moffs clung jealously to the idea that their counsel had value.

Moff Crowal, from the world of Valc VII, lifted her chin defiantly, but did not rise to her holographic feet. Valc VII was the Imperial world that pushed the border into the Unknown Regions, making her the farthest from the Yuuzhan Vong threat. This distance from danger in no way made her feel safe, and as always, she agitated for her backwater world needing more in the way of resources than could ever be justified.

"If this is a serious threat, Admiral, then we implore you to defend our worlds. If it is a *trap*, then we would likewise wish for you to keep our ships in Imperial space."

The admiral pressed his fingers together. "As I have told you all before, this is no trap. The threat to the New Republic is real. Their request for aid is real."

Moff Flennic's jowls shook with anger. "They should be allowed to crumble. Had they not destroyed the Empire, this threat would be as nothing. The Emperor would have dealt with it in an eye blink."

Bastion's own Moff Sarreti, young though he was, leaned forward with the sagacity of a much older man. "I fail to understand how, Flennic, you can make that statement. The New Republic defeated the Empire, and now the Yuuzhan Vong prey on them. It stands to reason that they would have beaten the Empire, as well."

Flennic's face contorted into a snarl. "Sarreti, I would have to ask this: Given your analysis, why would we commit our forces to defend the New Republic when, by your estimation, our forces are clearly inferior?"

Sarreti nodded slowly, acknowledging the logic of the question. "We should do it because it is the *right* thing to do."

Crowal snarled. "The *right* thing to do? Provide aid and succor to those who bleed us dry, destroying our economies, flooding our worlds with items that erode our culture? Oh, this *is* a trap, and you've fallen well and good into it."

Sarreti stood slowly, and Pellaeon knew that every move, every motion, no matter how seemingly casual, was deliberate. The young moff pressed his hands together and rested his fingers against his lips. His eyes focused distantly, as if he were lost in some wormhole of thought, then his hands fell to his sides. He began speaking in a low voice, softly, almost seductively.

"The wisdom of my elders is something that weighs heavily when I am given to consider serious matters such as this. Your experiences, from before the death of the Emperor, through the period of the warlords to now, holding together this fragile new Empire, these are all of value. My experiences are few in comparison, since I was young when the Emperor perished. My coming of age was in the midst of the Rebellion. My family fled Imperial Center when it fell, and eventually arrived here, where I entered the Empire's service.

"Perhaps, since my eyes were opened to the conflict only after the Empire's decline, I see things differently. I do not see through lenses of fury, of pain at losses, and of melancholy over the past. I view what the New Republic has done, and while, like you, I do not think they have done everything as well as they might, I am not blind to what they have done. Let us not forget that six years ago, had they wanted to, they could have crushed us. It was this Empire that had almost ripped them apart through treachery, and yet they did not punish all of us for the actions of a very few. They sued for and permitted us an honorable peace, as is evidenced by the fact that we have forces they can solicit for their aid."

Standing tall, he waved a long-fingered hand toward Pellaeon. "This request they have made of Admiral Pellaeon is no trap, no threat. It is an honest request, one that they have made not because of how we see them, but how they see us. They have *asked*, not *demanded*. They see us as their equals, and if we do not see the value in responding to that sort of overture, we are very blind and very foolish, and deserve to be swallowed whole by them or these Yuuzhan Vong or anyone else."

The young moff's comments had his colleagues nodding their heads, by and large. Pellaeon smiled at him and gave him a nod, then stood himself. He balled his fists and planted them on his hips, then nodded gravely.

"As always I find your commentary and advice useful, my moffs, but I must remind you that *I* command Imperial space. I summoned you to this meeting not to seek your advice, but to advise you and warn you. When we allow the people to know what is happening in the New Republic, and what our response to it will be, there will be plenty who react as some of you have. They will see no reason to support those they see

as enemies. I expect you will find it in yourselves to be per-
suasive to the contrary. I thank Moff Sarreti for his eloquence
and commend him to you as an example."

Flennic's hologram arched an eyebrow. "You will commit
our forces no matter what our opinion is?"

"You act as if you are surprised, Moff Flennic." Pellaeon
smiled slowly, his bristling white mustache broadening. "This
was your opportunity to voice your opposition, but you know
that your fellow moffs, by and large, will be in support of this
move. I wanted to inform all of you that I will be issuing a
mobilization order that will activate all reservists and call
some of those units into active duty. I will also issue a call to
all of our covert forces, both within the Empire and without,
to come to our aid. While some of you might have seen our
hidden forces as ones that would someday enable us to take
back the galaxy, the Yuuzhan Vong threat is one we must defeat. We will need everything we can summon, and then some."

Pellaeon glanced at an aide in the rear of the chamber. "I
am having sent to all of you the acceptable codes being used
by returning forces. You will not impede their travel in any
manner. In return for this cooperation I will not be summoning your personal bodyguard units and you will be given
latitude in using reserve units to maintain order."

Crowal shook her head. "You think you can distract us by
giving us soldiers to play with?"

"If you think that's what I'm doing, then, yes, I think you
shallow enough to be distracted." The admiral's eyes darkened. "Understand this: If the Yuuzhan Vong can defeat the
New Republic, we cannot stand against them. I suggest you
use the time I will win us in fighting against them to make our
worlds as secure as you can. If I fail, if you are made to play
with your soldiers, I hope I do not live to see the results. Pellaeon out."

The holographic images of the moffs vanished. Sarreti
came walking over to Pellaeon as the other three moffs drew
together in a group and filed from the room. The admiral noticed that the young moff remained standing on the floor, not

mounting the dais, allowing the two men to remain on an even eye level.

Sarreti smiled kindly. "You did not chasten them too badly for their poor manners."

"If I were to do that, they would gain the impression that their antics concern me."

"Good point." The younger man gathered his hands at the small of his back. "Bastion's forces will be glad to join you. I am still a reservist. If you require my service, I am certain my administration can function in my absence."

"I'd love to have you with me, Ephin, but I think I could use your efforts in organizing the other moffs."

"As long as I don't rebel against you?"

Pellaeon nodded. "I'd rather have the people with us than against us. Then again, if I mismanage things so badly that you need to rebel, better you running things than Crowal or Flennic."

"I trust that situation will not come to pass."

"That's my hope." Pellaeon sighed. "Now, if the Yuuzhan Vong will just oblige us and lie down and die, perhaps warriors like me can fade, and the future can be put in the hands of builders like you. At least, then, there will be a future."

CHAPTER THIRTEEN

"Lieutenant Solo reporting as ordered, Colonel." Jaina Solo stood stiffly just outside the open hatchway to Colonel Darklighter's cabin aboard *Ralroost*. She had no idea why he had sent Emtrey, the unit's M-3PO military protocol droid, to fetch her, but she was glad to get a chance to speak with him. The whole incident with her brother the week previous had left her stomach churning. *When I thought he was dead . . .*

"Come in, Jaina, please, be seated." Gavin Darklighter nodded her toward the bunk against the wall. He sat at a small table bolted to the cabin's opposite wall. On it he had a datapad, several data cards, and a small holocube displaying alternating images of his family. With just that holocube he'd managed to drain the small cabin of its sterility, despite the white walls and gray decking.

As she sat, he turned in his chair to face her. Though he was still a young man, gray had crept into his hair at the temples, and little lines traced back from the corners of his eyes. He'd assumed command of Rogue Squadron right after the peace with the Remnant, but the dozen and a half years he'd put in with it before then had been what marked him. To Jaina he was one of a handful of legends who had survived and even thrived within Rogue Squadron.

"Jaina, I should have spoken to you about this before now. What happened at Garqi was unfortunate. It was also necessary. Operational security demanded we let no one in-system

96

at the time know that the *Lost Hope* was meant to go down in flames."

Jaina nodded. "I've been told that only Admiral Kre'fey and the techs who had prepared the ship—as well as the task force—knew what was going to happen. I know you didn't know, so you couldn't warn me."

"Yes, I have been informed of how kind you've been in supposing what I would have done had I known what was going to happen. The fact is, however, I would not have told you." His looked straight at her, and she shivered. "The decision to keep that information secret came from above me, and I would have respected the security demands that would have kept me silent. And while I know you would have not let out any hint of what was happening, the judgment about whether or not to take that chance, again, was not one I would have made."

Jaina gripped the edge of the bunk to keep herself upright. She felt betrayed by his words, in great part because she had credited him with far more kindness than he was saying he possessed. She had trusted in him, and here he was saying he was not worthy of that trust. And while his voice rang with sincerity, he was plainly suggesting he would have remained silent no matter who or what was involved.

Her anger over that latter point surprised her. Jaina would not have thought she was deserving of special treatment, but her anger clearly indicated that some part of her did. After all, she was a Jedi, as was her brother, and that should have counted for something. The affairs of Jedi were being meddled with, and that wasn't right. Moreover, after all her family had done for the New Republic, shouldn't it have at least taken steps to stop her from being hurt? Didn't the New Republic owe her at least that much?

She quickly caught her outrage and broke it down. The umbrage at having Jedi affairs compromised, she realized, bordered very closely on the arrogant attitude that Kyp and his followers embraced. *Jedi have abilities others do not, but this does not make us any better than anyone else; and for the purposes of my time with Rogue Squadron, I am a pilot first, not a Jedi.*

That thought led her to explore the idea that the New Republic owed her anything. *My parents might have a debt that needs to be paid off, but it's not mine. The only way the New Republic will owe me anything is if I earn something from it. So far, in comparison to what my parents have done, I have done nothing.*

Colonel Darklighter leaned forward, his elbows on his knees, his hands clasped together. "I didn't speak to you earlier by design, and while I might have saved you some pain, I thought a little now would be better than a lot later. When I came into the squadron I was your age, and I had a burden: Biggs Darklighter was my cousin, so the Darklighter reputation landed firmly on me. Like you, I was young enough to believe I could do anything. I was lucky enough that those in the squadron accepted me, helped me along, and enabled me to uphold my family's honor.

"You have a much greater burden, and one that has shifted slightly. You've been born to privilege, whereas I was a moisture farmer's brat. My parents were no one; yours saved a galaxy, and continue to serve it. In that service they made enemies, and you're smart enough to know that once your mother left power, her enemies set about weakening her image, *and* that of the Jedi."

Jaina nodded. "I've met people who figure me for a spoiled Jedi brat. I work hard to prove them wrong."

"That's very apparent, and those of us in the squadron are very happy you're with us. There are others on this ship, however, and in the service, who don't have the view of you that I do." He sighed. "Part of what happened here was to show them that we play no favorites. There isn't a single person here who didn't feel for the death of your brother, and none of them would have liked to have been in your boots when the *Lost Hope* exploded. All of them know how much you must have been hurting. And when they learned that your superiors had purposely not let you know—not let any of us in Rogue Squadron know—what was happening, they realized they've got more in common with us than they imagined. They realized that the problem of the Yuuzhan Vong is serious enough that the New Republic isn't playing favorites: not for Rogue Squadron, not for the Jedi, not for any Solos."

The young pilot closed her eyes and rubbed one hand over her forehead. As he explained it, everything made sense. Jaina discovered she'd inherited from her parents the narrow belief that it was her role, her family's role, to be saving the galaxy. The fact was that their actions were crucial, but it was the hundreds of thousands of sapient beings that made up the Rebellion that had been able to capitalize on and maintain the victories others won. Blowing up the Death Star certainly eliminated threats to the galaxy, but it hadn't liberated a single Imperial planet. That had taken lots of others working hard.

And they needed to be shown that hard work is going to be vital here. She opened her eyes and looked up at her commander. "Colonel, I—Boy, this is humbling, and I guess I didn't realize I needed to be humbled."

Gavin laughed heartily, then nodded. "You didn't need it as much as others might have thought you needed it. You're not the first pilot in this unit to be taken down a notch or two, and remember, *all* of us were treated similarly. Rogue Squadron *is* the best unit in the New Republic, but now our comrades know we're all on equal footing when it comes to how we are treated."

He held up a finger. "One more thing that I hope you'll take away from this. In my time with Rogue Squadron I've seen a lot of people die. I've lost a lot of friends, people I was close with, and some I was *very* close to. What Admiral Kre'fey managed to do is remind all of us, through the persons of your brother and Corran, that none of us are immune to death out here. He reminded us that we may be called upon to make sacrifices we don't want to make, and that's good. If we go out there thinking we're invulnerable, we'll get stupid. Stupid people die, and all too often, they take friends with them."

"Yes, sir, thank you, sir." Jaina had already seen, in the simulations she'd flown after Garqi, that she was flying sharper than before. She had more of an edge, and she knew she'd need it against the Yuuzhan Vong.

"Very good, Lieutenant." He straightened up in his chair. "Go find your squadron mates and tell them they have two hours before we report to the belly launch bay. Admiral Kre'fey thinks he has a way to neutralize some of the Yuuzhan Vong threat facing us, but we'll still be out there patrolling in case there's a miscalculation. I want everyone ready to go because, at the end of this little foray, I want to recover as many fighters as we put out there."

Sealed inside the cockpit of his X-wing, which was nestled deep in the lower launch bay on the *Ralroost*, Gavin never saw the Bothan Assault Cruiser revert to realspace. The second the capital ship's sensors became operational, they flooded Gavin's computer with systems data for Sernpidal. Launch control cleared him for launch, so he powered up his repulsorlift coils and nudged the throttle forward. The X-wing picked up speed as it moved into the launch tube, then burst through the magnetic containment bubble at the end and looped up to the rendezvous point.

He raised his right hand and flicked a canopy switch that locked his fighter's S-foils in attack position, then checked his shields, lasers, and finally his target acquisition system. "'*Roost*, Rogue Leader here. Scopes are negative for an immediate threat."

"Copy, Leader. Commence run."

"As ordered." Gavin flicked his comm unit over to the squadron tactical frequency. "One flight on me. Two, you're with the snoop. Three, take low. So far, so good, but be careful."

Gavin checked his scopes again and saw some movement out at the fringes of the system. The data came from the *Ralroost*'s sensors and registered the distant craft as coralskippers. Short of making a microjump through hyperspace, they couldn't get to the *Ralroost* in less than four hours, by which time the ship should have been long gone. *And if they* do *get to the* Ralroost *before then, it* will *be long gone.*

Admiral Kre'fey had agreed that the slamming of a moon into Sernpidal had not just been a terror attack. The resources it required demanded some other gain, since Sernpidal was hardly a threat and could have been useful for whatever the sorts of things were that the Yuuzhan Vong were doing with Dubrillion. Getting a mission in to see what was going on there was very important.

A standard scouting mission would generally appear at the fringes of a system and employ probe droids or just long-range sensors to learn what it could. Kre'fey assumed the Yuuzhan Vong would place defenses at the edges of the system to prevent this strategy from working. The admiral had his astronavigators run countless analyses of data from the *Millennium Falcon*'s outbound run. Using that information, they created models that showed how the planet would break up over time. The models helped determine how the fragmenting world would change the gravitic profile of the system as it slowly broke apart. They found a point very close to the crushed world where a ship could get in and out, yet intrasystem jumps would be difficult for the Yuuzhan Vong.

So, we're dropped into that space and get to go. Gavin brought his fighter around and headed into the labyrinth that the debris from Sernpidal had created. While the moon's fall had shattered the world, it had not done as complete a job with it as the Death Star had with Alderaan. Gavin had flown through the Graveyard of Alderaan, but the remains of Sernpidal were bigger than the asteroid-size shards of Alderaan.

He could see huge chunks with what were once coastlines etched on them. He suspected, were he to fly in close enough, he would see the ruins of cities. The idea of doing that, aside from being well outside mission parameters, held no appeal for him at all. *My job is to get past the debris screen and see what else is going on here, if anything.*

The screen of coralskippers at the edges of the system did suggest the Yuuzhan Vong wanted to protect something, but until Gavin threaded his flight through fragments of the planetary crust and around stone that had been molten and

flowing until frozen by the vacuum of space, he had no inkling of what the Yuuzhan Vong would be doing. Once he did
make his way through, and brought his X-wing out into the
light of Sernpidal's sun, his mouth went dry.

"Emperor's black bones!"

Gavin heard the curse over the comm and almost snapped
at the lack of comm discipline, when he realized he'd been the
one to say it. "Snoop, are you operational?"

"Affirmative, Leader. Pods deployed."

"Good, get it all."

Gavin couldn't be certain what he was seeing because,
while he had seen similar things, it had never been in space.
With his wife, back on her homeworld of Chandrila, he'd
gone diving and had marveled at the life hidden under the
surface of the water. Having come from a desert world, the
idea that much of anything could hide beneath the waves just
hadn't occurred to him. He had come to love diving and especially watching the teeming life around various reefs in the
Silver Sea.

Clinging to the sunny faces of Sernpidal's fragments were
things that looked very much like snails, only huge. *Large
enough to house a flight of X-wings!* He could see where
some of them had worked their way down along the rock,
leaving a softened trail behind them, as if they were eating the
rock. In their wake came countless smaller creatures of a
similar design. They seemed to be following up on specific
veins of minerals the large ones had exposed.

The snails clinging to the rock were not the only ones he
saw. Others—a cloud of them—drifted out to a nexus point
that seemed vaguely equidistant between most of the fragments. There Gavin made out a stony lattice somewhat ovoid
in shape and easily the size of a small moon. Some of the
snails, both big and small, moved over it, layering rock across
it. Some of the snails, with decidedly different shells than
those eating rock, were being incorporated into the lattice,
along the spine and located in a couple of other places. Slender filaments that glistened in the sunlight linked them, calling to mind images he'd once seen of nerve plexuses.

They're growing a ship, a huge ship. Gavin glanced at his range finder and saw he was still a good forty kilometers from the skeleton. *That's as big as the Death Star was.*

"What do we do, Lead?"

Gavin heard Major Varth's request for a mission and immediately started picking out targets. He stopped only when the absurdity of it struck him. One proton torpedo might have killed a Death Star, but this thing had no shielded reactor exhaust port. *It has no reactor. It is alive . . . or will be.* Even a direct hit by every proton torpedo in the squadron would only thin the work force, not even cripple it.

"Nine, we do nothing. We're here as eyes." The words tasted bitter in his mouth, but he could say nothing else. "Someone wiser than me will have to figure this out, Rogues. Let's hope they can."

CHAPTER FOURTEEN

Corran Horn knelt on one knee in the brush near the rendezvous site he'd worked out with his local contact. He wore a padded combat suit that had been supplemented with some duraplast panels encasing his arms and legs. They, like the padded suit, were a motley pattern of red, gray, and purple, matching them to the vegetation on Garqi. Sunk as he was back in the brush, his suit made him all but invisible to the naked eye.

His contact was late, and while Corran sensed nothing out of the ordinary through the Force, it didn't lessen his apprehension at all. Of course, had the Yuuzhan Vong been closing in to ambush him, he'd have felt nothing through the Force. As a hedge against that possibility, Jacen, Ganner, and the Noghri had set up a perimeter. Corran was certain that if anything happened to them and somehow they were not able to use their comlinks to get him a message, he'd pick up their distress through the Force and be alerted.

Having an alarm because I'm losing someone, though—that's nothing I want. The mission to Garqi had, so far, passed a week without incident. The *Best Chance* had gotten well away from the crash site, and the Yuuzhan Vong seemed unable or uninterested in following up the little bits and pieces of the trail they'd left behind in making their escape. They'd brought the ship to ground at an agri-combine facility about forty kilometers north of Pesktda, the world's capital, and secreted it away in buildings that had once housed the large harvester droids.

Going in, they'd expected the Yuuzhan Vong to wreak havoc with the droids that were used to do all the farming on the world. The harvester droids of various shapes and sizes had been uniformly reduced to amorphous blobs of melted durasteel that stained the ferrocrete thoroughfares around the facilities. The crops themselves were close to time for harvest, but without the huge machines, there would be no way to get it all in. This worked to the team's advantage, since it made living off the land much easier.

Corran found it in himself to grudgingly admire the Yuuzhan Vong's stand on machines. The world of Garqi was not terribly important in the overall scheme of things, but it *did* manage to produce a lot more food than the local population could use. Assuming the Yuuzhan Vong could actually eat the same food as the people of the galaxy they were invading, Garqi was one huge welcoming fruit basket waiting to be devoured. *If I were the commander here, I would have harvested the food,* then *destroyed the machines because, barring machines of my own, there is no way all this can be gotten in. But he obviously decided it was better to let the food rot than to use hated machines to harvest it. Interesting stand on principle.*

This left open the question of what the Yuuzhan Vong were doing on Garqi. The survey team had seen no people as they slowly made their way in toward the capital. At the appropriate local times, they set their comlinks for the frequencies and scramble codes the New Republic had set up in the event an attack from the Remnant had overrun Garqi. For the first several nights they heard nothing, and then, four days in, they caught a quick burst of sound that, when fed into a datapad and decompressed, became a long text message to anyone who had survived the crash down south of Pesktda. The message included a list of times and places to meet, with several of the sites within easy range for the team.

Ganner and Jacen had both argued that the message was a trap, but Corran had disagreed. "If the Vong aren't going to use machines to harvest crops, which have obvious value, they aren't going to use one on a task with little chance of return. Besides, the Vong haven't shown a skill for guile. We stake out one site, watch it, see what happens, then make a meeting at the next site."

The Noghri offered no opinion one way or another about whether or not they were going to be walking into a trap. Corran suspected that because a Noghri had been killed by a Yuuzhan Vong who was trying to murder Leia Organa Solo, *all* Noghri saw themselves honor-bound to avenge that death. The reputation of the Noghri as being very lethal was quite well known, and Corran was more than happy to have them angry with the Yuuzhan Vong.

At least I know they're not going to let themselves get out of control. He had no similar assurances concerning Jacen and Ganner. Ganner's enmity toward the Yuuzhan Vong stemmed from acts he'd witnessed on Bimmiel. While Corran didn't think Ganner would be stupid and precipitate trouble, he did figure him for doing his utmost to take the fight to the Yuuzhan Vong. That desire to engage the Yuuzhan Vong could get Ganner in a lot of trouble.

Jacen was another case altogether. On Belkadan he'd been defeated and captured by a Yuuzhan Vong warrior. While he had engaged and defeated warriors on Dantooine, and killed a lot of Yuuzhan Vong slave soldiers there, as well, he still hadn't the distinction his younger brother did of having fought and possibly slain upwards of a dozen of the warriors on Dantooine. Corran didn't think Jacen would go on a killing spree just to even up the score, but that put him a long way from being able to predict the younger man's actions.

A sense of determination tinged with apprehension came to Corran through the Force. He looked to the south where a solitary young man ambled up the trail through the rain forest. Because of the Force, Corran had no trouble spotting him, yet the way the man moved through the forest would have made tracking him tough for anyone else. Clearly the man had lived on Garqi long enough to learn how to avoid detection in its forests.

Corran gathered the Force and projected the image of someone moving swiftly through the brush off to the man's left. The man turned quickly, bringing a blaster carbine around to cover the movement. Corran slipped from his hiding place and closed with the youth. The young man's hand came up to press against his right ear—Corran assumed he was comlinked to someone else who'd seen the Jedi move—then the man spun and leveled the blaster at him.

A jolt of fear rolled out of the man, but he quickly shut it down. "Green."

Corran nodded. "Yellow."

The youth smiled, straightened up, and lowered his blaster. The agreed-upon challenge had been a color in the visible light spectrum, and the countersign the color immediately contiguous with it. "I'm Rade Dromath."

Drawing closer, Corran found something familiar in the man's face. The name likewise tickled at his memory. "Dromath, the name's familiar."

"My father was with the New Republic. He died during the Thrawn war."

Things slowly trickled back into Corran's brain. "Your mother, she was from Garqi."

The tall, blond man nodded. "Dynba Tesc. She fled the Empire, met my father, and married him. She came back after he died."

A shiver ran down Corran's spine. "I met her once, here. How is she?"

The young man shook his head. "She's dead. The Yuuzhan Vong got her in the first wave. Because of the stories she told of the old days here, of fighting against the Empire, and being so close to the Remnant, she'd prepared things. Wasn't like she was a nut about it, but just hid some things away. Her foresight is why we're alive—the Resistance, that is."

"Sorry to hear she died." Corran sighed. He remembered Dynba Tesc as a naive but enthusiastic woman who'd been brave enough to oppose the Empire on a world where no rebellion was really necessary. Her stand on principle, though it made trouble for her, had enabled him to escape the same world and eventually join Rogue Squadron. "She was very special, your mother."

Rade squinted his blue eyes and nodded. "Okay, now I know you. Horn, the one who got her off Garqi."

"She got herself away. I was just along for the ride."

Rade smiled. "My father was her hero and the love of her life, but she remembered you fondly and was proud of your successes."

A pang of regret arced through Corran. *I should have gotten in touch with her, should have known to do something when her husband died.* He shook his head. "If we have time, you'll have to tell me more about her. This isn't the time or place, I suspect. I'll call my people in, you call yours. You have a safe place nearby?"

"Right, a klick east of here. The Yuuzhan Vong haven't been anywhere near it."

Corran quickly contacted his team. Jacen and Ganner arrived first, followed by three of the Noghri. Corran didn't mention that three more Noghri were out there, knowing they would act as a rear guard. Rade brought in four people: two women, another man, and a female Trandoshan. Together they headed east and found a half-buried, overgrown bunker that appeared to predate even the Empire.

Once inside, Rade explained. "In the early days of the colony they practiced slash-and-burn agriculture. They'd clear whole areas, overplant, exhaust the land, then move on and allow the forest to reclaim everything. This bunker once housed the agridroids working this area."

Jacen Solo leaned against a rusted girder that curved up to support the arched ferrocrete structure. "We saw what the Yuuzhan Vong did to the current crop of droids. We've not seen any signs of their setting up villip paddies or anything else I saw on Belkadan."

Ganner nodded. "This is such a fertile planet, I assumed they would be growing things here."

"They are." Rade shivered. "Tomorrow, we'll show you. They're growing an army."

* * *

Before dawn they set off on a long trek west and then south, to the outskirts of the capital. There, just west of the Pesktda Xenobotanical Garden, Rade led them to a hillside from which they could study a complex of buildings that had been part of Garqi Agricultural University. Several blocky buildings ringed a central rectangular grassy redsward. Pouring out of the dormitories came file upon file of tall and fit men and women. They lined up in ranks facing the rising sun, with little reptilian creatures bustling about, snapping orders.

Jacen lowered his macrobinoculars. "The little reptoids are like the troops used against us at Dantooine."

Ganner leaned forward, peering intently at the cadres. "The people down there have growths like the ones we saw on the slaves at Bimmiel."

"And like the slaves on Belkadan, but these growths are more regular."

Corran studied the humans and agreed with both assessments. Coral growths—generally white and smoother than he'd seen before—had come up through the humans' flesh. The browridges and cheekbones had thickened, presumably to protect the eyes, and little horns curved up through the scalp. Bony buttons capped knuckles, while short, sharp spikes grew from elbows, wrists, and knees. From cadre to cadre these growths varied in size and location, and a couple of cadres even had bony armor plates growing on chest and back, arms and legs. The fourth cadre actually had humans who were encased in the stuff, looking almost like stormtroopers carved of ivory.

Rade sighed. "These are the latest. The Yuuzhan Vong have been here for a month and produced two earlier cadres. They train them, then release them into sections of Pesktda that have been cleared of life. The little reptoids and some of the Yuuzhan Vong warriors are released to hunt them. Not all of the machines have been destroyed here, so we can tap into surveillance holocams and get images of the fighting there. We've seen some Yuuzhan Vong casualties and the cadres are getting better, which is why we think they are growing an army here. These are prototypes, and once they find one that works well, I guess they can transform anyone into a soldier."

Corran ran a hand over his chin, then lowered his macrobinoculars. "This answers the question of why they were content to let some of the farms go untended. They've herded the others together at a combine, I assume, picking produce by hand, which is more than enough to keep everyone fed and healthy. They harvest the best of the people, transform them, and work from there."

"That's it. My people and I are in contact with some other resistance groups. We can stage a raid and liberate the prisoners, but we can't stop those who have been transformed, and frankly, we can't stop the Yuuzhan Vong from reestablishing control."

The frustration and weariness filling Rade's comments tightened Corran's chest. He glanced at the other two Jedi. "Suggestions on what we can do?"

Jacen scratched idly at the flesh below his right eye. "I know we should do something, but our mission here is to scout out Yuuzhan Vong operations. We could attack their experimental station and destroy everything, but we don't know if that would be a crippling blow or just a minor setback. The repercussions could be horrible, though, if the Yuuzhan Vong decide to punish the locals for something we did."

Ganner squatted on his haunches. Despite being dressed in a garish combat suit, he managed to keep an air of dignity about himself. "A strike at the experimental facility is a key. We ruin their work and maybe take away some samples so we can have our people working up a way to counter what the Yuuzhan Vong are doing to people here. I mean, we're here to collect data, and samples would be hard data, and data we need."

Corran nodded slowly. "I think you're both on the right track, but hitting the experimental facility isn't going to do it. If we do that, what will the Vong know?"

Jacen frowned. "That we were here, that we know what they've been up to."

"Right. Now, on Bimmiel we used genetic manipulation to

counter the threat of their insects, so we have to assume they know we not only use machines but can manipulate the machinery of life." Corran pointed back at the cadres. "I think it is safe to assume that the modifications done to each successive cadre builds on the work done to earlier generations. This means their experimental line will continue, unless they know we have enough data to be able to counter it. If we can obtain samples without their knowing it, we might be able to work up some sort of inoculation against what they're doing. I mean, if these implants function like, say, warts, then preparing a body's defenses to fight them at the first will prevent the growths from sprouting."

Ganner scratched at the back of his neck. "You want a covert run to kidnap a couple of cadre members from their beds?"

"No, that will give them evidence that we've been here. I have another idea." Corran smiled. "The next time they're out there running a cadre through a war game, we'll be there, too. We snag some of the cadre and get out, letting the warfare cover our escape and the fact that a couple of bodies are missing."

"Are you just choosing to ignore the fact that we'll be on the same killing ground with Yuuzhan Vong warriors and their little surrogates?" Jacen shook his head. "Kind of heightens our chance of discovery, doesn't it?"

Ganner straightened up and rested a hand on Jacen's shoulder. "He knows that, Jacen, but those chances are high no matter where we are on this rock. We know they're there, but they won't know we're there until too late."

"And if they figure it out, Ganner? What then?"

The handsome Jedi smiled coldly. "They'll learn that as deadly as their experimental troops may seem, they're nothing compared to a trio of Jedi."

CHAPTER FIFTEEN

Shedao Shai watched the gold-downed Caamasi from a high window. The New Republic's envoy, clad only in a brief loincloth, struggled beneath the burden of carrying broken blocks of ferrocrete from one side of a courtyard to another. The task was mindless, providing for Elegos a perfect opportunity to think of nothing save the pain wracking his back and shoulders, knotting his thighs, making his feet burn. The alien had started the day standing tall, but now, as dusk came on, he hunched over his burdens and moved them along one staggered step at a time.

The Yuuzhan Vong leader turned from the window and nodded at his subordinate. "Yes, Deign Lian, I heard you. The New Republic's forces were able to study our shipwomb at Sernpidal. I do not find this as great a concern as you do."

"Master, I would ask you to reconsider all I have laid before you." Deign Lian hid behind a mask and was bolder for it, this Shedao knew. He, too, wore a mask—one that was more terrible in aspect than that of his aide—but it concealed a face that could make Deign tremble. "Master, the ship we identified at Sernpidal was the same one that was at Garqi. Their scouting run there was aborted when we attacked, but not so at Sernpidal."

"Not so because we did not attack." Shedao Shai raised his clawed left hand and slowly curled it into a fist, driving his talons into his palm. Ligaments popped deliciously, and he perceived a slight shudder running through his aide's shoulders. "Have we determined yet how their ship was able to jump into the heart of the system? There are limitations to their capabilities, are there not?"

"Shapers have analyzed patterns and have determined what we believe to be the parameters for their travel. We will be able to pinpoint these places in the future and defend them."

Shedao's hand opened, and he ran his thumb across his bloody fingertips. The wounds in his hand had already closed, so he smeared the blood on his right shoulder and down across his chest. "Would not it be more effective for our shapers to study the infidels' machines than to guess about or work from information that might be incomplete?"

Deign's eyes widened, expanding beyond the size of the mask's holes. "Master, to do that would soil them. They would be sullied and tainted. They would have to atone for such blasphemy."

"Then they atone." Shedao Shai snarled and turned back to the window. "How is it that those who create the Embrace of Pain, modify and refine it, fail to use it? How is it that they shy from those things that make us purer? They should welcome the chance to wallow in the filth of the unbelievers, because through proper atonement they will reach a closer union with the gods *and* win for us knowledge that will make our battle against them so much swifter."

"Master, if ordered, they will obey your command."

"You suggest that I should not give that command, Lian?"

"Master—" Lian's voice softened slightly. "I believe your close congress with the alien has . . . shifted your perception about the infidels."

Shedao Shai glanced over his shoulder at his subordinate. "You are suggesting what, exactly, Deign Lian?"

"Master, people have begun to speak of how much time you spend with this Caamasi. They speak about how you have shown him the Embrace of Pain, how you have introduced him to the Boiling Caress. You spend time with him, watching him, talking to him, teaching him about us, revealing our secrets to him."

"I see. And this is considered a threat?"

"If he were to escape, Master."

"Could he, Lian? Could he leave this place?"

"No, Master, we would not permit it."

Shedao Shai spun and closed the gap between them in two blurred steps. He grabbed his aide by the shoulders and slammed him back into a wall, cracking the panel. "*We* would not permit it? *You* would not permit it? You suppose, somehow, do you, that *I* would permit it? That I will somehow let him escape me? That I will somehow let him talk me into releasing him? Is this what you think?" He slammed Lian against the wall again, then let him go.

The Yuuzhan Vong subordinate fell to his knees, then pressed his face to the floor. "No, Master, we only fear—*I* fear—for your union with the gods. Your congress with this alien will change him and could change you."

"Is that what you truly think?"

"Fear, Master, fear."

"Then master your fear." Shedao Shai spun on his heel, took a single step away, then turned again, fast, catching Lian beginning to rise. Shedao flicked a foot out, clipping Lian in the chin. The kick spun the subordinate around and battered him against the wall a third time, then left him huddled as paint and plaster dust settled over him.

Shedao Shai pointed a quivering finger at him. "You are not *my* master, I am yours. What I do to learn about the enemy is mine to do. Yours is not to question me. Yours is not to listen to the gossip of my inferiors. You are here to undertake the menial tasks that are beneath me, so I may concern myself with more important matters. If this does not suit you, I can find you a world to administer."

"No, Master, no!" Deign held his hands up, though whether to ward off another kick or beg forgiveness Shedao Shai could not be certain. "I meant no offense, Master, but to acquaint you with the murmurings of those who might plot against you."

"If there are plotters against me, Lian, you should have had them eliminated." Shedao Shai folded his arms over his chest. "Now, go down there and send Elegos to me. I will be in the tank chamber."

"Yes, Master." Deign rose slowly, sliding up the wall. "At once, Master."

Shedao Shai waited until Deign had staggered several steps toward the door. "One more thing."

"Yes, Master?"

"Remove your mask before you speak to him."

"Master?" The terror in his aide's voice had a piquant quality to it. "You cannot—"

"I *cannot*?" Shedao Shai closed slowly with his trembling aide. "You will remove your mask, send Elegos to me, then install yourself in the Embrace of Pain. If you are out of it before the sun rises again, I will kill you myself."

"Yes, Master, as you will it."

Having set aside his own mask, Shedao Shai watched one of the large predatory fish swimming slowly through the watery cylinder. He'd studied the fish a lot, watching it and its fellow tear into meat, ripping away great bloody hunks. Bits of flesh slowly sank through the water when they fed, to be snapped up by the other fish. Bones tumbled to the bottom of the tank to be cleansed by snails and other small creatures. *Nothing is wasted. The harvest of pain brings bounty for all, as it should be.*

He'd ordered the shapers who now oversaw the aquarium's operation to stop feeding the fish humans or their remains. While the spectacle had been one that was amusing—as always, watching creatures deny the centrality of pain was amusing—Shedao had sensed a reduction in the nobility of the predators. Presenting them captives diminished these great hunters who could take much tougher prey in the wild. To deliver to them anything they could not recognize as prey they usually caught for themselves was to mock them.

Shedao Shai smiled as best he could. The shapers and priests, the intendants and many of the workers—these were all classes of Yuuzhan Vong society who had become lazy. The warriors were the true hunters. They were the Yuuzhan Vong who clung most closely to the truth of the universe. And yet, he was willing to admit to himself, not all of them were faithful to that concept. Deign Lian had shied from it, and Shedao suspected that even a night in the Embrace would bring him little enlightenment.

Elegos held himself erect as he entered the chamber. He moved fluidly, not giving in to the pain in his body. Shedao Shai could see that he hurt. The motion of his arms was restricted. He limped almost imperceptibly as if a hipbone ground in its socket with each step. *Still, he does not deny the pain, but comes to embrace it. He is learning well.*

Shedao Shai turned from the fish and nodded to him. "You have worked hard today and yet accomplished nothing."

The Caamasi smiled slowly as if even the muscles of his face produced pain. "On the contrary, I understand even more your belief that pain is the only constant. My rational mind wishes to reject this idea, but can only do so if I disassociate myself with the reality of my physical self."

"You realize that is folly. Why?"

The Caamasi's shoulders slumped slightly. "Philosophers debate whether or not we are creatures of elemental material, or if we somehow have an ethereal nature to us—something that is more than our body and its functioning. Proof of that is impossible to find, so we are left having to accept that, perhaps, we are nothing more than creatures of meat, bone, and blood. If so, we are born in pain and die in pain and know pain throughout. To deny this is to express a belief in the unprovable, which is a fraud we perpetrate upon ourselves. You do not allow yourself to be deceived in this manner."

Shedao Shai nodded solemnly. "You understand things better than many of my own people. And yet, you do not fully accept this to be true."

"You have told me you believe in gods. Are they not extra-corporeal creatures? Does not their existence suggest that you may have a spiritual component to your existence?"

"No more so than the ability of these fish to breathe water

should suggest you, too, somewhere, somehow, have the capacity to do so." Shedao Shai shrugged. "The gods are the gods. They are aspects of pain and of the universe. We can join their fellowship if we are true to reality."

Elegos's head came up. "When all you are is pain you transcend your physical form?"

"Yes."

"Then it would seem there is more I need to endure since I have not transcended yet."

"You are fatigued, and I shall let you go rest, soon." The Yuuzhan Vong leader tapped talons against the transparisteel aquarium. "Deign Lian brought me news of events in our holdings. It seems your assessment that the New Republic would withdraw their probes in light of the failure at Garqi was incorrect. The same ship appeared at Sernpidal to see what we were doing there."

"Did it find out?"

Shedao Shai refrained from granting Elegos a smile. *Yes, play our little game. Don't ask me what we are doing at Sernpidal, merely inquire if that information is no longer proprietary.* "It could be they did. Our forces were misdeployed and did not stop them. They scouted the system and withdrew. There is, of course, a chance that they will fail to correctly analyze the data they collected."

The Caamasi cocked his head to the side. "You do not believe that."

"No. The leader who placed his ship where he did is too wise to make such an error." The Yuuzhan Vong lifted his chin. "This was the same ship that helped evacuate Dubrillion and fought us at Dantooine. I believe you told me the admiral commanding it was a Bothan."

"I believe you asked me to confirm information you had from prisoners interrogated here." Elegos pressed his lips together in a thin line. "I am certain that if the ship is yet commanded by Admiral Kre'fey, he'll again turn up where you do not expect him."

"So you sought to fool me with your earlier assessment?"

The Caamasi shook his head. "The admiral's appearance at

Sernpidal surprised me *and* you. I merely am predicting, on the basis of this fact, his continued unpredictability."

"I see." Shedao Shai granted Elegos his smile and received a solemn nod in return. "It strikes me you are not stupid enough to believe I learn nothing of you or your people from these games we play. I have learned, such as broaching the subject of these games, something we have not spoken of before, which surprises you. I am able to surprise you, Elegos. In this same way I will surprise your Admiral Kre'fey."

Shedao pressed a hand against the transparisteel sheet as a large gray fish swam past. "This admiral is a Bothan. How does he compare to this Chiss admiral you mentioned? Does he study art, too, to learn about his enemies?"

"He does not have Thrawn's habits, but is considered highly skilled."

The Yuuzhan Vong's eyes narrowed. "But he is a Bothan, a species about which much is known and much has been communicated. They are duplicitous, these Bothans. Few trust them, and many revile them. They slaughtered your people, did they not?"

"They did some, and more of them are not to be trusted, true." Elegos shifted his shoulders stiffly. "But to judge Admiral Kre'fey by other Bothans is a mistake you should not make."

"Well played, Elegos." The Yuuzhan Vong clapped his hands together. "You force me to choose now to believe what you are telling me, or to assume you are tricking me so I will believe the opposite."

"If I am here to learn from you, and to teach you, then tricking you would be stupid." The Caamasi clasped his hands behind his back. "I warn you fairly."

"There are those, Deign among them, who think I could be scared by your words, or influenced into acting against our best interests. They believe my time with you has tainted me."

"Perhaps it has."

"Has your time with me tainted you?" Shedao Shai watched him closely. "Have you learned enough of pain that you would share it with others?"

"Inflict it upon them? No." Elegos's violet eyes all but closed. "Violence is upsetting to my people, horribly so."

"But you have killed in the past."

"Only to save others from that horror." The Caamasi shook his head. "I would not willfully inflict pain."

"Even if the victim wished the pain?"

"Such as strapping you into the Embrace? No. I would not do that."

"And if I threatened to kill a person for every minute you did not do it?"

Elegos's expression hardened. "Any people who are subject to such a capricious order of death are beyond my protecting. If not killed *then*, they could be killed later, at your whim. They would never be safe as long as they were in your power. I would let you kill them, knowing you would be denying them greater pain by taking such quick action."

The Yuuzhan Vong leader turned away, slowly, and let talons trail across the transparent wall between him and the water. "You have learned much, Elegos, and have taught me much. Chief among it is this: Your people, blasphemers, heretics, and damned though they may be, have a resilience that may prove troublesome."

"A good lesson for you to learn."

"Indeed, and one to test." Shedao Shai smiled, enjoying the twisted vision of his face he saw in the transparisteel. "One we will test when next the New Republic sends its forces against us."

CHAPTER SIXTEEN

Anakin Solo felt pretty good about himself. Once Luke, Mara, and Mirax returned to the *Pulsar Skate*, a discussion began concerning the possible places Daeshara'cor could have gone from Vortex. It was agreed that the chances that she knew her cover had been blown were slender, so she would proceed to the next place where she might be able to get information about a twin for the *Eye of Palpatine*.

The logical choice for such a place was Belsavis, since the first *Eye* had traveled there. The difficulty with that idea came from two directions. The first was that Belsavis was an inhabited world that would certainly have raised an alarm if another *Eye* showed up there. The second was that while the first ship had a mission that would take it to Belsavis, there was no indication that the second had a similar mission.

Anakin retreated to access the *Skate* computers and approach the search more systematically. He pulled down records of ships leaving Vortex with their stated destinations, then cross-referenced those worlds with an index of the availability of Imperial records there. One world popped immediately to the top of the list: Garos IV.

Garos IV was known primarily for the University of Garos, located in the capital, Ariana. Garos IV had not joined the New Republic until after Thrawn's defeat. Whereas Ysanne Isard had destroyed many covert files in the computers on Coruscant when the world fell to the Rebellion, no such destruction had taken place on Garos IV. Scholars descended on the world to use the secret Imperial files to complete studies of the Empire. It struck Anakin as highly possible that Daeshara'cor would access these files in continuing her quest for a weapon to use against the Yuuzhan Vong.

Luke agreed, so Mirax plotted a simple short hop to Garos IV. Actually skirting the Nyarikan Nebula made plotting a course somewhat tricky, but between Whistler and R2-D2, the work was done quickly and the trip made in record time. This heightened hopes that they would arrive before Daeshara'cor had a chance to escape. Anakin entertained great hopes that he'd be side by side with his uncle, heading to the university to apprehend her.

His good feeling evaporated when Luke told him he would be waiting behind on the ship yet again. With the others gone, Anakin scowled, and the very weight of it seemed to press him deeper into the copilot chair. "It's not fair to be stuck here."

Chalco laughed. "Well, I hope you're not complaining about the company, because Whistler here would be mighty put out if you were."

The young Jedi scooted back up a bit in the chair and glanced at Chalco standing in the cockpit hatchway. "I just wanted to be doing something, you know?"

"I know, and you are."

"Yeah, waiting."

"Waiting here because *we've* got the best chance of catching her."

Anakin straightened up in the seat. "How do you plot that course?"

The short man laughed aloud. "C'mon, smart boy, you're the one who figured out she'd come here. You should be able to get the rest of it."

"Okay, she comes here for the information. She goes to the university, then will come back here to fly away." Anakin looked up. "Not very enlightening."

"Okay, a clue. Why am *I* here?"

"To help spot her."

"Why?"

"You saw her on Coruscant."

"So did every Jedi there. Why am *I* here?"

Anakin's jaw dropped. "You're here because you know spaceports the way Daeshara'cor knows spaceports. And she knows spaceports because she spent lots of time at them. Since the extent of her formal training was at the Jedi academy, she's not going to be comfortable in some crowded university setting."

Chalco scratched at his chin. "University has a lot of folks to keep an eye on, lots of memories to mess up, if she doesn't want to be seen."

"Right. So she's not going to go to the university herself. She'll find another way to get the university's records delivered."

Chalco smiled. "Now, your uncle said we should keep to the spaceport, but I think there are a few areas nearby where the sort of folks she'd need can be found. If we expand our search area, I think we can tag her."

The young Jedi's blue eyes narrowed. "Master Skywalker is rather specific about his orders."

"Was that an order, or suggestion? I mean, if we saw her here, and she left, he'd expect us to go after her, wouldn't he?"

"That's true." Anakin glanced at Whistler as the droid moaned in a low tone. "We wouldn't go far, Whistler, and we can keep in comlink contact with you. Then again, I could comlink Master Skywalker and ask permission to explore."

Chalco interlaced his fingers, bridged them, and started cracking the knuckles. "You could do that, but if we're wrong and she was at the university, and your uncle decides to come back here, he'll miss her."

Anakin shot Chalco a sidelong glance. "You know, that kind of circular logic is why you get in trouble a lot."

"Got me where I am today, kid, which is in a position to help you get this Jedi of yours back on the straight and narrow." He got the sort of sloppy grin on his face that Anakin recognized his father wearing—usually right before his father wanted to do something quite risky. "Let's go, kid, up off your butt. Time to go hunting."

You know better than to do this. Anakin heard the little voice in his head warning him off, but the fact that it sounded more like Jacen than it did himself pushed him away from the sensible course. Jacen had impulsively gone up against a Yuuzhan Vong warrior; but Anakin told himself his mission was nowhere near as dangerous. *I'm just going out to find someone we need to find.*

He stood, shunting away the twinge of foreboding niggling in the back of his mind. "Let's go."

Ariana's spaceport sat on the outskirts of the beautiful city. The battle to liberate Garos IV had been brief, so not much was damaged. Since the world was largely self-sufficient, the fluctuations in the New Republic's economy really didn't affect it that much. In fact, the influx of scholars had increased the university's reputation. As it expanded to accept more students, the business that catered to students and faculty likewise expanded. An economic boom followed, which allowed rebuilding painlessly and resulted in Garos IV showing up regularly on lists of worlds where the living was desirable.

Despite the world entering into an economic golden age, the area surrounding the spaceport had the usual mixture of industrial zones along with a seedy assortment of cantinas, casinos, cheap hotels, and other places of diversion. The garish holographic signs, the grime, and the powerful spoiled scent emanating from alleys—all of these things assaulted Anakin's senses. While he'd been well aware of such places—and knew his father, of late, had been spending a lot of his grief time in them—this was pretty much the first time they'd taken on a harsh reality for him.

Chalco did nothing to insulate Anakin from this nasty domain the way Lando Calrissian might have, or his father. *Or Chewie.* The man had told him he couldn't go out in his Jedi robes, so they found some clothes aboard the *Skate* and fixed him up. Anakin assumed they'd belonged to Corran, and they were only slightly too big. That worked to his advantage, though, since he needed to hide his lightsaber inside the nerf-hide jacket. He found a little hook there that let it hang in his left armpit.

Properly attired, and with his brown hair messed up by Chalco's rough rubbing, Anakin followed the man through the streets. He did note the change in Chalco's gait as bits of swagger entered it. The man puffed up a bit, nodding, winking, pointing at people as they wandered along. It seemed as if he was making himself obvious on purpose, and that truly did seem to disarm some of those folks on the street. Anakin kept getting a sense of curt dismissal from most folks, or a sense of idle curiosity about him.

He was very careful to keep the Force close to himself. He knew he was fairly powerful as far as the Force was concerned, but by no means did he have full control over it. He assumed Daeshara'cor would be running with the Force held close, as well, and he didn't want to give her the chance to detect him before he could find her. Worse than following Chalco off on some silly errand would be to tip Daeshara'cor to their presence and start her running in earnest.

As they went along, Anakin's admiration for Chalco slowly began to blossom. The man made his first stop at a news agency, where spacers could come in and download into their datapads the news feed from a variety of worlds. There he made some inquiries, quietly, and emerged grinning.

"What now?"

"I have a new place to look. I'll talk there, I'll get another place, and so on until we find her."

Anakin turned sideways to slip between two hulking Ithorians, then caught back up with Chalco. "How do you do it?"

"Do what?"

"What you're doing. You manage to survive without really doing anything. You act like you know these people, but I'd bet you've never seen a one of them before. You just talked to that guy and he told you something."

Chalco's stubble bristled as he smiled. "I don't know these specific people, Anakin, but I know them by type. The guy in the news shop, he hears a lot of rumors. People expect him to know things. He barters for information. I asked about secret Imp files at the university, he sent me to a guy."

"But you didn't pay him."

"Sure I did." Chalco nodded. "I told him that a shrewd operator on this rock could make a lot of money in the short term buying up bulk lots of rooms in hotels."

"What?"

Chalco pulled Anakin into an alley and bent down a bit so they were face-to-face. Farther down the alley a ragged Gotal looked at them, but a snarl from Chalco sent him shambling down to the far end. "What I told him only makes sense, Anakin. This world is a nice world. Lots of people would want to live here. Now, the refugees coming from the worlds the Yuuzhan Vong have hit, they'll end up here, too. They'll need rooms and someone will pay for them. This guy buys blocks—or, more like, passes the information on to someone who will buy them—and someone will buy them off him. Inside a year he can double his money. I gave him information for information."

"I never thought—"

"You never had to, kid, but I know your father did." Chalco straightened up and tousled Anakin's hair again. "Sure, I thieve a bit, but pretty much I'm a trader, like your father or Talon Karrde. I carry my inventory in my head. I look at things, I figure out the angles, and I make something out of them."

Anakin frowned as they moved back onto the street again. "Okay, I understand that, but don't you see that what you're doing is harmful?"

"Harmful? Get out of here."

"No, think about it. Let's say the rooms get bought up and the price is raised to make it hard on the refugees."

Chalco smiled. "The government will help them out."

"Sure, but where does the government get its money?"

"Taxpayers." The man winked at him. "I know where you're going, but, hey, kid, you think I pay taxes?"

"Nope, but the people you thieve off do. If they have less

money, they don't have the things you want to take. You pay no matter how you try to Hutt out of it."

Chalco's mouth opened and then closed with a snap. "You want me to starve, don't you?"

"No, just to consider the consequences of your actions." Anakin sighed. "If you give information that allows speculators to profit off other speculators, the only folks getting hurt are going to be those who put their money at risk. The greedy people get hurt, not folks who have had their lives destroyed."

"I get it. That leaves me what to work with? Produce futures? Commodities? They'll do." Chalco arched an eyebrow at Anakin. "You know, that 'smart boy' comment I made earlier, I didn't mean nothing by it."

"Yeah, I know. Let's go."

Their second stop took them to a curio shop. Anakin waited on the street while Chalco went in. Even before the man returned Anakin could sense the pleasure pouring off him. "Told you something, did he?"

"Yeah, where he sent the other person looking for that same information." Chalco smiled carefully as he hustled Anakin along. "Said he'd forgotten about it, but his cash account came up short at noon. He played back the surveillance holocam output and caught his conversation with a Twi'lek. She must have blanked his memory, but the holo still had her, just like your uncle told me it would. She talked to him three, maybe four hours ago."

"That means we're close."

"Very. The guy he sent her to won't be around for another half hour."

Anakin waited for a blue landspeeder to turn a corner before crossing the street. "What did you trade him?"

"Told him I was private security, undercover, tracking her. Promised him his money back, plus the reward." Chalco shrugged. "I'm sure once he found the till off, he pocketed even more credits than she stole, so he's already been paid."

"That works."

The man nodded. "And you know, I got this odd feeling of,

um, I guess, satisfaction knowing I've, ah, cheated a cheater. Weird, huh?"

"Not at all. It's about as close to justice as there can be in that case."

"Well, nobody gets hurt, unless that guy's boss figures the way I did, that he hit the till for his share." Chalco cut down an alley. "C'mon, it's over here. The Violet Viska."

Anakin blanched at the cantina's entrance. A sculpture of a viska formed an archway over it, leathery wings two and a half meters long arching down, leaving the viska's two-meter-long body at the top of the arch. A pair of arms sprouting from the center of the torso were drawn up, just waiting to dart down and grab a victim. The creature's head sported a forty-centimeter-long, needle-sharp proboscis. Viska, which were more commonly known as the great bloodsucking fiends of Rordak, fed exclusively on blood, and Anakin had to wonder at what sort of establishment would choose such a nasty creature as its emblem.

The interior, which smelled of warm ale, hot sweat, and boiling coolant, had no viska hanging from the shadowed rafters. Anakin felt sure this was because the thin layer of grease over everything would have made maintaining a grip on prey all but impossible. He slid into the booth to which Chalco directed him, then furiously wiped his hands on his pants, hoping to clean them.

He watched as his companion sauntered over to the bar and started talking with the Baragwin behind it. The heavy-headed alien nodded, then pointed to a doorway in the back. Chalco spun, winked at Anakin, then held up a hand to keep him in his place. The man cut through the crowd and made his way to the doorway, then disappeared through it.

Anakin frowned and tried to look nonchalant as aliens of every sort wandered past. He was determined that he'd not feel abandoned, but that didn't stop doubt from creeping into his mind. *I should do something, because if Daeshara'cor is in there with whomever Chalco is meeting, he's in a world of trouble.*

Anakin started out of the booth, then he caught a hint of

movement near the front door. He turned just in time to see the tail of a cloak whisk through the doorway. *And lekku, too. That was a Twi'lek, and of Daeshara'cor's coloration.*

He dashed to the doorway, sidestepped a gaggle of Jawas, then looked right and left down the alley. Deeper into it, off to his left, he saw the cloaked figure running away. Anakin sprinted after her, elation blossoming in his chest. He opened himself to the Force and tried to get a sense of her.

He *did*, but it came from behind him. As he slammed into a brick wall, he realized she'd projected into his brain an image of herself fleeing. *It's an old trick and I fell for it.*

Stars exploded before his eyes. He rebounded and fell hard to the ground. Anakin blacked out for a moment, then the world swam slowly back into focus.

Daeshara'cor stood over him, her head-tails twitching nervously. "Anakin Solo . . . If you're here, then Master Skywalker is. That's not the encounter I wanted, not this soon." She waved a hand, and Anakin felt his body slowly rise into the air. "Still, all is not yet lost. And with you in my possession, I may be able to win after all."

CHAPTER SEVENTEEN

Jacen Solo remembered well having heard that military service was hours of sheer boredom punctuated by seconds of absolute terror. He'd not disbelieved what had been said, but had never experienced it himself. Even fighting on Dantooine he'd never been bored, and the terror, well . . . *I was too busy to be scared.*

On Garqi, waiting in the Wlesc neighborhood, just east of the Pesktda Xenobotanical Garden, he had plenty of time to let the terror sink in. He and the others had been deployed in underground tunnels that used to allow service droids to pass unseen beneath the streets. The conduits themselves carried fiber-optic cables that formerly allowed for communications between buildings through normal comm channels. Images were collected by surveillance holocams and so on, though the Yuuzhan Vong had destroyed as many of those as they could.

The Yuuzhan Vong lack of understanding of technology hurt them and helped the resistance fighters immeasurably. While the invaders had destroyed many holocams, they'd not ripped up the cables. By simply attaching a new camera to a cable, then plugging into the line through the conduit, or hooking a comlink into the line so the images could be pulled remotely, or using any of dozens of other methods, Rade Dromath and his people had been able to collect and archive hours and hours of Yuuzhan Vong war games.

Corran had ordered virtually all of the holovid duplicated and stored in the *Best Chance*. After studying the most recent exercises, he formulated their plan for pulling out samples of the breeding program. The Yuuzhan Vong had appeared fairly ruthless in how they dealt with the prototype soldiers, so everyone agreed that if they could get only parts, they would get parts. Preferably, however, they would capture a live soldier and see if they could smuggle him off the world, so others could work on him and perhaps redeem him.

On Belkadan Jacen had encountered beings that the Yuuzhan Vong had enslaved; through the Force, he had gotten a disturbing sense of them. It most closely equated to hearing static on a comlink channel. It wasn't right, and was definitely wrong, and it seemed to get stronger the longer the slaves existed. Jacen felt certain that whatever the growths were that the Yuuzhan Vong grew on their slaves, these growths were killing them.

By the same token, he'd also fought against the little reptoid slaves on Dantooine, but he hadn't sensed them dying. It was as if their implants entered into a symbiotic relationship with them. There had been ample evidence that the Yuuzhan Vong were able to exert some remote-control capabilities over the slaves, since their discipline remained terribly strong despite a slaughter, until Luke had destroyed what passed for a Yuuzhan Vong command vehicle.

What Jacen found disturbing, as he waited in the darkness at the base of an access tunnel, was that the modified humans in the streets above felt less like the Belkadan slaves than they did the reptoids. Both had diminished senses through the Force—he felt as if he was sensing them at great distances even though he knew they walked not five meters above him. From the humans he could sense muted emotions, including fear, but also a lot of pride and determination. Some even exuded confidence, and those around them seemed calmer.

He adjusted the holovision goggles he was wearing, and his gloved fingers brushed the tiny scar under his right eye. When he'd been captured by the Yuuzhan Vong they had tried to implant something beneath his flesh. They'd even succeeded, but his uncle had it out of him in minutes, so it had not begun to grow. *If it had . . .* He shuddered.

The feed into the goggles came from a holocam secreted in a second-story window, looking down to the access hatch cover beneath which he waited. The cam itself was immobile, but by switching to other cams, he could expand the view of the plaza above him. The expanse of ferrocrete was dotted with fountains and benches. Planters divided it, making it into a simple maze that showed burn marks and bloodstains from previous battles. According to the fighting they'd watched, things usually funneled into this place toward the end of the exercises, with chaos reigning. At the appointed moment, the resistance forces would move in, eliminate as much as they could of the Yuuzhan Vong force, and hustle a sample or two out.

The virtue of a simple plan was that there was very little that could go wrong, but entering a battle pretty much guaranteed that *wrong* was what was happening already. It seemed apparent to Jacen that cleaning up after the battle would have been preferable, but Corran insisted that battle-damage assessment teams would probably be swarming over the place the instant hostilities ceased.

But there was something more in his planning. Jacen had watched Corran and found him constantly walking a thin line. Clearly the resistance force wanted to hurt the Yuuzhan Vong and hurt them badly. It seemed to Jacen that Rade wanted Jedi sanction for whatever he planned to do, less to absolve himself of any guilt for excess than to know that someone who was supposed to be able to handle problems was agreeing with his plan.

Ganner, too, seemed to be itching to engage the Yuuzhan Vong. The older Jedi had never come out and asked Jacen how it felt to kill a Yuuzhan Vong warrior, but he'd given Jacen ample opportunities to describe his fights against them. Ganner would smile at him and say something like, "Well, you're the expert here. How will you go after them?" Ganner seemingly sought reassurance that he could stand against them.

What am I looking for here? Jacen shivered. He remembered the frustration and humiliation of his defeat by a Yuuzhan Vong warrior on Belkadan. Later, on Dantooine he *had* succeeded in killing warriors, but he knew they were young and not terribly seasoned. Then the Yuuzhan Vong had sent the reptoids against them, and Jacen had not so much fought them as he'd butchered them. *If there had been any doubt in my mind about the ignoble nature of killing and warfare, that erased it.*

Yet there, on Dantooine, he had been doing what Jedi of legend had been doing for generations without end. All the songs, all the stories, pointed to Jedi defending the helpless, defeating the tyrannical, and restoring order. On Dantooine he had fulfilled the role everyone expected of him, and done it well. While the Jedi may have had their detractors in the New Republic, none of the survivors of Dantooine were among them.

They all saw us as glowing examples of the Jedi, but is that what I want? He'd long wrestled with the paradox of the Jedi. His uncle had been made into a weapon and directed at the Empire. Luke Skywalker had redeemed his own father from evil and had destroyed the fount of evil in the galaxy. He had continued to oppose evil up to and including the final battle with the Empire and even beyond that. As nearly as he could tell, Jedi were meant to be warriors.

The problem was that Luke Skywalker's training had been incomplete. The Emperor's drive to eradicate the Jedi had been so thorough that what information about them did remain seldom included any good instructional material. Much of what seemed to be solid was left behind by the Emperor with deliberate errors in it. Following those paths would lead one to the dark side and might even usher in a new age of the Sith.

Jacen knew, in his heart, that there was something more to being a Jedi than being a warrior. In his uncle he saw glimmerings of it, though Luke had so many demands on him that trying to focus on anything aside from problem solving was impossible. And watching Corran balance between sanctioning a bloodbath and planning an operation that would certainly take lives, Jacen also saw something more than just a warrior. Corran insisted again and again that everyone focus on the objective, which was gathering data. If Yuuzhan Vong got in the way and had to be killed, so be it, but the job was one that would help others, not quench a thirst for blood.

In them, and others, Jacen saw hints of philosopher and teacher. He appreciated that because it suggested to him a different course, but he wasn't sure that was for him either. *I keep seeing the paths I don't think I want to take, but all that does is leave me in one spot.* He shrugged. *There has to be another path.*

A double-click sound came through his comlink, calling him to preliminary alert status. He played out the cable to his goggles and climbed the ladder rungs sunk into the ferrocrete tube. He climbed to within a meter of the access hatch and waited. Clinging there, he reached down and touched the hilt of his lightsaber. *At least, for now, being a warrior is a good thing.*

Through the goggles he watched a mixed force of reptoids and Yuuzhan Vong warriors enter the plaza through the south end. The reptoids hurried forward, crouching behind planters and benches, wading through fountains. Anxiety pulsed from many of them, and several clearly had been wounded. At least one stumbled while running forward and never got back up, though a thin ribbon of dark blood raced on ahead of him.

The Yuuzhan Vong warriors, by way of contrast, strode into the plaza with the air of soldiers on parade. Only three of them came—one for every twenty of the reptoids—but they looked magnificent in their armor. Silver highlights flashed from the edges of the black armor as they marched forward. They had small villips on their right shoulders and turned their heads to speak at them. The other warriors nodded in response or spoke back, then issued orders to their reptoid charges.

Suddenly a mixed cadre of what once had been humans attacked from the buildings surrounding the plaza. Many ran normally, but those more heavily armored loped along awkwardly, sometimes on knuckles as well as feet. All of them uttered inarticulate war cries, and many, though carrying blasters, brandished their weapons as if they were no more useful than clubs.

As crude as the human ambush had been, it proved effective initially. The Yuuzhan Vong right flank broke, pulling back, and would have fled had the warrior in their midst not whirled his amphistaff and used it to behead the first human within reach. As that twitching body hit the ground, the little fighters regrouped and counterattacked. They drove the humans back to a line of planters, then engaged them with their own amphistaffs.

On the right the human attack faltered, then the reptoids charged. The humans fell back, drawing the reptoids deep into their lines—lines that consisted of the most recent cadre of humans. Though more bestial in form than the other groups, they also appeared to be more cunning. As the reptoids forced a salient into their line, the wings folded in, cutting the enemy off and falling upon them savagely.

Jacen shifted to a holocam view that took him farther from that knot of breaking bodies, then a tone ripped through his comlink. He tugged the cord from his goggles, killing the images, then summoned the Force and blew the hatch cover up and away. He scrambled to the surface and ignited his lightsaber.

All around the plaza the resistance ambush closed on the Yuuzhan Vong. Blasterfire from snipers in the building splashed the various villips posted to study the war games. Red bolts burned through the fleshy communications pods, bursting them like overripe fruit. A couple of snipers tried to shoot the villips from the Yuuzhan Vong warriors' shoulders, but succeeded only in hitting the warriors themselves, spinning them around, but not putting them down.

Ganner rose through a conduit just as Jacen had, but did it by force of telekinesis alone. He looked magnificent, popping up there, at the rear of the Yuuzhan Vong formation. The hatch cover, a heavy metal disk, whirled around him and crushed the first reptoid to get close. The disk clanged to the

ferrocrete and rolled around in a lazy circle, drawing a line
after as it passed through the blood pooling from the broken
reptoid.

The centermost Yuuzhan Vong warrior spun and snapped
an order that parted the reptoids heading toward Ganner.
Bringing his amphistaff up with two hands, he pumped it in
the air. He said something, and Jacen was certain, from the
tone, that it was a challenge. The warrior began to twirl his
amphistaff, waiting.

Ganner thumbed his lightsaber to life, producing a sulfurous-
yellow blade over a meter in length. With his free hand he
waved the warrior in. Contempt masked Ganner's face while
his movements appeared casual, almost sloppy, compared to
the tightness of the Yuuzhan Vong's approach.

The Yuuzhan Vong warrior flew at Ganner, smashing his
amphistaff down with terrific force. Ganner blocked the
blade high, then smashed his left hand up into the warrior's
face mask. He caught the edge of it with the heel of his hand,
spinning the warrior away, then Ganner laughed loudly, and
some of the humans hooted a chorus of ridicule after him.

The Noghri moved against the Yuuzhan Vong slaves like
rancors through Jawas. Fists and feet blurred as they struck,
crushing bone and pitching their reptilian foes to the ground.
Jacen had seen Noghri fight before, and had even sparred
against some, but never had he seen them attack without
holding something back. Here they were pure killers, and the
ease and economy of their motions belied their lethal power.

A trio of reptoids closed with Jacen. He parried a slash
from a staff, then riposted his green blade through the reptoid's chest. Two blaster bolts from snipers burned hot and red
through a second reptoid. Jacen shoved the reptoid on his
blade off, letting the rolling body trip up a third reptoid.
When that one fell at his feet, he slammed the dark end of his
lightsaber against the reptoid's skull, knocking him out.

The Yuuzhan Vong warrior fighting Ganner had recovered
and tugged his face mask back into place. His amphistaff
spun into a blur. The warrior came in fast, attacking low and
high. Ganner blocked some cuts, ducked back from others,

then one grazing slash opened a red line on his left thigh. Ganner snarled, and the warrior yelled and increased the violence of his assault.

Ganner leapt back, limping, his leg faltering. Jacen saw him go down, falling back on his haunches. Ganner raised his lightsaber in a weak defense as the warrior charged forward, amphistaff raised for a two-handed blow that would crush Ganner's skull.

Blaster bolts sizzled through the air, but none touched the Yuuzhan Vong warrior. Jacen glanced at the hatch cover, gathering the Force to hurl it and shield Ganner, but there was no time. He hoped a bolt might catch the warrior, or Corran might be able to project an image into his brain to save Ganner, but that did not happen.

Ganner had already saved himself.

The Yuuzhan Vong warrior, in his furious, headlong rush, stepped into the hole from which Ganner had emerged. His right leg sank into it up to midthigh, then his leg got trapped, and Jacen could hear it snap halfway across the plaza. The warrior's torso smashed into the ground. His helmet and faceplate bounced off, then Ganner's backhand slash carried away his head from the eyes up.

One of the other Yuuzhan Vong warriors shrieked aloud, shattering the momentary silence that marked the other warrior's death. In an instant the knotted balls of humans fighting reptoids separated. Humans and reptoids sorted themselves out. They appropriated new weapons from the dead.

The Yuuzhan Vong warrior screeched another command.

The human thralls turned, snarling, and galloped toward the resistance members. Malice burned in their eyes, replacing any vestige of humanity that might once have been there.

CHAPTER EIGHTEEN

Luke rose from the chair he'd been occupying in the office of the director of the University of Garos library and paced out into the outer office before answering his comlink. He left Mara and Mirax behind to deal with the director's questions. The director was a bureaucrat who took great pains to explain every procedure she was doing as she went along, reducing her work pace to something slower than that of a wet tauntaun on Hoth.

If she'd just let Artoo jack into her system, we'd be done in no time.

"Skywalker here. What is it, Anakin?"

"Greetings, Master Skywalker."

"Daeshara'cor?" A jolt ran up Luke's spine. He sought through the Force for a sense of her or Anakin. He found them, but very distant and small, as if they were actively trying to diminish their presence in the Force. "Anakin had this comlink frequency."

"He is fine. A bit sore, but unharmed." Static ate at her voice, erasing traces of stress. *If there is any.* Luke realized she'd dialed down the signal power to make it more difficult to trace. *If she keeps with training, this conversation will be short, then she will move.*

"Daeshara'cor, we need to talk. What you are doing is not right. It will not help the situation."

"Master, if I thought you could understand, I would have

spoken to you. I know you cannot and it is not a failing of yours." She hesitated for a moment, then plunged on. "You'll be blocking access to the information I need, so I propose a trade. The data I want, for your nephew. Think about it. Daeshara'cor out."

"Blast!" Luke wasn't really aware he'd yelled out loud until Mara and Mirax both came out of their chairs and into the antechamber. The anxiety rolling off them reached him before he focused on its mirror on their faces. "Daeshara'cor found Anakin, somehow, and took him."

Mara's green eyes narrowed to malachite slits. "How could she? Do you know she has him? Perhaps she just nabbed his comlink."

"I can't get a good feel for him through the Force. Her, either. She's definitely hiding, and he's holding himself close, much as he did when you two were running on Dantooine. Her getting his comlink means he's out and about somewhere—and that somewhere has got to be with her."

Mirax snapped a comlink into a socket on her datapad, then frowned as words scrolled up on the screen. "Whistler says Chalco talked Anakin into checking out local information sources. Says it's a standard investigative technique, though Whistler's got the old CorSec disdain for amateurs playing detective. They left the *Skate* about an hour ago, and Whistler's not heard from them since."

Luke closed his eyes and rubbed at his forehead. He felt Mara's hand stroke his back and smiled at her. "Thank you."

"What do you want us to do?"

The Jedi Master opened his eyes and sighed. "Daeshara'cor wants to trade Anakin for data files relating to the *Eye of Palpatine* or anything else, I suspect. Now, if what little I've understood from what the director is telling us is true, there are no such files. So, no exchange."

"That's one problem." Mara scowled. "The second is that Daeshara'cor can't let Anakin go, since she knows we won't let her get away and continue this search. She has to keep him. She may not have figured that out yet. She will, though, and she isn't going to like it. She'll know we have to move against her."

"But without data to trade, we can't even get close."

Mirax held up a hand. "Look, negotiations and trading are what I do. We could dummy up a data card and stuff it full of reports and things that only the swelled brains here can understand. We slice a few to have key phrases she can scan for, and she'll think it's all legitimate at first glance. That's all we need to draw her out. Do you think she would put Anakin in a life-threatening situation?"

Mara nodded, but Luke disagreed. "I don't get that feel from her."

"Luke, she's seeking superweapons."

"I know, but I don't think she's really considered what the result of their use is. We all know the story of Alderaan. We know what happened to Carida. We remember the Krytos virus, but somehow, getting your brain around the idea that billions of people are dead is very tough. You can feel very bad, devastated, over the death of one person, but can you multiply that a billion times when a planet is destroyed?"

"Especially a planet full of the enemy?" Mara shrugged.

"Despite what she has done so far, Mara, she's not yet strayed to the dark side. She has always been good." He sighed. "If we knew what had set her off, we could help her."

"Big if." Luke's wife nodded slowly. "I think Mirax's plan has merit. Let's do it."

Luke smiled and returned to the director's office. "Forgive me, but something urgent has come up. I really need your help."

The woman smiled. "I'm ready to assist in any way I can."

"Good, thank you, then just back away from your terminal." Luke glanced at R2-D2. "Yank down everything you can on the *Eye* project's history, then a data card's worth of the most technical stuff you can find. We're baiting a trap and we can only afford bait that's irresistible."

Anakin shifted uneasily. He'd gotten his first inkling of how serious Daeshara'cor was about her quest when she'd threatened to kill him if she so much as sensed him reaching for the Force. Now she sat, two lightsabers on her lap, comlink in hand.

She switched off the comlink and looked over at him. "You heard. It will be you for the data. You won't be hurt."

Kneeling there in the corner of a dingy, unfurnished apartment, with his hands bound behind his back and to his ankles, Anakin sighed. "You mean I won't be hurt more than I am already."

"That can't be helped. I can't have you loose."

"That's not what I meant, Daeshara'cor." He shrugged as much as he was able to. "I always admired you, how hard you'd worked. Why are you doing this?"

She sighed. "You wouldn't understand."

"No? Why not? Because I'm not a Twi'lek? Because I grew up on Coruscant and then at the academy?" He frowned at her.

Before she could say anything, the apartment door flew in with a crash. Chalco stepped into the doorway, a blaster carbine in one hand, and a ratty gray *thing* wrapped around his throat. It looked as if someone had yanked a strip of hide off a Talz and made it into a stole, which then had been dragged behind a Podracer during some endurance rally.

"Hold it right there, Daeshara'cor." Chalco growled in low tones. "Don't worry, kid, you're safe now."

"Think so?" The Twi'lek brought her lightsaber to hand and ignited it. The blade splashed bloody highlights over Chalco's face. "Leave now and you won't be hurt."

"I'm not the one who's going to hurt, sister." His trigger finger twitched, launching a blue stun bolt at the Jedi. Her lightsaber came up with ease and around, batting the blue bolt back at him. It hit Chalco in the right knee, then raced like lightning up his body and around his belly. The involuntary twitching of his muscles quickly erased the shocked look on his face, then he collapsed to the floor.

Using the Force, Daeshara'cor dragged him into the room, then shut the door behind him. She kicked the blaster from his hands and slid him over next to Anakin.

The man lay there for several seconds, then blinked and began to whisper. "I don't get it."

"Get what, Chalco?"

"She wasn't supposed to be able—" A shiver shook him. "They said it would make a Jedi powerless."

Daeshara'cor frowned at him. "What are you talking about?"

"The miriskin."

Anakin arched an eyebrow at his friend. "Ysalamiri skin? Is that what that thing is?"

"Yeah. Cost, too."

"Um, Chalco, that only works if the ysalamiri is alive."

The Twi'lek sniffed. "And the closest that thing you're wearing ever was to being alive was being touched when someone pulled it off a loom."

Chalco groaned.

"Did you tell Skywalker?" She extinguished her light-saber. "No, you wanted to get me yourself. Okay, I still have a little time."

Anakin looked up at her. "You were going to tell me why you're doing this."

"No, I was going to tell you why you couldn't understand." The Twi'lek's eyes hardened. "You come from a life of privilege, Anakin. You and your siblings were hailed as heroes from the moment you were born. You held a fascination for billions. Expectations for you were great, *are* great, and to your credit, you shoulder all that very well. Still, it puts you where you cannot understand the rest of it."

"What I can't understand is why you want to find some weapon capable of killing billions. Could anything have been that bad in your life to inspire that?"

"Can you not imagine wanting to kill billions?"

"No."

"Not even to protect your family? To save your mother? Your father?" She regarded him openly. "Wouldn't you trade the life of a billion Yuuzhan Vong to bring back Chewbacca?"

A lump immediately choked him. Anakin fought his face scrunching up. He tried to blink away tears, but felt them searing his cheeks. He sniffed and tried to wipe his nose on his shoulder, but couldn't. His lips trembled and he remembered Chewbacca as he last saw him, brave and defiant. *And then nothing . . .*

Anakin sniffed again, then lifted his chin, stretching his throat. "A billion lives or ten billion lives would not bring him back. And the killing of a billion Yuuzhan Vong still wouldn't match the heroism of his death. Chewie went through so much. He was a slave my father freed—"

"Then he would understand."

Anakin frowned. "I don't—"

"No, and you never could." She turned away and began to fiddle with the comlink's settings. "I need to talk to your uncle again."

Chalco slowly roused himself and pulled himself up against the wall. "I'd try to untie you, kid, but, ah, my fingers aren't working too good yet. My head . . . my head is throbbing."

"Mine, too." Anakin shoved off from the wall and righted himself again. His head hurt, his knees were sore, and his throat ached. Daeshara'cor's comment about Chewie had hurt horribly.

He caught sight of a vein pulsing at Chalco's temple. It kept time with the pounding in his own head, as if it were hammering his braincase. He sighed.

His head came up for a second, then he let it hang again lest Daeshara'cor notice him. Carefully, slowly, concentrating very hard, he pushed his discomfort aside and touched the Force.

Daeshara'cor spun as he gathered it to himself. She took one step toward him, then the blaster carbine rose from the floor and careened solidly into her forehead. Her eyes flickered, then she sagged to the floor.

Anakin sank back on his heels and reached out through the Force to find his uncle. He did, and quickly, for Luke was far closer than Anakin expected.

Anakin opened his eyes and saw Chalco looking at him with a huge, self-satisfied grin. "What's so funny?"

"You're lucky I happened along. Without me, she'd have gotten away cleanly."

"You think dealing with you tired her out?"

"No, not hardly."

"And klonking her with the blaster, that was something you did?"

"Nope." Chalco shook his head. "But if I'd not brought it along, you'd have had nothing to use against her."

Sighing, Anakin used the Force to slide the blaster carbine over to Chalco. "Now, pump a stun bolt into her to keep her out, and then you can see if your fingers are well enough along to untie me."

"Give me a minute."

"I would if we had one, but my uncle is on his way." Anakin gave the older man a smile. "Now, knowing he's going to be upset that we're here, in this situation, do you think it's better I'm all trussed up, or free?"

"Gotcha. You are a smart kid." Chalco whipped the miriskin from around his neck and tossed it off into another corner. "Our secret about that?"

"Sure, Chalco, our secret. We're in enough trouble as it is." Anakin smiled. "My uncle doesn't need to know everything."

CHAPTER NINETEEN

I'm not going to kill the people I should be protecting!
Jacen snarled, then summoned the Force, shoving back hard
against the onrushing throng of armored human slaves. The
two in the lead stumbled back, knocking down others of their
number. Jacen grabbed one of the fallen humanoids and
shoved it back, low, slamming it into the knees and thighs of
the other slaves. Bodies flipped high in the air, then crashed
back down.

Off to his right, Corran and his silver lightsaber entered
the fight. He swept past and through two reptoids, spilling
smoking bodies left and right, then met the Yuuzhan Vong
leader on equal footing. The Jedi feinted high, then slashed
low. The lightsaber's argent blade sparked off the vonduun
crab armor covering the Yuuzhan Vong's shins, but did not
penetrate to the flesh.

The warrior took a half step back, then scythed his staff
around in a cut that came at Corran's left flank. The Jedi spun
inside the arc of the cut and parried it wide with the blade
held in his right hand. This left Corran standing with his back
to the Yuuzhan Vong's front, just for a second. He continued
his spin, pivoting now on his right foot, and brought his left
foot up in a roundhouse kick that cracked his heel against the
Yuuzhan Vong's face mask.

The Yuuzhan Vong staggered backwards and caught his
legs against a planter. He fell back, off balance, and found his

limbs trapped by the branches of a spindly ornamental fruit tree. Corran closed and slashed at him twice. The first cut traced a scar across the Yuuzhan Vong's armored belly, then the return stroke opened him from hip to hip.

The third Yuuzhan Vong warrior hissed an order, which started the reptoids pulling back. Before he had any chance to organize any sort of defense or retreat, resistance snipers targeted him. A hail of red blaster bolts shot down at him from all angles, jolting him. He wobbled and lurched, raising a hand to ward off the sting of the energy weapons. His vonduun crab armor might have been proof against an errant bolt or two, but such concentrated fire burned through it. The Yuuzhan Vong spasmed, throwing his limbs wide, then collapsed to the ferrocrete decking.

The reptoids, bereft of any leadership, scattered. Ganner slashed two down and the resistance fighters killed more, but none came in Jacen's direction. Instead, nearest him, a thrall snapped an order that brought several of his fellows with him. They retreated in good order to the north, back into the building from which they had launched their attack.

Corran raised his blade and circled it over his head. "Move it. Grab two of the guys Jacen put down. Let's go."

Two of the resistance fighters each grabbed a downed thrall and started to drag them off when a black ovoid form screamed overhead. It vanished beyond the line of buildings to the south, but Jacen felt a sour taste growing in his mouth. "That was a coralskipper, Corran."

"Sithspawn!" Corran glanced at his chronometer. "We have to get out of here fast, and we've got at least two hours before our ride will be here. As we planned it, people. Get the prisoners out in the vehicles, the rest of us will pull the Vong off."

Ganner nodded grimly. "I've heard the Pesktda Xenobotanical Garden is worth seeing."

"Yeah, well, don't figure you're going to get time to read all the exhibit signs."

Ganner frowned, but Jacen smiled. "Hey, at least he thinks you can read."

The older Jedi's return comment was swallowed by the

reappearance of the coralskipper. The ship came down and hovered ten meters above the plaza. Its nose-mounted plasma cannon spat out a bolt that sizzled over the Jedi's head and melted a two-meter-wide furrow in the ferrocrete.

Corran pointed west. "Go, now! I'll distract it."

Ganner started sprinting west, but Jacen grabbed Corran's sleeve. "You know what you're doing?"

"Nope, but that's never stopped me before." The Corellian Jedi winked at Jacen and stood, then darted east. He waved his lightsaber in the air and shouted. "C'mon, sparky, I dare you."

The plasma cannon's muzzle swiveled in Corran's direction like a bug's eye on a stalk. The Jedi set himself, lightsaber in hand, ready to deflect the bolt. Light began to glow gold in the muzzle.

"Go, Jacen, go!"

The young Jedi frowned and gathered the Force to himself. He grabbed the hatch cover Ganner had used as a weapon and flicked it up into the air. He slammed it against the cannon muzzle and summoned all the strength he could to hold it there. Jacen felt an immediate shock of pressure through the Force, so he redoubled his effort.

The hatch cover glowed red, then white, then evaporated from the center out. A little spurt of plasma squirted down, and Corran batted it from the air with ease. On the coralskipper, from the nose back, little golden lines traced their way along the ship's black body. They seemed to define where bits and pieces of it had grown together. Then a nova filled the cockpit and blew out the viewports. Burning plasma geysered into the air, and the ship hung there for a moment before dipping its nose and plunging into the ferrocrete.

It hit hard enough to ripple the surface, knocking Jacen down. Pieces of the ship shattered and started bouncing across the plaza. Jacen began to comprehend his danger from them, but before he could act, Corran came sprinting over, hauled him up by his shoulders, and pulled him clear. A huge section of the coralskipper's tail toppled over on the spot where Jacen had fallen.

He smiled up at Corran. "Thanks for saving my life."

"Sure, now don't ever disobey another order."

The young Jedi blinked in confusion. "But I saved *your* life."

"Details, details." Corran pulled him along as they sprinted to catch up with Ganner and the majority of the resistance fighters. "I lead this expedition, I get to decide the risks and who assumes them. You almost got yourself killed."

Jacen frowned. "But since I saved your life, you managed to save mine."

Corran's eyes narrowed, but he smiled. "You know, if you're going to keep using logic against me, I'm just going to have to send you home."

"Yes, sir."

His chest heaving as it hadn't in years, Corran crouched in the shadow of one of the Xenobotanical Garden's out-buildings. The retreat from the plaza had been easier initially than he had expected. While the human thralls did come after them, they did so with little organization. Corran had no desire to slay the thralls, but the resistance members seemed to regard setting their fellow Garqians free of their torment as a sacred duty. Corran had previously acknowledged on Bim-miel how those who could not be cured had to be destroyed, but he was glad he didn't have to be the one pulling the trigger.

He glanced across the small pathway to where Jacen Solo knelt on one knee. The boy had impressed him. *Boy? Emperor's black bones, he's a young man, and growing up fast.* The use of the hatch cover had likely saved Corran's life. The fact that the plasma reflux blew out the plasma cannon and splashed plasma all through the interior of the coralskipper had been an added benefit. What he liked more about Jacen, though, was the way he had paced Corran in their retreat.

Along with several of the resistance members, the two of them formed the group's rear guard. Ganner and four of the Noghri went with the main body, while the remaining two Noghri were heading away with some resistance fighters and the two prisoners. The action the rear guard faced had not been that serious until a larger Yuuzhan Vong transport had descended. From that point forward, Yuuzhan Vong warriors entered the fight, and they clearly were something more than thrall trainers.

Corran ducked as a hum rose and a slender, dark shape flew at him. The razorbug sailed past his head and landed in the dust a couple of meters behind him. It sprouted arms and legs and, if allowed to, would have taken wing again and returned to the warrior that had thrown it.

The Jedi reversed his lightsaber and twisted the handle. The blade went purple and more than doubled in length. The coruscating purple blade tapped the bug, instantly converting the moisture in it into vapor. The bug popped crisply, spraying legs and chitin everywhere.

"I hate those things."

Jacen nodded, then pointed off to the right.

Returning his blade to its normal focal length, Corran ducked his head out past the edge of the building. He caught a fleeting glimpse of a Yuuzhan Vong warrior, then nothing. *These warriors are very good. We're not going to see them until too late.*

Ganner's voice poured through his comlink's earpiece. "Perimeter secure. Ithorian section is ours."

Corran double-tapped his comlink's microphone, then glanced at Jacen and pointed toward the gardens and the tall grove of bafforr trees. The young man nodded, then took off at a run, cutting left and right at random intervals to make hitting him with any sort of missile weapon tougher. *Good for you, Jacen.*

The eldest Jedi came up out of his crouch and gritted his teeth against the pain in his legs. He danced back from his shelter, watching for movement, then turned and sprinted. Like Jacen, he juked, and even threw in a few skips.

Two razorbugs arced past him, then a fatter, blue thing hit the ground and exploded off to his right. He cut through an archway and dodged right, then heard something skip off the ferrocrete. He almost stopped for a half second, hunkering down in the archway's shadow, to ambush the next Yuuzhan

Vong through, but he knew he'd be overwhelmed by those following him.

No, into the bafforr grove. That's going to be our chance.

The bafforr grove was a rarity from Ithor. The towering trees, with their dark green foliage, were semi-intelligent and certainly a big reason why the Ithorians worshiped the Mother Jungle. The Ithorians' decision to transplant bafforr trees to Garqi signaled their belief that the Garqians shared that uniquely harmonious bond with their environment that the Ithorians had with theirs. Corran hoped that, through the Force, the Jedi could link with the trees and get an idea where those hunting them were. He was far from sure if that plan would succeed, but it was the best they had to work with at the time.

Corran arrived at the heart of the grove and dropped to one knee near Ganner, Jacen, and Rade. On their faces he could recognize the fact that they knew they were dead. He knew it, too, but every second they could buy would be one more second that the *Best Chance* could use to get its cargo aboard and out.

He looked up at Jacen. "I should have sent you out with the ship."

Jacen shrugged. "I'm just the copilot. We get off this rock, we get off it together."

"It's a deal." Corran glanced at Ganner. "Tried to read the trees?"

Ganner nodded wearily. "There is something there, but it's very vague and subtle."

Rade pointed at the yellow pollen staining the ground. "It's spring. The trees are devoting a lot of energy to growth and reproduction. They are budding, after all."

"I see that." Corran sighed. "My grandfather once told me that a blood meal is nourishing for plants. One way or another they're going to gorge."

Jacen pointed back toward the archway. "They're coming."

Back at the arch some reptoids and thralls darted through, taking up covered positions. Resistance snipers hit a few, but had no clean kills. More of the Yuuzhan Vong experiments and slaves came through, but they huddled there, around the gate, waiting. Their anxious glances told Corran what they waited for. When it came, he couldn't help but be impressed.

One by one, seven Yuuzhan Vong warriors stalked through the arch. They moved quickly enough, but not hurriedly. While they did not choose to stand in the open, they *did* stand and didn't seek heavy cover. A few blaster bolts reached out and struck them, but their cerulean armor skipped the bolts off.

Rade raised a hand. "Wait for good shots. At this range, the armor isn't giving."

"Different armor, Rade. This is the serious stuff." Corran remained on one knee and watched as the last Yuuzhan Vong warrior came through the arch. "Oh, yeah, we're just going to have a fun time now."

Jacen glanced over at him. "Your definition of *fun* and mine don't exactly match."

"Not you I'm worried about. It's them." Corran scraped two fingers through the yellow bafforr pollen and streaked it beneath each of his eyes. "Not quite as nifty as their battle masks, but it's something."

The warrior Corran took to be the Yuuzhan Vong leader stepped forward of their line. Rade started to give an order to cut him down, but Corran raised a hand. In a low voice he said, "Remember, we're playing for time here."

The Yuuzhan Vong brandished his amphistaff and began shouting in a high voice. "I am Krag of Domain Val. Garqi is mine. Surrender and you live."

Corran stood, but Ganner eclipsed him. "I am Ganner Rhysode. I am Jedi. Before you can engage our leader, you must go through me."

"Didn't know you cared, Ganner."

"I don't, Corran, but the last time I let you fight the Yuuzhan Vong, I had to lift you into a ship and save your life. A gram of prevention is worth a kilo of cure."

One of the Noghri likewise stepped out between the Yuuzhan Vong and Ganner. "I am Mushkil of Clan Baikh'vair. The way to a Jedi is through me."

Tension rose in the air. For Corran it was all but palpable, and even the bafforr trees could seem to sense it. A flurry of yellow pollen began to drift down, as if the bright playful color could somehow leech the malevolence from the air. He saw yellow spots dapple the shoulders of Ganner's combat suit and mottle the Noghri's flesh, adding a gay note to what had only been grim before.

Then a single blaster shot burned through the air, spinning a reptoid around and dropping him to the gravel-strewn garden pathway. The tension exploded like thunder, and though Corran knew his action was suicidal, he charged with the others at the Yuuzhan Vong line. Blaster bolts, hot and red, filled the air, knocking down reptoids and thralls, leaving the Jedi and Noghri matched number for number with the Yuuzhan Vong warriors.

But not for long.

Mushkil did reach Krag Val before either Ganner or Corran could. The Noghri hurled a knife as he closed, but the warrior's spinning amphistaff flicked the blade up high and away. Then, even before the knife had time to fall to the ground, the Yuuzhan Vong had closed, swept the Noghri's legs from beneath him, and stabbed down. He impaled the Noghri on his amphistaff's tail. Blood spurted straight up as Krag Val pulled his weapon free and engaged Ganner.

The Jedi's sulfurous blade slashed low at the warrior's legs. Krag Val pivoted on his left foot, pulling his right foot back, letting the lightsaber scar the armor on his left shin. Ganner's rush carried him past the warrior. As he turned to bring his lightsaber into play again, the Yuuzhan Vong slashed down. Ganner reeled away, his left hand trying to keep his torn face together.

Corran drove at Krag Val, but Jacen got to him first. The younger Jedi slashed high, letting the Yuuzhan Vong block with his amphistaff. Jacen kept the pressure on, grinding the blade against the amphistaff, then kicked out with his right foot, catching the warrior on his left knee. The joint straightened, then locked and would have broken, but the warrior hopped backwards.

Jacen arced his green blade around, stroking it through the

scar Ganner had cut on the left shin, and took the warrior's leg
off at midcalf. He leapt above an amphistaff blow, then
slashed down and caught Krag Val's right arm at the juncture
of his elbow. Sparking and smoking, the lightsaber sawed
through it, freeing the arm and amphistaff.

Corran streaked past Jacen and leapt over the fallen Ganner.
He blocked a slash meant to decapitate the downed Jedi, then
whipped his blade down and around in a cut that scored a
warrior's breastplate. That warrior fell back, for a moment
blocking one of his fellows. This gave Corran a chance to step
on the dark end of Ganner's lightsaber and kick it up into the
air. He grabbed it in his left hand and held it with the blade
trailing back behind him. He let the tip of his silver blade
drift, as if he was going to connect the pollen dots on the
Yuuzhan Vong's armor with it.

"C'mon, you two. Let's go." Corran stamped a foot and
feinted at the warriors he faced. "I don't have all day."

They glanced at each other, then one took a step forward,
but it was a halting one. Corran knew it wasn't a feint. The
step ended abruptly and too much weight shifted onto that
foot. In an instant Corran lunged high with his silver blade,
then spun to the right, slashing Ganner's trailing blade across
the warrior's knee.

As he came around he brought the silver blade down and
across in a parry he hoped would pick off the attack coming
from the other warrior, but the blade met no resistance at all.
He tightened the arc and left the blade pointed straight at his
second foe. If the warrior came at him, he'd impale himself.

But that's not going to happen. Corran stared, wide-eyed,
at the warriors. The soft, leathery tissue that covered the
vonduun-crab-armor joints had begun to swell, stiffening
limbs. Dark fluid oozed from holes beneath the warriors'
armpits, flooding down to erode the pollen stains. The swelling
forced the warriors upright, then, stiff-limbed, they toppled
over. Breath came short and shallow for them, and Corran
had no doubt the armor's swelling was suffocating them.

All around him the Yuuzhan Vong warriors were down,
along with two more Noghri. Ganner had risen to hands and

knees, his left glove covered with blood. Jacen stood over the body of another dying warrior while the resistance blasterfire broke the slaves and sent them scurrying from the garden.

Jacen looked stunned. "What happened?"

Corran waved a hand through the air. "If I had to guess, their living armor had a nasty allergic reaction to this pollen. It's swollen up and is killing them." He swept his silver blade around in a circle. "We have to burn this all down. Everything."

"What?" Jacen pointed at the bafforr trees. "They're semi-intelligent. They saved us. How can we burn them down?"

"We have to. We have to burn the entire garden." Corran nodded at Rade. "Gotta be done. We know bafforr pollen can affect vonduun crab armor, and quickly, too. The Yuuzhan Vong don't, otherwise we'd never have been allowed to retreat here. This knowledge is vital, and we have to delay the Vong figuring out what happened here."

The youngest Jedi shook his head. "What if it's just the pollen from this grove? What if this grove's genetics are unique?"

"Take cuttings then, Jacen, take pollen samples, as much as you want." Corran turned to Rade. "We need to start four fires, so the Yuuzhan Vong can't trace this grove as what we're trying to destroy by having the fire's epicenter be here. We'll also need to knock out the fire suppression system here to make sure it all goes. Their dead have to burn, too."

The resistance leader nodded. "I'm on it."

Jacen shook his head. "This place, so much greenery. Can't you feel the Force here, Corran?"

"I can, Jacen, but we have to look beyond it." He dropped to a knee beside Ganner and helped one of the resistance fighters press a bandage over the left side of Ganner's face. "The Vong *will* figure out what happened here, eventually. I just hope what we're doing earns us enough time that we can mount a defense of Ithor. If we can't, that world will die, and with it will go our best chances for driving the Yuuzhan Vong from our galaxy."

CHAPTER TWENTY

Jacen looked at the digital readout on the sedative injector in his right hand. *One dose left.* The two captives had received enough of the drug to keep a small gang of men down for a week, and still they could move—though, not much, given how tightly the Noghri had bound them. Just how tough the Yuuzhan Vong's creations were slammed into him, along with bloody visions of a long war against them.

He turned from the back end of the *Best Chance*, sidled past where Ganner sat with a reddened pressure bandage against his face, and slipped out the hatch. Jacen crossed quickly to where Corran stood talking to Rade. He nodded to the both of them, but waited for their conversation to end before he said anything.

The Garqian smiled wearily. "I appreciate the offer, Corran, but I'm not going to take up one of those open slots you have on the ship. I can't abandon my people, and they'd refuse an order to evacuate. We're here for the long haul."

"I'm not being altruistic here, Rade. You've got great intel on the Vong, and we need it."

"But what you need more is us being active here, making the Yuuzhan Vong think the whole Xenobotanical Garden fire was just a terrorist act." The resistance leader clapped the elder Jedi on the shoulders. "Your coming here meant a lot, and we'll get more information out to you. You have to go so you can find a way to turn our people back into our people. We need to be here to make sure there are some folks remaining to welcome the returnees back."

Corran's green eyes narrowed. "You're not being abandoned, you know. We'll be back to liberate Garqi."

Rade's smile broadened. "Better hurry back. We're planning to do the job ourselves."

Jacen held up the injector. "Our guests are down, but I'm not sure for how long. There's one dose left. Can I give it to Ganner?"

"Did he ask for it?"

The young man shook his head. "He's suffering, though."

Corran thought for a moment, then nodded. "Ask him if he wants it. If he says no, give it to him anyway."

"Are you joking?"

Corran shook his head. "He's a Jedi and he's in pain. I don't want him twitching TK that breaks something. We can't go until we get a signal, and I want us ready to sky when that happens. Our escape window here isn't going to be that big."

The idea that he should shoot Ganner full of a sedative against his will struck Jacen as a gross violation of Ganner's privacy and dignity, and he almost suspected Corran gave him the directive because of the friction between the two older Jedi. But Corran's reasoning made perfect sense, and his deliberation before telling Jacen what to do suggested he was searching for any way around adding insult to Ganner's injury. The order, though it would be a blow to Ganner, would be for the sake of the mission. Clearly Ganner's wishes, or those of anyone else, had to be secondary to what they were doing. *Just as I should have left the courtyard when Corran ordered me to, regardless of the consequences.*

All of a sudden Jacen saw the role of a mission leader in an entirely different light. Before, he'd always seen the leader as someone in power, and he could see how that position would be desirable. It meant a person had been deemed superior to his fellows. His orders were to be followed, his dictates were law. For someone as young as he was, becoming a leader seemed like a promotion to adult status, and he had not looked beyond that point.

The other side of being the leader and what that meant blossomed full in his brain. Yes, Corran could give orders, but he bore the full responsibility for the consequences of those actions. The success or failure of the mission was on his shoulders entirely. Jacen had no doubt that if required to, Corran would order suicidal assaults—the stand at the garden had been one such. And even though such orders could be justified in the name of success, Corran would still have to live with the consequences of his orders.

And Uncle Luke, too . . . Jacen turned back toward the ship and reentered. His uncle had an even greater burden to bear, and Jacen was suddenly relieved that such a mantle did not rest on his shoulders. Not only was it bone-crushing, but Jacen was fairly certain that having to shoulder it would deflect him from discovering the sort of Jedi he should become. *Responsibility for others could blind me to my responsibility within the Force.*

He ducked his head and passed through the hatchway. He smiled at Ganner. "Corran said I can give you this last dose of sedative, if you want it."

"No, I don't need it."

Jacen nodded, then stabbed it toward Ganner's thigh. The injector got within five centimeters, then stopped as if he'd been trying to drive it through transparisteel.

Ganner glared at him. "Don't make me break the injector, Jacen."

If he can focus that much, he's not going to be twitching. "Sorry, Corran said—"

"Corran said what he had to say. I don't want a sedative. Not yet, anyway." Ganner turned his head and glanced at one of the Noghri. "Sirhka, your help, please."

The Noghri unbuckled himself from his seat. "Ask."

"The medpac has a Nilar field cauterizer." Ganner peeled the bandage away from his face. "Use it to close the wound."

The Noghri nodded and bent to retrieve the medpac from beneath Ganner's seat. He slid it out and opened it. From the box he drew a sixteen-centimeter-long stylus that emitted a close-focus, low-frequency laser beam that would burn the wound shut. The Noghri stood again, and for the first time, Jacen realized that some of the patterning on the Noghri's gray flesh was from scars—some of which he felt certain Sirhka had closed himself with a cauterizer.

"Wait a minute." Jacen held a hand up. The wound on Ganner's face ran from above his left eye, splitting the brow, down to his cheekbone and below, to his jawline. Blood bubbled in the lower part of the wound as Ganner breathed, and the amphistaff had clearly carved bone as it slashed his face.

"Wait for what?"

"We'll get out of here. You can get into a bacta tank. If he uses that thing, you'll have a scar."

"I imagine I will." Ganner looked at the Noghri. "You don't have to be fancy, just close the wound."

The Noghri nodded and reached out to pinch Ganner's flesh together. He stroked the cauterizer against the wound's seams, sending little puffs of white smoke into the air. The bittersweet scent of burning flesh got into Jacen's nose, and he couldn't snort it back out. As much as he wanted to walk away, though, he couldn't do that either.

Ganner gripped the arms of the seat, and his muscles tightened with every brush of the cauterizer. Jacen could feel some pain coming off him, but it was considerably less than the disgust that rolled off the injured Jedi. It seemed to Jacen almost as if with each touch of the cauterizer, Ganner was reliving the cut that had opened the wound.

"Don't worry, Ganner, you won't be fooled by one of them again."

Ganner said nothing until Sirhka dropped to a knee and began working on the wound on Ganner's thigh. The Jedi accepted a dressing soaked in disinfectant and swabbed it over the side of his face, clearing up the blood. Most of the red went away, save the angry line from forehead to jaw. The flesh on the line was clearly tender, but Ganner washed it thoroughly nonetheless.

"You don't understand, Jacen, the Yuuzhan Vong didn't fool me. I fooled myself." Ganner closed his eyes for a moment and sat back. He opened only his right eye. "Throughout this mission, since I first heard of the Yuuzhan Vong even, I wanted to prove that I was better than they were. I was furious that I did not get to engage a Vong on Bimmiel. The first one I killed this afternoon, I tricked into stepping into that hole. I knew he was a fool, and he died because of his stupidity. And somehow, I started thinking that I was a genius compared to the rest of them."

Little wisps of white smoke rose like a curtain between Ganner and Jacen as the Noghri closed the other flesh wound. "It wasn't a stretch for me to think I was brilliant compared to the Yuuzhan Vong. I've been thinking that for a long time compared to other Jedi. Your uncle, Corran, Kam—all of them—they aren't of our generation of Jedi. They knew the Empire—they fought it or served it. They are older. They don't know the Force the way we do, didn't have the training we did."

He nodded his thanks to the Noghri as Sirhka put the cauterizer away. "Krag Val made me pay for my arrogance in a way none of the others had. They could have. Your uncle could have broken me down. Corran could have been nastier, but I took their being nice as a sign of weakness. I mean, I teased Corran's son. I was being an idiot, and Corran endured it because the mission we were given was more important than his feelings."

Ganner sighed. "So, yes, I'll have a scar, and it will be good. The old Ganner, he had a perfect face over a perfectly arrogant attitude. Not so anymore. Every time I look in a mirror I'll be reminded that he died on Garqi, and I'm here in his place."

The cold edge to Ganner's voice sent a chill through Jacen. He wanted to protest that Ganner didn't need a ruined face to remind him of the sort of person he should be. Jacen couldn't bring himself to speak. *As we grow up, we change physically. Maybe Ganner needs this change, not to remind him of who he should be, but as a mark of who he has become. My uncle lost a hand doing that. What will happen to me?*

Ganner sighed. "Now, if you wouldn't mind . . ."

Jacen blinked. "What?"

"Sedative. I'll take it now."

Jacen frowned. "But you could have had it before to make all that easier."

"I didn't want it to be easier, Jacen; wanted it to be memorable." He smiled, then closed his eyes. "Wake me when we're safe again."

Jacen touched the injector to him and pumped a full dose of sedative into Ganner. Jacen smiled as the man relaxed. *Let's just hope, Ganner, that there* will *be a point when we're safe again.*

Wedge Antilles stood with Admiral Kre'fey on the *Ralroost*'s bridge. They both stared at the forward viewport and the system's brilliant spot that was Garqi. It seemed so far away, yet a simple jump through hyperspace could carry the ship there in an instant.

And might carry us into an ambush. Wedge slowly shook his head. "Think they're waiting for us?"

The Bothan admiral shrugged uneasily. "There is still a great deal we don't know about them, Wedge. We know that when we send a message from here to Garqi, it will take three and a quarter standard minutes to reach our people on the ground. We don't know if the Yuuzhan Vong have means by which they can communicate faster. The message that came in from Corran requesting a pickup was sent over twelve hours ago. The Yuuzhan Vong could have reacted to their operation and have summoned support. Sithspawn, we don't even know if the Yuuzhan Vong travel through hyperspace the way we do, or if they are faster than our ships are. Nor do we know how close they are to Garqi, or what their possible response time could be."

"We live and learn."

Kre'fey flashed fangs as he smiled. "*If* we live, we learn." Without looking back, he growled a question. "Sensors, no anomalous system readings?"

"No, Admiral, all is within normal limits. Fine gravitational fluctuation readings do not indicate any increased mass hiding around moons or asteroid belts. If the Yuuzhan Vong are hiding ships out there, they must be very tiny."

"Thank you, sensors." The Bothan turned and nodded to a dark-furred officer at the communications console. "Lieutenant Arr'yka, send a message to Colonel Horn. Tell him we are here to pick him up. Request transmission of his intelligence reports as he comes up. Deploy a communications relay drone here to capture and send out the report in case we have trouble."

"As ordered, Admiral."

The snowy Bothan then looked over at Tycho Celchu at the flight operations command center. "Colonel, if you would be so kind as to put our fighters on alert."

"Done, Admiral."

Kre'fey came full around, his eyes narrowing. "It would seem a decision to advance would be difficult, but it's really not. We made a bargain with Horn and his people. They go into danger, we get them out. I will uphold that bargain."

"I think you should, though others may question your judgment if the Vong are waiting for us." Wedge gave the Bothan a grim grin. "But then, hindsight criticism is always based on fantasy foresight. What we *should have known* will be touted as facts we chose to overlook."

"If you think I'm overlooking anything, do let me know."

"Yes, Admiral, I will." Wedge nodded toward Garqi. "Right now the only thing I want to overlook is Garqi's horizon and see a ship coming up to greet us."

"I agree. Helm, execute primary egress-vector plot. Look alive, people. We have heroes to rescue."

Jaina Solo, locked in the cockpit of her X-wing, didn't so much feel the microjump into the interior of the Garqi system as much as she picked up sensations of uneasiness from crew members who didn't like making jumps. As those impressions faded, she immediately got a launch authorization and jammed her throttle full forward. The fighter jetted down the launch tube and shot out beneath the belly of the *Ralroost*, between it and Garqi's spinning sphere.

She brought her X-wing up on Anni Capstan's port side

and began to orbit. "Sparky, sensors at full, filter for Vong flight characteristics."

The droid tootled an acknowledgment of the order.

Jaina resisted the urge to reach out through the Force to sense her brother. She'd been stung by the deception earlier, when the task force had been inserted into Garqi. Intellectually she understood the need for operational security, and she could remember the shock of everyone on board the *Ralroost* when the task force was believed dead. Gavin had been correct about the tragedy and subsequent revelation creating a sense of unity between the crew and the pilots. Not knowing made them all one, and using the Force now would violate that trust.

The latest briefing did *say they had casualties, including a Jedi.* She knew it wasn't her brother; no matter the distance from her twin she felt certain she would know if he'd died. And she did acknowledge there was a huge difference between casualty and fatality, but somewhere in the back of her mind she'd imagined Jedi were somehow special and not the sort of heroes to fall in combat. Logically, and based on even the most recent history of the Jedi, she knew that wasn't true, but the depiction of heroism in the Jedi tradition allowed her to accept the fantasy as true on an emotional level.

Right now the only possibility you should be dwelling on is vaping some Vong so the Best Chance *can make it home.* She checked her sensors, but they remained clean. "Nothing here, Lead."

Anni Capstan, her wingmate, reported on the squadron tactical frequency. "Twelve here. I have one contact coming up from Garqi. Looks like our people."

"Good, stand by."

Jaina was about to ask Sparky to punch up Anni's contact when the droid shrieked. Her primary sensor monitor lit up with one huge contact, then several smaller ones, all of which began leaking yet smaller contacts. She looked up through her cockpit canopy, and her mouth went bone-dry.

"Emperor's black bones!"

The Yuuzhan Vong had arrived, and in force.

CHAPTER
TWENTY-ONE

Corran Horn headed the *Best Chance* straight for the *Ralroost* and was happy to see X-wings pouring from the Bothan ship. A smile lit his face. He keyed the ship's comm system. "There it is. We're all but home!"

He heard a little gasp from Jacen and felt a burst of shock roll off the younger man. "Look at this! Corran, we've got problems."

"Thanks for the preview, Jacen, now count it off for me." He put enough of an edge in his voice to get Jacen to concentrate. "How much, what, and where?"

"Sorry, Corran." Jacen exhaled curtly. "I have one big contact, seven smaller ones, and then skips all over the place—at least sixty-four, but more coming all the time. Small contacts are corvette size, the big one is a Yuuzhan Vong cruiser. They are vectoring in at our aft. Their closure rate means they'll get us before we get to the *Ralroost*."

"Thanks, I think." Corran flicked the comm unit over to the tactical frequency for the Bothan Assault Cruiser. "This is *Best Chance* calling *Ralroost*. We can break off and go dirtside. You get clear."

"Negative, *Best Chance*, keep coming."

Corran recognized Admiral Kre'fey's voice. "With all due respect, sir, there's an asteroid belt's worth of Vong here. We are not worth risking the *'Roost* for."

"Your humility notwithstanding, Colonel Horn, I'm the

162

one who makes the decisions here. You come to us as fast as you can." The Bothan admiral paused for a second. "This possibility was not wholly unanticipated."

Ensconced in his cabin aboard the *Burning Pride*, with the cognition hood linking him to the ship's sensory apparatus, Deign Lian let the first shock of finding New Republic forces at Garqi roll off him. He had proposed to Shedao Shai an expedition to Garqi, ostensibly to check up on how Krag Val was doing with the slave conversion experiment. He intended, based on reports from his own agents in the Garqi garrison, to show that resistance had not been wiped out there, shaming Krag Val and bringing his master's judgment into question.

Shedao Shai had granted the request for the trip, but demanded that Deign take a large task force with him. Deign's inquiries as to why he should do it had been met with a withering stare. He'd acquiesced to the request because he knew it was a gross waste of resources, which would not look good for Shedao Shai.

And yet, somehow, he knew . . . Deign Lian shivered, then focused. The ship's sensors brought to him a holographic feel for the system and ships. His training allowed him to pick out the prize, the one ship running from Garqi and his forces, the one ship to which the infidels were sending their fighters.

As fast as he could think it, the order went out. His forces oriented on the small ship racing away from Garqi. *Get it, kill it, then kill all the rest of them.*

On the bridge of the *Ralroost*, Admiral Kre'fey turned away from the viewport as the blast shields began to close. He strode over to the communications station with deliberate haste but not a whiff of anxiety. He smiled at the Bothan sitting there. "Lieutenant, please invite Hammer Group to take up the positions outlined in Delta Case."

"As ordered, Admiral."

As she punched up the appropriate tactical frequencies and

began to relay orders, Kre'fey turned to Wedge. "Nasty little game to be played here."

"Our reinforcements should be useful, but they're not going to be enough."

"We're not trying to win the battle, Wedge, just trying to win some time." Kre'fey pointed toward his station on the bridge. "Sensors, give me a holographic feed of the system, and start relaying all our tactical data out to Coruscant through the drone we left at the edge of the system."

"Setting it up now, Admiral."

"Good, very good." He let a predatory grin slowly spread over his face. A low growl rumbled from his throat, summoning up a very fundamental piece of his Bothan psyche. It was something he set aside when dealing with humans, for they so often saw the malevolent side of it in Bothan politics. *We are predators by nature, and now I need that nature.*

"Remain here with me, Wedge Antilles." Kre'fey's words rolled out in low tones, born deep in his chest. "We might not be able to kill the Yuuzhan Vong here, but we *can* hurt them, and that might just be enough."

Jaina kicked her X-wing up into a portside barrel roll, then came around for a long glide to starboard. She stayed hot on Anni's port wing, the two of them angling in for a series of deflection shots on a skip squadron. "Ready when you are, Twelve."

Anni double-clicked her comm, acknowledging Jaina's comment. The pair of them adjusted their course, drifting a little more starboard, then closed on a knot of six skips jetting in at the *Best Chance*. In a flash of blue fire, a proton torpedo launched from Anni's X-wing. A heartbeat later a second missile raced from the starfighter.

Jaina's eyes narrowed. *If this works . . .*

The first proton torpedo approached the group of skips, and the Yuuzhan Vong fighters responded by putting up voids to catch the missile before it could hit the fighters. Using a tactic that had proved effective in the fighting on Dantooine, the New Republic had programmed the proton torpedo to detonate prematurely when it detected a gravitic anomaly, which this missile did.

The skips then found themselves on a course heading straight for a titanic cloud of energy. This shattered the formation. The Yuuzhan Vong pilots broke like birds in flight, twisting their ships about at acute angles. Some flew below, and others turned toward the attack. One pair broke away and up, and therein proved the efficacy of the new tactic.

The one flaw in the coralskipper design was that the dovin basals that manipulated gravity waves to provide propulsion *also* were the things that generated the voids. The New Republic analysts had noted that when voids were generated, the ability of skips to maneuver was diminished. It took Rogue Squadron's pilots to realize that the reverse might also be true.

The second proton torpedo caught up with two of the fleeing skips and exploded. One skip vanished amid the brilliant detonation. The other caught a part of the blast on its port side, melting the yorik coral and exposing the cockpit to vacuum. The stony ship stopped flying with any direction or purpose and just tumbled toward Garqi like so much other interstellar debris.

Jaina dropped her aiming reticle on the closest Yuuzhan Vong fighter and hit the splinter-shot trigger. Her quadded lasers spat out hundreds of underpowered laser darts at her target. A small void absorbed some of them, but quickly collapsed, allowing other shots to pepper the fighter's rocky exterior. The second she saw splinters getting through, she hit the main trigger, loosing a full quad burst on the fighter.

The sizzling crimson bolts converged on the skip, filling the nose with enough energy to make it glow white-hot. Molten stone peeled back, sloughing off like dead flesh. The skip began a slow roll, then shook and jerked, thrashing as the dovin basals died.

Anni clipped off a quick shot that damaged the other skip but didn't kill it, and then she and Jaina were through to the other side of the Yuuzhan Vong formation. Watching the sensors intently, Jaina brought her X-wing around for another run. Above her the battle had deteriorated, with skips and X-wings spinning and looping, streaking and rolling in a chaotic tangle. The proton torpedo tactic that proved so useful in the first pass would now have as much chance of taking out an ally as an enemy.

We're back to conventional tactics.

Beyond the fighters the capital ships had begun to slug it out. The *Ralroost's* two companion ships, a pair of *Victory*-class Star Destroyers, appeared above and beyond the Yuuzhan Vong cruiser. They launched barrages of concussion missiles and laced the enemy formation with turbolaser fire. The corvette-size Yuuzhan Vong ships intercepted many of the missiles and shots before they could reach the cruiser, providing an outer sphere of defense. Their shots back at the New Republic forces were picked up by shields, but those shields could not hold forever.

Jaina felt a shiver run down her spine. *Were this a sim it would be obvious that we're overmatched. It would be time to cut and run.* She sighed. *It's not a sim. We can't run. We can't win, so we just have to hope we hurt them enough that they don't really win either.*

Deep in the bowels of his ship, Deign Lian smiled. The advent of the New Republic reinforcements had surprised him, but a quick study of the situation showed that their intervention would only extend the time it took to kill them. While his coralskippers had taken more damage than he expected they would, and the new ships had deployed more mechanical fighters, his fighter force still outnumbered the enemy. Likewise, his capital ships outnumbered them and were more powerful.

He directed all his attacks at one of the smaller New Republic ships. The cannons on the Yuuzhan Vong ships vomited plasma bolts at it, hammering the shields. The enemy ship's sphere of protection began shrinking. Another volley or two and the shields would collapse, then the shots would melt their way through the enemy vessel, ridding it of its blasphemous parody of life.

And when that is done, I take the rest of them. The Yuuzhan Vong leader smiled slowly. *Forces will praise me for winning. My position will be such that when my master falters, there will be but one choice for his replacement.*

Admiral Gilad Pellaeon, seated in the chair from which Grand Admiral Thrawn had commanded the *Chimaera*, watched the holographic display of the battle raging at the heart of the Garqi system. He smoothed his mustache with the thumb and forefinger of his left hand, then stabbed his right index finger down on the command chair's comm button.

"Is force Spike deployed, guns?"

His combat command officer replied affirmatively. "Confirmed now, Admiral."

"Good. Helm, five seconds to jump. Positions from Gamma file. Tell Spike Lead he is cleared to jump to point blood-niner."

"As ordered, Admiral."

Pellaeon released the comm button and sat back, pressing his hands together. For decades he had dreamed of finding a New Republic task force in such a compromising position. He would plan out an ambush as he had done here, then order it executed. He smiled as he imagined their surprise.

"Oh, they will still be surprised, I imagine." He nodded slowly. "As will our targets."

Corran whipped the *Best Chance* through a roll, then brought the nose up in a half loop, before inverting and rolling out to port and diving. His sensors still showed two skips on his ship's tail. His maneuvers were keeping them from getting good shots in on him, but the Yuuzhan Vong were slowly herding him away from the *Ralroost*.

"Jacen, any more sedative in that injector?"

"Ganner took the last of it. Why?"

"Well, I always kinda figured I'd like to die in my sleep." Corran laughed aloud. "Just so you know, kid, you've impressed me on this mission. Might not mean much when we're free-floating atoms, but—"

"Sithspawn!"

"Didn't think that comment warranted profanity."

"No, Corran, multiple new contacts coming in. I have two Star Destroyers, one *Imp*-class and another *Vic*. And a bunch of something else. ID transponders list them as Imperial Remnant forces."

Corran smiled. "Let them know we're friendly, Jacen. Then hang on. We might just get out of this after all."

Sparky screeched as dozens of tactical fighter contacts sprayed themselves over Jaina's aft sensor screens. She broke to port in a barrel roll and glanced down at her monitor. The craft looked like nothing she had ever seen before. It had a TIE fighter ball cockpit, with the twin ion engine pod at the back of it. Unlike TIEs, though, this one had four arms emerging from the junction of engine and pod. They jutted out and forward, as if fingers closing on the cockpit, splaying out in an array that was faintly reminiscent of an X-wing's laser positioning for combat.

A sharp keening pealed through her comm unit, then resolved itself into a human voice. "Get clear, Rogues. They are ours now. Spike Lead out."

What? Who?! Jaina's jaw dropped open as the clawlike fighters blasted past her, three sets of four, all grouped in tight formations. They twisted and turned as if the pilots shared a brain, moving with precision that took her breath away. Their weapons blazed out with green splinter shots, then loosed paired bolts that hit the skips with incredible accuracy. Cockpits became volcanoes. Dovin basals boiled and exploded. Skips crumbled as the thirty-six clawcraft that had just appeared in the system raked their way through the dogfight.

The two Star Destroyers that had at the same time appeared shifted the balance of the capital ship battle. One interposed itself between the enemy and the stricken *Taanab Sunrise.* Its shields had collapsed and a dozen fires burned in holes in the hull. The new *Victory*-class Star Destroyer, *Red Harvest,* soaked off incoming fire from the Yuuzhan Vong, while using its weapons to crush one of the enemy corvettes.

The other one, the *Chimaera*, joined the *Ralroost* in targeting the Yuuzhan Vong cruiser. The enemy vessel spawned a plague of gravitic anomalies. They managed to absorb the assaults directed at it, but killed all maneuvering capability from the ship. *It can hold us off like this until the dovin basals tire, and we have no idea how long that will be.*

"Rogue Leader to all Rogues, recall is ordered. Back to the *'Roost*. We have achieved our objective and we're heading home."

Jaina blinked, then stretched out with the Force. She felt her brother's presence, safe and whole, on the *Ralroost*. *Now, if we can just get back.*

She glanced at her sensor screens and frowned. The skip traces were few and far between, and all heading toward the Yuuzhan Vong cruiser. The clawcraft wove intricate patterns through what had been the battleground, with quartets of them escorting X-wings back to the Bothan ship. One small formation curled down and came around, taking up a position around Jaina and Anni.

"Don't worry, Rogues, we have you now. We'll get you home safely."

The patronizing tone in Spike Leader's voice made Jaina grit her teeth. "Who are you?"

"We're simply the best combat pilots in the galaxy." A momentary spark of static burst through the comm channel. "We are a Chiss House phalanx, on loan to the New Republic by my father, General Baron Soontir Fel."

CHAPTER
TWENTY-TWO

What Shedao Shai saw on the surface of Garqi did not please him. Coming down to the planet in a shuttle, he had seen a blackened scar below, but standing amid it magnified its obscenity. Charcoal crunched beneath his feet. The dry scent of burned wood filled his nostrils, and occasionally a hint of charred flesh made it through, as well.

Pleased that the mask he wore hid his shock and disgust, Shedao Shai looked down at the subordinate who lay prostrate before him. He carefully placed his foot on his inferior's neck. "You say, Runck Das, that Krag Val fought valiantly here before dying. How is it that you did not die with him?"

Runck spit cinders from his mouth. "Commander, Krag Val ordered this one to remain behind, preserving information for you, guarding against a different attack by the resistance. I wanted to be here to guard him, but I had been ordered to remain behind."

Deign Lian snorted from Shedao Shai's left. "Obey a foolish order and you merely reveal yourself to be a complete and total fool."

The Yuuzhan Vong leader's left hand snapped out. Stiffened fingers slapped against Lian's throat, punching a coughed gasp from him. The subordinate staggered back a step and began to bring his hands up to his throat. They stopped halfway, curling down into fists, then loosened again and slowly drifted back to his sides. Lian dropped to one knee and bowed his head.

"Your. Pardon. Master."

Shedao Shai regarded Lian coldly, then returned his gaze to the Yuuzhan Vong beneath his foot. "What happened here? Tell me all."

Runck's fingers clawed into the ground. "We can only surmise and only have information from some Chazrach who ran from here."

"And what you surmise is?"

A gray tongue licked lips free of black specks. "Krag Val, as is proper, announced a challenge to the enemy leader. Silverblade did not answer it. Yellowblade did, then one of the others, not a *jeedai*, answered. Krag Val cut down the first, then Yellowblade. The third *jeedai* slew him. Silverblade engaged others and must have slain them. Our slaves broke and ran. The enemy burned this place to the ground, consuming the bodies of their dead and ours."

Shedao Shai's right hand convulsed into a fist. He pounded it against his armored thigh, breaking the grip and letting each finger slowly straighten. "And by the time you got here, the conflagration had spread. You could find no way to track them?"

"No, Leader, there was nothing we could do."

"Wrong, Runck of Domain Das." Shedao Shai shifted all of his weight onto the subordinate's neck, then twisted his foot, popping skull from spine. "You could have been faster."

He glanced quickly at Deign Lian. His subordinate hesitated, then started to lower himself to the ground.

"Don't be stupid, Deign Lian." The Yuuzhan Vong leader left Runck's body twitching out its life and stood over his aide. "What have you learned from letting your prey escape?"

Deign Lian's eyes studied the blackened ground. "That the infidels are cunning. They laid a trap for us. Had you not insisted—"

Shedao Shai kicked him in the chest, dumping him onto his left flank in a black cloud of dust. "If that is the lesson you learned, you are no smarter than Runck."

"But, my leader—"

"Think, Lian, truly think." Shedao slowly spread his gauntleted hands. "You see this ruin around you and you come away with an impression of cunning? Analyze the battle you were involved in. The truth is obvious."

"I have tried, Commander."

"Not hard enough, Lian." Shedao suppressed a shiver spawned by his subordinate's incompetence. "They arrive and deploy to recover the *jeedai*. You arrive and deploy to deny them their prize. Your force is superior. Then they bring in reinforcements in two waves? The second wave's delay gained them no tactical advantage. One of their ships took serious damage because of the delay. Moreover, given where the second wave appeared in the system, there are a limited number of points from which they could have come. Few of them allow for convenient access to the New Republic, but not so this Imperial Remnant."

The Yuuzhan Vong leader slowly paced a circle around his aide. "More importantly, even the arrival of this force was not enough to defeat you and drive you away from the planet. They took their prize and retreated. My supposition is that the second wave was from the Imperial Remnant, here for their own reasons, and they decided to intervene."

Lian nodded slowly. "My leader's wisdom is boundless."

"If it were that, I would have sent more ships with you. I would have been here myself."

The aide looked up. "How did you know to send ships with me?"

Shedao Shai paused for a moment. "The earlier appearance of the New Republic ship made no sense. If they wished a scouting run on Garqi, it could have remained at the system fringe while their fighters flew in close, gathered data, and retreated. This was largely their activity pattern at Sernpidal. The only reason for them to be here was to deliver the ship that was reported downed. Analysis of the crash site showed us all we would expect."

"I fail to see—"

"Indeed." Shedao Shai snorted. "You and those who explored the ruins of the ship. They were so afraid of being tainted that they missed the obvious. Why would we find traces of the crew of a stricken ship when they could get into escape pods?"

"But there were no indications of life pods—"

"Exactly, there were none." The Yuuzhan Vong leader rubbed his hands together. "Now we know the escape ship was hidden in the downed one, the bio-trace material merely bait. It was an elaborate ruse."

"But why?"

"Lian, how can you be so stupid?" Shedao Shai opened his arms. "We are standing amid their reason. Go, now, and determine what that reason was. Find out why they destroyed this place. Those who fell here demand it of you. Do not fail them, or me."

"As you command, Master."

Shedao Shai turned his back on Lian and waited for the sound of his aide's footsteps to fade to nothingness before he turned around again to regard his silent, golden shadow. "And what do you make of this destruction, Elegos?"

The Caamasi shrugged with his full body. "This was a garden. It had no military value. They were pursued here, made a stand. Collateral damage."

The Yuuzhan Vong let a little chuckle roll from his throat. "Do you think me fooled so easily?"

"Do you think I seek to fool you?" Elegos's dark eyes remained wide open and innocent. "If Deign Lian cannot figure out why this place was burned despite the time he has now spent here, how am I to know with only an hour's inspection?"

Shedao Shai began to walk deeper into the scorched scar, then waved his right hand to indicate Elegos should accompany him. When the alien caught up, he glanced at him. "How is it you abide their company, Elegos? You are thoughtful and peaceful; they are neither. I see it here. I saw it at your world of Bimmiel. How do you stand being with such dishonorable creatures?"

Elegos frowned. "What dishonor? The New Republic risked much to recover a force sent here. There is much honor in that."

"Yes, perhaps there is, but it pales in comparison to the other things." Shedao Shai forced his hands open and spread them. "As you said, this place has no military value, but they destroyed it. Why? And this mission of which you speak. They took dead bodies and used them as refuse to plant on a ship."

"Even you believe the body is a vessel, Commander Shai; this I have learned from you."

Shedao Shai turned and stabbed a finger at Elegos. "Yes, but a sacred vessel. One to be honored and cherished. We have ways, rituals, that show respect for all a fallen ancestor means. I have shared with you the results of such rituals. Here—"

The Yuuzhan Vong leader found his hand and finger quivering as rage coursed through him. He thought for a second to hide it, but instead resisted that impulse. "Here bodies were burned where they lay. Limbs were not straightened. Comrades were not placed together. They were treated as if they were rubbish, and not only *our* bodies. This I could understand, after a fashion, but their own?"

"The treatment of dead Yuuzhan Vong bodies you can ascribe to ignorance." Elegos squatted near a carbonized skeleton. "Of their own people, perhaps haste. We, too, honor our dead, when possible. With your forces gathering, that clearly was not possible."

"It could be as you suggest. I have learned much from you, but now I need to learn one more thing."

Elegos glanced up, the sun flashing white from his golden fur. "I do not think there is more I can tell you, Commander Shai."

"Oh, there is." The Yuuzhan Vong pressed his two fists together. "At the mention of a *jeedai* called Silverblade you started, almost imperceptibly. When I mentioned Bimmiel, you again gave a sign of recognizing something. I shall assume you know this *jeedai*, Silverblade."

"I have never denied knowing Jedi."

"But Silverblade you know very well."

The Caamasi nodded and slowly stood. "His name is Corran Horn."

"Ko-run Horn." Shedao Shai let the words roll around in his mouth. He linked the sound of them to the taste of the *jeedai*'s blood from Bimmiel. "You didn't tell me he was the one who killed my kin at Bimmiel."

"You never asked."

"If you are willing to be that coy, Elegos, you not only know him, but you care for him. You think to shield your friend from my wrath?"

The Caamasi lifted his chin, exposing his throat. "Perhaps, Commander Shai, it is you I am shielding."

"You care for him, *and* fear for him." Shedao tapped an index finger against his battle mask's chin. "Your loyalty is laudable, though to such a disreputable character? Impossible to understand. You are wiser than that."

"Corran is not a stupid or dishonorable man, despite how you read what you see here." Elegos gathered his hands at the small of his back. "None of the Jedi are stupid, nor are most of the leaders of the New Republic. You put too much weight on their ignorance of your ways, and you are swayed because of how little of them you understand."

"But, Elegos, you have taught me well. I understand much about them."

The Caamasi ventured a small smile. "And through my time with you, I have some understanding of your ways. I am even led to believe that some sort of accord could be reached. This war does not have to go on forever."

"No, I would not want that." Shedao Shai folded his arms across his chest. "If I were to open a dialogue, I would need an envoy I could trust implicitly. I have nonesuch among my people."

Elegos's eyes half shut. "I could be your ambassador."

"Indeed, an excellent idea." Shedao Shai nodded slowly, then turned and beckoned Elegos to follow him. "Come along. I will prepare you to deliver a message to these *jeedai*—a message they cannot possibly fail to understand."

CHAPTER
TWENTY-THREE

Though there had been peace with the Imperial Remnant for over six years, Corran still felt a sense of dissonance as he watched Admiral Gilad Pellaeon enter the briefing room aboard the *Ralroost*. Admiral Kre'fey greeted him warmly, shaking his hand. The Imperial admiral acknowledged Master Skywalker with a nod, then turned and smiled at Corran.

"I had a chance to study your initial report from Garqi. Good work."

Corran blinked, then nodded. "Jacen Solo prepared the report, I just corrected some spelling. I'll pass your comments on to him."

"Please do." Pellaeon took a seat across from Corran at the lozenge-shaped briefing table. That left Admiral Kre'fey at the head, Master Skywalker at the Bothan's right hand, and Corran on Luke's right. "We have quite a situation here."

Kre'fey seated himself. "We do, on several different levels. I cannot thank you enough for having intervened when you did. The intelligence assets you have in the New Republic are clearly very thorough."

"Not as thorough as you might imagine." The Imperial officer leaned forward on his elbows, pressing his hands flat against the table's black top. "We can speak plainly, and will need to before the politicians arrive. I brought my force here after I heard of your abortive raid. My assumption was that either you *had* inserted assets onto the planet, or that a previous attempt to exfiltrate assets had been rebuffed. It suggested something of value on Garqi that I wanted to know about, so we had been there for two days by the time you arrived."

"The data we recovered would have been yours immediately, regardless of what my superiors might have said." Kre'fey scratched with claws at his throat. "And, yes, we must speak plainly because the politicians are going to complicate things incredibly."

Corran sighed and slumped down in his seat a bit. The task force had leapt to the edge of the Garqi system, rendezvoused with the Imperial force, then had plotted a course directly for Ithor. Admiral Kre'fey issued a call for reinforcements, scientific teams, and a lot of support that raised alarm on Coruscant. While they did say they were sending what they could, a report also came in that Borsk Fey'lya and a number of the key senators and ministers would be coming to Ithor, as well. Once there, no one had any doubts, they would begin to interfere with what really needed to be a military operation.

"I harbor no illusions, Admiral Kre'fey: the moffs will be as opposed to my helping you defend Ithor as your leaders will be to having Imperial forces operating in the New Republic." Pellaeon's eyes narrowed. "They are not going to see this the way we do. The battle for Ithor will determine the course of the war against the Yuuzhan Vong. If we win here, they are blunted and can be driven back. If we lose here, I am not sanguine about the New Republic's chances for survival—nor those of Imperial Space."

"We are in dire circumstances, to be certain." The Bothan's eyes tightened. "You should know, Admiral, that we have no access to any of the Empire's old superweapons. Reports of their destruction are true, no matter what rumors to the contrary still circulate."

Pellaeon smiled. "And we have none, either. It is just as well, because those weapons were difficult to employ in defense."

"And the Remnant bringing them into the New Republic, for whatever reason, just would not be tolerable." Kre'fey nodded. "The defense of Ithor will be difficult enough without having superweapons entering the mix."

"It's true, this isn't going to be easy." Luke brushed a hand over his mouth. "We have a couple of problems here on Ithor. The first is scientific. It is possible to take grafts from bafforr trees of the line that produced the pollen on Garqi; however, the trees take years of growth before they become mature enough to produce pollen. Even if we take samples away and plant groves all over the New Republic, it could take as much as a decade before the plants would be able to produce the pollen we need."

Corran frowned. "But Ithorians are well known for their skill at cloning and genetic manipulation of botanicals. My grandfather maintains an ongoing correspondence with them concerning the stuff he does. They should be able to synthesize the pollen we need."

The Jedi Master winced. "This leads us to the second and more difficult problem we face, regardless of whether synthetic pollen would be as effective as the genuine thing. Ithorian society is based on a religion that worships the forest and world and life. If we were asking them to produce something as medicine, something that would further life, they would agree in a heartbeat. We're asking them to manipulate the stuff of life to create a weapon. They won't do that."

Kre'fey arched a pale eyebrow. "There is no way to appeal such a decision?"

Luke shifted his shoulders uneasily. "I have spoken with Relal Tawron, the high priest who replaced Momaw Nadon as the Ithorian leader. The fact that the bafforr trees on Garqi contributed pollen to the fight means they would be willing to let us harvest pollen and create new groves. They take the action on Garqi as the trees' consent to opposing the Yuuzhan Vong. He is, however, reluctant to modify or abandon other tenets of their faith. For example, the Ithorians apparently allow no one to set foot on Ithor."

Pellaeon shook his head. "I doubt the Yuuzhan Vong will abide by that rule."

"Relal knows that, and is willing to be somewhat practical

in that matter, but it will require concessions on our part. Our people on the ground will have to be blessed, will have to observe certain restrictions."

The Bothan admiral sat back in his chair. "The high priest must realize that any restrictions are likely to be forgotten in the heat of battle."

Luke nodded. "He would not say that, but that is the sense I got from him. He is in a precarious position. The Ithorians are very peaceful. This invasion and even the preparation for it could shatter Ithorian society."

Corran leaned forward. "We are all agreed, though, that the destruction of the Pesktda Xenobotanical Garden on Garqi is only buying us time. The Vong will attack Ithor. Given the threat it presents, I could see them just popping into the system and using dovin basals to pepper the planet with asteroids. One solid impact and pretty much everything dies."

"We can screen the planet against that, though." Pellaeon nodded. "Asteroids would take long enough to come in that we could pulverize them."

"I would also have to think, Corran, that given how the Yuuzhan Vong view biological things the same way we do machines, they would want to learn more about Ithor." Luke closed his eyes for a second, then opened them again. "The report of what you saw on Garqi could be a blueprint for what they could do with Ithor."

"No argument there, *and* we've not had another Sernpidal in this second wave, so the Vong leadership seems to be approaching things in a more logical manner." The Corellian Jedi shrugged. "Standard defense, then? Engage in space to make landing troops difficult, then fight them as they come down and on the planet?"

Kre'fey nodded. "I would prefer to stop them in space, but to neglect a planetary defense would be silly. We have some elite troops, both from the New Republic and Imperial Space, that can take up positions on the ground. They're disciplined enough to work within the Ithorian strictures, at least until hot light starts flying."

The New Republic admiral looked to his Remnant counterpart. "That decision, though, will be up to you, Admiral."

Pellaeon looked startled. "What are you saying?"

Kre'fey smiled carefully. "You are the senior officer here,
with far more experience than I have. I've fought the Yuuzhan
Vong several times and never come away with a clean victory,
so I am not seeing something. I would like you to be in command of the defense of Ithor."

Corran arched an eyebrow. "Well, the politicians won't
like that at all."

The Bothan flashed fangs for a second. "We can package
the defense nicely, all this joint planning and everything, but
when the battle comes, I still want you in charge, Admiral. By
that point it will be too late for them to object."

The human admiral nodded slowly. "You will be second in
the chain of command, of course."

"Honored, yes."

Pellaeon smiled quickly. "And then who? Master Skywalker?"

The Bothan glanced at Luke. "Jedi fought on the ground at
Dantooine and again at Bimmiel. Will they have a role here?"

Luke pressed his hands together, and Corran caught a faint
impression of emotional pain from his Master. Jedi were not
combat troops, but were trained to fight in ways that would be
very useful on Ithor. Because Ithor teemed with life, it fairly
well pulsed with the Force, so Jedi would be drawn to defend
it, as well. Still, things they might be called upon to do would
be outside the boundaries of strictly defensive action.

The Jedi Master glanced at Corran. "Your thoughts?"

"No question we have to help with the defense." Corran
sighed. "In essence, the whole of the planet will be held
hostage. I'm not sure there is anything we could do here,
short of slaughtering innocents, that would be of the dark
side. And I'm fairly certain there will be no Vong innocents
on the planet."

"If there are Yuuzhan Vong who surrender?" Pellaeon
asked.

Luke shook his head. "The slaves they use as proxy troops

can't surrender, and the Yuuzhan Vong themselves, well, I have a hard time believing they would surrender to us."

"I don't know as how I'd trust any of them who *would* surrender." The Corellian frowned. "On Dantooine, didn't Mara run into some who had killed civilians, then used ooglith masquers to take on their appearance for the purpose of slaughtering more civilians?"

The Bothan tapped a talon on the table. "Good point. We will have to review normal rules of engagement and inform our people that surrenders may not be respected. Not knowing about the Yuuzhan Vong, about their culture and traditions, makes the task of figuring out how to fight them so much more difficult. We can guess, we can make inferences, but we just don't know."

Pellaeon smiled. "Grand Admiral Thrawn set great store by studying the art of a culture as a key to understanding it. I don't know what he would make of the Yuuzhan Vong, but the few Chiss that came in from the Unknown Regions took to fighting them very eagerly."

"Yes, the Chiss in their clawcraft." Kre'fey smoothed fur at the back of his neck. "You can rest assured that Coruscant did not like hearing that there was a whole contingent of Thrawn's people lurking out there. I'm sure many of them fear you'll use the Chiss to carve a new Empire from the New Republic."

The human admiral shrugged. "I might have, had I known they were there, but I was not privy to all of Thrawn's plans. When we issued a recall to all Imperial agents and troops, no matter where they were, this contingent showed up with Baron Fel's compliments, and led by his son."

Corran shook his head. "Who would have guessed?"

"I knew." Luke's declaration came in a low voice, so low that Corran wasn't certain he'd heard it. "Back during the Bothan crisis, when I went to find Mara, we found Admiral Parck and Baron Fel. They were overseeing an effort set up by Thrawn, including a facility to clone a replacement of Thrawn. They indicated there was fighting going on in the Unknown Regions, that they were holding back some sort of threat to the Empire out there. They were no threat to us, so passing on the information about their existence out there would have been a distraction for the peace process."

Kre'fey blinked his gold-flecked violet eyes. "If certain ministers knew you'd withheld this sort of information, they would take it as proof positive that you desire some sort of Jedi hegemony to rise up, and you thought you could use the Chiss to make that happen."

Corran frowned. "That's nonsense."

"Oh, I know, I'm just telling you what will happen if that information gets out. For our purposes, though, we know we have someone holding that flank for us. This is good." The Bothan glanced at Pellaeon. "How much in the way of military forces will you be able to bring here?"

"My staff is still working up plans. At least one operational group: four Imperial Star Destroyers, eight *Victory*-class Star Destroyers, and assorted support vessels. We can have them all here, or stage some at Yaga Minor to make a drive at Garqi, since we have to assume they will be staging from there."

Kre'fey nodded. "I can draw comparable strength, though a number of the ships will have to be staged at Agamar. They will threaten Garqi and also reinforce the escape route for anyone fleeing the Yuuzhan Vong. If we have to, I can pull those resources from Agamar, but then we know that world will fall."

Corran's heart sank at the Bothan's words. As much as he would have liked it to be otherwise, the chances were that Agamar would face a Yuuzhan Vong assault and would be conquered. Its conquest might precede that of Ithor, allowing the Yuuzhan Vong to secure an even closer staging area, but even slight pressure on Agamar could pin down New Republic forces, denying them to the defense of Ithor. The Yuuzhan Vong had to attack Ithor and do it quickly, lest the New Republic be able to reinforce it enough that it couldn't be taken.

The real problem with the loss of Agamar was that it would, in effect, cut the Remnant off from the New Republic by shutting down a key hyperspace route between them.

Aside from Ithor, the nearest New Republic world would be Ord Mantell, but getting from Yaga Minor to Ord Mantell was not easy and involved a lot of minor jumps and a long time. Corran wasn't certain, in the long run, how much help the Remnant would be in the fight against the Yuuzhan Vong, but since they'd just helped save his life, he was inclined to want them in the fight for the long run.

Pellaeon shrugged stiffly. "This is ever the plight of the military man. We know where we can deploy our forces for best effect. That is a rational decision based on numbers and analysis. We both know that Ithor is the key here. The Yuuzhan Vong have to come in sufficient force to take it. If we strip defenses from elsewhere, we provide a tempting alternative target. Some people suffer so others will not. We can provide the best response as per our brain, but it isn't the *right* response according to our hearts."

He spread his arms wide. "We have approximately two weeks before your leaders get here, and I imagine some of mine will arrive, too. In that time we will have to come up with a plan in which we show them we are splitting responsibility and risk to the gain of all. This means we will make concessions to political considerations that we don't want to make, in essence slipping binders on our own wrists before we go into this fight. I don't like that any more than you do, but the alternative is for our leaders, fighting between and among themselves, to impose their own binders on us.

"I'd much prefer the binders I choose than theirs." The man's eyes sparkled. "After all, if I tie myself up, it's with the knowledge I can get out of the binders. And in this coming fight, if we can't do that, everything—Ithor, New Republic, and Imperial Space—is doomed."

CHAPTER
TWENTY-FOUR

For Jaina Solo, the absurdities of the reception would not end. To begin with, the reception was a formal affair that took place on the *Tafanda Bay*, one of the Ithorian herd ships, cities that drifted lazily above the jungle. The transparisteel-domed ships, with their own ecosystems and loaded with plant life, were kept warm and very humid. In everyday clothes she didn't mind it, but dressed up in formal Jedi robes, she found the atmosphere heavy and oppressive.

Just having such a formal affair on a planet that was going to be the focal point for an enemy assault struck her as wrong. She would have preferred to be up on the *Ralroost* with the rest of Rogue Squadron. It annoyed her, too, that she had been invited because of her status as a Solo and a Jedi, not as a member of Rogue Squadron. Colonel Darklighter had been chosen to represent the squadron, and Jaina got a distinct impression that the New Republic's protocol experts were afraid the pilots might actually speak their minds and disrupt things.

The tension of those gathered in the room seemed almost as oppressive as the humidity. They had been gathered into a large hall that was open, though overarching tree branches made glimpses of the night sky through the dome few and far between. More impressive than the trees, though, was the way the wood covering the floor and paneling the walls had been fitted together. A rich gold in color, with dark streaks of grain, the strips formed a mosaic through which the lines flowed effortlessly. Jaina could have followed the grain with her eyes forever, but knots of diplomats kept eclipsing it.

From years of watching her mother attend—and attend to—such functions, she knew diplomatic contacts operated in an unreal world. Mortal enemies would be unfailingly polite face-to-face while plotting ruthlessly behind closed doors. Even Admiral Kre'fey and Colonel Darklighter would withhold criticism of political limits placed on their operations so the impression could be created that all was well.

She sighed. *At least that means people will be polite to the Jedi.*

"Such a sigh. Did it relieve the weariness in your spirit?"

Jaina turned and smiled, recognizing the voice. "Yes, Ganner, a bit." She kept the smile in place despite the little shock she felt at seeing the livid scar on his face.

The older Jedi sipped a cup of wine, then gave her a little nod. "I suppose, perhaps, I should try a sigh."

"Why? Oh." She glanced past Ganner in his robes of blue and black, toward a knot of Jedi paying court to Kyp Durron. "I had heard there was some trouble."

Ganner gave her a wry grin that made him a different sort of handsome in her eyes. "My experiences on Bimmiel and especially Garqi were . . . sobering. Since many Jedi have been called here to help oppose the Yuuzhan Vong, and are eager to do so, my sharing rather frank views about how dangerous the Yuuzhan Vong are is not welcome. Realism becomes synonymous with defeatism in their eyes."

"Probably didn't help that you saved Corran's life on Bimmiel."

Ganner snorted a quick laugh. "No, it didn't. I don't regret it, however. The lessons I've learned working with him are lessons I needed to learn. I'm glad I lived long enough to do it."

She glanced down for a moment. "I'm sorry you got hurt."

"I'm not." His blue eyes narrowed. "Before I got this scratch, it was easy to believe in my own invincibility. I was arrogant enough to think of myself as perfect. That's a trap Kyp, Wurth, Octa, and others in his cabal are falling into.

They think that because they've not been hurt, they *can't* be hurt. That's not an illusion I harbor anymore."

"I don't think I have many illusions anymore, either." Jaina shifted her shoulders to relieve some of the stiffness in them. "We have been simming a lot to prepare us for the Vong assault. I must end up dead half the time I fly."

Ganner winced. "Not good."

"Well, not as bad as it might sound. Part of the time we sim flying skips, to help train the others. The Imps we are able to smoke, but the Chiss are just deadly."

"I've felt their presence, but haven't seen any of them."

"Neither have I, except on my aft scope, drilling my X-wing or skip." She glanced toward the front of the grand courtyard in which people had been gathered. Up there had been raised a dais, with Relal Tawron and his attendants greeting the various New Republic functionaries. "Looks like home team introductions have started. The Remnant's people will be next and then, maybe, the Chiss."

"It will be interesting to get a look at them." Ganner waved his hand in the direction of the dais. "After you."

"Thanks." Jaina almost hesitated, both because of Ganner's courtesy—which she had not expected—and because of her desire to see the Chiss herself. *It's their leader I want to see.*

She started to blush for a moment, but chased that sensation away with a burst of irritation. In all of the simulations she had flown well. Perhaps she hadn't always been the best pilot in the squadron, but she'd been close to it. Every time she'd simmed against the Chiss and been shot out, their leader had been the one to kill her. She never had the sense that he was picking on her specifically, but to double-check that she pulled the statistical data from the simulator battles.

Over and over again the Chiss leader had gone after the hottest of the enemy pilots, picking them off in descending order. None of them made it easy for him, and both Wedge and Tycho had managed to kill him once, but in every statistical category the simulators measured he was skewing the bell curve to the high side. And that would not have been so bad, she decided, if he and the Chiss didn't keep to themselves. She didn't mind being shot out, but she hated the idea of being dismissed for dying.

She and Ganner slipped toward the front of the crowd as Luke and Mara Skywalker were welcomed. Polite but muted applause arose from the assembled dignitaries, with most of it coming from the Ithorians. They clearly welcomed a Jedi presence on their world, though Jaina sensed that Borsk Fey'lya would be perfectly happy if those Jedi died in the defense of Ithor.

Next came the Imperial Remnant's contingent. Admiral Pellaeon came first and moved down the long line of dignitaries with an economy of motion that suggested he wanted nothing but to be back planning Ithor's defense. A wave of emotional warmth rolled off him as he greeted Admiral Kre'fey, Colonel Darklighter, Luke Skywalker, and Wedge Antilles. It lessened slightly as he shook hands with Jaina's mother, then took his place beside her as the other Imperials were introduced.

Several moffs had made the trip to Ithor, and all of them looked like tired functionaries save for Ephin Sarreti, the moff from Bastion. What impressed Jaina about him was the genuine sense of enthusiasm pouring off him as he greeted Borsk Fey'lya and the New Republic's other ministers. He exchanged comments with each of them, apparently impressing them with his knowledge of their lives or homes. Shock exploded from most of them, with tendrils of suspicion snaking out in its wake.

Ganner half smiled. "Well, now, there's a plaything to keep Chief of State Fey'lya occupied."

"Good, give him less time to advise the military about the defense of Ithor."

Any comment Ganner might have been about to offer died as a new and strong presence sent ripples out through the Force. Jaina knew from having been around people like her father and Wedge Antilles that these ripples didn't come from any conscious use of the Force; some people just so brimmed with life and confidence that they shone like a magnesium flare in darkest night. She rose up on tiptoes to see who it was, then felt a shock run through her.

At the head of a dozen blue-skinned Chiss came a human walking along with a crisp formality to his step. Taller than she was, but not as tall as Ganner, he had a wiry muscularity about him that his black uniform could not hide. His black hair had been cut short, which showed off a white lock that traced the line of a scar that started at his right eyebrow and ran back into his hair. His pale green eyes seemed tinged with a chill that matched his manner. Only the red stripes along his pants legs and cuffing his sleeves seemed at odds with his solemnity.

He mounted the dais at a step, leaving the Chiss in their white uniforms to file along the front of the platform and stand at attention. He bowed sharply to Relal Tawron and shook his hand. The Ithorian high priest turned to introduce him to Borsk Fey'lya, but the Chiss leader bypassed the chief of state and the rest of his cabinet. He marched along until he met Admiral Kre'fey, again executed a stiffly formal bow, and shook hands. He repeated this process with Colonel Darklighter and Luke Skywalker.

As he moved down the line, gasps and hubbub began to rise in the crowd. It increased as he bowed before Wedge, then smiled and allowed the older man to enfold him in a hug. Before Jaina could figure out what was happening there, the Chiss leader greeted Admiral Pellaeon. Ignoring the Remnant moffs, the young man then stepped off the front of the dais.

He's coming straight at me!

He drew himself up before her, straight of limb and muscularly taut, then snapped his head and upper body forward in a bow that was not as deep as that given the others, but was nonetheless respectful. "I am Jagged Fel." He straightened, and she started to blush as his green-eyed gaze raked her over. "A Jedi, too. Fascinating."

Jaina blinked. "Too?"

"In addition to being a superior pilot. You are a difficult kill."

She wasn't sure why, but she smiled at him. "You meant that as a compliment."

Jag Fel nodded. "Among the Chiss it is high praise indeed. I was only a bit better than you at your age."

"Which was what, about two years ago?" Ganner asked mockingly.

Neither Fel's expression nor his sense in the Force betrayed any embarrassment at Ganner's question. "Yes, just before I took command of my squadron."

Wedge Antilles stepped down from the dais and approached them. "Colonel Fel."

"Yes, Uncle?"

"You should return to the dais and greet those people you bypassed." Wedge nodded toward Borsk Fey'lya and his confederates. "They're fairly important."

Fel shook his head. "They're politicians."

Wedge lowered his voice. "The impression is that you skipped them because they are not human."

Fel turned to face the dais and raised his voice. "If they believe I did not greet them because they are not human, they are stupid. I did not greet them because they are politicians."

A Sullustan senator stepped forward. "A convenient label behind which you hide your xenophobia."

Surprise stiffened Fel's spine, and disbelief flooded his words. "You are accusing *me* of having an antialien bias?"

Pwoe, A Quarren senator, opened his hands. "It floods from you, Colonel Fel. Your uniform is cut on Imperial lines, harkening back to the uniform of your father's 181st Imperial fighter group, one of the most effective Imperial units at suppressing the Rebellion. Your formality. Greetings like that were last seen at the Imperial court. The disdain with which you bypassed us makes it more than obvious."

Fel shook his head. "Where I come from—"

Borsk Fey'lya cut him off. "Where you come from is an archaeo-Imperial community. Grand Admiral Thrawn gathered his most staunch and reactionary followers and set them up like a pocket of infection. You've festered out there, hating every moment we have been in control of what was once your empire. You've inherited the attitudes that oppressed us for ages, and now, here you are, ready to resume control, all under the guise of helping us."

"Stop, please." The Chiss leader held up a hand. "Don't make even more of a fool of yourself."

Borsk Fey'lya's violet eyes blazed. "How patronizing! You have to tell *me* what is best for *me*! You, born to privilege, have no idea what it is like to be discriminated against because of your species. You have no idea what it is like to sacrifice to win freedom." He flicked a hand at the dozen Chiss before the dais. "You even dare parade your nonhuman subordinates before us, reminding us of how Imperials should always be in the lead."

Jaina felt a cold calm come over Jag Fel as his hands slowly unknotted. "Where I come from, Chief Fey'lya, *I* am in the minority. *I* am the alien. If you remember *anything* from the history of your precious Rebellion, it is that Thrawn was uncompromising, and that is a trait of his people. I was raised among them, raised *with* them, judged by *their* standards. I met those standards. I exceeded those standards."

He took a step forward and pointed at the Chiss men and women who had accompanied him. "I *won* command of my squadron. These people competed to join that squadron. They wanted to fly with me, not because I am a *man* or because I am an Imperial, but because I am a superior pilot and leader.

"And as for fighting for my freedom, I've been doing that in the Unknown Regions for all my life. My mother gave birth to five children. My older brother died fighting, as did a younger sister. Why are we out there? Why are we fighting? A threat to the New Republic like the Yuuzhan Vong has long been anticipated. You remember the devastation of the Yevethan Great Purge? There were things in the Unknown Regions that would have made it look insignificant, save we were there and stopped them."

Fel pressed his hands together. "You accuse me of xenophobia, but you ignored the fact that I greeted my host, an Ithorian, and immediately greeted Admiral Kre'fey, a Bothan. You saw what you wanted to see. This is what you accuse me of, accuse Imperials of: that we saw only bestiality where there was sapience and nobility. I have come here to help defend you against the Yuuzhan Vong, and yet what you choose to see is some specter of the past."

He looked around the room. "*That* is why I bypassed you. I came to fight a war, not to play political games. My mission is to help you maintain your freedom, not to help you gather more power to yourself, or to take it from you."

Leia Organa Solo stepped forward, holding a hand out to forestall any rebuttal by the New Republic's Bothan leader. "We want that help. From you, from the Remnant, from all the peoples of the New Republic. Working together is the only way we will defeat the Yuuzhan Vong and save Ithor."

People began applauding her mother's words, and Jaina joined them. With public agreement, the politicians retreated a bit, and it would have been easy to imagine the situation had been solved. Still, Jaina found herself haunted by what Fey'lya and the others had said. The vehemence in their words had previously been directed at her mother, with similar accusations of her desire to take power away from nonhumans. *And whispers about the Jedi, blaming them for the loss of Garqi and Dubrillion, somehow suggesting the Jedi brought the Yuuzhan Vong down on the New Republic. They make me wonder if we're not being positioned to take the blame if Ithor falls.*

Jag Fel turned and looked at her, and Jaina wondered if, somehow, he were reading her mind. She met his stare unflinchingly. "We *will* save Ithor."

He nodded. "We *will* win the battle for Ithor. Its salvation, well . . ." He spared a glance for the knot of New Republic politicians. "Its salvation is in other hands and, I am afraid, is beyond our ability to control."

CHAPTER
TWENTY-FIVE

Jacen Solo clasped his hands at the small of his back. He'd answered his uncle's call for the Jedi to assemble in a small grove on an upper level of the *Tafanda Bay*. Though he could still feel Jaina's presence in the floating Ithorian city, he was a bit surprised that she had not come to the meeting. Given the impression he was getting from her, he knew she was simming again, and he momentarily resented how the squadron was keeping her separate from him and the Jedi.

Standing there, between Ganner and Anakin, Jacen caught himself thinking negatively about his sister and probed his own feelings. He felt a tinge of jealousy because she clearly loved flying with Rogue Squadron, and Jacen was very proud of how well she had succeeded in her role as a fighter pilot. He knew she'd not abandoned her Jedi heritage or training, but was just finding another way to employ it.

Following in Corran Horn's tradition of serving the squadron. Jacen glanced down the line and saw Corran. Jacen had accepted the task of trying to be the sort of Jedi that Corran and Luke had become. He acknowledged doing good and necessary work on Belkadan and Garqi, but still he had a sense of dissatisfaction haunting him.

Memories of the slaughter on Dantooine reminded him what the worst of that Jedi tradition could be. He knew that none of them had been given any choice by the Yuuzhan Vong: they had to kill soldiers, or many more people would have been killed. They had been acting as defenders there, so there had been no hint of the dark side attached to their actions. *And yet many creatures died.*

Jacen found himself once again returned to a philosophical question that he could not see a way around. If the Force was something that bound all life together, could killing be in any way justified? *The Jedi Code says there is no death, only the Force, but the death of billions on Alderaan and Carida was enough to send shock waves through the Force.* If that was true, then didn't lesser deaths also have an effect?

As certain as he was that he didn't have an answer for that basic paradox, he knew there was one out there. Anakin had suggested that in his search he was circling the answer, and he couldn't fault his little brother's insight. *But in circling something, I know at the very least there is something to circle. Now I just have to find what it is I'm circling.*

Two things served to rock Jacen out of his internal journey. The first was the arrival of Relal Tawron, the Ithorian high priest, along with Luke. Until the Ithorian showed up, Jacen had no idea why they had been called together, and the solemnity with which the high priest and the Jedi Master moved suggested that the reason for the meeting was most serious.

The entry of Daeshara'cor into the room, slipping through the hatchway after Luke and taking up a position beside Octa Ramis, likewise underscored the seriousness of the situation. Ever since Luke had arrived at Ithor, the Twi'lek Jedi had been kept secluded, at her request. He knew Luke had spent time with her, but he had offered no explanation for her search for superweapons.

Luke Skywalker stood before the two dozen Jedi and inclined his head toward them. "Brothers and sisters, Relal Tawron is here to prepare us for what will be our part in the coming struggle. Listen well to what he has to say. Though we are here to save Ithor, we could, through negligence, destroy it. That cannot happen."

The Ithorian nodded acknowledgment of Luke's words, then looked over the Jedi in silence for a moment. He interlaced his fingers and let his hands rest against his belly, then slowly began speaking in a voice that was as resonant as it was low.

"We welcome you, the Jedi, here, and thank you for what you will do for us. I speak not just as myself, but for the Mother Jungle above which we drift and for the Ithorian people. We are one and wish for your communion with us."

He again studied the assembled Jedi. When his gaze fell upon Jacen, the young Jedi found a blush rising to his face. He knew of no reason he should feel ashamed, then realized that what embarrassed him was the sense of complete calm coming from the Ithorian. Jacen's own wondering about his future ran smack up against a confidence in Tawron's life and life choices. *He feels about himself as I wish to feel about myself.*

Relal Tawron opened his hands and spread his arms. "You all have heard that no one is allowed to set foot on Ithor. This statement is materially correct in its translation into Basic, but not absolutely true. We have pilgrims who do go down into our world, tending the forests, visiting sacred places from before technology allowed us to build floating cities, and to survey damage done after storms or fires. Before they make such journeys, they prepare themselves spiritually.

"You will journey to the surface if needs be. We wish, then, to prepare you, so you will accept the world as your mother, and the world will accept you as its children." The high priest's eyes blinked slowly. "In order to do this you need to become other than yourself. No one is allowed on the surface; those who are allowed are not themselves."

Jacen frowned for a second, but caught a glimpse of Corran nodding to himself, so he assumed the mystery was not impenetrable. He recalled some of his early training in which he was required to open himself to the Force, to let go of himself so the Force could fill him. *To become one with the Force, I had to become more than I had been before, but that meant casting off the image of who I thought I was.*

"Each pilgrim, in making the journey to the Mother Jungle, wishes to become closer to the jungle. To facilitate change and growth, the pilgrim looks at pruning aspects of herself that keep her from being one with the world below. So it shall be with you. You must think upon that part of yourself that closes you in, and that is the part of yourself you need to modify. You will share those things."

"Out loud?" Wurth Skidder, over next to Kyp Durron, shook his head. "This is a waste of time. We should be getting ready to fight the Vong."

Luke frowned. "This is more important than that, Wurth."

The Ithorian high priest pressed his hands together. "If you feel we are wasting your time, you may be excused."

"What?!" Wurth folded his arms across his chest. "We're here to save your world."

"You need to save yourself first, Jedi." The Ithorian spoke quietly from both sides of his mouth. "Until you wish to be saved, the Mother Jungle can do you no good."

"I don't under—"

Kyp laid his left hand against Wurth's folded arms. "The confusion is ours. We understand, Relal Tawron, and will respect your customs."

The Ithorian nodded assent, then spread his hands again. "The public declaration is meant to enlist everyone in aiding the pilgrim in making the transition toward unity with the jungle. In sharing the burden we, as diverse a community as the plants and creatures that make up the Mother Jungle, function together in a complex ecosystem. It is only through functioning together that we can succeed."

Luke Skywalker turned toward the Ithorian. "If it would be permitted, I would like to go first."

"We would be honored, Master Skywalker."

"I renounce responsibility." Luke's eyes narrowed, and Jacen could feel shock rise from some of the other Jedi. "For a long time, I've felt weighed down by being sole heir to a Jedi tradition. I've cheated you. You're all my coheirs. I know you'll accept shares of the responsibility I've carried around with me. I have every confidence in you."

A chill ran down Jacen's spine. He'd never had any doubt that his uncle trusted him, but their relationship was more than student and Master. A lot of the trust bled over from the family ties. For the first time he caught a sense of what it might have been like to be Ganner or Corran or Daeshara'cor. Luke's renunciation was a gift to them all, one that bound them together and tied them to the jungle.

The other Jedi began to make their own declarations. They came in no particular order, but were voiced as each person felt his time had come. Jacen listened to them, less trying to understand their words than marveling in the sense of peace their declarations seemed to kindle in them. He desperately sought that aspect of himself that locked him away from such peace, so he could feel inside how they felt.

Anakin surprised him by stepping forward fairly quickly. His little brother's shoulders straightened, and his voice did not waver. "I give up self-assuredness. I want so much to be right, to do the right thing, that I don't look to see if another answer would be a better answer. Judging yourself right is a destination. I'm just on a journey."

At the far end of the line, Daeshara'cor looped one lekku back over her shoulder. "I renounce hatred. The description of the Yuuzhan Vong taking slaves made me hate them as I hated those who had enslaved my mother. That hatred made me do stupid things. No more. I will stop the Yuuzhan Vong because they must be stopped, but I will not hate them."

"I'll ditch fear." Corran ran his left hand over his mouth. "All my life I've been afraid of failing—my father, my wife, my children, my friends, all of you—but no more. Failure is not part of the menu here, so fearing it, fearing anything else, is pointless."

Ganner nodded once, sharply. "I can do without pride. It's blinded me to many things, not the least of which is how deadly the Yuuzhan Vong can be. The jungle doesn't need a blind guardian."

Octa Ramis slipped past Daeshara'cor. "Mourning a friend the Vong took from me has blinded me. I'll lay him to rest."

Fear. Pride. Hatred. Even his brother's retreat from assuming he knew more than he did. All of these things struck Jacen as laudable. *Yet none of them is right for me, at least, not right now.* He sighed, feeling a thousand questions bubbling up through his mind. *Which one is right for me?*

His jaw dropped open as his flesh puckered. As his surprise at the answer shook him, he almost laughed, though to do so would destroy the dignity of the ceremony. The simplicity of the answer astounded him, and yet the peace that settled over him as a result of discovering it almost made him giddy.

He stepped past Ganner and Anakin. "I renounce the need to know, now, what I will become later. In looking to my future, I have ignored the present and my role in it. The present is too critical for me to do that anymore."

Even before his uncle nodded to him, a warmth had begun to spread from his heart throughout his body. He'd not abandoned his search for his place as a Jedi, just drained the urgency from it. That energy he redirected into his efforts to defend Ithor. The sense of well-being he had as a result left him no question that he'd made the right choice. *I just have to hope I live long enough to continue on my path, be it a circle, or toward a goal.*

The Jedi all went through their declarations. Wurth renounced weakness with a vehemence meant to hide his insecurities. Kyp rejected pride, using words meant to suggest that the glory of one was the glory of all. He clearly was trying to bring all the Jedi together, as Luke had done, but from Jacen's new perspective the effort just seemed transparent.

Somehow Jacen knew that the high priest must have seen past the blinds Wurth, Kyp, and a few others raised, but the Ithorian gave no sign of it. "You Jedi, through your link with the Force, understand how life is woven together with life. You know how one thing touches another. Here, today, you are woven together with the Mother Jungle and the Ithorian people. Our fates are ever intertwined. We welcome your strength and sincerity. We offer you our support and love. As fibers woven are stronger than those alone, so shall we all be strong together, facing this threat."

The Ithorian lowered his hands, then shook hands with the Jedi Master. Luke remained at the front of the room as Relal Tawron made for the egress hatchway. The Ithorian paused only once, to rest his hands on Daeshara'cor's shoulders and whisper in her ear, then he exited the room.

Luke waited for the hatch to close behind the high priest, then stood there, shrouded in his cloak. "So you all know, our exact role in the fight has not been decided. From the computer system here you can pull an abstract of the various plans that have been floated for us. You can pretty much ignore any that were not initiated by Admirals Pellaeon or Kre'fey or by me. I will have assignments for us all."

Kyp frowned. "You cede us responsibility, but we have no part in deciding how we will be used?"

The Jedi Master smiled easily. "To you, I ceded responsibility for your own actions. To the military, I have ceded responsibility for what we will do. *How* we accomplish their goals, this we will all have input on. They will decide what must be done, and we will decide how Jedi can best accomplish those tasks."

He looked around the room. "That's all for now. May the Force be with you."

The Jedi broke down into little groups and slowly started to filter from the enclosed grove. Luke walked directly over toward Jacen and Anakin and opened his arms. He rested a hand on each of his nephews' shoulders. "I'm very proud of the two of you. The things you said, well, as the high priest has said, the jungle is no place for children. What you said shows you're not children."

Jacen rested his right hand on his uncle's mechanical one. "Thank you, Master."

"Me, too, Uncle Luke, thanks." Anakin smiled broadly at first, then composed his face much more solemnly. "I'm ready to do whatever you need me to do, no matter what."

Ganner chuckled quietly. "Given your experience fighting the Yuuzhan Vong, perhaps you should be given command of our contingent."

Luke arched an eyebrow. "I'm not sure that much responsibility should be placed on his shoulders just yet, but someday."

Daeshara'cor cut through the crowd of other Jedi and

paused a couple of meters shy of the group. "Master, if I could have a moment."

Luke turned toward her. "Please, join us."

"Yes, Master." The woman approached, then looked down at her hands. Her lekku twitched ever so slightly, betraying her nervousness. "I just wanted to thank you for trusting me, inviting me here, allowing me to participate in this ceremony. I have been doing a lot of thinking—self-examination. Until asked to articulate things here, I had not understood exactly why I had done what I did, or what that was doing to me. I had allowed my hatred to make as much of a slave of me as my mother had been. I don't regret opposing slavery, or opposing the Yuuzhan Vong, but I can't do it for the wrong reasons. Winning or preserving freedom is good; seeking retribution is not."

The Jedi Master nodded. "That's a lesson we all need to keep in mind. I'm glad to have you back with us, Daeshara'cor. The struggle we'll face will demand the best, and here, I think, we have the best."

Corran, who had joined the group, sighed heavily. "We'll just have to hope that our best is enough. I can't shake the feeling the battle for Ithor will be the last for some of us. If we can't stop them here, well, perhaps becoming one with the Mother Jungle won't be the worst thing that could happen."

CHAPTER
TWENTY-SIX

Freed from the Embrace of Pain, Shedao Shai reached out and grasped one of the device's slender limbs in his left hand. He hung on as tightly as he was able, then lunged his body quickly to the right. His left shoulder popped loudly, the sound echoing within his cabin aboard the *Legacy of Torment.* The arm slipping back into the socket sparked an argent explosion of pain and sent it rippling through him, weakening his knees. He might have dropped to the floor save that surrendering to the pain would have tarnished it.

And it would not do to let my subordinate see any weakness. He turned his head slowly to where Deign Lian stood, eyes averted to decking. "You have a reason to disturb me?"

"Commander, yes, many reasons."

"Then give me the best one."

The implied threat in his command shook Lian, and Shedao Shai took secret pleasure in that. His subordinate did not look up and could not quite rid his voice of a minor tremor. "My leader, we believe we have determined what it was that the *jeedai* sought to hide on Garqi."

"Really?" The Yuuzhan Vong leader kept his voice light, his tone questioning. "After so long? Why is it you think you have succeeded now?"

"As you will recall, Commander, we had great difficulty with the probes we were using in that area. We had a high failure rate on them. It was assumed that one generation of them had an undetected defect in the breeding. We employed another, and had similar results."

Shedao Shai nodded. "You have bored me with these excuses before."

Lian's shoulders shifted slightly. "The creatures we were using are a strain related to vonduun crabs. We employed another device while doing forensic examinations of the searchers that had failed. The searchers had inflammations of their respiratory systems, and with the new scanning creatures, we discovered pollen grains. The searchers died of an allergic reaction to the pollen. Vonduun crab armor had a more immediate and violent reaction to the pollen."

The Yuuzhan Vong leader held up his left hand, ignoring the grinding in his shoulder. The idea that their armor fell prey to a naturally occurring element in the environment stunned him. That revelation had serious implications. The first, on a purely military level, was that now the enemy had a weapon they could employ that would seriously handicap the Yuuzhan Vong warriors. He had no doubt the enemy would use it—he would not have hesitated were he as beset as they were. Suddenly every combat situation was a potential disaster.

The second and more fundamental issue was that of biological and botanical opposition to their invasion. Ever since the invasion had been ordered, one of the motivating forces had been that the enemy were machinists. They created machines that mocked the living with their pseudolife. Their reliance on machines marked them as defective, as weak, as contemptible, and certainly as deserving of death. They were infidels, blasphemers, and heretics with no help of justification of their lives.

But now, a living thing opposes us. He shook his head ever so slightly, realizing how dangerous was the battlefield that this development could lead him to. Just as a political faction had struck prematurely to gain control of the invasion, now the priesthood could use this new opposition to strengthen their influence. While Shedao Shai had every faith in the validity of the crusade in spite of this discovery, war was a task best left to those trained to it.

His eyes narrowed. "Who knows the information you have revealed to me?"

"Just myself and those who investigated it." The hint of a smile snaked its way across Lian's lips. "They have been isolated. No word of this will escape."

"Very good." He gave his subordinate a sincere nod. "You have isolated the plant that produced this pollen?"

"The bafforr trees, which are native to the planet they call Ithor. The world is within our current invasion corridor, accessible from Garqi." Lian lifted his chin. "I have taken the liberty of preparing a plan for the planet's annihilation."

"A repeat of Sernpidal's destruction?"

Lian shook his head. "No, Commander. My researchers have assured me that they can prepare an assault weapon with which we can seed the planet. Ithor is rich in organic matter. Destroying it will be simple."

Shedao Shai raked a talon over his own chin and down his throat, feeling it click along the folds in his leathery flesh. "Stand off the world, deliver the agent?"

"Most efficient, my leader."

"Indeed, but wasteful." Shedao Shai shook his head. "That is not how we will do it."

"Why not?" Impatience flashed over Lian's face. He flicked a hand toward the planet below. "Even the conquest of a planet like Garqi was not without casualties—and that is excepting the deaths in the garden. The infidels must be fortifying Ithor. They cannot allow us to take it from them. Fighting there will be fierce."

The Yuuzhan Vong commander lunged at his aide and flicked a backhanded slap at the younger warrior's throat. Lian's hands came up, but not fast enough. The blow landed, not hard, but hard enough to drive him back a step and wring a choked gasp from him.

Lian immediately dropped to his knees and touched his forehead to the deck. "Forgive this one, leader, for angering you." His harsh croak carried little contrition to Shedao Shai's ears, but the fear shooting through it brought him satisfaction.

"Do you think we will be defeated in taking Ithor?"

"No, Master."

"Do you think our warriors will shrink from the possibility of dying there?"

"No, Master."

"Good." Shedao Shai spun away from Lian and let his heel spurs click on the decking as he began to pace. "What you suggest would be most efficient, but would hurt us more than help. We need to show them that we will crush them no matter their preparations. So far we have not launched a solid military operation against any of their worlds. Yes, we took Garqi, but the opposition was minimal. The subsequent infiltration and exfiltration of agents taints that victory. As you point out, they *must* fortify Ithor. When we take it we will send a message out to the rest of the New Republic with the survivors. That message is that we are implacable and invincible. That is the message our enemies need to hear."

"With all due respect, Commander, this one thinks you have spent too much time with Elegos."

"Do you?" Shedao Shai turned slowly, allowing a heel spur to tease a squeal from the decking as he did so. "From him I learned much about our enemies. Now he will bear to them a message from me. His preparation for this role is complete, and now we know where we may deliver the message: Ithor. He will return to his people there and will not fail me."

"That is all well and good, Commander, but your concern with how they think—it . . ."

"It what?" Shedao Shai walked over to Lian and pressed his right foot down on his subordinate's head. "It has me flirting with heresy? Have I done anything that indicates I have abandoned our ways? Have I used a machine? Have I said I doubt what we are doing? Have I questioned the dictates of the gods or priests?"

"No, my leader, but—"

"But nothing, Lian. There is much Elegos could teach you, Lian, even in the few days he will remain with us." The

Yuuzhan Vong commander increased the pressure, mashing Lian's forehead against the deck. "You offer me a plan that will be effective from a tactical standpoint, but ineffective on a strategic level. Moreover, your plan could be considered blasphemy, since it would destroy a storehouse of life. Ithor could be a gift to us from the gods, requiring us to wrest it from the enemy, and you would destroy it rather than do what the gods wish and liberate it."

Shedao Shai pulled his toes back, cocking his ankle, allowing his heel spur to dig into Lian's scalp. Flexing his knee and lifting his thigh, he brought his subordinate's head up. Once he could see Lian's eyes, he pulled the spur free and stood there. He watched in silence until a thin ribbon of blood started dripping slowly on the deck.

"You are fortunate, Lian, for I will not let you disgrace yourself. You shall accomplish that which is the will of the gods." Shedao Shai folded his arms across his chest. "You will plan for me an assault on Ithor to commence a month from now. You will likewise plan a feint in force at the world Agamar. It will fall, or we will take it after we take Ithor. You will plan these assaults, using all the assets assigned to me."

"Commander, this is an honor, but should you not plan these assaults?"

"I will review and modify your plans. You are competent enough to lay the basic groundwork. While you do that, I will continue a job that only I can do." He nodded slowly. "Elegos will provide our first avenue of attack on the New Republic. Within a week he will be doing our work for us. Then I will have time to oversee what you have drawn up, correct it, and make it work."

"Yes, my leader." Lian nodded slowly. "It shall be done as you order it."

"One last thing."

"Commander?"

"No word of this pollen goes out to anyone. If your people can find a way to modify armor to be immune, good. If not, we will fight without living armor." Shedao Shai smiled. "We are the Yuuzhan Vong. Our cause is right and just. The gods armor us when we go into combat, and entering it in a dead shell is just a sign of our faith in them."

Deign Lian retreated to his cabin aboard the *Legacy of Torment* and closed and sealed the hatch behind him. The small, ovoid enclosure had almost enough room for him to walk through it without scraping his head against the ceiling. He kept his head ducked, not wanting to smear blood on the ceiling, then dropped to his knees at the small storage space beneath his bed and pulled forth a sclipune.

He gently set the creature on top of the bed so the line where the two halves of its shell met faced him. Reaching around to the sensory tissue at the hinge, Lian ran his fingers over it in the combination of movements to which the creature had been trained to respond. The upper half of the domed shell rose, revealing a villip nestled there like a pearl. The Yuuzhan Vong stroked the villip once to waken it, and felt his pulmonary arch quicken its pumping as the communications creature morphed with the features of his true master.

Lian ducked his head immediately. "Master, forgive this intrusion, but this one must report."

"Proceed." The villip voiced the command flatly, but it still contained a hint of his master's tone.

"It was as you suggested it would be. I offered Shedao Shai the plan to destroy Ithor, but he rejected it. Instead he would have us assault it in a most conventional manner. And, perhaps, in not so conventional a manner."

The brows on the face assumed by the villip arrowed downward. "Explain."

Lian kept his face expressionless and flattened his voice. He knew that in crafting his answer he was playing a dangerous game, but Shedao Shai demanded he play it. He was likewise certain that his master knew he was playing, but might not know the depths of his skill at political manipulation.

"He remains obsessed with the infidel. He has not enough time to spend on planning the Ithorian assault, he is so preoccupied. He is convinced eliminating the threat that is Ithor would be detrimental to the future of our assault because of how it would make the enemy feel about us."

"What matters how the infidels feel?" The villip did manage to communicate his master's scorn. "You will plan this assault for him, and plan it well. You will calculate the appropriate amount of force you will need to take the world, then advocate bringing a handful more ships. Shedao Shai will slash your estimates. He will be made to look a fool."

"As you will it, Master, it shall be done." Deign Lian nodded enthusiastically, then made a quick play. "Before long all praise shall gather to your name, Master. Soon, on the lips of many will be—"

"Quiet, fool!"

Lian dipped his head sharply. "Beg pardon, Master."

"Do not make me wonder about you. You are in position to see that the right things happen. I would hate to have to find another asset to replace you, but it is not impossible."

"Yes, Master." Lian let a dollop of fear swirl through his words. As long as the Warmaster thought as little of him as Shedao Shai did, Deign Lian could successfully play both of them against each other. Shedao Shai would have to lose this round so Lian could be appointed as his replacement, but then his political patron would have to fall. *Only then can I reach the ascendancy for which I was bred.*

"Continue your work. Report as needed and keep me apprised as the battle for Ithor unfolds. You are doing good work, the gods' work." The face on the villip assumed a serene expression. "When our conquest is complete, then you shall be rewarded greatly."

"Thank you, Master. This one is ever your loyal and obedient servant."

Lian reached up and closed the sclipune. He would have laughed, but a droplet of blood splashed on the creature's shell. Lian reached up and found his hair wet with blood, with the circular wound puckered and swollen. He probed it with his fingers for a second, then shrugged, pleased that it would result in yet one more scar.

He hid the sclipune away, then licked at the blood on his

fingers. All the indignities he suffered from Shedao Shai would be repaid in one grand surprise for his superior. *The only pity is, he will not see my hand in his downfall.* For an instant he regretted that, then shunted aside his regret.

That satisfaction I can forgo. It is a sacrifice I offer to the gods. He smiled broadly, confident they would find the sacrifice pleasing. By Shedao Shai's command, it would be a month until the battle for Ithor. A month more to endure humiliation.

A month before I assume the office that long ago should have been mine.

CHAPTER
TWENTY-SEVEN

Luke found Mara standing at the large viewport in the suite they'd been given on the *Tafanda Bay*. He caught a bit of surprise from her as he entered the cabin, but the spike leveled quickly as she recognized him. She'd been hugging her arms around herself as she looked out at the Mother Jungle below, and let them slacken slightly, but Luke laced his fingers through hers and hugged her from behind.

He kissed her neck. "How are you doing?"

Mara nodded confidently. "Good, very good. High Priest Tawron stopped by and graciously performed with me the ritual he did for the Jedi and others. I felt ashamed that I'd not been there with the Jedi, but—"

"It's okay, Mara. We would have loved to have you there, but we want you rested to be at your best."

She leaned her head to the right, gently touching her temple to his. "I know, and that's very sweet of you, Luke, but there are times I feel like a malingerer. In some ways Ithor seems so peaceful that maintaining an edge is tough for me. It's not so much that I like strife, it's just that I've been trained to deal with it. I'm at my best doing that."

"And you're one of the best doing that."

" 'One of'?"

Luke laughed lightly. "Let me amend that. The *best* at dealing with strife."

She turned her head and kissed him on the cheek. "Thank you. Mind if I just relax here in your arms for a while?"

"Sure, we have time."

"A day or two?"

"Well, sure, but standing here for a couple of days will be a bit much, don't you think?" Luke smiled. "We could get faint from hunger."

"Oh, good point, husband mine. Perhaps we should go lie down."

"Definitely like the way you think, Mara." The Jedi Master hugged her just a bit tighter. Outside the viewport a flock of triple-clawed manollium birds took off in a brilliant gush of color, to whirl and dive in a rainbow arc back down to another roost. "Wow. With all the planning and everything that has been going on, I have had little time to stop and see what it is we're fighting to protect."

"I've been watching for hours and there is always more to see." Mara turned within his arms and brought her arms up and around his neck. "Relal Tawron was very good for me. He told me that while the Mother Jungle is a peaceful place, it is not without violence and hostility. He noted that predators and prey are all part of the natural cycle. A predator kills prey and eats it, then bugs and microbes devour what remains, nourishing plants that provide food and shelter for the prey."

"And he likened you to a predator?"

Mara shrugged. "Actually he likened me more to a fire-storm burning a huge swath through the jungle during the dry years."

"Hmmmm, didn't think they got that much news out here."

"Oh, Jedi sarcasm. I'm wounded."

They both laughed aloud, and Luke kissed her again, on the lips and tip of her nose. "He gave you a bit of perspective with which to view your role in the upcoming battle?"

"Yes, one that allowed me to reconcile my nature with that of the Mother Jungle. And that's really the key: the Mother Jungle embraces it all because it is part of the natural cycle. What is unnatural about the Yuuzhan Vong invasion, about war, is that it's not for natural reasons. Politics, avarice, greed, jealousy—all of these things cause wars but are pretty much unrecognizable in nature. They occur when creatures try to divorce themselves from nature."

Luke smiled at her and hugged her very close. "That's one of the things I like the most about you, Mara. You're always on the move, always getting better and better. You continue to grow when so many would be content with sitting back."

"I can't sit back, Luke, especially now." Mara slipped from his arms. "There are so many things I want, and with the invasion, with my illness, I don't know if I will ever be able to—" Her lips flattened into a thin line, then she took his left hand in hers. "Maybe it's just all the talk of nature, but right now I really wish that we had . . . that I was carrying our child. I mean, I look at you and love you so much, Luke, and to even think that we might not be able to—"

She looked away from him, her other hand curling into a fist.

"Mara . . ." He kept his voice soft as he closed with her, letting their joined hands rest on her belly. He brushed a tear away with his thumb, then kissed her moistened cheek. "Love, we will get through this. I would love for nothing more than creating new life with you. One child, two, four . . ."

She pressed a fingertip to his lips. "I know you have a lot to do right now, but I need you to be with me, just for a bit, please?"

"As long as you need, Mara, as long as you desire."

A smile traced her lips. "We both know there isn't that much time in the universe. I'll take what I can get now. We complete each other, we complete our connection with nature. And from there, we trust in the Force to guide us into doing what has to be done."

Corran handed the last duraplast container up to the bald, heavy-set man helping to load the *Pulsar Skate*. "Looks like that's it."

The man nodded. "I'll secure the hatch and see to the passengers, then. Thanks for the help."

"No problem." Corran turned from him as the hatch irised closed, and walked over to where Mirax was checking off the last of her passengers against the list in her datapad. All around them the docking bay on the Ithorian city-ships bustled with activity. Countless ships, large and small, were loading refugees and equipment on as fast as they could. Once they cleared the bay, other ships would come and take their place. Throughout the city, and on all the other city-ships, similar evacuations were taking place.

The Jedi sidled up to his wife. "Got them all?"

"Uh-huh." She snapped the small device closed and slipped it into a thigh pocket on her cargo pants. "We're fueled and about ready to go."

Corran reached out and stroked her cheek with the back of his left hand. "You know I don't want you to go."

"I know, but you don't want me here, either." Mirax smiled and jerked a thumb at the freighter behind her. "I'm rolling this team out to Borleias. Climate there isn't quite optimal for Ithorian plants, but they think they can make changes."

"I'm sure it will work." He slipped an arm around her shoulders. "You going to be okay with this Chalco guy crewing the ship?"

"From what I've seen so far, I think he's worth trusting. We deliver the cargo, then I drop him back on Coruscant." She leaned her head against Corran's shoulder. "Then I'm coming back here."

"Mirax, don't."

She turned to face him, pressing her hands against his chest. "Hey, listen up, Corran. The last time you went off and fought the Yuuzhan Vong you barely escaped, and the time before that you were more dead than alive when they brought you back."

"Mirax, having you here isn't going to keep me safe."

"Maybe not, but I can certainly kill whoever it is who gets you."

Corran rested his hands on her shoulders. "First, I'm not planning on dying."

"Very few people do."

"True." He sighed. "Mirax, I don't want you here. The fighting is going to be nasty. What you're doing now, taking

Ithorians and their botanical bounty away, that's more important than anything I'm likely to accomplish here. You're going to be doing what you do well, and so will I."

Her brown eyes narrowed. "The chances of my being killed are rather slender."

"I know, and I like that." He gave Anakin Solo a quick nod as the youth went running up the *Skate*'s landing ramp, then touched his forehead to his wife's. "My grandfather died when my father was young, and I know you lost your mom young. I don't want that to happen to our kids, but the only thing worse would be if both of us die here."

"If we both die, Booster will take care of the kids."

"Now *there's* a comfort."

She lifted his chin with her hand. "Think of it as motivation to stay alive, Corran."

He ducked his head to kiss her hand, then looked up, his smile carrying all the way from his mouth to his green eyes. "I have motivation, love, and look at the record. The first time, they nearly killed me. The second time, I escaped in pretty good shape. Momentum and trajectory I've got—it's the Vong who should be worried."

Mirax smiled grudgingly. "You know, that cockiness of yours really drives my father nuts."

"But you love it."

"Well, when you were a pilot it was attractive." She shrugged. "In a Jedi Knight, well . . ."

"Yes?"

"Well, the Yuuzhan Vong should take it as a warning." Mirax kissed him once, softly, then her kiss hardened. Corran let his hands slip down and around her back to draw her into a tight embrace. In her kiss, in her body, he felt an urgency and intensity, fueled more by love than any sense of loss or fear. "I will miss you, Corran, so much."

"Me, too, Mirax." He clung to her fiercely. Through his mind flashed scenes from their life together. The first time he ever saw her, her face as she slept peacefully in the wake of passion, the tears and smiles after the birth of their children, and even that spark of pain hidden behind an impassive mask as she watched a child try and fail, knowing that she could not make the failure right. "I love you, Mirax. Always will."

"I know." She kissed him again, then smiled. "You know, I'd love to take the next twelve hours to say good-bye to you properly, but they need the ship berth."

"Bureaucrats have no romance in their hearts." Corran kissed her again. "Whatever you were thinking for us to say good-bye, figure that's how we'll say hello again, and take a week doing it."

"You have yourself a date." She kissed her fingers, then pressed them to his lips. "Be careful, Corran. I know you'll be brave."

Anakin found Chalco tightening the restraining straps on a couple of the Ithorians in the *Skate*'s lounge. "You weren't going to tell me you were leaving?"

Chalco patted the young Ithorian on the shoulder, then turned to face Anakin. "You've been busy doing Jedi stuff. I didn't want to interrupt. Mirax needed some help, and one thing flowed into another, you know?"

"That explains why you're here, but not why you didn't say good-bye."

The man frowned. "Always said you were a smart kid. It's like this, Anakin." Chalco leaned down, resting his hands on the youth's shoulders. "Going after Daeshara'cor, I kinda wanted to be a hero, and you saw how that turned out. I went to rescue you, and you turned around and rescued me. I guess I figured, well, I'm not really hero material."

Anakin frowned at him. "Hey, you *did* rescue me. As you said, if you'd not brought the blaster, I'd not have taken Daeshara'cor down. And, you know, what you're doing here, helping these people escape, is heroic."

"Sure, maybe, but not the sort of heroism you're going to need." Chalco patted him on the cheek. "Don't get me wrong. I'm happy I met you. Proud, in fact, to know a Jedi like you. I mean, we're friends, right? I'd like having a Jedi friend—and more important, I'd like having you as a friend."

"We're friends, Chalco."

"Good. Then, look, my friend, the reason I'm getting my sorry carcass off this world is so there will be one less person that needs rescuing, okay?" He smiled and straightened up. "And I was planning to comm you, you know. Leave you a message or something, so we wouldn't get weepy and all."

"I believe you." Anakin smiled, then looked to his right as a comlink on a shelf started to beep. "Should I?"

Chalco nodded. "It's Corran's."

Anakin picked it up and answered. "Anakin Solo here."

"Anakin, where's Corran?" Wedge Antilles's voice was easy to recognize even over the comlink. "I thought I was connecting with his comlink."

"You did. He's outside with his wife. I can get him."

"It's okay. Tell him to wait there. I'm on my way to that docking bay anyway."

Anakin frowned. "What's the matter?"

"A Yuuzhan Vong cruiser showed up at the edge of the system and dumped out a shuttle. Its ID transponder registers as the one Elegos A'Kla took out to meet with the Yuuzhan Vong." Wedge's voice became lower. "All we're getting is a recorded message, playing over and over. It's from Elegos, to Corran, conveying to him the compliments of a Yuuzhan Vong commander."

CHAPTER
TWENTY-EIGHT

Jaina Solo watched the auxiliary landing bay on the *Chimaera* from the pilot's ready room. From her vantage point she was able to look down on the bay and the *Lambda*-class shuttle situated between two X-wings. She and Anni Capstan had been scrambled to recon the shuttle, then a Remnant shuttle had tractored it and dragged it to where the *Chimaera*'s bay tractor beams could haul it in.

On her first recon pass she had recognized the shuttle for what it was, but only just barely. The landing gear were extended and the wings locked up. Because the shuttles were never seen in flight that way, it seemed out of place drifting there.

That impression was aided by the fact that all sorts of growths covered the shuttle. Jaina made runs close enough for visual contact—to see if there was a pilot at the controls—and the growths reminded her of algae and barnacles, just crusty things spreading over the shuttle's hull. A fairly thick concentration of them covered the landing ramp's outline, leading Jaina to wonder how the recovery team would open it.

Once the shuttle was pulled into the landing bay, the X-wings were ordered to land, then technicians in biohazard suits had hustled Anni and her from the bay. The both of them got scanned for alien life-forms, were pronounced clean, and allowed to wait in the ready room or head into one of the galleys to get something to eat. Anni ran off, and Jaina was

215

fairly certain she'd have found a sabacc game somewhere and in no time at all would be stripping crew members of whatever the Remnant used for credits.

Jaina decided to stay and watch. She remembered Elegos well from traveling with him, her mother, and Danni before she joined the squadron. The quiet calm he possessed amazed her. It didn't seem so much that he ignored the outside world, or was able to override emotions through logic, but that he looked at any problem, saw the core of it, and dealt with that instead of getting detoured by distractions.

In flying recon on the shuttle she'd heard the continuous looping of Elegos's voice. It sounded normal and even happy, but something about it disturbed her. She was hoping she'd see Elegos at the controls, or be able to sense him on board the shuttle, but nothing. Of course, before the appearance of the shuttle, she'd not known about Elegos's mission to the Yuuzhan Vong, and she was pretty certain that part of her shock at learning about it was what was tainting her feelings about the shuttle.

"What they have done there is unusual."

She turned as Jag Fel entered the pilot room. He wore a black flight suit with red stripes on the sleeves and legs. He wasn't as formal as he had been at the reception, but neither did he seem casual. Looking at him, she would have refused to believe he was Wedge's nephew if not for the resemblance around the eyes and nose.

"Pretty much everything the Yuuzhan Vong do is unusual, as far as I'm concerned." Jaina folded her arms across her chest and looked back at the deck. "They've spent an hour scanning the thing. I can't imagine there is much more they can learn without cracking it open."

"There isn't. That's not what they are doing." Fel came and stood beside her, his reflection easily visible in the transparisteel over the viewport. "They don't know what is in there, and they're just making sure that if it's harmful, they don't get blamed for releasing it."

"You say that as if it's a bad thing to be cautious."

He shook his head. "They know they cannot be certain of

what is in there. All they can do is reduce uncertainty to statistically insignificant levels. What they are wasting is time. We are at war. There is no absence of risk. There are times when one just has to do what needs to be done to win."

Jaina turned and looked at him. "In theory you're only two years older than me, but you're talking like you're old enough to be my dad."

He nodded once. "Forgive me. I was judging you based on your accomplishments, not your age."

She blinked and felt anger spike. "What is that supposed to mean?"

The flesh around Fel's eyes hardened. "You are a Jedi. You are a superior pilot in an elite squadron. The dedication and skill required for these things are well known. I made the mistake of assuming too much about you."

Jaina frowned. "I'm reading your tracking data, but still don't have a lock on your target."

Jag Fel sighed. "In Chiss society, there is no adolescence. Chiss children mature early and are given adult responsibilities very quickly. Those of us humans living with them were raised as they were raised. Intellectually I knew things were not the same here in the New Republic, but—"

"You think I'm a child?" Jaina gave him an icy glare. "You think I'm soft or something?"

Fel broke eye contact, and she noticed a blush rising on his cheeks. He raised a hand to ward off her comments, then shook his head. In doing that he peeled off a decade or two and seemed, to her, for the first time to be someone his own age.

"Not soft, no, not at all. You have determination and courage, but you lack—"

"Lack what?"

He frowned and glanced out at the shuttle. "You're not grim."

Jaina caught herself before she could proclaim that she was, in fact, grim—grim enough to outgrim him even. "Um, no, I mean, there are times, yes, but being grim takes such a toll."

"It does at that." He pointed a finger toward two men

walking across the deck. They were wearing environment
suits, but the clear headgear made them easily recognizable.
"My, ah, uncle . . . when he hugged me at that reception . . .
We'd met barely an hour before, privately, and he was surprised to learn who I was, but in no time after that . . . Where I
come from, there are men that I have never seen smile before,
and here he was, in the midst of a difficult situation, and he
was happy to meet me. Not because I was an ally, but because
I was his sister's son. And he accepted me despite the fact that
my mother's departure from the New Republic hurt him
deeply."

Jaina reached out and rested a hand on Fel's shoulder.
"Wedge is like that. Most people are. Life is too harsh not to
take what pleasure you can find in it, and certainly learning of
his sister and how her life has gone would be wonderful to
him. No matter how bad things might be, a joke, a smile, a pat
on the back help break the tension."

Fel raised his chin, and Jaina could feel his defenses re-
pairing themselves. "Among the Chiss, celebration is saved
until the job is done."

"Even if it is never-ending?"

"If it isn't ended, the celebration is false."

"No, it's necessary." She looked at him, at his strong profile, at the determination on his face, and felt a shiver run
down her spine. That he was handsome there was no dis-
puting, and the cockiness, which was backed by fantastic
skill as a pilot, had its charm. She admired the way he'd stood
up to the New Republic's politicians—most of whom dis-
gusted her because of the way they treated her mother. Even
the Imperial formality was attractive in a quaint sort of way.

I wonder if my mother saw my father that same way?

The second that thought occurred to her she pulled her
hand back from Fel's shoulder abruptly. *Oh, no, I am* not
*going to let myself fall for some guy who thinks grim is the
normal state of being. Not the time or place to even be
thinking about it.*

Fel glanced over when she pulled her hand away, then half
smiled. "The Chiss, despite the impression I might have

given you, *are* a thoughtful people. Deliberate, calculating, but not above a flight of fantasy or two. They are not averse to wondering where they would be, had life been different. Whom they would have met, how they would have met, what would have become of them."

"And you mention this because?"

"Because . . ." He hesitated, then looked out at the deck. "I was wondering what Uncle Wedge would have thought of my older brother."

Jaina smiled and looked out at the deck. "The only problem with those flights of fancy are that life never works as cleanly as we'd like. Sometimes a meeting is just a meeting. Other times it's a prelude."

Fel laughed lightly. "Had I said that, you would have accused me of talking as if I were your father's age again."

"I might well have, but probably not." She didn't glance at him, but did look at his reflection. "The nice thing about being an adolescent is being able to make mature decisions when you need them and being able to just flow along with life when you don't."

Corran felt extremely uncomfortable in the environment suit. He was sweating, but wasn't hot, since the suit's cold temperature had him shivering. The way the growths on the shuttle changed its outline, the way scales trailed along edges, then blossomed into a gush of gray-brown mineral crusts just had his flesh crawling.

He glanced over at Wedge. "You don't need to be here, Wedge. If anything happened to you, Iella and the kids would never forgive me."

"Oh, sure, and you think Mirax would forgive me if anything happened to you?" Wedge laughed easily. "You and me, just like that trench run on Borleias, 'cept this time you go first."

"Didn't I get ordered out on that run?"

"Yeah, you did. You going to pull rank on me here, *Colonel*?"

"You'd listen to that order as well as I did." Corran shook

his head. "And you're not feebleminded enough for some of the Jedi things to work. Okay, glad you're on my wing."

The two men approached the shuttle and walked to the area of the landing ramp. Techs had pulled up a wheeled set of steps that would allow one of them to climb up and touch the underside of the hull. A huge growth, looking to Corran a lot like a giant scab—complete with that dark-brown-tinged-with-dried-blood-purple color—covered the whole landing ramp. The growth changed color over by the access panel, becoming lighter in color and a lot spikier.

"What do you think, Wedge?"

"Well, your lightsaber ought to be able to core through the hull, but you never know what you're going to be cutting above." He folded his arms across his chest. "Since this is being presented to you with the Yuuzhan Vong commander's compliments, I'm not inclined to think he wants you carving up his handiwork."

"You're right there." Corran mounted the steps and took a close look at the growth covering the remote access panel. "This growth is a lot sharper than the others, with some of the edges looking serrated. And there are spines, almost like needles."

He raised a gloved hand toward the growth, and one of the spines shifted to orient toward it. In an eye blink a slender needle shot out, but failed to penetrate the glove. Still, it hit with enough impact to knock Corran's hand back a couple of centimeters. Corran aided and abetted it by leaping backwards and found himself on the deck, with Wedge steadying him.

"You okay?"

Corran nodded. "Yeah, I'm fine." He sighed. "If you were to send someone a token of your esteem, you'd want to make sure he got it, right? You'd lock it up and give him some sort of combination or code to open it, wouldn't you?"

"Makes sense."

"I was afraid of that." Corran freed his lightsaber from his belt with his right hand and ignited it, letting the silver blade splash cold highlights over the shuttle. He extended his left hand to Wedge. "Take my glove off. I'm going to touch it with my bare hand. Something weird happens, the hand goes."

Wedge frowned. "Are you sure this is wise?"

"Of course not, but I don't think I've got much choice." The green-eyed Jedi smiled. "I left enough blood on Bimmiel that the Vong have easily got samples. I'm betting that thing there is keyed to open when it gets another taste of me."

The older man stripped the Jedi's left glove off. "Wouldn't bleeding into a cup and offering that make more sense?"

"Um, sure, in a non-Corellian sort of way." Corran shrugged and climbed back up and raised his left hand toward the shuttle's belly. One of the spines shifted over and flicked a needle into his palm. It pulled back fast enough, and Corran stared at the bead of blood rising from the little wound. "Guess we should have thought about venom, shouldn't we?"

Before Wedge could answer, the edges of the scab cracked, with little brittle pieces of it falling to the deck to shatter like ice. Thick, glistening lines of mucus flowed from around the edges, linking the hull to the descending ramp. The lines stretched thin, then broke in the middle, half of it retracting to drip from the hull, the other slowly flowing into a sluggish crystalline pool on the deck.

Corran climbed off the stairs and headed up the ramp, his lightsaber still lit. Wedge came close on his heels, with a blaster in his right hand. Save for some bioluminescent lighting, the shuttle remained dark, with the lightsaber's blaze deepening shadows and stretching them into grotesques as Corran waved it about.

Throughout, the shuttle panels had been pulled open and smashed. Weird Yuuzhan Vong growths, some like roots, others just coral spikes, decorated the interior hull. They spread out in an ivylike pattern, but even as the two men entered the ship, the growths began to wither and sag. The external sheath on the long tendrils split, allowing black fluid to ooze out.

Corran shook his head. "I don't understand."

"I do. All that stuff was probably scanning us while we were scanning the shuttle. It was sending back information for as long as it took for the hull to be opened. Then it started dying, and dying so fast we aren't going to get anything useful out of analysis." Wedge pulled a piece of root from a wall, and it dissolved in his hand. "Something is metabolizing this stuff very fast. It's like having a compost pile decaying at light speed."

"Well, if that's the message Shedao Shai wants to send me, I don't know how to take it. I mean, I'm not the Jedi who was a farm boy, and I'm not planning on dying that fast, thanks." Corran held his lightsaber high to spread the light out. "Wait, what's this?"

Up toward the front of the passenger compartment, flush against the bulkhead that backed up to the pilot's compartment, sat a large and semiovoid shape, lying on its side. It had a seam running around the middle parallel to the deck and looked very much to Corran like the shell of a sea creature. It had a rough tan exterior, with stripes running from the spine to fan out along the front edge. Another of the stony growths with spines sealed the seam at the front.

As the two men approached it down the aisle between banks of seats, the villip perched on top of it took on the features of Elegos. Though the protoplasmic ball lacked his golden down, it did take on a yellow hue and even had purple streaks around the eyes. It looked much akin to a static holograph where the lasers had been misaligned—recognizable, but only barely.

The villip began to speak in Elegos's voice. "There is much I would tell you about the Yuuzhan Vong, but I have little time. Shedao Shai has taught me much. The Yuuzhan Vong are not mindless predators, but a complex species whose philosophy is much the antithesis of ours. I have not discovered the origin of their hatred for machines, but in other things I believe there is room for compromise. My mission to the Yuuzhan Vong has been difficult, but not fruitless, and I have hopes for continued progress."

The image molded onto the villip smiled. "In our many discussions, Shedao Shai was especially intrigued by the tale of Grand Admiral Thrawn studying the art of the enemy and gleaning understanding from it. For you, Corran Horn, Shedao Shai has great respect. He knows you were at Bimmiel. The two warriors slain there were kin of his. He knows you were at Garqi. He believes the two of you will meet in the future, so he has prepared for you the enclosed, so you may study his handiwork as he has studied yours."

"Every day here, my understanding of the Yuuzhan Vong grows, as does their understanding of us." Elegos's eyes softened. "It is my hope that I will be again with you, soon, in a time of peace. Please give my love to my daughter and friends. Fear not for me, Corran. Though difficult, this mission is vital if there is to be any chance at peace at all."

At the message's conclusion, the villip condensed back down into a ball, then rolled off to the left and dropped to the decking.

Corran looked over at Wedge and shivered. "I don't think I like Shedao Shai thinking the folks on this side of the firing line are the same caliber of genius as Thrawn was."

Wedge shrugged. "Well, it might make him more cautious."

"And might make him come at us with enough force that even Thrawn would have run." The Jedi shook his head. "Maybe we can talk the Vong into accepting some Noghri bodyguards."

"I don't think that's likely." Wedge nodded at the container. "You going to open it?"

"I guess. If Elegos had thought this was a trap, he would have found a way to warn me." Corran held his left hand above the seal and tightened it into a fist, letting a couple droplets of blood drip down onto the Yuuzhan Vong device. The growth cracked slowly, then crumbled. The shell case slowly opened. The lightsaber's glow flashed from gold in the interior.

"Sithspawn!" Corran felt his guts liquefy as he dropped to his knees. "Oh . . . oh, no . . . no."

The opened case revealed a work of art that clearly had been the result of many hours lovingly lavished on it. A fully articulated skeleton sat cross-legged, each bone washed with gold. The sternum, and the smooth caps at the ends of long bones, were gleamed with platinum. Scintillating violet gems burned in the hollows of the eye sockets. Amethysts had been powdered and layered onto the sides of the skull, flaring back in the exact pattern of Elegos's stripes.

The teeth, polished white, grinned coldly in the lipless mouth.

The Caamasi skeleton sat there, the head canted down to stare at the villip nestled in the triangle described by its legs. That ball of tissue hardened into mismatched features. The voice that emerged from it came equally harsh and halting. Its command of Basic was fine, but shaping its mouth around the sounds appeared to be difficult.

"I am Shedao Shai. You were at Bimmiel. You slew two of my kinsmen and left them to be gnawed by vermin. You stole the bones of my ancestor. These bones here I present to you so you may know the proper way to venerate fallen Yuuzhan Vong warriors."

The voice softened almost imperceptibly. "I regret that your actions forced me to slay Elegos. I want you to know I did it myself, with my bare hands. As I strangled him, I read in his eyes betrayal, but only at the first. Before he died, he understood the necessity of his death. You must understand it, as well."

The Yuuzhan Vong's eyes narrowed on the villip's surface. "We will meet, our respective forces, at the world you call Ithor. If you have any honor at all—and Elegos assured me you did—you will return to me the bones of my ancestor. If you do not, then it is you who renders our friend's death meaningless."

Corran felt Wedge's hands on his shoulders as the villip rounded itself again. The Jedi flicked off his lightsaber, sinking the cabin into darkness, all but hiding the skeleton displayed before him. He reached out with his left hand, seeking warmth, seeking something of Elegos's essence, but just felt cold.

"Wedge . . . he was . . . Elegos was so peaceful. He . . . he saved me and my sanity when I was with the pirates. He helped save Mirax." Corran hung his head. "And his murderer tells me that his death is *my* fault? Elegos never did anything to hurt anyone and is slaughtered to make a point?"

Wedge's hands tightened on Corran's shoulders. "To the Yuuzhan Vong, this was the only message they thought you would understand."

"Yeah, well, this Shedao Shai made his point." Corran heaved himself to his feet. "He wants those bones back, he'll get them, and in a big box, too. I'm going to pack his in with them, then the Vong can carry the whole stinking lot back to wherever they call home."

CHAPTER
TWENTY-NINE

The light from the holographic representation of the Ithorian system splashed over the faces of the people gathered in the briefing room. Luke watched it shift and change as Admiral Kre'fey altered the perspective. The image's center soared out around Ithor in a spiral orbit, flashing past the city-ships as they crept slowly away from what had been their home.

The Bothan Admiral froze the image there. "The evacuation is proceeding pretty well. The city-ships are not structurally sound enough to make the jump to lightspeed, even *if* they could be fitted with hyperspace drives. We can and will keep them screened from the Vong force, while any ships we can round up will evacuate the people."

Admiral Pellaeon nodded solemnly. "I would have never thought it possible to evacuate a planet's entire population."

Corran frowned. "We've not got them all away, not by a long shot. *And* there is plenty of life left behind on Ithor. We're just taking away the most mobile parts of it."

Kre'fey nodded and glanced down at the datapad he was using to control the holoprojector. "Best estimates are that we need a week or so to complete the evacuation, but that's provided the extra shipping I've requested can get here. Already the price of passage from worlds like Agamar is spiking, so anyone with a ship that can haul a load is heading up there to get 'self-loading freight.' It is a race against time, and the chances to win it are quickly slipping away."

The Jedi Master sighed, the gravity of the Bothan's words weighing his spirit down. "Nothing your cousin can do?"

Traest Kre'fey laughed aloud. "No, not really. His advisors fled back to Coruscant on one of the first ships to go."

Corran arched an eyebrow in surprise. "Borsk stayed behind?"

"He did."

The Corellian Jedi held both hands out, palms up, as if they were either side of a scale. "Brave, stupid. Brave, stupid. Not sure which I want to believe of him."

"As long as he does not cause trouble, I don't care which it is." The Bothan sighed. "Then again, the chances of his not causing trouble are minimal."

"And really immaterial." Pellaeon pressed his fingertips together. "Our engineers have finished the work on the ground station. The defenders, such as they are, are in position. Shells defending a shell, but it should be sufficient to fool the Vong."

Luke nodded. "Good. The Jedi are very close to finishing our preparations on the *Tafanda Bay*. I'd prefer more time to make sure things will work properly, run some simulations, but we go when we go. It's really up to the Yuuzhan Vong."

"It *is* that, definitely." Kre'fey hit a button on his datapad and the viewpoint's spiral continued on out in a long arc toward the depths of the solar system. There, nestled between an asteroid belt and a gas giant, sat the Yuuzhan Vong fleet. The ships almost appeared to be a group of asteroids slowly leaving the belt to orbit the gas giant, but their course pointed inexoribly in toward Ithor itself.

The fleet's image sent a chill down Luke's spine.

The Bothan Admiral sat back and smoothed the white fur on his neck with both hands. "Ever since they showed up in the system I've been running dozens of simulations of the probable course of battle. With the forces allotted to both sides, the outcome is fairly consistent. We engage in space, inflict damage on each other, then retreat to the opposite sides of the world. At their current rate of advance, we engage in three days, perhaps four. One big battle, then a standoff."

Gilead Pellaeon leaned forward and smoothed his moustache with thumb and forefinger. "I've requested reinforcements, and I know you have, too. What I don't like about the simulations I've run is this: The Vong can peel off a small contingent of their ships and send them after the city-ships once we've settled into our standoff. We have to react, shifting the balance of power here. Ithor will be open to them."

Corran's green eyes narrowed. "Can these reinforcements come into the system in a position to cover the city-ships?"

The Imperial Admiral nodded. "That would be relatively simple to accomplish, and would put them in position to help with the evacuation, too."

"And the evacuation is more important than killing any Yuuzhan Vong splinter force." Luke looked at Corran. "What is it?"

The Corellian Jedi blinked, then glanced down at his hands. "Well, it sounds as if what we really need, instead of just a standoff, is a truce."

Pelleaon nodded. "That would be most useful, but the fate of your Caamasi friend would suggest it's unlikely."

"Maybe not."

Luke looked hard at Corran as a spiked wave of conflicting emotions erupted from the dark-haired Jedi. "What do you have in mind? You've been planning something."

"Caught red-handed." Corran's lips pressed into a flat line. "I didn't mean to deceive you, Luke. I know that's not possible, but . . . You all heard what Shedao Shai said to me. I sent a message to Agamar. A day from now I expect to get those bones from the archeological team that recovered them. I'll have something Shedao Shai wants."

Luke shook his head. "You weren't planning something stupid, were you? Were you going to bring them to the *Tafanda Bay* and use them as bait?"

"I don't know what I was thinking. I hadn't gotten as far as planning." Corran looked at his open hands, then pressed them flat on the table top. "I just knew, I mean I *knew* I had to have those bones here. Maybe I'd shoot them into the sun and tell Shedao Shai I'd done that so he'd race his ship into the sun's gravity well trying to get them, and then get all burned up. I don't know."

Kre'fey scratched at his chin. "Trade the bones for a truce? I'm not sure that would work."

Corran shook his head. "It wouldn't."

Luke heard the uncertainty leave Corran's voice. "What do you mean?"

"I was wrong when I said I had something Shedao Shai wants. I have two things. I have the bones, and I have *me*. I killed two of his kin on Bimmiel, so he killed Elegos. He wants to kill me."

The Imperial admiral slowly smiled. "And you want to kill him."

"I wouldn't mind it." The Corellian Jedi's head came up. "What I propose is this: I challenge the Vong leader to a duel. He wins, he gets the bones. I win, I get Ithor. To set it up, we have a truce. How long do you want? A week? Two?"

"A week would be great, two would be better." Kre'fey nodded. "This could work."

Luke shook his head. "No, this can't happen."

"Master? Why not?"

"First, Borsk Fey'lya will never agree to it."

Kre'fey cleared his throat. "What my cousin does not know will not hurt him."

Corran nodded. "And if it does not work, if Shedao Shai does not agree, we don't have to explain yet another Jedi failure."

"Corran, it's still not right. You challenge him to a duel, you become the aggressor. You're coercing him into acting. That's not what Jedi do." *You're treading perilously close to the dark side, my friend.* Luke did not voice his concern because he wasn't at all sure how either Admiral would take it.

The green-clad Jedi sat silently for a moment, then slowly nodded. "I think I understand your concern, Master, but this goes back to the discussion at our meeting months ago. I can feel the focusing of Vong power. I know that to do this is to preempt Vong action. Elegos sent himself out to try to stop the invasion and, um, if I can do that, even for a day, the chances of more people escaping goes up. It may not be the choice we want to make, but it's the only one that seems to be offering itself at the moment."

"But the example you'll set. You'll be playing into Kyp's hands."

"I know." Corran closed his eyes and sat back. "I wish there was another way, Master, but this one just feels right."

Luke wanted to protest and forbid Corran from striking the bargain with the Yuuzhan Vong leader that had been proposed. He didn't because of the sense of calm radiating from his colleague.

The Jedi Master looked at the two military men. "You two approve of this plan?"

Pelleaon snorted. "Of one man taking a vigilante action to decide the fate of a planet and its population? That's the last thing the Empire would ever condone. Not only is it risky for the man on the spot, but it would encourage others to act in an insubordinate fashion if they felt their action was 'right.' Were he under my command, I would forbid this action, but he's not. I also recognize how absolutely desperate things are, and if this will work, I'm willing to work with it. The decision is going to be up to his commanding officer."

Admiral Kre'fey frowned. "I seem to remember there having been a good reason for recalling Colonel Horn to active duty, but it escapes me now." He sighed. "I agree with Admiral Pelleaon. I don't like this at all, but I think this is a chance we must take. Ships can only move so fast, so we need to win time more than the battle. At the very least this will win us time. If it safeguards Ithor, so much the better."

Luke nodded solemnly. "There is a great deal I don't like about this, but . . ." He glanced at Corran. "I trust your judgment. I know you will do the right thing."

"Thank you, Master."

Luke reached out and patted Corran on the shoulder. "We'll work out a way to get the message to Shedao Shai. I will get you the plans as soon as we have them."

Kre'fey stood and offered Luke his hand. "Just in case it never gets said, I appreciate the sacrifice you and your Jedi are making here. I wanted you to know that, in case we don't make it through to the other side of this conflict."

The image of Chewbacca flashed through Luke's mind for a second, then he banished it with the sensation of meeting the Bothan's firm, dry grip. "Thank you, Admiral. May the Force be with us all."

CHAPTER THIRTY

Jacen Solo watched the freighter captain accept the datapad back from Corran, check the receipt flashing on the screen, then wave forward the binary loadlifter with the brushed aluminum case. "You should know that Dr. Pace said she was going to protest this appropriation of Yuuzhan Vong artifacts to the highest levels." The captain shook his head.

"Noted." Corran gave the man a curt nod. "Thanks for the diversion here. I won't keep you."

"Not a problem. Your wife's done me some good turns in the past. Glad to return the favor." The man gave Corran a quick salute, then directed the loadlifter back to his freighter.

"Want me to get that, Corran?"

The elder Jedi hefted the case by its handle, then extended it toward Jacen. "Has your mind changed about this? You didn't like the idea at the briefing. Second thoughts?"

Jacen accepted the case and was surprised by how light it really was. "Not really. You're making part of this war personal, you against Shedao Shai. That's not right. It's divisive. It's of the—"

"Don't tell me it's of the dark side, Jacen." Corran held up a hand and shook his head. "I'm not in a mood—"

"Yes, you are, Corran, you're in a mood. And you don't want to hear it because you know it's true." Jacen got a step ahead of the other Jedi, glancing back at him over his left shoulder. "You're the one who told me we all have to be pulling in the same direction, but you're going off on your own. You want revenge for your friend. I can't blame you for that, but were the situation reversed, you'd be arguing with me to subordinate my feelings to what others thought was best."

"That's probably true."

"So, why doesn't the same work for you?"

"Because . . ." Corran frowned, then grabbed a handful of Jacen's tunic and tugged him down a side corridor. "Come here."

The two of them walked along in silence and emerged on a walkway that gave them a view across the expanse of the bowl that was the *Tafanda Bay*. Had Jacen not known they were floating over the Mother Jungle, he could have easily been led to believe that the Ithorian ship was a domed city nestled comfortably on the planet below. The transparisteel dome displayed a bright blue sky through which freighters streaked toward space, and the verdant foliage throughout the city let the white walls and walkways peek through only here and there.

"Look out there, Jacen. This is a city that is now abandoned by the people who love it, who labored to create it. Why? Because it's a target. We know the Vong are going to hit it, so we've moved the people and have rigged up some surprises for the enemy. We're doing that on the planet itself, too."

The youth nodded. "I understand that."

"Well, understand this: Shedao Shai, because of what I did at Bimmiel, because of what *we* did at Garqi, has decided I'm a target. He's going to be looking for me—and for the bones in that case—which means he's going to be distracted. That's what we want, because a distracted leader is one who will give us some time and, ultimately, is going to fail."

"I get that, but the rest of it . . ."

Corran sighed and laid a hand on Jacen's left shoulder. "Look, Jacen, I don't want revenge for Elegos. His death hurt me, deeply, but I knew him well enough to know that the last thing he'd want is someone slain in his name. You remember on Dantooine, he took to flying that shuttle because he was willing to take responsibility for killing, to shield others from having to bear that burden. If I went out after Shedao Shai in Elegos's name, Elegos would see that as *his* having thrust the burden of violence on me. I wouldn't do that to him."

"But you do intend to kill Shedao Shai."

Corran's face resolved itself into a solemn mask. "If the opportunity arises, yes. Look, Jacen, it's not about vengeance, which, you're right, would be of the dark side. It's about responsibility. Shedao Shai wants to kill me. If I don't engage him, then you or Ganner or someone else might be required to deal with him. Yes, he's dangerous, of that I have no doubt. He may well kill me and *then* he's your problem. Until then, he's mine."

Jacen shivered. "I don't know about that."

"Yeah, but you don't have to." The older man sighed, not wearily, but as if he were letting tension boil off. "I know what we are doing is right, Jacen. The battle here is for two ends. The first is to preserve Ithor and its fleeing population. The second, which is equally important, is to inflict a defeat on the Vong. We need them to know the easy course of their invasion so far isn't going to continue. If they pay a price here, they may reconsider further action.

"I don't expect you to understand it at your age, because I didn't until well past it, but I just know that what I'm doing is right." He smiled. "I can feel it in my gut. It's just what has to be done."

Jacen heard the conviction in Corran's voice and took heart in it for a second, then frowned as his mouth soured. "I felt that way about freeing the slaves on Belkadan, and you know how that turned out."

Corran looped an arm over Jacen's shoulders. "Um, kid, you've got a lot to learn about this morale thing."

"Just trying to be realistic."

"Yeah, I know." Corran smiled grimly and steered Jacen along to their staging area. "I have a feeling we're going to get realism washed over us in waves. I just hope we don't drown."

* * *

"Indeed, I am rather surprised to see you still here, cousin." Admiral Traest Kre'fey stood forward on the *Ralroost*'s bridge, watching the spacescape over Ithor. Out in the distance a number of dagger-shaped ships orbited the planet—with fewer of them belonging to the New Republic than to the Imperial Remnant. "I would have thought you'd have made your way back toward the Core with High Priest Tawron."

Borsk Fey'lya avoided shrugging, though fur did ripple at the back of his neck. "There were reasons I stayed."

Not the least being that Leia Organa Solo has not fled as your cabinet has? Traest left his thoughts unvoiced, though he felt the chief of the New Republic might have read them in his feral smile. "And reasons you wished to speak to me?"

"Speak to you? No." Fey'lya smiled carefully. "I wanted you here as a witness." He nodded toward the communications officer. "You may put the connection through now."

Lieutenant Arr'yka looked to the admiral for permission.

Traest held a hand up for a moment. "And whom do you want to speak with?"

"Admiral Pellaeon." Fey'lya nodded toward the *Chimaera* glimmering in the distance. "Since you are not so bold as to champion your own cause, it becomes incumbent upon me to do so. I will demand the leadership of this operation fall to you. It is a New Republic world; you should be leading its defense."

"I see." A hint of a growl entered Traest's voice, then he nodded to the lieutenant. "Open communications with Admiral Pellaeon, please."

The two Bothans waited in silence for a handful of seconds, then Pellaeon appeared in life-size holo as imposing as he did in life. "Yes, Admiral Kre'fey?"

"My compliments, Admiral. I did not want to disturb you, but Chief Borsk Fey'lya wishes to urge you to give me command of the Ithorian defense. Before he did that, I thought I would let him hear your orders concerning the matter."

The human nodded and smoothed his white mustache with

his left hand. "As per Imperial directive 59826, if I am replaced as commander of the Ithorian defense, all Imperial ships and personnel are to be withdrawn to Bastion immediately."

"Thank you, Admiral. Sorry for wasting your time. Kre'fey out."

The Bothan admiral turned to face his cousin. "Will that be all?"

He could see by the crest of fur rising at Borsk Fey'lya's neck that it would not be. "This is an outrage! The Remnant has no place defending this world. It is *our* world. *We* must be in command of the defense. There can be no other way!"

Traest extended his right hand toward Fey'lya, palm up, fingers clawed, and unsheathed his talons. "On Coruscant you agreed to leave the defense of the New Republic to the military. I warned you that if you tried to interfere, I would withdraw my forces to the Unknown Regions. I can and will yet do that. If I do, Admiral Pellaeon will pull his forces out. Ithor will be defenseless."

Fey'lya's violet eyes widened. "But you can't. The troops you have on the ground would be abandoned. And the Jedi . . . you would not leave them—"

"No? Try me. You don't care about the Jedi. If you had your way, they would all perish here. You'd praise their sacrifice, build memorials to them, then happily dance on their graves." Traest's amethyst eyes hardened, letting light glint from the gold flecks in them. "As for leaving Ithor behind, you have no idea where I've sent the refugees. There will be Ithorian colonies throughout the New Republic and Unknown Regions. Yes, it will take years before the bafforr trees can produce their pollen again, but I can spend that time building up armies to come and crush the Yuuzhan Vong. I warned you before that is what I would do, and I will. One word from me and the dependents for every warrior in my command will be moved to worlds of my choosing."

"You are insubordinate! I will remove you from command." Fey'lya turned and pointed at two Bothan security officers standing beside the access hatch to the bridge. "Arrest Admiral Kre'fey and conduct him from the bridge."

Neither of the Bothans stirred or gave any sign they'd even heard the command.

Traest peered down his nose at his cousin. "We are in a war zone, cousin. Your power ended when you entered this system. You have a choice—" He was cut off by Pellaeon's sudden holographic appearance.

"Forgive me, Admiral, but the Vong have reached attack range. They have launched; we have incoming. It has begun. Case Seven, it appears."

"Thank you, Admiral. Case Seven it is." Traest looked through the Imperial's vanishing hologram. "Case Seven, slave our targeting computers to telemetry from the *Chimaera*. Scramble all fighters. This is not a drill, people. Fight well and we'll live to see the Yuuzhan Vong repulsed."

Traest stepped in close to Fey'lya and dropped his voice to a whisper. "The choice I was going to offer you was to return to your quarters, or to get on a ship and flee before the enemy deployed its forces. That latter choice is gone now, but I offer you another. You can remain here, on the bridge, and silently show your support for those who will fight to save your life, or you can slink away in terror and hope the Yuuzhan Vong attacks never breach your cabin's bulkheads."

Fey'lya lifted his chin. "You may have contempt for me now, cousin, but in my day, when Imperials were our enemies, I spilled blood. I've known combat, and I've not run from it."

"Good, because the Yuuzhan Vong are worse than anything you ever faced." Traest raised his voice so everyone on the bridge could hear him. "Yes, cousin, your help here would be wonderful. If there is a need, I will let you know what to do. Until then, just having you here, honoring my staff with your presence, is more valuable to our effort than you could know."

Jaina Solo's X-wing sailed out high above the *Ralroost* and rolled left to come into position within Rogue Squadron's formation. Anni Capstan dropped in on her starboard S-foil and drifted back a couple of meters. A quick glance at the displays showed her screens up at full, her inertial compensator field expanded to protect them from Yuuzhan Vong dovin basals, and her weapons systems fully charged and green.

"Eleven hot and green."

Sparky hooted and started painting tactical data on her primary monitor. In an eye blink a dozen Yuuzhan Vong targets scrolled past. The monitor displayed a huge Yuuzhan Vong cruiser, bigger than anything she'd seen before. It bristled with long spines of yorick coral, though the core of it seemed to have started life as an asteroid onto which the other pieces had been grafted.

Three smaller cruisers—all the size of the ship they'd fought at Dantooine—surrounded the largest cruiser, then eight more ships were positioned in support of the rest. From all of them boiled skips, forming a cloud of contacts. Through all that Sparky managed to pick up a series of medium-size ships that Jaina took to be troop carriers.

Fleet command immediately downloaded tactical designators for the Yuuzhan Vong ships. The biggest was designated a grand cruiser. The smaller ones became assault cruisers, and the smallest were tagged light cruisers. The quickchat designators of *grand*, *salt*, and *light* were appended to the files, though Jaina assumed the pilots would come up with their own designators just to spite the tactical planners.

The troop carriers earned the name crate. Jaina knew they had to be jam-packed full of Yuuzhan Vong warriors. The soldiers would be helpless until they got into atmosphere and on the ground, and an attack on them didn't need to destroy the crate, just open the hull enough to let the atmosphere out and cold in.

Gavin's voice crackled over the comm channel. "Rogues, we have the crates. Lasers if you can, torps if you can't. Better us killing them up here, than having them on the ground."

CHAPTER THIRTY-ONE

"It's huge, Admiral. It masses as much as a Super Star Destroyer."

Pellaeon turned slowly away from the viewport on the *Chimaera*'s bridge, knowing he would win the battle as much by the demeanor he showed his crew as he would by firepower or tactics. "We'll have to see, Commander, if we can trim mass from it, shall we?"

The *Chimaera* sat in the center of the defender's formation, deep in the well of a cone. Arrayed around and ahead of it were four other *Imperial*-class Star Destroyers—two each from the New Republic and the Remnant. Then nine *Victory*-class Star Destroyers, three Bothan Assault Cruisers, and a Mon Calamari star cruiser ranged out further along the cone. Beyond them came a scattering of smaller ships, from frigates on down to a couple of freighters with more guts in the crew than weapons on the hull.

"Firing solutions for the grand, please; fire at will." The Imperial admiral turned and watched the turbolaser batteries on either of the ship's flanks fill space with hot red bolts of energy. Some of the weapons emitted a nearly constant stream of small bolts that sprayed back and forth at the target. The voids the Yuuzhan Vong used to shield their ships sucked them up greedily, though when a few began to get through, the other guns unleashed a concentrated torrent of fire.

Those heavier bolts flashed in at their targets. Pellaeon expected them to hit and melt gaping holes in the grand's rocky hull, but voids swallowed those bolts, as well. The admiral's eyes narrowed as he studied the large ship's ability to absorb the punishment his guns were doling out.

"No good, sir." The weapons-control officer let frustration bleed into his words. "These snubfighter tactics may work against skips, but not against the big ships. They have enough shielding to hold us off."

"That's possible, quite possible." Pellaeon frowned, and ran his right hand over his chin. "Or have they learned how we fight?"

Jaina scattered laserfire over a skip, then drilled a quad burst into its aft. Coral slagged off into a frozen comet tail. The dark little Yuuzhan Vong ship started to roll and began on a course that would burn it into a golden streak high in Ithor's atmosphere.

"Sticks, break starboard."

Without thinking, Jaina reacted to Anni Capstan's warning. She jerked her stick to the right and feathered the adjustment jets to pitch the X-wing into a barrel roll to starboard. A plasma blast from a skip sizzled past her ship, then hot after it came molten chunks of coralskipper. Anni's fighter blazed through, sparks still trailing from her shields, and Jaina dropped onto her aft, then slipped slightly to port.

They exchanged fire with a pair of skips, then blew through the Yuuzhan Vong screen to get in among the crates. In comparison to the fast-moving skips, the crates were bloated floaters, just inviting a quick run and a pair of proton torpedoes. Each of the troop carriers sprouted hornlike projections that spat plasma bolts at incoming fighters, but they were clearly meant more for antipersonnel use than antifighter tactics. Dodging the streams was easy, and a burst of splinter shots actually scored some hits on the hull.

"Sparky, watch our tail, we're making a run." Jaina slipped her X-wing back into the lead, then leveled out and started in on one crate. As it fired plasma toward her, she abruptly kicked her X-wing up on its port S-foil and dived down at another. She snapped off two bursts of splinters fore and aft, then drilled a quad burst into the boxy craft's spine. Coral went from coal black to white-hot in an instant, then evaporated.

Got it! Jaina keyed her comlink. "Finish it, Twelve."

"As ordered, Sticks."

Suddenly Sparky started shrieking. Jaina's secondary monitor showed a pair of skips lurking dead center in her aft scope, slipping in behind Anni. "Twelve, break off the run."

"Sithspawn!" Anni's voice rose with panic. "I'm hit!"

Jaina jerked her stick to starboard and pulled back to climb, but it was too late. Anni's X-wing trailed flames from two engines. The fighter had tucked itself into a tight spiral and slammed full force into the crate Jaina had shot up. Jaina caught a pulse of pain from her wing mate and then nothing.

Anni!

Jaina!

Down on Ithor, hidden with the Jedi squad waiting for the Yuuzhan Vong, Jacen doubled over as pain exploded in his stomach. He struggled for breath, feeling as if a vibroblade had been shoved into his guts. The physical pain in his middle slowly began to ease, but not so the heartache flooding through him.

In an instant Corran was beside him, his hand on Jacen's back. "What is it?"

Jacen coughed a couple of times, then caught his breath. "My sister, she's . . . something happened . . . up there."

"How bad?"

Jacen blinked and reached out with the Force, then raised his face to the night sky. He could still feel her out there amid the flashes of laserfire and the golden debris streaking across the sky. "She's okay, but someone close to her got vaped. I get that much very clearly."

Corran nodded, then he and Ganner slapped Jacen on the back. "You have to figure she'll be safe."

"Why's that?"

"Because, Jacen," Ganner offered, "there's nothing you can do for her down here. We'll just make sure that what comes down isn't going back up again to bother her."

The youngest Jedi nodded. "You think they're going to take the bait?"

"Do glitbiters suck spice?" Corran gave Jacen a confident

smile. "The Vong have managed to surprise all of us a number of times. It's their turn to be surprised, and a nasty surprise it will be."

With his head ensconced in a cognition hood, Deign Lian surveyed the battle. He had chosen to color the carrier bearing Shedao Shai red and watched as the enemy fighters broke through coralskipper cover to start shooting up the carriers. Their weapons spat hot light at Shedao Shai's ship, but none hit. The outer shell of carriers was gradually carved away, but the majority of them hit atmosphere and began their descent onto the night side of the planet.

Lian then turned his attention to the fleet battle. In an eye blink he designated one of the small infidel ships as a target. The *Legacy of Torment*'s gunners focused on it, launching a salvo from a half-dozen plasma cannons. The first shot to hit the ship splashed around its shield like mud on an egg. The subsequent shots, all golden and boiling, ate through it like acid. The last one blew unabated through the ball that had once been a metal construct in which warriors had huddled.

More infidels to feed the gods.

With a flicker of thought, Deign Lian shifted the representation of the battle. Instead of seeing it as it might appear in visual light, the *Torment*'s analytic neuroengines layered colors over the images, letting him assess the damage done to the fleet. Coralskippers became gold and red sparks flitting through the void, growing darker until they winked out of existence. The larger ships started gold, but took on reddened spots or stripes. It pleased him that so few of his ships were reddened.

That pleasure faded quickly as he realized that Shedao Shai was the reason for their successes. His superior had analyzed the infidel's small-fighter tactics and anticipated the capital ships using a version of them. His countertactic, of deploying a dovin basal screen of sufficient strength to pick off the weakened shots, succeeded in conserving energy for the intense fields needed to arrest the full-power shots.

It does not matter. He might win today, but his victory will just blind him to what needs to be done in the future. Deign

Lian smiled. *And if he loses, to him goes all blame, and to me will fall the glory of having made the best of his feeble plan.*

Colonel Gavin Darklighter rolled to starboard, then spiraled down after the escaping crates. "Got my wing, Deuce?"

Kral Nevil double-clicked his comm, replying in the positive. Gavin checked his scopes and found six more Rogues coming on hot. *Only eight of us left?* A shudder shook him. At once he was happy that so many of the Rogues were still operational, but the losses still sent icy tendrils through his guts. *Anni, gone, and others whom I never got a chance to know.*

He snarled angrily, then felt his mind go very cold and clear, as his fury became arctic and infused his body and mind. He suddenly felt as if he was more than a pilot in a machine, that somehow he and his fighter had become one. *As closely linked as a Vong pilot and his machine.* He let his right hand ride lightly on the stick despite the bump of entering the atmosphere and cruised on in after one of the crates.

Gavin sailed in at its aft and scattered splinter shots at it. The crate projected a void that swallowed the red darts, then its aft guns started spitting plasma sparks at him. The New Republic pilot took his fighter down enough that the crate's own voids shielded him from the fire, then he laced the carrier's belly with splinter shots. The void shifted down to pick off those shots, and the plasma fire resumed.

Gavin smiled and tugged back on his stick. His nose came up just enough to pulse a quad burst at the crate's aft. The lasers hit it hard, with one carving a black furrow up along the side. The other three burned holes in the back. Gavin followed them with more splinter shots, not figuring they'd do more damage to the carrier, but every one that got through the hole would wreak havoc on the cargo.

That crate broke left and dived hard for the jungle below. Gavin ignored it and brought his X-wing around on the same heading as the rest of the crates. In the distance gleamed a white building complex nestled amid the jungle, and twenty kilometers north of it, the lone remaining herd ship, the *Tafanda Bay*, rode in the sky like a peaceful metal cloud. Four of the crates broke off for the herd ship, while the rest bore in at the ground target.

Gavin flicked his weapons control over to proton torpedoes and targeted the space between two of the crates heading for the *Tafanda Bay*. He glanced at his monitor and read the range to target. "Catch, program the torps for detonation at two klicks or proximity void detection."

The droid beeped once, solidly, then Gavin hit the trigger. The paired missiles burned blue through the sky, and his sensors reported voids appearing behind the crates. The Yuuzhan Vong had clearly learned the proton torpedoes would go off when they detected a void, so these crates projected their voids far behind them. In space, the amount of energy from the blast would be insignificant at that range.

But we're not in space, are we, boys? The exploding proton torpedoes did two things. The first was to pulse out a shock wave that traveled faster than the speed of sound and pushed a lot of atmosphere in front of it. That dense chunk of air slammed into the two crates, boosting them forward and starting them to tumble. It raced past, dissipating as it went, but even the two leaders were bounced around a bit.

The second thing the explosions did, by superheating air and blasting it out in all directions, was to create a void that a lot of air rushed in to fill. The resulting turbulence whirled the spinning crates around. Gavin had no idea how the Yuuzhan Vong pilots and the living components of their ships were able to track up, down, direction, speed, or altitude, but he knew that at the heart of a whirlwind he'd have had a hard time thinking about any of that.

Apparently, so did the Yuuzhan Vong. Their ships fell from the sky, careening through the jungle. No explosions resulted from their impacts, though trees toppled, scarring the dark canopy.

Gavin watched them fall, then focused on the rest of the crates. They were already quite far and quite low, and too close to the herd ship to risk another proton torpedo shot. He smiled to himself. *Did what we could to slow them down. Now they're not our problem.*

CHAPTER
THIRTY-TWO

The first Yuuzhan Vong carrier swooped in at the *Tafanda Bay* and pulled away sharply at the last moment. The herd ship, which had no guns, presented no obvious threat to the invaders. The second carrier came in level and blazed away with the two small plasma cannons mounted on the cockpit's roof. Golden gouts of plasma slammed into the transparisteel of a veiwport, melting it like ice beneath a blowtorch.

The carrier then used a void, centering it on the hole, to suck molten transparisteel away. The void pulled in some atmosphere, tree branches, and small uprooted plants by the time it had cleared out a hole big enough to let the carrier land. The boxy ship entered the *Tafanda Bay* and moved forward to a green promenade. It touched down lightly, opening hatches through which poured a legion of little reptoid shock troops.

From the ship's aft emerged a half-dozen Yuuzhan Vong warriors, all tall, lean, and terrible. They bore their amphistaffs and wore armor, but it hung loosely on them. They seemed to move uneasily in it, and as Anakin Solo watched them alight from the ship, he supposed their uneasiness came from wearing the dead shell of a creature instead of the living vonduun crab itself.

He studied the small screen on his datapad, occasionally hitting a key to provide himself another view from one of the many holocams located throughout the city. He switched to the one nearest where the first crate had landed and caught the quick flash of something before static filled the little data window. Another view showed two Yuuzhan Vong warriors pointing at the smoking, sparking ruin of a holocam.

One of the warriors plucked a flat, disk-shaped bug from a bandolier he wore across his chest and sent it whirling out toward the cam through which Anakin watched them. Anakin flinched, having felt the sting of the razorbugs on Dantooine. The toss missed, but the bug came flying back to its master for another try. Anakin switched to yet a third cam, but the landing of the second crate cut off his view of the warrior throwing the bug.

Daeshara'cor rested a hand on his left shoulder. "It's time, Anakin."

He shut the datapad off and started to pocket it, but she turned and looked at him. "Leave it. No reason to drag it along."

The remark surprised him for a second. She was right. He didn't need it for what they would be doing. In fact, it would be a little extra weight, something that might slow him down. If they defeated the Yuuzhan Vong, he would have all the time in the world to come back for it. *If we don't . . .*

He smiled, then slipped the datapad into the pocket on the left thigh of his combat suit. "The Yuuzhan Vong hate machines. It's not a living thing, but I don't want to leave it for them."

The Twi'lek smiled briefly. "Hadn't thought of that. C'mon, Anakin, let's go teach them the error of their ways."

Anakin stalked after Daeshara'cor, slipping through a broad doorway and into a wide corridor. Planters mounted into the walls brimmed over with purple vines, while gold-leaf ivy ran along the ceiling. Daeshara'cor walked down the center of the passage, which, because it had been built for Ithorians, was sufficiently large to make her look almost childlike.

He wondered for a moment why she was walking down the middle of the corridor. He knew she wasn't afraid of the vines, then he noticed he was doing it, too. *Neither of us is slinking along.* Approaching the coming battle boldly hardly made sense, since the Yuuzhan Vong were lethal. *But to cower as we approach would give them a victory even before the battle is joined.*

Irrational though he knew that explanation was, it felt right to him. Watching her, seeing the set of her shoulders and the straightness of her spine, he realized that to be truly brave took more than deciding you weren't going to be scared. You had to allow yourself to believe you were brave, and you had to do all the things you could to promote that feeling. *You have to give yourself the chance to be brave.*

They reached the end of the corridor and crouched down. The corridor connected with the large series of forested plazas that ran down the belly of the herd ship about three levels above the greensward. The reptoids had spread out in little knots of six, moving along the walkways that edged the plazas. Anakin knew the Ithorians had not been taking tactics into account when they created the herd ship. Still, the fact that the walkways curved often and moved up and down, as if the path were on a hillside, meant that the Yuuzhan Vong troops could pretty much see only twenty meters in front of them, and that in the best case.

And the foliage choking the greensward made looking from one side of the herd ship to the other almost impossible. That mattered little to the Jedi. Though they could not sense the Yuuzhan Vong themselves, their client troops had a presence in the Force. Moreover, the Jedi could pick one another out within the city. While none of them had direct telepathic connections, having a sense of where someone was, and a comlink for talking to them, was almost as good as a brain-to-brain hookup.

Daeshara'cor keyed her comlink. "Team Twelve in place."

"Copy, Twelve. Race starts in five."

The Twi'lek nodded to Anakin. She brought her lightsaber to hand and covered the ignition button with her thumb. "Anakin, I just want to say thanks."

He frowned. "What for?"

"I got myself lost before, and you found me." Daeshara'cor smiled. "That's a debt so huge I can't repay it. If I had succeeded . . . I'd have hated myself forever."

Anakin's reply died amid the electronic squealing of an MSE-6 mouse droid rolling along the walkway as fast as it could. Guttural barks and hisses chased it. It paused just in front of the corridor where they waited, spun in a tight circle, then shot on down the walkway past them. Pursuing hotly came a half-dozen reptoids. So focused were they on the small droid that none of them even spared a glance at the corridor.

Anakin flicked his left hand at one of the middle reptoids and used the Force to boost it into the air. The Yuuzhan Vong slave caught its heels on the walkway balustrade, starting the creature somersaulting in flight. Screaming, it crashed through foliage and landed with a crunch below.

The surprised look on the second reptoid's face died as Anakin slammed his lightsaber against the side of its head, then hit the ignition switch. The purple blade swept up through the top of the creature's skull, then came around to parry an amphistaff strike from one of the two lead reptoids. With two hands on the hilt, Anakin parried the amphistaff wide to his left, then pivoted on his left foot and side-kicked the reptoid in the face.

As that creature pitched backwards, the other one lunged with his amphistaff at Anakin. The young Jedi felt the fire of the amphistaff's sharpened edge grazing the inside of his left thigh. Anakin whipped his lightsaber around in a backhanded slash that separated the reptoid's triumphant grin top from bottom.

Spinning back, he saw Daeshara'cor standing above the bodies of her dead reptoids, then the two of them went over the balustrade and dropped to the level below. Anakin landed astride the reptoid he'd pitched off the upper level. It had clearly shattered its spine in the fall.

Anakin turned to his right and saw a Yuuzhan Vong warrior coming along the walkway. "Quick, the corridor. Go!"

Daeshara'cor darted down the corridor that ran below the one in which they'd hidden, and Anakin made to follow her, but the reptoid clutched at his right ankle. He tried to shake his foot free, but the creature clung to it for dear life. The Yuuzhan Vong roared a challenge and charged, his amphistaff whirling.

Turning to face this challenge, Anakin set himself as best as he was able. He raised his lightsaber to a guard and was ready to parry the warrior, when the reptoid slammed a fist into the wound on his left leg. Pain shot up through him, dropping him to one knee. He looked up and saw the bladed end of the amphistaff slashing down at his face.

Suddenly Anakin felt himself jerked back by the Force as strongly as if he'd been strapped to an X-wing making the jump to light speed. Her lightsaber burning scarlet, Daeshara'cor stepped onto the walkway, interposing herself between the Yuuzhan Vong and Anakin. The warrior, whose strike had carved through the reptoid instead of Anakin, dropped back into a half crouch, with his amphistaff held waist high, the bloodied tail pointing at the Twi'lek.

The Yuuzhan Vong thrust at her twice. Daeshara'cor sidestepped one lunge, then batted the second aside. She pressed an attack, cutting twice at his head. The Yuuzhan Vong retreated, drawing her forward, as he brought his amphistaff up to block the slashes. Reversing his amphistaff, he parried a lunge to his left, then riposted. Daeshara'cor brushed his attack wide, then pivoted and extended her left leg in a kick that doubled the warrior over.

Anakin smiled, then saw Daeshara'cor stagger and collapse against the walkway. As she slid to the ground, her right arm left a dark bloody streak on the wall. The amphistaff coiled at the feet of its warrior, then slithered up his leg and into his grip, a red tongue darting from its fanged mouth.

It bit her when he reversed it. She's been poisoned.

Anakin rose to his feet, fury racing through him. He summoned the Force to himself, feeling it surge. He couldn't feel the Yuuzhan Vong through it, but he could easily use it to collapse the walkway beneath his enemy or shatter tiles into a jagged hail that would flense the Yuuzhan Vong alive. He could do hundreds of thousands of things that would leave the Yuuzhan Vong shrieking in untold agonies.

I can avenge Chewie, avenge Daeshara'cor, avenge the people of Sernpidal. Right here, right now, starting with this one Yuuzhan Vong warrior. He smiled coldly and nodded solemnly at his enemy. *I can show him what a true Jedi can do.*

The Yuuzhan Vong advanced almost casually. He spun his amphistaff as he came. He reached Daeshara'cor's feet and she moaned. He flicked a glance in her direction and slashed his amphistaff at her throat.

In a heartbeat Anakin realized that a *true* Jedi wasn't concerned with what he could do to the enemy, but what evil he could prevent the enemy from inflicting. Using the Force, he brought Daeshara'cor's lightsaber up enough that it deflected the amphistaff strike. The Yuuzhan Vong weapon buried itself in the balustrade, splitting tile with a thunder crack.

The Yuuzhan Vong had almost tugged his weapon free of the wall by the time Anakin reached him. The lightsaber's violet energy beam swept low, shredding a knee. As the Yuuzhan Vong warrior began to fall, the Jedi brought his weapon up and around in a stroke that caught the invader between left shoulder and neck, angling down into his chest. The dead armor held for a second or two, then melted.

The warrior slid, lifeless, off the blade.

Anakin dropped to a knee beside Daeshara'cor. Her green flesh had begun to take on a milky hue, and he did not think that was good. He flicked on his comlink. "Team Twelve, one down."

"Copied, Twelve, pull back to the opal grove and the med station."

"As ordered."

Anakin thumbed his lightsaber off, then extinguished hers. He clipped her lightsaber to his belt, then hefted her up over his shoulder. Casting a glance behind himself, and summoning the Force to strengthen him, Anakin carried Daeshara'cor deeper into the Ithorian city. *I don't know if we can save it, but I hope we can save her.*

* * *

Traest Kre'fey turned from the holographic display of the battle when his shields officer called out to him. "What is it, Commander?"

The cream-colored Bothan snarled. "Port shield is down to 5 percent. The next shot will—"

Something slammed into the hull outside the bridge and shook the ship. Kre'fey, off balance from his turn, dropped to the decking. He gathered his hands beneath him and heaved himself up. Sharp ferroceramic shards fell from his body to litter the deck, and he noted that blood covered some of them. It took him a second to realize that whatever had hit his ship had managed to spall off the bulkhead's internal sheathing. *Had I remained upright . . .*

He glanced toward the communications stations and saw what little was left of Lieutenant Arr'yka twitching on the deck. "Comms officer is down. Get someone on that station! Shields, what happened?"

Grai'tvo tore the right sleeve off his uniform and used it to staunch the wound on his forehead. "Shield were low. A skip got through, hit us. It was just too powerful for us."

Too powerful for us . . . Kre'fey growled a quick laugh. "Yes, that's it, that's the solution."

Grai'tvo shook his head. "Admiral?"

"To the Yuuzhan Vong defenses." Kre'fey looked at his gunnery officer. "Give me a 50 percent boost on the power of splinter shots."

"It'll slow the rate of fire."

"I know, but they're putting up weak voids for our weak shots. Make the shift and we can sting them." Kre'fey turned toward the communications station. "Give me Admiral Pellaeon."

Borsk Fey'lya nodded and wiped blood off the console with his sleeve. "Call going in, waiting for an answer."

"Thank you, cousin." Kre'fey crossed to the station. "Are you certain you want to be here, given the danger you're in?"

The New Republic's leader nodded solemnly. "Better to die here than waiting below for the Yuuzhan Vong to find me."

Kre'fey smiled and patted Fey'lya on the shoulder. "Do

good work here, cousin, and there won't be any Yuuzhan
Vong left for you to fear."

Shedao Shai moved through the jungle in the midst of his
troops. Above him the troop carriers—save for the one serving as his ground-force command center—streaked skyward
to carry reinforcements down to the planet. The grounded
troops consisted of a dozen Chazrach for each Yuuzhan Vong
warrior. He'd broken his force into four components. One
squad remained with his ship. He deployed triads on his left
and right flanks, knowing the trio of squads in each triad
would be enough to delay any enemy they met. In the center
he led an ennead, with a triad at point, one in reserve, and the
core triad with which he moved.

He intended to conduct only a reconnaissance mission in
force, because he knew he had too few troops to do much so
soon. The villip on his left shoulder whispered in his ear.
"Master, we have reached the facility now. You will want to
see this."

"On my way." In his scout's voice he had heard something
that began to sap his resolve to only reconnoiter the enemy
building. They had met no resistance in the planet, which allowed him to imagine the enemy would collapse when
pressed. The battle for Dantooine showed that was not necessarily true, but Elegos had told him the Ithorians were paci-
fists. *If they lead things here . . .*

Shedao Shai cut through the ranks of his troops and began
to run through the darkened rain forest. Though he knew his
people controlled this section of the planet and that he was in
no danger, he could not shake a sense of hostility. *No, not
hostility, just opposition. We are not wanted here. We are not
hated, but definitely not wanted.*

For the barest of moments he entertained a flicker of doubt
concerning the invasion. The gods had given them this mission because they were champions of life, yet here was a
world where he felt foreign—truly felt like an invader. He did
not go so far as to wonder if the priests had lied, or if their
mission was a mistake. Instead he wondered if he was pur-

suing the gods' wishes in the proper manner, then decided that the uneasiness he felt was from means, not ends.

He quickly found his forward force and crouched next to its leader. "Report."

"We have movement there." The Yuuzhan Vong warrior pointed at a sprawling white complex of ferrocrete. The building rose to three levels, with each stepped back from the one below. Towers rising from the uppermost floor provided ample advantage, and the muzzles of weapons seemed to bristle from walls and viewports. "It is defended."

"We expected no less."

"It is defended by automatons." A tremor entered the warrior's voice. "They have no respect for us. They dishonor us by letting their machines do their killing for them."

Shedao Shai rose and stared defiantly at the white building before him. He pointed to it, allowing his tsaisi to slither into his hand and stiffen. "They mock us. They mock our gods. Let us break their toys, then they will have to come to us. And when they do, we will break them, as well."

CHAPTER
THIRTY-THREE

"I copy, thanks, Range Lead." Corran looked at the other half-dozen Jedi with him. "You heard that. General Dendo says they have taken the bait. Gavin's flyby pinpointed the transport they're using as a command center. Saddle up. We're going in hot."

Corran, clad as were the other Jedi in black combat suits, climbed aboard a speeder bike that had a brushed aluminum case strapped to the back of it. He punched the ignition button and felt the engine thrum to life. A small holographic image of the darkened jungle popped up between the handlebars, painting in luminous details the trees hidden by darkness.

He smiled. Through the Force he could feel those trees and avoid them. *This will just paint any Vong lurkers for me as the thermal bleed from their bodies will betray their presence even if they are hiding.*

Corran looked around for a moment, then smiled at Jacen, swathed in shadow. "What are you looking at?"

The younger man pointed at the case. "That case. Kinda hard to miss."

"It is, isn't it." Corran nodded confidently. "But then, having it be noticed is the purpose of this exercise. Shedao Shai is going to find himself in a fight, and with this, we can remind him once again what he's fighting for."

* * *

At Shedao Shai's order, the Yuuzhan Vong ennead surged forward, breaking from the jungle to sprint across open ground at the Ithorian building. Red laser bolts began to burn out from the walls, with splinters of light streaking in every direction. Around Shedao Shai ran Chazrach, howling and barking. In their midst went Yuuzhan Vong warriors, longer and leaner than their minions, racing forward in a sea of bobbing heads.

The Yuuzhan Vong leader stalked forward, seeing his troops as silhouettes in the light of the enemy fire. Energy darts exploded through Chazrach chests, clipped limbs, spun the diminutive warriors around to drop them smoking to the ground. Some of the wounded mewed and writhed, others struggled to their feet to keep going. Shedao Shai did not waste the time to dispatch the seriously injured, instead granting them the grace of dying in pain to redeem their failure.

Concentrated though the laserfire was, the automatons controlling the weapons lacked the flexibility to shift their tactics as the situation evolved. All the variables they were given to consider changed constantly, so each second brought new calculations and spastic motions imperfectly mimicking the living enemy they faced. Different machines responded at different speeds, causing them to leave one vector open while doubling up on another that no longer presented a threat. Slaves to their programming, the machines could not eliminate the extraneous and concentrate on what was vital.

As a living creature has long evolved the capacity to do. Shedao Shai saw one of his warriors go down and reached his side in a heartbeat. He tore the amphistaff from the lifeless hands, began to whirl it over his head, then charged forward, letting his fury and outrage fuel his assault.

Yuuzhan Vong attack bugs filled the air around him. Some struck targets and exploded, crumbling walls, destroying computer-controlled gun mounts, and reducing automatons to shrapnel and sparking limbs.

A living foe would continue fighting, but not these things.
The Chazrach swarmed over the wall and raced up the

ramps to the next level. From the roof towers more laser-fire poured down, though the guns failed to depress enough to rake the building's upper terraces. Shedao Shai smiled grimly at that fact, since no living creature—no *intelligent* creature—would have made that mistake. *A true warrior would hoist the weapons from their mounts and spray that lethal energy over us. These automatons are not even as intelligent as beasts.*

Well-thrown explosive bugs blasted the top of one tower off, sending a triumphant shout throughout the Yuuzhan Vong host. The squeal of metal as amphistaffs were ripped from metal and the snap of sparks as coufees sliced cables wove themselves into a percussive symphony of destruction. More explosions split the night, and a second tower crashed down with enough force to shake the whole building.

Shedao Shai found himself shrieking victoriously with his ennead, but his cry died prematurely. He stepped back, a cold sense of dread seizing him as Yuuzhan Vong warriors and Chazrach flooded into the building. Something was not right, and not until he realized that the impact from so light a structure as the tower should not have been able to send more than a minor tremor through the building could he pinpoint what was wrong.

This is not a permanent structure. He looked around again, his eyes widened with growing horror. An orgy of havoc surrounded him. Chazrach were beating consoles into debris. Circuit boards were yanked from their middles, rainbow ribbons trailing out like colorful intestines. Even his warriors appropriated wires and gaskets, adorning themselves with relics of the vanquished.

His force had lost all its cohesion and discipline. The razing of the facility and the shattering of its technology continued deep inside, with shouts luring more and more of his troops into the white building's heart. *It is what they wanted, what they expected when they put their abominations here. They knew we would take offense and lose our minds.*

Shedao Shai vaulted the low wall and began to back away from the building. He shouted for his troops to retreat and heard his call repeated. The Chazrach near him came away immediately, and more of their brethren began to flee, but none of the Yuuzhan Vong warriors. *No, of course not. They would not take orders from Chazrach to leave off their sacred duty.*

He started to use his villip to get the command center to issue a recall, but a rumble began to build, shaking the ground, and Shedao Shai knew it was too late.

The New Republic defenders, having long acknowledged that hitting a target was tough if there was no target, decided to provide the Yuuzhan Vong with something to attack on the surface of Ithor itself. They defended it with automated blasters and peopled it with droid shells, cobbled together from spare parts and just enough circuitry to allow the machines a little motion. They knew that using what appeared to be droids to defend the target would likely unhinge the Yuuzhan Vong and get them committed to a frenzy of destruction. Toward this end they constructed a building rather hastily, not worrying about a lot of internal support structures or a deep foundation.

Despite not providing a deep foundation to the building complex, the defenders *did* dig a hole beneath the building. This hole they filled with explosives and then laid the building slab over the top. The detonators for the explosives were wired to one of the computers stored in the heart of the building. Once General Dendo armed it by a comm signal, the detonation sequence would begin only if the computer shut down.

Having an amphistaff shoved into it and twisted accomplished this end rather nicely.

The resulting explosion shattered the slab and filled the basement with fire, consuming a half-dozen Chazrach that had wandered down there. The expanding fireball then vaporized the next floor, taking with it the Yuuzhan Vong warrior, his amphistaff, and the computer he'd destroyed. The blast cracked what few internal supports had been placed in the building, and as the fireball collapsed, the building collapsed in on top of it.

Walls buckled and the uppermost floor pancaked into the second one. The exterior walls cracked and sagged in, albeit unevenly, providing some room for survivors to hunker down. Smoke and dust poured out through broken viewports, with the wailings of the trapped and wounded following closely behind.

Shedao Shai picked himself up off the ground and snarled. The villip on his left shoulder started chattering, but the whine of blaster bolts tearing through the jungle on his right flank alerted him to his immediate problem. The fact that he heard nothing from his left flank displeased him even more. He snapped an order into the villip, ordering a withdrawal, and began to stalk back through the night.

How could I have allowed this to happen? His eyes tightened. *Elegos!* The Caamasi had been so open and peaceful, so intelligent and honest, that Shedao Shai had discounted the sort of cunning and guile such an ambush would require. *They might have even anticipated what I thought of them based on my contact with Elegos. These people are not the Chazrach. Their conquest will not come easily.*

Shedao Shai let an angry howl split the night. *It will come, though, and it will be at my hands.*

Mara heard Anakin's call and the order he'd been given to head to the opal grove. She reached out with her senses and picked him up, then got flashes of trouble in the vicinity. She keyed her comlink. "Jade moving to intercept Twelve."

Mara felt the Force flood through her. She'd been waiting deep in the Jedi formation, across the green strip from where Anakin had been stationed. The fighting on her side had not been fierce, so she'd not been asked to move up. As she raced along a walkway, then vaulted the balustrade to drop to the next level below, she found out why.

The Yuuzhan Vong had made a solid drive at the center of the Jedi formation. Kyp Durron and Wurth Skidder, both bleeding from numerous cuts, faced four of the warriors. Beyond them, coming down the walkway, Anakin had stopped at the top of a small rise. He'd set Daeshara'cor down and, with two lightsabers, was holding off a knot of the reptoids.

The idiots should have called for help! Mara thumbed her lightsaber to life, splashing a cold blue glow over the Yuuzhan Vong. She launched herself into a long, flying somersault, then ducked beneath the slash meant to open her from hip to hip. She stabbed her blade through the space between the Yuuzhan Vong's legs, then cocked her wrist and stroked the blade against the back of his left knee. Tugging, she came up and through the limb, severing it completely.

Snarling, the warrior began to go down. Mara leapt above the weak return slash, then came down with a heel hard on the fallen Yuuzhan Vong's wrist. Bones crunched and the amphistaff rolled free. Mara batted aside the warrior's other hand, scattering fingers, then stabbed her blade through his throat.

Mara spun as Wurth shrieked. The man reeled back, his right forearm bent where no elbow existed, and bent in a direction that no elbow could take it. His lightsaber was nowhere to be seen. His Yuuzhan Vong foe whirled the amphistaff, sending a hum through the air, and pressed his attack. With the flick of a finger, Mara send a handful of dirt from a planter flying into the warrior's face. The Yuuzhan Vong clawed at his eyes to clear them, giving Kyp Durron a chance to slash him across the belly.

That Yuuzhan Vong warrior sighed all too peacefully as he collapsed. Another warrior arced his amphistaff at Mara, opening a cut in her left shoulder. Mara parried the return slash, then spun and kicked the warrior in the chest. He pitched back, then caught his heels on his dead comrade's body. As he went down, Mara disarmed him with a cut through the wrist, then stabbed him through the chest and melted his heart.

Kyp's violet and white blade swept up in a mighty cut that sliced through the Yuuzhan Vong's chest from right hip to left shoulder. The Yuuzhan Vong spun away from the blow and staggered several steps, clutching at his ruined middle. He held the cleaved breastplate closed as if that would save him, then sat back against a wall and slid to the ground in a pool of his own blood.

Mara jabbed her lightsaber toward Wurth. "Get him out of here. I see blood—it's a compound fracture. Cauterize it with your lightsaber if you have to."

Kyp's eyes narrowed. "He'll survive. I'm not going to leave you here."

"I don't need your help, Kyp. He does. Just go on while there's still time. Do it."

He stared at her through a mask of blood flowing from a scalp wound. "I know my duty."

"Then do your duty toward your friend." She snarled as she ran toward Anakin. "Get him clear!"

Up on the walkway, the twin lightsabers had allowed Anakin to hold off the reptoids, but the four of them were pressing him closely. Mara gathered the Force to herself to make the leap up to his level, but before she could launch herself, one of the reptoids shifted his grip on the amphistaff and swung it around at waist height. His blow bisected his target.

Then the reptoid lunged and caught the second of his comrades with a thrust to the chest. As the third looked on in amazement, Anakin lashed out with his purple blade, burning the surprise from that reptoid's face. A quick lunge with Daeshara'cor's scarlet blade killed the last reptoid, who thrashed out his last moments of life at Mara's feet as she landed.

"What did you do, Anakin?"

"Nothing." The boy smiled and looked past her. Mara spun and saw Luke standing there, all serene and calm in the midst of the chaos.

The Jedi Master waved them toward him with a hand. "Let's go. Anakin, you lead."

Mara extinguished her lightsaber, then tossed Daeshara'cor over her shoulders in an emergency carry. "What did you do?" She took great comfort in his presence.

"Swapped images of Anakin and the other reptoids in that one's mind. Wasn't much of a trick."

"But an effective one." She nodded. "You saw Kyp and Wurth."

"Ahead of us. You can see the blood." Luke touched his hand to the middle of Mara's back. "You should have called me to help."

"I figured you heard my comm and would come if needed." She laughed lightly so he'd know she was smiling. "And I'm glad you did."

"Thanks for saving Anakin."

"I owed him." Her smile broadened as she saw Anakin warding a corridor entrance with his twin blades. "Besides, a century from now, when Jedi are singing ballads about the great Jedi hero, Anakin Solo, I want to be known for being a bit more than the woman he saved at Dantooine."

"Oh, I think, Mara," her husband said quietly, "*that* won't be a problem at all."

Aboard the *Legacy of Torment*, Deign Lian saw the weapons on one of the infidel ships flash. Their golden-red bolts lanced down at one of the smaller ships in the Yuuzhan Vong formation and blew through the voids raised to intercept such weak shots. The energy projectiles boiled yorick coral on the hull, converting it from solid to vapor, which jetted back out into space.

Two shots that hit along the dorsal ridge exposed the living ship's main neural channel to the cold of space. Tissue froze instantly, imposing an icy block that prevented data from flowing to and from the bridge and the forward part of the ship. The dovin basals there, being deprived of sensory data about incoming enemy fire, dropped into a standard wait state, positioning voids as best they could, to protect themselves and the ship.

Heavier shots poured down from the enemy ships. Some sank into the voids, but the rest punched past the defenses. They peppered the hull, walking in a line from prow to midship. Half-melted yorick coral panels broke off and whirled free. The front half of the ship disintegrated under the barrage. *Agony's Child* twisted in flight, snapping off the skeletal

structure that had been its front half, and began to orbit Ithor
as a new, dead moon.

What is happening? We had a strategy. Deign Lian watched
as another ship came under a withering assault. It began to
glow white and spread out like ice on a hot rock. *That can't be
happening!*

In an instant, Deign Lian knew what he had to do. He issued an order to all ships, commanding them to pull back to
the daylight side of the world. He concentrated his own fire
on the smaller enemy ships, discouraging pursuit, and slowly
let the world's green disk eclipse the enemy force.

Seething, Deign Lian pulled his head from the cognition
hood. *He knew this would happen. That is why he is down
there. He did this on purpose, to shame me.*

The Yuuzhan Vong nodded solemnly. *And he sent for reinforcements. He'll not have them from me. I hope he is dead. If
he isn't, I might just have to kill him myself.*

The Jedi jungle task force hit the Yuuzhan Vong command
center hard. Jacen triggered two shots from the speeder bike's
blaster cannon. They struck a Yuuzhan Vong warrior, spinning his headless body around and smashing it against the
hull of the crate. Other blaster shots killed reptoids, though
several Jedi dismounted to finish the last few with their lightsabers. Jacen knew it was less because they wanted the kill
than it was to prevent themselves from feeling so distant and
insulated from the life they took.

Corran leapt from his speeder bike's seat and tugged the
case free of its bindings. With his lightsaber unlit in his right
hand, he ran to the crate. Jacen followed close at his heels,
and Ganner came right behind. Jacen pounded up the landing
ramp with his lightsaber at the ready, but found Corran alone
in the ship's interior save for one cowering reptoid tucked
down in a corner.

The elder Jedi stood before a bank of villips and studied
them. Most bore the likeness of a Yuuzhan Vong, though
Jacen could not really tell them apart. A few of the villips
slackened and smoothed as he watched, leading him to as-

sume the Yuuzhan Vong or villip paired with it was out of commission.

"How do you know which one to talk to?"

Corran had set the case down and had his left hand pressed to his mouth. "I'm looking for one who looks important. Chances of Shai being here are slender, but whoever is in command would have his . . . well, whatever the Vong have that passes for ears."

Jacen shrugged. "Sort on ugly?"

"That might work." Corran smiled suddenly. "It's a good day for our team. Can't forget that ugly face." He reached out and slapped a particular villip none too softly. "Shedao Shai, this is Corran Horn. I own your command center, and it's my people harrying your flanks. You have some regular New Republic commandos on your right, and Noghri on your left. Bct the left is *real* quiet."

The Yuuzhan Vong villip visage hardened. "You have less honor than a ngdin."

Corran glanced at Jacen, but the young man shrugged. "I don't know what it is, but it doesn't sound good."

"I might not have any honor, but I do have a packet of bones here. I think you wanted these."

"Their return does not mitigate your treachery."

"They haven't been returned yet, pal. I have a deal for you. You don't agree, I send these bones into the sun."

The Yuuzhan Vong's eyes became slits. "Your deal is?"

"What we both want. You, me, our seconds: the bones against Ithor. You win, you get the bones. I win, I get the planet." Corran's voice took on an edge. "Our forces have a truce until we can fight this out. We each recover our dead, then you and I settle this."

"You bargain like a merchant." The villip's lip curled into a sneer. "Elegos would have been ashamed at how low you've sunk."

"Well, you've taken care to see we won't ever know what he thought, haven't you? You and me, Shedao Shai; the bones against Ithor."

"How long until we meet?"

Corran hesitated for a moment. "A lunar cycle. I'm a Jedi. I want to fight under a full moon."

"Remember the lesson of Sernpidal. I can make it so you *will* fight beneath a full moon. Two planetary cycles. There is a tabletop mountain west of here. We will do it there."

"Two weeks."

"Four days."

"Ten."

"I tire of this game, *jeedai*." Fury poured through the words. "A week. No longer."

Corran nodded. "A week."

The villip's face softened for a second, then sharpened. "Seven planetary cycles from now, a truce until then. It shall be done."

"Good, very good. I'll see you then."

"Yes, you shall." The villip's voice sank to a gravelly growl. "Come prepared to die."

CHAPTER
THIRTY-FOUR

Admiral Pellaeon stood on the *Chimaera*'s bridge, his hands clasped behind his back. He stared at the hologram of his New Republic counterpart. "Yes, Admiral Kre'fey, I agree that we got away better than I expected in all this. The Jedi truce is longer than I had hoped."

"I agree, Admiral, and we are putting the time to good use." The Bothan paced slowly, the holocam panning to keep him in the center of the image. "The modification we made to our gunnery seemed very effective and took two of their smaller ships down quickly. I'm not certain how they will respond in the future, but by switching tactics in a battle we can take advantage of their weaknesses. I have fleet techs working on the modifications now."

"As do I," Pellaeon replied. "You expect the Yuuzhan Vong will not live up to this agreement if their fighter loses?"

"That, or my cousin will urge an immediate and full strike if Horn dies. This bargain has not proved popular here." Kre'fey scratched at his snowy throat. "Regardless, we know we will face the Yuuzhan Vong again. I have some new ideas, the files on which I am transmitting to you now. I have a ship in reserve to help us, if you think we should proceed."

"I'll review the files and let you know." Pellaeon gave his New Republic counterpart a nod. "Do wish Horn the best for me. Were I forty years younger, I would offer to take his place."

"He will appreciate hearing that, sir." The Bothan flashed fangs in a smile. "I don't think there's a person in the fleet that wouldn't say the same thing. Well, maybe *one*, but there is always an exception to the rule."

Corran slowly screwed the butt cap onto his freshly recharged lightsaber. "So, Chief Fey'lya, I'm getting the impression you don't approve of my having made this deal with the Vong leader. For the four hundred twenty-seventh time, in fact."

The Bothan stabbed a clawed finger at him. "And I'll make the point a thousand times more, if I need to. You had no right, no authority to usurp the New Republic's perogative to make war with your stupid duel. I will make that point until you understand it and recant this bargain."

The Jedi's green eyes hardened. "Perhaps you need to understand something: I don't give a bucket of Hutt spit for what you think. I would remind you that because of your unwillingness to sanction the Jedi, I was recalled into the New Republic military. I made that deal under that authority."

"You were not the ranking officer on the ground."

"Actually, I was. General Dendo was wounded."

"But you didn't know that."

Corran gave him a toothy grin. "You telling me I couldn't have felt it through the Force?"

That brought the Bothan up short, but earned Corran a frown from the third person in the crowded cabin, Luke Skywalker. "Corran, now is not the time to play such games with Chief Fey'lya."

"You're correct, Master. No time for games at all." The Corellian Jedi glanced down at the lightsaber in his hand. "Chief Fey'lya, you've forgotten our history. Over a decade and a half ago you forbade me to do something. I resigned from the New Republic military, as did the rest of Rogue Squadron, and we accomplished our goal anyway. So, consider this my resignation from the military again. Your authority over me ends now."

Fey'lya blinked his violet eyes, then glanced at Luke. "Master Skywalker, order him to leave off from this duel."

"No."

The Bothan's eyes became amethyst slits. "The Jedi sanction this duel?"

Luke stared back. "A week from now, I'm going down to Ithor to act as Corran's second."

"So then, the Jedi claim the right to determine Ithor's fate."

The sly tone in Fey'lya's words sent a spark of anger through Corran. "He's right, Master, the Jedi can't be caught in that trap. I quit being a Jedi, too."

"You can't."

"Okay, fire me." Corran frowned. "Um, there are parts of the Jedi Code I don't buy into, and these robes chafe. There's insubordination for you. Ditch me. This is one trench run you don't need to make."

The Jedi Master slowly shook his head. "What you do not understand, Chief Fey'lya, is that Corran has acted to preserve life. Even if he falls, he is but one life lost against all those we are evacuating. One family will weep, not many. And *when* he wins, Ithor will be safe and the Yuuzhan Vong will know this invasion will not be without gross cost to them."

Corran's flesh tightened as Luke spoke. Looking at Borsk Fey'lya, it became apparent that while the Bothan heard the words, their true meanings never penetrated his brain. *He's off figuring how he will spin this, win or lose, to his advantage.*

Corran flipped his lightsaber around and offered the dark end to the Fey'lya. "Here, take it, go down and fight him yourself."

"No, I couldn't."

"I know that, Chief, and not because I think you're a coward." Corran shook his head slowly, then reversed the blade, leaving his thumb poised over the ignition button. "This fight isn't *your* fight, it's mine. I'm suited to it, and since losing is not something I can do, I won't."

The Bothan half-snarled at him. "If you fail, you will join Thrawn and Vader in the minds of the people."

"*If* I lose, Chief Fey'lya, Ithor will be forgotten in the

bloodbath that follows." Corran purged himself of anger and set his face in a calm mask. "It is to prevent just that which brings me to fight Shedao Shai. The preservation of life and freedom are the only reasons ever to fight. In their cause, I *will* win."

Anakin shrugged his mother's hands off his shoulders as he stared through the medical bay's viewport. In the wardroom, covered with a white sheet to her throat, Daeshara'cor lay on a bed, barely moving. He could tell she was still breathing, but her breaths came shallow and hurried.

Leia spoke in a soft voice. "You don't have to go in there."

I don't want to, but I must. Anakin sniffed and nodded to his mother. "She's . . . she asked for me. I have to."

"Do you want me to go with you?"

He swallowed hard against the lump choking him. "No, I can do this. Just, um . . ."

"I'll wait here."

"Thank you." Anakin brushed away a tear and entered the medical bay. Droids busied themselves with other patients. He moved over to the left side of the bed and rested his hand on Daeshara'cor's hidden wrist.

She started for a second, then opened her eyes. Her surprised expression changed into one of happiness, though it lingered for only a second or two. Weariness washed from her, and Anakin could feel the spark of her life dimming. "Anakin."

"Hi. How are you?" Anakin squeezed his eyes shut for a moment. "Stupid, stupid . . ."

Daeshara'cor slipped her left hand from beneath his grip and the sheet, then brushed a tear from his cheek. "It's okay. The venom—"

Anakin sniffed. "Corran was bitten. They saved him."

"Human chemistry . . . different from a Twi'lek's." She lowered her hand and grabbed his, squeezing as hard as she could, which felt terribly weak to him. "There is nothing they can do. I'm dying."

"No! Not fair—you can't!" Anakin snarled as hot tears splashed down his cheeks. "Not you, not like—"

"Chewbacca?"

Anakin's knees buckled, and he started to go down but found a chair beneath his butt. He covered his face with his hands and felt Daeshara'cor stroking his hair. "I made a mistake and he died. I made a mistake and you are dying."

"There is no death . . . there is only the Force."

He looked up through tear-blurred eyes. "It still hurts."

"I know." She managed a weak smile. "Anakin, you have to know . . . even though I am dying . . . I would not change things . . . neither would Chewbacca."

"How can you say—"

She stroked his cheek, her fingers feeling cold against his skin. "He died . . . I die . . . in service to life. You saved me from the darkness. I saved you . . . not in recompense, but so you can continue serving life, the Force."

He reached up and covered her hand with his. "I will never be as good a servant as you or Chewie."

Daeshara'cor smiled again, maintaining it though the corners of her mouth quivered. "You already are, Anakin, and will be greater. As you heal, you will be stronger than anyone can imagine. We are proud of you, so proud . . ."

Her voice faded, along with her smile, as life drained from her. Anakin pressed her hand harder against his face, but found her touch fleeting and faint. As he watched, she became lighter, then translucent, and finally disappeared as the sheet that had covered her collapsed.

CHAPTER THIRTY-FIVE

Luke Skywalker, enshrouded in his black cloak, stood silently at the southern edge of the mountain clearing. To the west the mountain continued to soar. Its exposed granite seemed almost as if it were a long, solemn face, peering down on this flat greensward just below the level of its chin. Luke realized his own grim expression aped that of the mountain, and he found no reason to change that.

Toward the center of the clearing sat Corran, cross-legged, his back to his Master. Peace and well-being radiated from him, with only tiny bits of anxiety leaking out from time to time. He wore his Jedi robes, green over black. His bare hands rested on his knees, and his shoulders rose and fell slightly with his breathing.

So closely was Luke concentrating on Corran that Shedao Shai's appearance with his second surprised the Jedi Master. The Yuuzhan Vong commander was nothing short of magnificent, clad in a sleeveless scarlet robe opened down the middle. Beneath it he wore boots and a gold loincloth with tails that reached knee level. His leathery gray-green flesh shone as if it had been polished, and a hardened mask of ebon inlay hid his face.

He bore an amphistaff, which he stabbed tail-first into the ground. He raised a gauntleted hand, the dying sun glinting from his bracer, then pressed the hand back over his heart. "I am Shedao Domain Shai. This is my subordinate, Deign Domain Lian. He will stand as witness to this combat."

Corran remained seated. "I am Corran Horn, late of the New Republic Armed Forces, a Jedi Knight. This is my Master, Luke Skywalker. He will stand as witness to this combat."

The Yuuzhan Vong pointed at the case behind Luke. "Those are the bones of Mongei Domain Shai?"

"As we agreed, yes, seven days ago."

"Very good." Shedao Shai shrugged his robe off. Though the Yuuzhan Vong warrior was cadaverously slender, Luke could tell that did not translate into weakness. The warrior plucked the amphistaff from the ground, whirled it in a blurred circle, then snapped it to a stop against the back of his right arm, the hissing head at his wrist and the sharpened tail stabbing up into the blue sky. "You are the murderer of Neira Shai and Dranae Shai, my kinsmen."

Corran stood, slowly and deliberately. Luke could feel the Force gathering in him, swirling around him. "And you murdered my friend, Elegos A'Kla. It is not over the past we fight, but to win the future."

"You, perhaps." The Yuuzhan Vong drew himself up tall and straight, then bowed his head toward Corran. "I fight for the honor of the Yuuzhan Vong and Domain Shai."

The Corellian returned the nod. "So much risk for such a paltry gain."

Amphistaff spun and lightsaber rose. A slash blocked high, a low cut burning grass but not leaping legs. Combatants slipping past each other, turning, striking, blocking. The amphistaff's hiss rivaling that of the lightsaber. Weapons flashing forward, retreating, then riposting.

Luke felt the Force wreathing Corran. It strengthened him and quickened him, but could not predict for him what his enemy would do. The amphistaff cut and stabbed, always missing Corran by centimeters, or being parried aside. The Yuuzhan Vong managed to whirl his amphistaff around in time to parry Corran's lunges, or to bat away slashes. They seemed, the two of them, to be perfectly matched. *Defeat will come from a single mistake.*

The argent lightsaber whirled in a grand arc, then sliced in at Shedao Shai. The Yuuzhan Vong warrior moved to block the cut, but Corran dipped the blade beneath the staff. He whipped his lightsaber up in a stroke that should have split the Yuuzhan Vong from groin to throat, but Shedao Shai danced back, leaving only the smoking tails of his loincloth fluttering to the ground in his wake.

Corran closed and lunged at Shedao Shai's upper chest. With two hands on the amphistaff, the Yuuzhan Vong parried the argent blade high, then ducked his head and whirled around in a circle. The amphistaff snapped straight against Shedao Shai's right forearm, then he lunged.

Pain exploded from the Jedi as the amphistaff's tail stabbed deep into his guts. The tip tented the back of the robe over Corran's right hip, then the Yuuzhan Vong yanked the amphistaff free, spinning the Jedi to the ground. Corran curled around the holes in his right flank, drawing his knees up. His lightsaber lay smoking on the grass.

Luke wanted to reach out, to help quell Corran's pain, but he held himself back. The Jedi Master drew some small comfort from the fact that the strike had not severed Corran's spine. *Could have gotten arteries, and his guts are holed, but he could survive this, if Shai gives him a chance.*

Shedao Shai drew back several steps, then tugged off his mask and tossed it aside. He raised the gore-streaked amphistaff to his lips and harvested incarnadine fluid with his tongue. His lips closed for a moment, his eyes following, then he nodded.

"I vowed I would taste your blood as you die, and now I have done that."

Corran coughed once, pain flaring through the Force, then rolled up to his knees. "Good for you, pal, glad you're happy." He winced as he scooped up his lightsaber and staggered to his feet. "Had I been in your boots, I would have vowed something else."

"Oh?" The Yuuzhan Vong's eyes opened a slit. "And what would that have been?"

"I've have vowed to taste my blood *after* I was dead." All sense of pain vanished from the Jedi as the Force again enshrouded him. Corran waved the invader forward with his bloody left hand. "So, is this inability to make a clean kill a Vong thing, or just a Domain *Shai* thing? You're so sloppy those bones won't want to come home with you."

Shedao Shai's eyes snapped open. Though Luke could not read him through the Force, the fury and hatred coursing through the Yuuzhan Vong was unmistakable. The warrior darted forward, bringing the amphistaff up and around in a two-handed overhead blow. He smashed it down on Corran's upraised lightsaber, driving the Jedi back a step.

Again and again he rained the blows down with bone-jarring impact. Corran retreated, giving up a step or two with each attack. As Shedao Shai's fury built, so did his strength, forcing Corran to raise his left hand from the hole in his side to the hilt of his lightsaber. Another blow battered the silver blade, and another, buckling Corran's legs, dropping him to his knees.

Shedao Shai towered over him, rising up on his tiptoes to deliver that final blow. The amphistaff rose and crashed down, set to bash the lightsaber back into its wielder, slaying an infidel with the blasphemous weapon he embraced.

With a flick of his thumb, Corran killed the blade and sagged forward.

Overbalanced because his weapon met no resistance, Shedao Shai buried his amphistaff deep in the ground and stumbled a half-step forward. The surprise registering on his face widened his eyes, then his lips peeled back in a feral grin as Corran pressed his lightsaber against the Yuuzhan Vong's stomach. The lightsaber hissed. Argent light poured from Shedao Shai's mouth a second before he vomited black blood and collapsed to the ground, his spine severed, his belly smoking.

Luke ran to where Corran was dragging his legs from beneath the Yuuzhan Vong's body. "Stay down, I'll get you out of here."

"Wait." Corran clutched at Luke's shoulder. "Help me up for a moment."

The Jedi Master complied with the request.

The Corellian Jedi pointed his lightsaber at Deign Lian. "You witnessed this fight. You know our bargain. Take his body and go."

The Yuuzhan Vong waved Corran's comment aside. "I witnessed, but I will not take his body. He died at your hands. He is no longer of the Yuuzhan Vong." Deign Lian gestured uncaringly. "His body is yours."

Corran shook his head. "I've no use for it."

"Then our business is concluded." The Yuuzhan Vong spun on his heel and disappeared beyond the edge of the clearing.

Luke started to turn Corran toward where they had landed their shuttle. "Let's go."

"Wait, just a second." Corran pointed at the mask Shedao Shai had discarded. "I want that mask."

"Why?"

Corran's eyes closed for a moment as pain washed over him. "Elegos's bones. They're watching something. That mask will show him that the Vong are not invincible, and for Ithor at least, there will be peace."

CHAPTER THIRTY-SIX

Upon his solitary return to the *Legacy of Torment*, Deign Lian assumed command of the Yuuzhan Vong fleet. Appropriating Shedao Shai's suite, he immediately issued an order, the preparation for which he had begun over a month before when he realized it was the most expedient way of dealing with Ithor. Shedao Shai had rejected it, but Deign Lian's other master had approved.

From a dozen coralskipper sockets that had been refitted launched twelve seed-shaped, yorik coral pods. While not nearly as sophisticated as a coralskipper, these unpiloted craft did possess a rudimentary intelligence. It enabled them to use the dovin basals to lock onto Ithor's planetary mass and speed their descent into its gravity well. Their outer sheaths began to heat up and ablate as they entered the Ithorian atmosphere. The twelve pods fanned out, streaking through the sky on courses that spread them all over the daylight side of the planet.

In the *Ralroost*'s medical bay, Admiral Kre'fey turned away from where Corran Horn floated in a bacta tank, and raised his comlink to his mouth. "Kre'fey here. Report."

"Sensors here, Admiral. The *Rainbow* reports a dozen gravitic anomalies from the Yuuzhan Vong fleet." The Bothan officer growled. "It looks like coralskipper traces, but they've gone into the atmosphere. *Rainbow* is reporting airbursts."

"Airbursts? I'm on my way to the bridge. Relay the data to the *Chimaera*." The admiral flicked off his comlink and turned to ask Luke Skywalker what he might make of such strange behavior. His question went unasked as the Jedi Master winced in pain and slumped against a bulkhead.

The airbursts over the Mother Jungle vaporized each Yuuzhan Vong weapon's payload, expanding into a vast cloud. The aerosol droplets descended over the jungle in a fine mist. The bacteriological agents in the mist touched down unharmed. The jungle was to them what a herd of tauntauns would be to a hungry wampa ice creature. The bacteria began to metabolize everything and reproduce in an exponential progression.

Black slime teeming with bacteria dripped from high leaves on down, streaming along branches. So quickly did the bacteria work that the fetid fluid seemed almost acidic. Branches fell, splattering the bacteria over other branches and onto arboreal creatures. A leather-winged shamarok flitter launched itself skyward, but black droplets on its wings quickly holed them, sending the beast circling down in a spiral of agony to crash on the ground.

An arrak snake slithered over and scooped the flitter up. Opening its jaws, the snake began to swallow the rare treat, but the bacteria went to work on it, too. As it devoured the flitter, the bacteria devoured it, opening ulcers in its flesh and consuming it from the inside out. The snake lashed out its life in a painful frenzy, then melted into a stinking pool of protoplasm that started in on the organic matter on the ground.

That pool slowly spread as grasses wilted and flowed into fluid. Falling branches splashed more of the protoplasm about, creating colonies all around the parent puddle. As the branches themselves liquified, they created enough protoplasm to let it flood out of the small depression on the ground, washing into the colony pools. In fits and starts, a black flood began coursing through Mother Jungle, gnawing at roots, toppling whole huge trees, then melting them almost before the echoes of their fall had died.

Nothing that lived on Ithor could resist the bacteria. It

soaked into the ground, destroying insects and other microbes. It coursed through wormholes and gushed into rodent
warrens. Creatures taken unaware had a putrid wave wash
over them, dissolving flesh, leaving bone, then cresting again
to destroy the skeletons.

The wave ate its way along roots, both up and down. Sometimes a plant that had a shallow root system would simply
topple. Other times, the bacteria attacking a sturdier plant
would surge up through its circulatory system, devouring the
core. Black sap would begin to drip here and there, staining
the trunk. A steady trickle would start, and branches would
fall, with protoplasm pouring free. Finally a torrent of foul
nectar would gush forth as the plant's bark split and the whole
thing collapsed.

The bacteria attacked relentlessly and fast. Its metabolism
of the planet's life released a lot of hydrogen and oxygen. The
planet's temperature began to rise, the oceans darkened, and a
stinking shadow stole over the face of Ithor.

In no time at all on a human scale, the bacteria reached the
place where Shedao Shai's lifeless body lay on the ground.
His flesh resisted the bacteria for a moment or two, but the
agent found egress through the wound Corran had opened in
him. The bacteria ate into him, consuming him bone and
sinew. His skeleton fell apart, then his bones cracked and
oozed black as the marrow was devoured. Finally the bacteria
liquefied his skull, removing the last trace of his presence
from the world his death was meant to save.

Pellaeon stared hard at the holographic representation of
Ithor. "I agree, Admiral, they've done something. Oxygen,
hydrogen, temp rising. If Skywalker is right, that all life is
being devoured . . ." The Imperial admiral shivered, unable
to conceive of ever using a weapon that could metabolize a
planet.

Commander Yage looked up from her position at the
sensor station. "Admiral, the Yuuzhan Vong fleet is moving.
They're coming up on an outbound vector."

"Vector alpha-seven?"

"The only one open to them."

Pellaeon nodded at the small image of Kre'fey in the corner of the planetary scan. "They're outbound alpha-seven. Time to move. Ithor cries for vengeance."

Deign Lian smiled as he looked at the villip bearing his master's face. "It is done, Warmaster Tsavong Lah. Shedao Shai is dead. The threat of Ithor is no more. I have the fleet moving out."

"Splendid." The villip's image smiled, making the warmaster's face seem almost pleasant. "You have done well, Lian. The *Legacy of Torment* is yours. When you get to Dubrillion, I shall have orders waiting for you."

"I understand, Master." Deign Lian nodded solemnly. "This one awaits your pleas—What was that?"

A jolt shook the *Legacy of Torment*, knocking the villip off its perch. Deign Lian reached for it, then another, heavier tremor shook the ship. The Yuuzhan Vong crashed to his knees. *Something is wrong, very wrong.* Ignoring the shouts from the villip on the floor, Deign Lian ran from the cabin and sprinted toward the bridge.

In the week Corran's challenge won for the New Republic, Admirals Kre'fey and Pellaeon had not been idle. In studying the performance of Yuuzhan Vong ships, both large and small, they had discovered a vulnerability they thought they could exploit.

Snubfighter pilots had noticed that projecting voids cut into a skip's ability to maneuver. The two admirals wondered if the reverse would also not be true, especially in the case of the Yuuzhan Vong capital ships. Toward this end Kre'fey had summoned the *Corusca Rainbow* from the fleet arrayed to defend Agamar and had it jump in where one of Ithor's smaller moons hid it from the Yuuzhan Vong fleet. As the Yuuzhan Vong started to move out, the Interdictor cruiser jumped into close orbit around Ithor and brought all four of its gravity-well projectors on-line. That effectively doubled the mass of Ithor, steepening its gravity well and slowly beginning to suck the *Legacy of Torment* back toward the dying world.

The Yuuzhan Vong at the helm of the *Legacy* immediately moved to counteract this effect. They brought more dovin basals under helm control, reaching out to latch on to moons and the sun. They slowed the slide, then stopped it. They slowly began the climb back out onto the exit vector, and by the time Deign Lian reached the bridge, his ship was again on the move.

Unfortunately for Deign Lian, the *Legacy*'s crew, and even the living ship itself, the *Corusca Rainbow* had done more than jump in and power up its gravity-well generators. Its gunnery officers computed firing solutions for the Yuuzhan Vong grand cruiser. Their telemetry was fed to the main defender fleet. Every snubfighter boiling out of the ships, every cruiser, every Star Destroyer, used that data feed to provide targeting information for their proton torpedoes and concussion missiles.

Barrage after barrage arced over the curve of Ithor's expanding atmosphere. They slammed into the voidless *Legacy*, shattering yorik coral plates. The energy released by their detonations incinerated neural tissue and boiled dovin basals. The first wave completely disintegrated the aft hull, opening the ship to the void of space. Yet, before air and crew could be sucked out, another wave hit, vaporizing more of the ship and igniting the vessel's atmosphere. Fire flashed into the *Legacy*.

Deign Lian knew a moment of agony as a fireball expanded into the bridge. He would have screamed, but the air was burned from his lungs before he could make a sound. For the half second of clarity his mind possessed, he could hear Shedao Shai counseling him to embrace the pain, to make it part of himself so he could know union with the gods. His last thought was to surrender to the pain, to allow it to consume him, denying himself the ultimate goal because he could not bring himself to admit that Shedao Shai had shown him the one true way to reach it.

The assault cracked the skeletal structure that held the *Legacy* together. It broke into three parts, the most forward of which surged up away from the planet for a moment. The burning aft descended toward Ithor, picking up speed. The central piece hung in space for several seconds, then began its slow, tumbling fall to the planet. The prow, with its dying dovin basals quitting one by one, likewise succumbed to Ithor's embrace.

It really did not matter that the *Legacy* was burning when it hit the planet's atmosphere. The friction from entry alone would have produced enough heat for the hull to ignite the oxygen-rich atmosphere. Fire flared out, quickly wreathing the planet. The superheated atmosphere expanded, flicking out little tendrils that bounced snubfighters around and buffeted the New Republic's fleet. One flare did reach out and caress a small Yuuzhan Vong corvette, causing the ship to explode, but the rest of the ships had pulled far enough away to escape.

The Yuuzhan Vong fleet—what was left it—sped along its outbound vector and disappeared.

Ithor, once a peaceful planet, blazed in their wake. With it burned the hopes of the New Republic.

CHAPTER
THIRTY-SEVEN

Admiral Gilad Pellaeon paused at the landing ramp on his shuttle, turned, and shook Admiral Kre'fey's hand. As he did so, he felt a sense of profound loss. "You do know, Admiral, that I wish things could have turned out differently. I found working with you fascinating, even enlightening. Imperial Space will benefit from what I learned here."

The Bothan nodded. "I know that, Admiral, and share your feelings. I also know, despite what others might whisper, that you harbor no antialien bias. I have never felt anything but respect from you, and have nothing but respect and admiration for you."

"Thank you, Traest." The Imperial officer broke his grip and clasped his hands at the small of his back. "Had we managed to defend Ithor, to save it, I am certain my people would not be recalling me. They are scared, of course. That weapon would have been tough to stop no matter what. I'm not sure having fleets orbiting worlds could prevent the Yuuzhan Vong from doing that to any world they choose. But if I don't have the fleet at home, the civil population will panic, and we are as good as lost if that happens. We have, in microcosm, the problem you have in the New Republic."

"I only wish it were as simple a problem as that suggests." Kre'fey looked around the aft landing bay on the *Ralroost* and the knots of Ithorian refugees huddled here and there. "You don't have the best hope for the New Republic being

blamed for the loss of Ithor. You don't have every little admin-
istrative sector deciding it has to defend itself. Ithor's destruction has sent terror storming through the government. Some
people want to appease the Yuuzhan Vong, others want to fight
them, and I have no doubt, some would willingly ally with
them if they were given the chance to destroy old enemies."

Pellaeon nodded. "In some ways, victory over the Empire
was the worst thing that could have happened to the New Republic. Your hatred of us united you. Now forces seek to di-
vide you for their own gain. You are fortunate, though,
because your role in all this has been nothing but praised."

The Bothan sighed. "My cousin is being lauded for his
brave action in the first encounter. He comes out looking like
a hero. He finds it expedient to elevate me to his side, making
him yet greater, which is what the people want."

"It's what they need: heroes to believe in."

"I know, Gilad, and I would not deny them heroes, but I
would rather they believed in you or the Jedi, instead of
someone who made the best of being at the wrong place at the
wrong time." Traest scratched his head. "I feel sorriest for
Corran Horn."

Pellaeon nodded slowly. "Yes, the man who lost Ithor."

"Oh, then you've only seen the early news holos. As the
week has dragged on he's become the man who killed Ithor."

"Someone had to take the blame." The Imperial admiral
smiled. "You know, for the half hour between his victory and
the planet's death, I was proud of what he did, the stand he
took. He'd won the day and managed to save countless lives.
Now it is all for nothing."

"Worse than nothing. The Jedi are being held up to ridicule; the military will have senatorial oversight." Traest smiled.
"Any chance Imperial Space is recruiting?"

Pellaeon laughed aloud. "And I was thinking I would ask
you to save me a spot in that empire you'll carve out of the
Unknown Regions."

"It would be my pleasure, sir." The Bothan flashed teeth in
a friendly smile. "I will keep you informed of how we are
faring."

"I'd appreciate that, and will reciprocate." Pellaeon nodded, then looked at the other two men walking up to him. "General Antilles, Colonel Fel, what have you decided?"

Jagged Fel clasped his hands at the small of his back. "I'll be sending one of my squadrons back with you, sir. They will carry a report back to my father. I'll remain here with two squadrons, liaising with Rogue Squadron. I hope, sir, you understand my desire to stay here."

"Understand, yes. Respect and envy, even." Pellaeon offered the younger man his hand. They shook, then Pellaeon shook Wedge Antilles's hand. "This is not the last you shall see of me, my friends. Right now, my people are afraid of helping you. There will come a time when they are more afraid of *not* helping you. I will return then. I just hope it won't be too late."

"That is our hope, as well." Traest Kre'fey again shook Admiral Pellaeon's hand. "May your course plots be easy and your orbits safe."

"The same to you." Pellaeon nodded and started up the ramp. He looked back once, just to make sure he would remember them because he was not certain at all that he would ever see them again. Then the landing ramp retracted, and his shuttle carried him home.

Jaina still felt numb, sitting there in the *Ralroost*'s meditation cabin. Anni's death left a hole in her life, which both surprised and horrified Jaina. The surprise came from her having known the woman for only such a short time. *Yes, we flew together and bunked together, but* . . . Anni had liked to gamble, and no one in their right mind would gamble with a Jedi so Jaina had found other things to do in her off time. When they were together, they did get along wonderfully, and she knew Anni liked her, and she'd liked Anni.

That they had become closer than Jaina had thought during her stint with Rogue Squadron shocked her. That she had not known more about Anni came as an even bigger surprise. Colonel Darklighter had said he was recording a message to go to Anni's family and asked if Jaina would like to send one at the same time. It was then that she realized she didn't know Anni *had* a family. Anni had never talked about her life outside the squadron, and Jaina had been a bit closemouthed about her own family life, assuming that Anni already knew as much about it as she would care to.

She glanced at the data card in her hand. She'd sent off a message to Anni's family and had quickly gotten a reply. The holovid transmission captured on the data card had shown an older woman, clearly Anni's mother, eyes red from crying, doing her best not to break down. She told Jaina that Anni had enjoyed having her as a friend and wing mate, that Anni always talked about her in every message she'd sent home. Anni's mother added that she had some things of her daughter's that she wanted Jaina to have, and that she would like to meet her if Jaina ever made it to Corellia.

I didn't know. I should have known. I . . . Jaina covered her eyes with her left hand. Tears leaked out between her fingers. A sense of guilt compounded the loss. Intellectually she knew that there was nothing she could have done to save Anni, but that didn't stop her from feeling that she should have found a way to keep her friend alive. *Now I know how Anakin feels about Chewie.*

She sniffed and straightened up, swiping at tears as the cabin door opened. She glanced at the silhouette and managed a weak smile. "Did Mom send you?"

Anakin shrugged and sat down on the floor. "I kind of nudged her into it. She knew you wanted to be alone. She didn't want you to be alone, but she didn't want you to think she thought you were too much of a kid to get through it. I hinted and she suggested."

"You must have somewhere else you'd rather be."

He shook his head. "No, I wanted to talk to you. Figured this would be the best place. It's the only place I'm not underfoot."

Jaina frowned. "Plenty of Jedi here."

"Sure, but they're all wounded or caught up in what's going on with Corran. A bunch of them, like Wurth, wonder how it is I manage to kill Yuuzhan Vong warriors without much more than a scratch and they get hurt." He sighed. "I make them doubt themselves, and they're not very good at controlling that idea."

"I can understand that, I guess. Not that they should take it out on you." She smiled at her little brother. "Why did you want to be here?"

"You lost a friend. I did, too."

"And misery wanted company?"

He shook his head resolutely. "Nope. I thought, well, look, when Daeshara'cor died, she said some stuff that made me think. I thought, maybe, well . . ."

Jaina softened her voice. "What is it, Anakin?"

"Well, she let me know, let me see that for her, it wasn't so . . . I mean, it was bad that she died, but . . . she wasn't mad at me . . ." His voice broke, and he smeared tears across his face with a hand. "Your friend Anni had to know you were safe. She didn't die hating you."

"Anakin, thank you." Jaina sniffed. "I want to hope you're right. I just . . . I need to have my heart and my head and everything sort things out."

"Yeah, that seems like the hard part." He nodded slowly. "I'm flying that same course myself. If you want a wing . . . sorry."

"No, Anakin, that's okay." She reached out and tousled his hair. "I'm glad you're willing to fly on my wing. We can do this together, little brother. I think that would work out just fine."

Corran let the door to his tiny cabin slide shut behind him, then leaned back against it. A little cough shook him, reigniting the pain in his abdomen. He'd already undergone two of the three bacta treatments the Emdee droids had prescribed for his wounds, and had ample evidence that the bacta had succeeded in helping his nerves to regenerate.

He rested with his back against the door, less because of true fatigue than a reluctance to do what he had come to do. Threading his way through the *Ralroost*'s passageways had been draining. Dodging groups of Ithorians in the narrow corridors made the journey hard, but it was not their physical presence alone that wore him down.

Through the Force he could feel their anguish. After his wounding he'd slipped into a Jedi trance and had been transferred immediately to a bacta tank. He had been floating there, barely conscious, when the Yuuzhan Vong attacked Ithor. He could feel life on the planet being extinguished, as if something were blotting out all the stars in the sky one by one.

He'd been out of the bacta when the atmosphere ignited. The stunned shock of the *Ralroost*'s crew had hit him first, then the flood of grief from the distant city-ships slammed hard into him. The Mother Jungle, the living entity that had created the Ithorians, that had nurtured and sustained them, the entity they loved and dedicated their lives to preserving, had been destroyed. From their ships they saw the atmosphere burn like a solar corona around the planet, leaving in its wake a charred, sterile cinder.

That wave of horror and grief retreated, leaving every Ithorian feeling as hollow inside as Corran had when . . . He glanced at the Yuuzhan Vong shell lying on the bunk in the small cabin. He took one step toward it, then sank to his knees. He touched a finger to the latch-creature, ignoring the sting of the needle as it drew his blood.

The shell slowly opened. Bioluminescent tissue shed a pale green light that glowed softly from Elegos' bones. It danced a bit in the gems that replaced his eyes, but in no way conveyed any of the life Corran had seen in what they imitated. Elegos' skeleton peered down at him, and Corran fervently wished he could catch at least the hint of a smile there.

The Jedi sank back on his heels and looked up into the jeweled eyes of what had once been his friend. From inside his robe he drew the mask Shedao Shai had worn. He rubbed a sleeve over its black surface, erasing a smudge, then reverently set it in Elegos' lap.

"Your murderer is dead."

Corran wanted to say more, but his throat closed and the glowing image before him blurred. He covered his eyes with a hand, smearing tears against his cheeks, then swallowed hard. He wiped away more tears, then took a deep breath and set his shoulders.

"His death was supposed to save Ithor. It didn't. I know you'd be horrified to think I killed him for you. I didn't. I did it for Ithor."

The gold skeleton stared down at him, cold mercilessness glinting from the gems in its eye-sockets.

Never any fooling you, was there, my friend? Corran screwed his eyes shut against more tears, then opened them again. He looked away, unable to stand Elegos' dead gaze.

"That's what I told myself. It was for Ithor. That's what I told everyone. Managed to fool some of them—most of them, I think. Not Master Skywalker. I think he knew the truth, but the chance to save Ithor had to be taken."

He glanced down at his right hand and could again feel the weight of his lightsaber in it. "I had myself convinced, I really did, until . . . There was a point in the fight. I'd turned my lightsaber off; Shedao Shai had overbalanced himself. His staff was buried in the turf. I shoved my lightsaber's hilt against his stomach."

A shudder quaked through Corran. "There was a moment there. A nanosecond. I hesitated. Not because I thought of life as sacred and that taking any life was horrible—the way you would have, my friend. No . . . No, I hesitated because I wanted Shedao Shai to know he was dead. I wanted him to know *I* knew he was dead. If he was going to see his life flash before his eyes, I wanted him to take a good look at it. I wanted him to have a nice *long* look at it. I wanted him to know it was all for nothing."

Corran's right hand curled into a fist. He hammered it against his thigh to loosen it, then flexed his fingers as wide open and straight as he could.

"In that one moment, Elegos, I dishonored your sacrifice. I betrayed you. I betrayed the Jedi. I betrayed myself." Corran sighed. "In that one moment I crossed the line. I walked on the dark side."

He raised his head and met Elegos' bejeweled stare. "You Caamasi had a saying: If the wind no longer calls to you, it is time to see if you have forgotten your name. The problem I have, my friend, is that I heard the dark side calling to me. Without your help, without your guidance, I'm not sure how I can deal with that."

Jacen Solo studied Corran Horn as the elder Jedi sat gathered into a tight ball in a chair. Bacta had healed the physical wound the Corellian had suffered, but a certain amount of psychic agony still poured from him. As far as Jacen could see, Corran had done everything right, hadn't been out of control or acting like a rogue Jedi, and yet that was how he was being portrayed in the news reports about Ithor.

Ganner paced impatiently. "I just can't believe it. Corran puts his own life on the line, nearly dies to save Ithor, and has been transformed into 'yet another world-killing Jedi.' Vader to Kyp to Corran. I'm surprised they didn't build a link to Caamas in there."

Luke pressed his hands together. "People are giving in to their fear. They're not thinking clearly at all. We need calm."

"Calm isn't all we need, Master. You will need something more." Corran blinked slowly and looked up. "You have to disassociate the Jedi from me."

Ganner's surprise pulsed out. "Abandon you?"

Corran nodded slowly. "Borsk Fey'lya has already managed to point out a number of things. I was not an officer in the New Republic Armed Forces when on my rogue mission to Ithor. He's noted my presence there was counter to Ithorian custom and law. He has made me complicit in desecrating Ithor because I invited Shedao Shai to meet me there."

Ganner frowned. "I've seen one report that suggests you should have known that a fallen Yuuzhan Vong leader is always immolated, so that by killing Shedao Shai there, you guaranteed the death of the world."

Mara snorted disgustedly. "That little bit of Vong cultural lore, that's from that supposed holojournal of Elegos A'Kla? The one he was supposed to have recorded while with the Vong, even though they would have smashed every bit of technology he took with him?"

The Jedi Master held a hand up. "We know that is a fraud. Someone did it and is publishing it to make money."

Jacen snarled. "And is making a bunch of it, too. That thing is selling wildly. It's because people are afraid."

"And morbidly curious." Ganner shook his head. "There *is* no doubt about it, the death of Ithor is a serious shock. Dubrillion, Belkadan, even Sernpidal—hardly anyone recognized those worlds. Ithor, on the other hand, is as well known as Coruscant."

Corran sighed. "And now is a sister world to Alderaan."

"Which takes us back to Uncle Luke's first point. People are giving in to their fear. We can't do that. If we abandon you, Corran, that's what the Jedi will be doing."

The Corellian Jedi managed a weak smile. "Thank you, Jacen, but it's not really a question of giving in to the fear of others, it's a question of being overwhelmed by it. Master, you *must* repudiate me. Borsk Fey'lya is looking to avert a disaster. He can do it only by laying the blame on someone else. Right now he's playing off memories of Carida and Alderaan. He's dropping the blame on the Jedi. You have to let it land on me."

Luke shook his head adamantly. "The Jedi are not going to abandon you to political maneuvering."

"Luke." Mara leaned toward her husband from her chair and rested a hand on his shoulder. "I love you dearly, but this is a fight we can't win."

"Yes, we can, Mara."

"Okay, perhaps we can, but the effort we expend in doing it is going to detract from our ability to help people." She sighed. "If we're waging public opinion wars when we should be fighting the Yuuzhan Vong, we will lose horribly. Right now Borsk Fey'lya has given us a way out of this mess, and that's to let Corran shoulder the blame for the loss of Ithor. All it will take is for you to issue a statement saying Corran's actions were undertaken without your consultation or consent."

Luke's face closed up. "That's not true."

Corran sighed. "From a certain point of view it is. You had reservations all along about the duel. You had concerns over what fighting the duel would do to me. In fact, you noted many times that the Jedi are not warriors."

"Corran, I was your *second* in that fight."

"You chose to support me despite my errors because the opportunity offered through the duel was one that protected many."

A sense of resignation rolled off Luke Skywalker and surprised Jacen. "Uncle Luke, are you going to agree to this?"

The Jedi Master looked up. "I can't fault their logic."

"I can! They're saying that lies told by Borsk Fey'lya and others are enough to destroy the reputation of a Jedi Knight. For the sake of making our lives a little easier, you're going to pitch Corran aside. It isn't right. I won't stand for it."

"Yes, you will, Jacen." Corran nodded wearily. "This is what has to be done."

"You're letting the ends justify the means." Jacen blinked his eyes in amazement. "Can't you see that? To save us some pain, you become as evil as Darth Vader or Thrawn."

"Jacen, if you look at the short-term ends, that's how you can read it. I get hammered, but at least the Jedi won't. That means you are still free to do the jobs that need to be done. If I didn't do this, I'd deserve the reputation for being evil."

Corran sighed heavily and unfolded himself from within the chair. With elbows planted on knees, he held his head in his hands. "I'm *not* totally innocent here. Far from it. Some of the things Master Skywalker feared, some of the things you feared, Jacen, about vengeance and the dark side, they were true. I'm going to need time to sort them out. My being disowned, well, we get some good out of it. For the Jedi. For me."

Concern washed over Luke's face and flooded his voice. "Corran, whatever you need . . ."

"I know, Master, thank you. I think, I *hope*, it's just time."

Ganner scratched at the scar on the left side of his face. "What will you do if you leave the Jedi?"

Corran shifted his shoulders uneasily. "Well, Coruscant isn't home anymore. I have exchanged messages with Mirax. We'll return to Corellia. I can do things there. My grandfather still has enough pull with politicians that I can have asylum.

Maybe Corellia can be motivated to do some positive things concerning the refugees created by the Vong. Worse comes to worst and I hook up with Booster to use the *Errant Venture* to help out."

He looked at Luke. "You know, despite problems I may be having, I'll be there if you need help. It's just, right now, I think this is the best thing I can do for the Jedi all the way around."

"I think you're right, Corran." Luke reached up and patted Mara's hand. "You're making a tough decision much easier."

Jacen just shook his head. He couldn't believe it. The Jedi had done exactly what they were supposed to do at Ithor. They had helped whisk refugees away, evacuating the entire planet. They opposed the Yuuzhan Vong, putting themselves at risk to discourage the invaders. They'd suffered casualties and fatalities and had even won a duel that should have guaranteed the safety of the world. Their efforts had prevented countless deaths, and yet enemy treachery and political manipulation resulted in a Jedi being blamed for a disaster he had done all he could to prevent.

And my uncle is accepting that this is what must happen. Jacen had long known that the heroic mold in which Luke and Corran had cast themselves as Jedi was not to his liking. It seemed a poor fit, and that fit worsened as the Jedi bowed to political considerations. *If we serve life and the Force, how can we let politics turn one of us, all of us away from that duty? We can't! There has to be another way.*

He sighed. *I have to find that other way.*

"Jacen."

The young Jedi straightened. "Yes, Corran?"

"You're idealistic, and that's good. I know this doesn't sit well with you. I can see that in your eyes. Yours, too, Ganner. I appreciate that, but I need the both of you to do something for me. Something I can't do."

Ganner nodded. "Name it."

Corran looked at the both of them, and when his green-eyed gaze met Jacen's eyes, the younger Jedi felt a jolt. "Some Jedi, like Kyp and Wurth, will take my leaving as a good sign. They'll consider the sort of discussion we've had here just a display of weakness. When I leave, they'll think they've won some sort of victory. No persuasion on your part will change their minds. It will just lower you in their estimation. It will make their plays for power that much more effective."

He glanced at Luke. "You have to support Master Skywalker. If the Jedi aren't together in opposing the Vong, Ithor will be just one more tragedy in what's going to be a very long list."

"I'll do it." Ganner smiled. "Thanks for providing me an example to follow."

"Don't follow it too closely, Ganner. Be yourself. Set an example for others."

Corran shifted his gaze to Jacen. "What about you?"

Jacen started to open his mouth, then closed it. Thoughts and emotions ran rampant through him. He wanted to agree, but it meant committing himself to a direction he wasn't certain was for him. *A direction that will take me away from where I need to be.* Yet, despite his ambivalence, he nodded. "I'll do my best."

"I'm sure that will be more than enough." Corran straightened up, momentarily shaking off his weariness. "I'm sorry to abandon you. My ability to help . . . There are things I have to do. I just hope you are able to handle the Vong. If there ever comes a time when folks look forward to the return of the man who killed Ithor, well, we know that means the invasion is completely out of hand and things are truly beyond saving."